DARK
MATTER

DOUBLEDAY

NEW YORK   LONDON   TORONTO   SYDNEY   AUCKLAND

Garfield
Reeves-
Stevens

DARK
MATTER

PUBLISHED BY DOUBLEDAY

a division of Bantam Doubleday Dell Publishing Group, Inc.
666 Fifth Avenue, New York, New York 10103

Published in Canada by
Doubleday Canada Limited,
105 Bond Street, Toronto, Ontario M5B 1Y3

DOUBLEDAY and the portrayal of an anchor with a dolphin are trademarks of
Doubleday, a division of Bantam Doubleday Dell Publishing Group, Inc.

BOOK DESIGN BY DIANE STEVENSON/SNAP HAUS GRAPHICS

Library of Congress Cataloging-in-Publication Data applied for

Canadian Cataloguing in Publication Data

Reeves-Stevens, Garfield, 1953–
Dark Matter

I. Title.

PS8585.E445D37 1990   C813'.54   C90-094522-2
PR9199.3.R44D37 1990

ISBN 0-385-24756-7

October 1990
FIRST EDITION
RRH

For Paul Till

Good friend
Talented artist
Brutal chainsaw killer

Oh well, two out of three ain't bad.

One

STOCKHOLM

ONE

"**L**et me explain it to you again," the teacher said, gently sliding the scalpel across the forehead of the student so the first blood of her understanding welled up in a sudden crimson thread. The teacher smiled. It was going to be a good lesson.

The student did not react. She could not move in any way because of the white nylon cords holding her to the high-backed wooden chair, but her eyes had not flickered when the scalpel had pierced her. Instead, the young woman had focused on the larger knife the teacher held beneath her face, above the mottled blue and white wool of her sweater, distracting her attention from what was really to be done. The fact that she had not felt the scalpel's passage through her skin meant the local anesthetic that had been injected into her scalp had taken hold. The student could be entered now without the unproductive diversion of pain.

"You see," the teacher said, replacing the large, distracting knife on the equipment tray, beside the other gleaming probes and scalpels and the Huntington electric bone drill, "the final problem is to understand the *Beginning*. Of time, of space, of mass and energy. Of everything. And to do that, we must know how to combine the four basic forces of the universe into one, to unite relativity with quantum physics the way things were in the first instant of the universe's birth. And that's not as easy as it sounds, let me tell you.

"Take relativity and quantum physics. Mutually exclusive! Even Einstein saw that right away." The teacher paused, riveting eyes flashing as brightly as any scalpel in the glare of the room's brilliant illumination: five old gooseneck lamps beside the tray on a scarred and rickety birch veneer table, all carefully arranged in a ring around the student's head. The teacher sought out the student's eyes, looking for that meaningful contact so important when seeking to inspire true understanding.

"The problem, as Einstein saw it, was that Bohr's work in quantum physics suggested that information could travel from one part of the universe to another at speeds greater than the speed of light, in conflict with Einstein's own theory of relativity which had already established lightspeed as the fastest rate at which anything in the universe could move."

The teacher resumed the cutting. The incision now followed the student's hairline across her forehead, continuing on both sides across the temples. In an ordinary operation of this sort, the teacher knew the scalp would have been shaved and prepped with an antiseptic to lessen the possibility of infection during recovery. But recovery was not the point here.

Suddenly, the blade scraped metal within the student's blood-matted blond hair and the teacher snapped a latex-gloved hand away as if it had touched a live wire. The student moaned through the white cloth of her gag, a soft cloud of warm breath escaping into the frigid air of the unheated flat. "Don't worry," the teacher said to her, putting a reassuring hand on the student's thin shoulder, "it won't be much longer." Carefully, the teacher felt at the edge of the incision until what the scalpel had hit was found. The object was withdrawn and held before the student's eyes with a gentle laugh and kindly smile. It was a bobby pin.

"That's all," the teacher said reassuringly, then flicked it aside to land on the yellowed tile of the room they were in; the kitchen of the abandoned apartment, judging from the grid marks of interrupted paint on the wall where cupboards had once been attached and appliances installed. The teacher tossed the scalpel away also and chose another with a longer blade. It slipped between scalp and skull, separating the connective tissue there, freeing the epidermal layers from the slick surface of the underlying cranial bones.

"So anyway," the teacher continued, "Einstein created a *gedanken*, that is, a thought experiment—with Boris Podolsky and Nathan Rosen—to illustrate his objections. It's called the EPR Paradox." Another pause. "Would you like to hear it?" The student didn't nod, only moaned. Less like the sound of a terrified teenager this time. More like the sound of a wounded animal.

"Good," the teacher said, delicately arranging the student's scalp to hang like a hood from the back of the chair. Then the teacher was busy with dabbing at the blood that oozed out over the whiteness of her skull, and painting a quick-drying surgical plastic sealer along the edges of the incision. The amount of blood produced by the scalp was always a problem, and often made the procedure look far worse than it actually was.

"Of course, by the time Einstein and his coworkers formulated their paradox, Heisenberg had already established his principle of indeterminism, or uncertainty, with which, I assume, you're already familiar." Mucus bubbled from the student's nose as she wheezed with rapid breaths. The teacher took a sterile wipe from the tray and delicately cleaned her off. "In simplified form, Heisenberg was able to show that we can never know everything we think there is to know about anything at the atomic level, with any idea of precision. We can determine the momentum of an electron, let's say, but just by the act of measuring momentum we change the electron's nature so that we can't know its position. And if we measure the electron's position, then we can't know its momentum. It's one or the other, you see. Yes, no. Off, on. No middle ground. A quantum decision." The teacher paused to sniff the cold air. Urine soaked the student's jeans. She began to shiver.

"Shh, shh," the teacher said softly. "We'll be finished soon." The first burr was attached to the Huntington—a number twenty-seven for a hole precisely one-quarter centimeter in diameter.

"Now, not even Einstein doubted Heisenberg's work, but with the EPR experiment he seemed to find a way *around* it. Which might have meant that Heisenberg's ideas weren't absolutely correct." The drill burr clicked into place. The teacher tapped the start button and the Huntington whirred to life, heavy, black, and smoothly vibrating in gloved hands. "What Einstein and his coworkers did was to describe an experiment in which pairs of electrons were produced such that the total momentum of each electron pair and the relative separation between the two electrons could be known from the beginning."

The teacher held the tip of the Huntington to a point on the student's skull approximately one centimeter above the central spot still hidden by the skin left between her eyebrows. Then the start button clicked again. This time, it was held down and a high-pitched whine echoed in the almost empty room. Thin tendrils of what looked like smoke curled up from the drill bit, but it was only a fine suspension of minute bone particles caught in the rising column of air warmed by friction-heated bone. In an operating room, a surgical nurse would keep a constant stream of sterile water flowing over that point of contact. But the teacher had long ago realized that, so far, at least, there were no assistants who could keep pace with the Work that must be done.

The drill stopped. Using a soft plastic squeeze bottle of water, the teacher flushed the hole the drill had made, checking to see that the outer membrane of the brain had not yet been penetrated. The teacher smiled. It hadn't been. Practice made perfect.

"Then, you see, by measuring the momentum of only *one* of the electrons in a pair and deducting that from the total momentum possessed by both, we could know the momentum of the other electron, *without* having to directly measure it." The teacher chuckled softly again. "Just like a story problem. The same technique enables us to determine an electron's location, again without direct measurement." The teacher checked the student's eyes to make sure she was still conscious. They were wide, staring, intensely alert. The teacher nodded in satisfaction. "Of course, that was in complete violation of Heisenberg's Uncertainty Principle." The second appropriate point on the left side of the student's skull was found, just below the outward curve of the frontal eminence. The drill sang again.

When the second hole was finished, flushed, and checked, the teacher drilled five more in an arc roughly parallel to the curve of the coronal suture running across the top of the student's cranium, then drilled two more on the right side of the frontal bone to match the first pair. In the past, the teacher had always thought of this next stage as connecting the dots. The Huntington's drill burr was carefully replaced by a circular cutting disk. It spun smoothly as the teacher tested it.

The student's nose bubbled again and a thin trickle of blood was flooding the corner of her left eye. The teacher pulled back on the sleeve of the pale green trench coat worn as a surgeon's gown, and checked the watch there—a liquid crystal display of an analog-style watch face, each tick of the second hand a discrete jump. It was 2 P.M., sunset. Still two hours before the ceremony. Plenty of time. But there was also a small drop of blood on the watch's face. And a second drop beaded on the exposed edge of the black sleeve sticking out from the trenchcoat. But the teacher wasn't concerned. There would be time for correction of the problem. There always was.

"Now, Einstein's apparent circumvention of the Uncertainty Principle was awkward, but not, of and by itself, insurmountable. This was 1935 after all, and quantum physics was still in its formative years. No, the real point of the experiment, again as far as Einstein was concerned, was that quantum physics maintained that neither property—momentum nor position—was real until an observer had observed it. However, according to the EPR experiment, by determining the momentum—or position—of the second electron by making an observation of the first electron, the second electron's correlated property was indeed made real, even though no direct act of observation had been performed on it. And what's more," the teacher added, thoughtfully taping a thick wad of surgical gauze to the student's brow to absorb the flows of blood to come, "it didn't appear to matter how far apart the electrons were when the observation was made. Do you understand?"

The student moaned softly.

"I'll take the gag off soon," the teacher said. "Don't worry."

The teacher dropped the bloody wipes on the floor, kicked them to the side to avoid slipping on them, then reached for the Huntington again. "Let's try once more. Even if the electrons were half the universe apart, billions of parsecs, the measurement of the first would cause an *instantaneous* change in the second. Instantaneous. Faster than the speed of light. Relativity is not upheld. Causality is not preserved." The teacher gestured impatiently with the Huntington as no comprehension appeared in the student's eyes.

"Listen to me: It meant that quantum physics was not a *complete* theory. Do you have *any* conception of the ramifications of that conclusion?" The teacher leaned down to her, close enough to smell the cinnamon fragrance from the coffee shop where they had met and the student had been beguiled. She had said her name was Margareta. *"Do you understand?"*

The teacher looked at her, eyes fixed and unblinking, searching for some sign of connection. But it wasn't there. She didn't understand. The teacher nodded sadly. Just like all the others. But she would understand soon. And so would the teacher.

The Huntington whined again and the teacher brought the spinning cutting disk down to the first hole drilled. For an instant, the whole saw began to pull away as it cut into the skull. Then the teacher's grip tightened and held the Huntington in place, guiding it from one hole to another until all had been connected. But when the teacher pulled the instrument away, took pressure from the button, felt vibration fade, there was still a high-pitched whine in the room. It was the student. Screaming.

The teacher put the Huntington back on the equipment tray. "It's all right. I know you can't feel anything. The injections I gave you deadened your skin and scalp. And the brain has no pain receptors of its own. You're just scared, that's all." The teacher held a clean wipe to the student's nose. "Go ahead, blow." Weakly, she did. "That's better now, isn't it?" The wipe fell to the floor to join the others.

"Just give me a minute here and I'll take off that gag," the teacher said, then selected a Hagstrom probe from the tray and slipped the long silver blunt blade of it exactingly beneath the now separated section of bone that lay exposed on the student's head. "Gently, gently," the teacher whispered as the blade cautiously wiggled back and forth, seeking purchase. The student suddenly trembled and the teacher stopped all movement to avoid premature trauma. "Take a deep breath and hold it," the teacher advised her. "Not much longer."

The student stopped trembling and though not deep and slow, her breathing became at least regular. The teacher hooked a corner of the loose bone, lifted gently, and with the sound of a small balloon popping, it was out.

The shallow cup of cranial bone fell to the floor, no longer needed. Then the teacher took a smaller scalpel from the tray and quickly sliced along the glossy protective membranes lying beneath the level of the skull. As the teacher lifted them away, they made the sound of thin tissue paper tearing.

"There now," the teacher said, trying to flick the clinging leaf of membrane from the glove's fingers. "There now." The teacher compressed the thin sheet into a ball and rolled the surgical gloves off around it. They joined the other refuse on the floor in the corner. Then the teacher held bare hands before the student, empty like a magician's about to pull wonders from thin air. "That wasn't so bad, now, was it?"

The student stared up at those hands, awake and aware beyond all reason.

"So to continue," the teacher said, reaching for the student's gag, "what makes the EPR experiment such a paradox is that first, relativity *is* clearly upheld. Countless experiments have proven that Einstein was right about *that* theory, at any rate. Second, without causality, that is, the concept of action followed by reaction and not the other way around, classical physics and everyday life would be impossible, and both are demonstrably real." The teacher smiled. "After all, we *are* here, and it *is* now. And third, it's not a thought experiment anymore. The instantaneous effect is also *real.* It's been demonstrated in labs using pairs of correlated photons!

"Anyway, Einstein proposed that his experiment proved that there was still more to quantum physics than had been previously described. Sometime in the future, he believed, additional discoveries would be made which would make the improbable world of the quantum reasonable and deterministic, qualities that would bring the universe into line with Einstein's personal philosophy of the way things should be. Toward the end of his career, you know, he was a very conservative man. 'God doesn't play dice with the universe,' and all that."

The teacher tugged on the last knot of the gag and pulled the cloth strip away. The part that had dug deeply into the student's mouth was flecked with blood. She moved her jaw back and forth, opened her mouth to scream, but could only cough hoarsely, groggy and disoriented from her ordeal.

"And that's where John Stewart Bell came in. About thirty years later, he wrote a paper which came to be known as Bell's Theorem." The teacher crossed over to the small pile of soiled wipes on the floor in the corner of the room to get something to wipe the student's mouth, but the soaked pieces of cloth and gauze had already frozen together on the filthy tiles. The teacher returned to the student and pulled up her sweater to wipe off the spittle on her chin. Beneath her sweater, the student's skin was as pale as her edema-swollen face, as her heavy white bra, as her opened skull.

"Now, Bell's Theorem suggested that, contrary to Einstein's beliefs, there were no more underlying levels of reality to be discovered beyond quantum physics." The teacher tucked the sweater back down around the student to keep her warm. "No 'hidden variables' as they were called. No unknown rules that were controlling things at unsuspected levels yet to be discovered. In other words, the secret of the Beginning of all things must be hidden in what we can already observe, not in an unknown place." The teacher squatted down in front of the student, ignoring the stench of her urine, and reached out warm hands to hold hers, swollen, cold, and blue. "Now, you must listen very carefully to what I'm going to tell you next, because this is where I'm going to need your help. Do you understand?"

The student stared at her teacher. In the frigid air, the heat of her fading life steamed up madly from her exposed brain. Her mouth opened but she said nothing.

"Do you understand?" the teacher snapped, pulling harshly on the student's bound hands, jarring the chair with a wooden squeal against the floor. "Do you?"

"*Ja,*" the student finally said. Her voice was dry, hard to hear.

"Good," the teacher said, then stood before her, knees against hers, looking down into her eyes, down into her open body.

"Bell's Theorem was an intriguing start, but only a start." The teacher raised gentle hands to the student's shoulders, looked down compassionately upon her. "He proved that there were no hidden variables only by stating what *couldn't* be. Do you understand? He came at the whole question of what *could* be by ruling out all those things that *couldn't* be. He went at it backward. Do you understand?"

"*Var så god, det gör ont . . .*" the student whispered uncertainly, eyes glazing.

The teacher's hands were poised above her. "Whereas certain workers have come at it from the other side, not the negative side, but from the positive. And now there is a corollary to Bell's Theorem, taking it into higher dimensions. The corollary confirms Bell's original work but opens up a whole new level of understanding. Not a new level of existence. But a new way of understanding it. The corollary's practical result is that whole new areas of experimentation are opened up to the most modest of accelerators at much reduced energy levels. Do you understand?"

"*Nej,*" the student said, vapor puffing from her mouth like an escaping spirit. "*Nej.*"

"Good," the teacher said, ignoring her protest. The teacher's hands moved through the mist trailing from the student's head, fingers held motionless there, above the pulsing surface of the naked, living brain. "But even that corollary was a start, just the first look into the quantum. There are more answers there, waiting. The answers to . . . everything." The teacher could see it now, in the student's eyes, that meaningful contact so necessary when seeking to inspire true understanding. It was going to work. The teacher's fingers brushed the surface of the student's brain.

"And now, to help find those answers, we need to look again." The teacher applied pressure. "Into the quantum." Felt the fissures, the folds of her soul and her knowledge and her personality. "Into the reality that underlies it all." The fissures parted, warm, wet, enveloping. "Into Planck time." The student's muscles stiffened, trembled, she jerked left and right against her bonds as the teacher pushed in deeper, searching, looking. "The instant of transition . . ." She sang as a child. "From one to another . . ." She howled with rage. "From all to nothing . . ." Moaned with passion. "Into the quantum . . ." Pushed deeper. "Into the quantum . . ." Deeper. "Into the . . ."

A moment passed.

The student slumped. From life to lifelessness in that one instant.

"Yesss," the teacher sighed, holding that moment. "Yesss." The teacher had felt it. "Oh, yesss." The moment of transition.

And as if staring down onto a sunlit field, the light pure and brilliant to all the senses, the teacher saw the answer to the problem that had been presented and the teacher knew *more.*

Slowly, the teacher slipped coated fingers from the empty shell of the student, wiping the blood and small clumps of other matter on the green trenchcoat.

"Good," the teacher said. "Now we both understand."

The lesson had ended.

The teacher was *inspired.*

TWO

Charis Neale was late and there were few things she hated more than that feeling of hopelessness and loss of control. The interruption of order, the break in routine, the chaos of it was an affront to her. Everywhere she looked, the street was clogged with vehicles, nothing moving. Glaring white headlights and multicolored store signs were smeared and indecipherable through the frost and fog of her window, the scene outside as disrupted as her plans.

She leaned forward and rapped against the glass partition separating her from the limousine's driver. He turned his head to her reluctantly. It was the tenth time she had spoken to him since they had left the hotel less than twenty minutes ago.

"This is useless," she shouted through the glass. "Which way is the *Stadshuset?* I'll walk from here."

The driver gestured futilely toward the trail of red and orange brake lights stretching out before his car. *"Fröken Neale*, too cold, too cold," he said with a heavy Swedish accent. "Stay, please. A few more minutes." But when Neale opened her door, he stopped trying to convince her to remain, glad to be rid of her.

Neale slammed the door behind her and weaved through four

lanes of unmoving, bumper-to-bumper Volvo taxis and black limousines. The sidewalk, like the road, was dry and perfectly cleared of snow. Her feet were already cold in the thin Maud Frizon evening shoes she wore, but at least they would stay dry for the walk to Stockholm's city hall.

The sound of her hard soles on the sidewalk was crisp and quick as she made her way past the unmoving vehicles to the next major intersection. The street sign there was at least four feet long and read *Hantverkaregatan*, but Neale didn't have the slightest idea of where she was in the city. She just followed the trail of cars.

After a few blocks, her rapid breaths trailing to vapor behind her, she no longer felt the cold of the December night. She thought only of her anger at why she was late. Thirty-five years old, one doctorate in high-energy physics, another in math, and she was *still* nothing more than an assistant. Still writing up the notes in the lab, and handling all the loose ends everywhere else. While the others always got the credit. And the recognition.

She turned the corner, passing a gridlocked intersection which was devoid of honking—typical for Stockholm, but eerie for someone used to Boston. At the end of the next block, overlooking Lake Mälaren, the *Stadshuset* rose dramatically before her, the three golden crowns of its central tower gleaming in the festive lights blazing around it. Also typical for Stockholm, the only vehicles from which passengers emerged were those directly in front of the building, as if no one cared that traffic wasn't moving and everyone was late.

Only in this country, Neale thought. So many meaningless rules. So many affronts to intelligent behavior. Pedestrians frozen by "Don't Walk" signals in the middle of the night when the nearest car was five miles away. No more than three winners for each Nobel Prize so the fourth member of the team couldn't share, could only be a footnote. An assistant.

She cut through the motionless lineup of cars again, crossing over to the main, black granite entrance facade of the building. And what would have happened this evening if the Nobel committee did allow four people to share in a prize? What if she had had no choice but to have been present at the presentation ceremonies three hours ago at the Concert Hall, instead of missing them completely? Who would have been the assistant then? It would have been the end of everything, not the beginning.

She ran up the low, broad stone steps to the main doors, pushing past those who merely walked to join the Nobel Prize celebrations. She hated this city. She hated this interruption in her work. What had all this nonsense to do with the pursuit of true science? The search for pure order and total understanding?

She burrowed her way through the swelling of the crowd before the doors, forcing her way past the partygoers and the hangers-on. She missed Harvard. She missed the control it gave her. The certain knowledge that she knew where everything was, where anyone could go, and how all the systems operated, including the police. But who knew how the Stockholm police might operate? Who knew what Interpol was geared to respond to? What madness had brought her here? Why did she do what she had just done? What she had always done.

But Charis Neale knew the answer before she had even finished asking herself the questions. She cut through the orderly lines waiting in front of the coat check counters, holding her Dignitary Pass before her so its official power could part the way. The clerk glanced once at the pass, then took Neale's long, silver tapestry coat with a smile. The Nobel Prize ceremonies were like a national holiday to the Swedes and they were used to dealing with visiting Americans. Much rude behavior was forgiven at this time. Though Neale doubted it was ever forgotten.

The banquet had ended and dancing and further celebration had moved into the Golden Hall. Before entering the boisterous throng, Neale stopped for a moment before the inlaid mirror of an elegantly carved wooden pillar to check her hair and gown. She smoothed a few errant strands of long blond hair, tucking them back into the tight bun she had drawn her hair into, perfectly contained and orderly. Her narrow face was suitably placid and unrevealing—a convincing show of composure brought by years of practice. The flush to her cheeks would be attributed to the winter air or to the supposed excitement of the event.

She shifted the snug, Fortuny-pleated silk of her gown, then tugged on the silver and crystal embroidered jacket of her outfit, centering it around the pushed-up fullness of her breasts above the gown's low neckline. Her appearance was going to cost her a great many annoyances this evening. Incredibly dull invitations from drunken scientists and reporters. Pawings by politicians and students. Nothing she had not experienced before. But knowing what faced her, she still would choose to wear exactly what she wore. Not for the panting audience of dullards, but for the one person who counted. The one person for whom she did all that she did. Her answer.

"Dr. Neale? We didn't think you'd be attending." The voice was hesitant and weak. Neale recognized it without turning, and forced a smile to her lips as she turned.

"Hello, Mrs. Weinstein. How was the ceremony?"

April Weinstein's mouth fluttered somewhere between a polite frown and a gasp of shock as her eyes caught sight of Neale's outfit. She was an old woman, her sparse hair dull gray and stiffly piled too high. Her own gown, bright blue, high at the neck, and long in the sleeve, made her look to Neale like the mother of the bride at a Vegas wedding chapel. And she was thin, much too thin, with a sallowness to her complexion that not even her thickly laid on and far too bright foundation could hide. The rumors of her illness were painfully more than rumors, Neale decided.

"It was just lovely, my dear," the old woman replied, pointedly not offering her hand. "Such a shame you couldn't be there." By her sarcastic tone, Neale knew the woman meant "as a recipient" and not as a member of the audience.

Neale returned Mrs. Weinstein's smile in kind. She stepped forward and spoke up so she could be heard over the confusion of the multilingual crowd and the dance music beginning to echo out from the enormous Golden Hall. "Well, it was really Dr. Cross's night to shine, wasn't it? And how lovely that after so many years of your husband's work being ignored, he was finally able to get here with Dr. Cross's help."

April Weinstein pursed her lips into a web of wrinkles.

Neale smiled consolingly and continued. "Your husband has often told me how much he looked forward to winning a Nobel. He's often told me so many things."

"Ah, there you are!"

Neale felt Adam Weinstein's thick hand slide lightly across the back of her waist as he came around to join her and his wife. The portly physicist, condemned to a tuxedo at least two sizes too small, stood beside his wife and gave her a quick peck on her cheek.

"We were worried you weren't going to show up at all," Weinstein said. He reached out exuberantly to take Neale's hand in both of his and Neale felt his eyes drop to her breasts. Neale smiled once more at Weinstein's wife as the old woman watched her husband watching Neale.

"Your wife was just telling me how lovely the ceremony was, weren't you, Mrs. Weinstein?"

Adam Weinstein slowly let Neale's hand slip from his. The hunger in his eyes was the same as it had been when she had been an undergraduate and he had been her prof at Harvard. He was notorious for approaching female students and politely, if explicitly, describing just what he would like to do to them and what he would like them to do to him. The only way he had survived to tenure was because he knew exactly how the university's system of faculty discipline worked: He never approached his own students, and he never propositioned anyone more than once so that the occasional indignant charges of harassment against him had never been easy to establish. Neale still remembered exactly what he had said to her before she had transferred to his department, and she could still see that same invitation in his eyes. Just as she could see so much else about him that everyone, including himself, thought was well hidden.

April Weinstein tugged on her husband's arm. "Adam, shouldn't we go back inside? The interviews . . . ? And . . ."

Weinstein shook his head impatiently. His face was flushed with more than the cold or excitement and Neale could hear the first hint of slurring come to his words. *Why not?* she thought. The physicist had a lot to celebrate tonight. More than anyone could know. Neale glanced at the arm Weinstein's wife tugged at. The sleeve of Weinstein's jacket ended two inches too short and pulled tightly against his beefy forearm. His shirt cuff was stained with food from the banquet, a portrait of a man whose appetites controlled him.

"In a minute, a minute," Weinstein protested. "No, really, Charis, what happened to you? I mean, I thought that . . . well, you know, only having the three of us up there. I thought that you understood that . . . well . . ."

Neale reached out to Weinstein's shoulder, more to bother his wife than to reassure the man. "Adam, I *do* understand. And the important thing is that the Nobel committee has legitimized the Cross Corollary to

Bell's Theorem." She saw Weinstein's eyes flicker beneath his bushy, salt-and-pepper eyebrows as she gave the corollary the name the physics community had bestowed upon it. "That gives us a firm theoretical foundation for the eventual consolidation of the three fermion families into one superfamily. We've got a strong hint at how gravity can fit within the standard model, and we've got everyone with an accelerator frothing at the mouth to see if they can prove the corollary's new interpretation of the Higgs boson and the graviton as braided versions of the same particle. My God, Adam, NASA's even considering adding a Cross accelerator module to Space Station when they start orbital construction next year. How could I not be happy with having a part in turning modern physics around one hundred and eighty degrees? A large part, a small part? What's the difference?"

April Weinstein hooked her arm around Adam's. "The difference," she stated defiantly, "is that what everyone's going to remember is that it's the *Cross* Corollary, and not the *Weinstein*-Kwong-Cross Corollary. It's . . . it's just not fair!"

Neale shrugged and took her hand away from Weinstein. Fame, and the attention it brought, was the last thing she wanted, now or ever. There was only one reason for all that she did, she reminded herself. One reason above all.

"As I'm sure your husband has told you, Mrs. Weinstein, the pursuit of science isn't fair. It's not the first time the proper workers haven't been granted recognition. It won't be the last, either. Good scientists just have to come up with some way to deal with that reality so they can keep going on with their work." She stared into Weinstein's eyes. "Isn't that right, Adam? We all have to deal with it, one way or another, don't we?"

He was so easy to read that Neale almost laughed. She could see the anger in him. And the shame. Because she knew how he dealt with the pressures of research and the agony of devoting his life to a field that only a handful of people in the world could understand. Scientists and children, what was the difference? Certainly not curiosity and the desire for bigger and better toys. And the things they'd do to get those toys.

Weinstein looked away, but not before Neale had been able to see that despite his anger, and his shame, there was still the hunger in him.

His eyes swept over her gown's neckline once more as he turned to his wife. "We better go in, pet," he said.

April Weinstein walked away with her husband without saying anything more. After a moment, Neale followed, wondering how Weinstein would deal with his appetites once his wife had succumbed to cancer. She had an image of a runaway reactor heading for meltdown. Neale was thankful that if the rest of this evening went as had been planned, then Weinstein's future plans, no matter how twisted, would never again be her concern.

Once through the huge doors leading into the Golden Hall, Neale paused for a moment, struck by the swirling effect of the intricate mosaics that covered the walls. They seemed to pulse with the noise and the music of the twelve hundred guests and she wondered what kind of person would have the patience to design something so complex and so useless. There was so much wasted time in this world. So much wasted opportunity.

The heat of closely whispered words suddenly flooded her ear, though the background noise was too intrusive for her to even guess what had been said to her. Neale spun quickly, coming face to face with Lee Kwong. The physicist's dark eyes were heavy-lidded and moist. His lips glistened and his straight black hair sprayed out in two different directions. He was drunker than Weinstein had been.

"Hello, Lee." Of course, Kwong's eyes did not fly to her breasts. What she had that he coveted was not attached.

"I said, you look lovely this evening, Dr. Neale." Kwong adjusted the black tie he wore. "Very . . . hot. Listen, Adam is not going to be able to keep his sweaty hands off you, you lucky girl."

"I've already seen Adam. He was a perfect gentleman."

Kwong laughed with a high, wild cackle. Then he stopped and coughed. "I'm sorry. I am so amused when you lie. You do it so badly."

"Taught by experts," Neale said. She nodded at the young man in the dark suit who stood behind Kwong, waiting to be invited to step forward. He had long blond bangs that fell over his forehead, and a shy smile. He held two flutes of champagne.

Kwong reached out for one. "Listen, I'd like you to meet my new friend, Gustav. Gustav is a student at Uppsala, aren't you, Gustav?"

The young man gave Kwong a glass of champagne, then held out his hand for Neale. His English was slow, but good. *"Goddag.* I am very pleased to meet you. Do you help Lee with his work?"

Kwong caught Neale's eye and she saw the message in his face. "Sometimes," she said, smiling graciously and shaking Gustav's hand. She turned to Kwong. "Have you seen Anthony any—"

"It must be very exciting to work with Lee," Gustav interrupted.

"Very much so," Neale agreed.

"He is avoiding me," Kwong said.

"I am the study of botany," Gustav announced earnestly.

Neale smiled at Gustav again. "Of course, Uppsala is where Linnaeus worked, isn't it?" Then she frowned at Kwong. "Why would he be avoiding you? Especially now? Does he—"

"Very famous Swede," Gustav continued excitedly. "World famous. Great man."

"He doesn't know anything," Kwong said.

"Are you certain?" Neale knew better than to assume anything about what Cross knew or didn't know.

"More than ten thousand species of plants Linnaeus described." Kwong signed at Gustav's interruption. "Of course I'm certain."

"Then why—"

"But he became a professor of medicine at Uppsala and—"

Kwong held his hand to Gustav's cheek and shushed him. "This is Gustav's first Nobel Prize party. He is quite taken by the glamour of it all, aren't you?" The physicist winked at Neale. "Remind you of anyone?"

Neale had seen the resemblance right away but had decided not to say anything. One way or another, Kwong was determined to have Cross. In the meantime, he made do with whatever and whoever was at hand.

"When was the last time you saw Anthony?" Neale asked.

Kwong shrugged. "At the banquet."

"And you're positive that he doesn't know what . . . arrangements have been made?"

Kwong turned back to Gustav, hiding whatever else there was in his eyes. "Look, I have already answered that. You are acting nervous, Charis. And that is a sign of guilt."

"I have nothing to feel guilty about."

Kwong's dark eyes flashed at her. "As I said, you do it so well."

"What?"

But Kwong didn't answer. "Gustav tells me there is a magnificent view of the old city from the tower. He is going to take me up there."

"And the . . . meeting?"

"Follow Adam's lead. It is going to be better than you thought. Really."

"Better . . . ?" That meant Kwong and Weinstein had changed the plan somehow, added an unanticipated detail. But that was impossible. Not without telling Neale.

"To the tower?" Kwong asked Gustav.

"Ja!" Gustav swung his champagne flute exuberantly forward to meet Kwong's and the two glasses exploded into shards.

"Damn you!" Kwong's shrill cry cut through the noise and the music as his face darkened with the full force of his infamous temper. He shook his hand free of the loose splinters of glass but Neale saw several glittering fragments stay embedded in his palm. Blood began to flow from the wounds.

Kwong stared at his hand as if stunned, transfixed by the sight of his own blood. He looked at Neale and waved his hand uncertainly. "Charis . . . could you . . . ? What do I do?"

Neale didn't move. Two white-jacketed waiters were already picking up the glass from the polished dark wooden floor. She couldn't bring herself to go near the blood, now running down Kwong's wrist, sopping into his white cuff and formal jacket. Not blood. Not again.

Neale's and Kwong's eyes met and held. She could see that something was close to erupting within him. He was about to say something, shout something, probably that they'd both regret. Then Gustav brought out a white handkerchief and placed it carefully around Kwong's hand.

"Idiot! There is still glass in it!"

Gustav pulled back his hands and the handkerchief floated to the ground, spotted with blood.

"Why don't you go find a bathroom and get cleaned up," Neale said, still not moving. "One of the foundation people must know a doctor here."

Kwong held the wrist of his injured hand as if it belonged to someone else. "Fine, right, of course. So much for the tower." He stormed off toward a distant door.

Gustav hung back for a moment, unsettled. "He hates me."

Neale didn't have the strength to deal with the boy, but it would be to her advantage to have Kwong's attention compromised, especially if there had been a change of plans. "No, he doesn't," she said. "Go follow him. It'll be all right."

Gustav smiled like a praised puppy and moved off through the crowd. *How could* any *of them survive without me?* Neale thought. And then she felt two hands move around her waist and she didn't jump or pull away because even in that split second of awareness that preceded the conscious recognition of who it was behind her . . . she knew. Just as she had always known. And always would. Forever.

There was no more reason to be upset at the events of the day. Anthony Cross had returned to her.

THREE

Neale closed her eyes as she felt Cross circle around her and the confusion of the Golden Hall dropped away. He must know what she wanted now, what he must do. And he did.

Neale felt his lips on hers, perfect, warm, and gentle. She breathed in the scent of him, felt him fill her senses, and wondered how she had survived even the past ten hours of their separation. His lips withdrew, brushed back against hers, then pulled away again. She felt his hands take hers. She opened her eyes.

And Anthony Cross was there, just as he was supposed to be, as perfectly and as suddenly as he had first appeared to Neale in the desert seven years earlier. She felt the same sudden ache in her heart now as she had then.

Cross's hands tightened on hers, every move a lover's caress. His dark eyes bore into hers and she could see his pupils dilate, a simple sign of pleasure which not even a person as brilliant as Cross could control.

"God, you're beautiful." His words made up for everything, even Adam Weinstein's hungry stares.

"I wore this for you." Neale pulled him closer to hug him again. She could feel his mouth draw up into a smile against her cheek.

"Too bad," he whispered as well as he could against the sounds of the celebration. "Because I'm going to have to rip it off you as soon as I get a chance."

Kwong and Weinstein and being late and cleaning up meant nothing now. Life was ordered again and Neale was in control. And all because of the one reason for everything in her life: Anthony Cross.

Cross hugged her to him as if he were conscious of nothing else, focusing all his concentration and awareness just on her. Neale absorbed the force of it greedily. She could see the people passing nearby, on their way to the refreshment tables or the dancing area, glancing over to stare at Cross. She couldn't blame them. Even if they didn't recognize him as one of the youngest Nobel Prize winners ever, or as the American physicist whose name was slowly acquiring the same public recognition as Einstein's, they couldn't help but notice Cross's smile—incandescent and infectious, Hollywood's loss.

The portrait of the American team that had appeared on the cover of *Time* when the Nobel Prize announcements had been made had exquisitely captured that smile, the youthful leanness and intensity of his face, the clarity of his eyes that could peer into depths unimagined. Neale had seen that image of Cross pinned up in universities around the country where it had captured a generation of young girls who had not the slightest idea what it was that Cross did. The portions of the cover showing Lee Kwong and Adam Weinstein, who looked much the way people imagined physicists should look, were invariably folded under or cut away completely to leave Cross on his own. But any jealousy Neale might have felt was tempered by her knowledge that, of all who were captivated by those riveting eyes in that picture, she was the only one who knew what it was like to gaze into the real things, and to understand the passion, the vision, and the genius behind them.

Cross stepped back again. "When you weren't at the ceremony . . . and the banquet, I got so worried. Adam didn't think you were going to come at all. I felt . . . alone."

Neale saw the pain of that word in Cross's eyes. He had no brothers and sisters, his foster parents had died before he had turned twelve, and Neale had never heard him say anything about his birth parents, even when she had asked. The researchers from *Time* had also not had success in uncovering anything at all about his early life. At the age of twenty-nine, hailed by the press and scientists around the world, facing a life full of the promise of staggering achievement, Anthony Cross *was* alone, separated from the ordinary world by accidents of fate as well as by his brilliance. Neale couldn't bear to see his pain. Never could. Which is why she did all she could to spare him from the unpleasantness of a world which he knew nothing about: the real world.

"Unavoidably detained," Neale said lightly and when she saw that Cross was not going to ask her why, she relaxed. One thing fewer to worry about this evening. Easier for everyone. "But you know I wouldn't miss this."

"You should have been part of it," Cross said. "The academy follows an antiquated rule structure that completely disregards the realities of modern research in physics. Only *three* people! It's—"

"It's all right, Anthony. I don't mind. Really." She could see that he couldn't detect the lie in her voice as easily as Kwong claimed he could.

"But they'll listen to me now, Charis. I can get them to change the rules. I can—"

"Bravo, m'lad!"

Cross and Neale both turned to see Henry Appleby, the octogenarian British chemist, saluting them with his gnarled walking stick. Cross instantly went to the man and placed both hands around the one Appleby offered, greeting him enthusiastically.

"Quite a day! Quite a day!" Appleby said excitedly, not giving up Cross's hands.

"Professor Appleby, may I introduce you to Dr. Charis Neale. She is the 'fourth man' on the Harvard team."

Appleby kept shaking Cross's hand. "'Fourth man,' y'say? Shame. Damned shame. Happened to that woman who worked with Cricks, Wilkins, and Watson, didn't it? What was 'er name?"

"She couldn't share their Nobel Prize because she was dead, Professor," Neale explained.

"Of course, she was. Like a doornail. Takes the bloody Swedes so damn long to make up their minds. The work I won for I did fifteen years ago—1980! Took 'em this bloody long to figure out what it was I'd done! But still, what a day."

Two bemused younger men wearing Oxford ties came up behind

Appleby, gently took his arms, and whispered reminders about what his physician had said and the interviews still to come.

Neale and Cross smiled as Appleby was led off, still chattering, without realizing that his audience had changed.

"That's what I'm going to do at the rest of the interviews when they ask how it feels to win the Nobel Prize," Cross said.

"What's that?"

"Point to Appleby and say 'just like that.' Better than any bunch of words I could put together."

Neale hooked her arm around Cross's, the rest of the day a distant memory to her as Cross told her of what he had done and how he had felt being on the stage with the King of Sweden. How Weinstein had almost not been able to get out of his chair when his name had been called. How Kwong had jumped out of his own *before* his name had been called. Cross talked about meeting the princesses, and the grim and unsmiling Soviet economists who had won the Riksbank Nobel Prize—the first for the U.S.S.R. in twenty years—for their penetrating analysis of the market factors that had almost caused the collapse of the EEC during the first three years of German reunification. "Can you believe it? *Soviet* economists!" Cross shook his head like a boy at a circus, marveling at the gaudy wonder of it all. Neale squeezed his arm more tightly against her, treasuring that expression and that moment. That was why she struggled—to protect Cross from all the dangers around him which he didn't see, or chose not to acknowledge. She had to keep him safe from Kwong and Weinstein, and their political machinations and personal faults which could destroy Cross's career, and to which he was so naively oblivious.

They began to dance and Cross kept talking, only for Neale. "And the Blue Hall? The one through the doors over there where they held the banquet. It's red! I don't get it. I kept asking those aides, 'If it's a *red* hall, why do you guys call it the Blue Hall all the time?' And none of them knew!"

"You're glad you came now, aren't you?"

"Are you?"

No, Neale thought. Harvard was better. The known was always better than the unknown. "You deserve the prize, Anthony. Of course I'm glad we came."

"But I still don't believe the hype, you know."

"A by-product," Neale said. "None of this is necessary. The dancing, the medal, the check. They're just symbols. An equation representing reality without being real themselves."

"And what do the symbols represent?"

"Power, Anthony. The power to choose your areas of study. The power to obtain allocations and funding. The power to be left alone."

Cross stopped dancing and held her tightly. His eyes never moved from hers. "Is that important?"

He just doesn't understand. "Of course it is. For a scientist, those are the three most important conditions to work under."

"Good," Cross said, and spun her wildly away, keeping one hand linked tightly with hers. Neale laughed, surprised by the suddenness of his move. He swept her back. "That will make things much easier."

"What will?" Neale's feet were beginning to tire in her tight shoes. She wondered if Cross could be convinced to sit down quietly someplace.

"Our agreeing like that. On what's important."

"Why wouldn't we agree?" She could see his eyes begin to stare away, as they did when he became irretrievably caught up in the pursuit of one of his ideas. "Anthony?"

"I can't imagine why. It's just that, you know, sometimes people have a hard time understanding me."

That was true enough, Neale knew. Even at the level of understanding represented by the members of the Swedish Academy of Sciences, most scientists were no different from the teenage girls who stared with hopeless longing at Cross's photo: They just didn't understand the man's work. "Not me, love. Never me."

Cross continued to look past her, peering beyond the walls of the hall, just as he stared out the window of his Harvard office at the sun, hard at work. "I know." His voice was so soft that Neale had to strain to hear him. "You understand me. And you always have, haven't you? Ever since the beginning."

"That's right," Neale said. She carefully lead him away from the other dancers, hoping that Kwong would stay busy with his hand or his blond student for a bit longer, to give Cross time to recover from the excitement of the day before he heard the bad news his research partners had in store for him. "Ever since the beginning."

He held her hand tightly and Neale promised herself she would never let go, never leave him alone and unprotected, just as she had sworn she would that day in the desert when Anthony Cross had first appeared before her eyes as whole and as complete as a suddenly observed electron, made real by a single act of observation.

Hers.

She had been furious. That's what she remembered most about those moments just before she had met Cross for the first time.

The helicopter was too hot, too noisy, and far too cramped. The fact that they had blacked out the windows, actually blacked out the goddamned windows so she couldn't see the desert—as if she didn't *know* they were in New Mexico, for God's sake, as if she couldn't find the old A-bomb test site on a Landsat map *anytime* she wanted—it made her want to scream. And she would have if she had thought that either of the moronic pilots could have heard her through their stupid-looking radio headphones. Screaming her rage would not have bothered her in those days when proper behavior was something to be scorned as something suitable only for suits and the great unwashed, before conformity and studied obscurity had become so vital to her survival. It had been a different Charis Neale who had arrived in the desert that day.

When the helicopter finally began to slow and descend after the fifty-minute flight, the copilot waved at Neale, motioning her to come forward.

"It's okay!" the man yelled over the wild thumping of the rotor. "You can look outside now!"

Neale lurched up to the front of the helicopter, swearing all the way at Adam Weinstein, the lecherous prof back at Harvard who had talked her into signing up for this so-called research project. And she swore at the two grown men in the headphones who behaved like little boys when they got behind the wheel or the yoke or whatever they called it of this thing. Her words weren't audible in the roar of the cabin, but the copilot grinned at her from behind his mirrored sunglasses, obviously reading her lips.

"Oh, great," Neale moaned as she braced a hand against the backs of the pilots' seats and looked out the front canopy. She had spent almost an hour in the air fuming at being prevented from seeing the scenery and now, when they finally told her it was all right to look out, there was nothing to see. The helicopter was so close to the ground its down draft was creating a sandstorm and she might as well be looking into the middle of a cloud. She heard the pilots laughing at her and then the helicopter touched down with a thud and she slipped forward, both hands sliding onto the men in front of her, one hand nearly hitting the copilot's lap. She fell to one knee as she twisted away from him and the two men laughed even louder.

Those were the feelings that raged through her as she crouched by the side hatch of the helicopter, forced to wait for the copilot to spring it open. She was twenty-eight years old and had spent eleven of those years in universities, which left her knowing very little about life other than it was *serious* and that macho helicopter pilots had no place in it.

The side hatch popped open and swung back with a clang that made her jump. She knew the copilot had done it on purpose, she just knew it. Outside the helicopter, the main rotor still spun, still stirred up the sand, obscuring everything beyond.

"Watch your step, beautiful," the copilot said, extending an arm behind her.

"You touch me and I'll break your fucking arm, asshole," she spat at him.

The copilot grinned again. She could feel his eyes all over her shorts and bare legs. "Might be worth it," he said.

It was the final provocation. Neale threw her canvas duffel bag out of the helicopter and jumped down after it.

"Not till the rotor stops!" the copilot shouted, but she ignored him, grabbed her bag, and started walking into the wall of blowing sand.

And then, as if she had suddenly wakened from a dream, the whine of the rotor stopped, the sand disappeared, and the most perfect man she had ever seen was standing in front of her, appearing so abruptly that she stopped only inches from colliding with him.

Without knowing why, Neale felt herself caught in a bizarre conflict, like a compass needle swinging back and forth trying to find true north. She was full of anger at the men who had brought her here, full of frustration at how dismally her doctoral thesis was progressing, physically stiff and sore, and dreading the six days and nights she knew she had to spend camping in the desert. And yet here was this man in front of her—who had just appeared in front of her—and he had eyes that stopped her completely. Eyes that looked *into* her, not at her, with a smile that didn't leer; it was a smile that cared. She had to concentrate not to follow through on her first reaction, which was to reach out and gently brush the windblown hair away from those haunting eyes.

She didn't know how long they stood there, facing each other in the desert. It could have been an hour. Probably it was only a moment. But it was the moment when she recognized that he was someone whom she knew, though she had never seen him or felt anything like this before.

There was something that joined them in that desert, in that moment, though Neale's rigid, scientific mind could not conceive what it might be. And as she wrestled with her conflict, swinging erratically, trying to find her one true direction, she suddenly realized that her anger and her discomfort and her dread were gone. Completely. Wiped out by the calming presence before her. The only thing she could do at that moment was wonder, *Who is this guy?*

With perfect timing, it was then that the man held out his hand, politely, awkwardly, as if he might also be experiencing some of what she felt, and said, "I'm Anthony Cross."

She took his hand in hers and as she introduced herself, she threw all her scientific ideals and concepts of the seriousness of life away, and couldn't help thinking that their hands were a perfect fit. That they were meant to be together. No matter what.

Ten hours later, on a blanket beneath the desert moon, far from the flickering Coleman lamps of the campsite, she found out how well the rest of their bodies fit together.

"I've never done this before," she told him after. "I mean, making love right away like this." Of course she had, once or twice, but she knew that it paid to have her lovers think that she hadn't. And she felt an unreasonable desire to have Cross think the absolute best of her.

"Neither have I," Cross said. In his case, Neale was inclined to believe him. He was only twenty-two.

"Must be the desert air," she said, astounded at how quiet the night was, enjoying the warm breeze as it took the sweat from her body.

"Or low-level radiation left over from the fifties affecting our endocrine systems." Cross said it so earnestly that Neale rolled on her side to stare at his face in the moonlight.

"You're not serious? Are you?"

Cross kept his eyes on the stars. "Well, that *is* what we're doing here. Measuring the long-term decay products of those early tests."

She was worried by his expression. "Weinstein told me that the residual radiation at this site was virtually nonexistent."

At last, Cross laughed and rolled up against her. "It is, don't worry. We'll just be measuring it with more sensitive tests and technology. There are some oddball anomalies around that no one ever thought to look for before." He kissed her, lightly, appreciatively, with nothing to prove, unlike some of the heavy breathers back at Harvard who somehow equated sexuality with how far they could stick their tongues down her throat.

"Are you always that accepting of what people tell you?" he asked.

"Only for what geniuses tell me."

His smile left suddenly. "Is that what you think I am?"

"You tell me, bright boy. Twenty-two years old and six months away from a doctorate in high-energy physics. That's pretty impressive. I'd say you're either a genius or your father is rich enough to buy off Weinstein and the rest of the physics department. Hey, maybe that explains the helicopter. If the university was paying the full shot on this, they would have had me *walk* out here. With a blindfold so I wouldn't see any of the goddamned top-secret government sand."

Cross shook his head. "The helicopter's courtesy of Shannon Industries. They're funding some of the project, not my . . . family." He was silent for a few moments. "I guess that makes me a genius."

"You don't sound too happy about it."

He sat up and wrapped his arms around his legs, hugging his knees close to his chest. "I don't think it's anything to be happy, or unhappy, about. I don't think I had a choice in the matter."

She ran her hand along his back. His skin was smooth, unblemished, perfect. The only thing he wore was a heavy bracelet of densely twisted copper wire that looked homemade. "Would you have chosen anything different if you had had a choice?"

"I'll add that to my list," he said.

"What list?"

"The list of things I want to find out."

Neale smiled. She remembered when she had been twenty-two, full of the idealism of science, the heady quest for new knowledge for the betterment of humanity, before she had discovered that science, just like every other organized endeavor, had its own netherworld of politics, and old boys, and bureaucracy as mind-numbing as anything the IRS could dream up. God, this kid was cute. She hated to think of the day when his dreams would be destroyed by reality. She wondered how she could help him survive it.

"Is it a long list?" Neale asked, sitting up beside him, kissing his shoulder.

"Twice as long as half of it," he said and she could feel his silent laugh.

"Spoken like a true theoretician." But Neale was worried. To have come this far by twenty-two, the kid must have skimmed through Harvard so fast that he would have no idea how the infrastructure of the scientific community operated. He'd be open to manipulation by aging professors who would try to steal his youth and enthusiasm to add luster to their stagnant careers. She had known Cross only a handful of hours but she could already tell that he needed guidance if his early promise was to be fulfilled. It would be important that he not be alone. She wondered what it was about him that made her know that so clearly. She wondered what it was about herself.

"I'm serious, Anthony. What's on that list? What do you see yourself heading for?"

He turned then, gazing at her for the first time since they had been joined together, and it was as if, for just a moment, someone else looked out at her, judging her, coldly and calculatingly.

Charis Neale didn't flinch. She didn't look away. Somehow she knew a decision was being made and she was prepared for it.

Cross reached out to her then and held his fingers to the side of her face. "What do you see?" he asked.

"Someone . . . who shouldn't be . . . alone," she said, overwhelmed with the sudden seriousness of the moment.

"I wish . . ." he began, but never finished the thought. He took his hand away. "First on the list, I want to find out how much the decay product curves from the samples on this test site deviate from the standard projections."

Neale blinked as if she had missed something, as if one Cross had left and another had replaced him. Her lover had suddenly turned back into a physics nerd. *Oh well,* she thought, *that's what I am, too.*

"Do you think they *will* deviate?" she asked, still taken with the task of keeping up with his sudden change of mood.

"Absolutely. My data will show that the radiation effects of the bombs tested here were much more powerful than originally predicted."

"Why?" Atomic bombs were old news as far as she was concerned.

But she saw the passion in his eyes as he talked about his project and she had no doubt he was in the right field. "Because there are still a few surprises left in physics," he said fervently. "I mean, I just know it, almost like I can see it right in front of me. There are things going on in atomic reactions that no one knows anything about. Extremely high-energy reactions that are taking place in small quantities, sure, but if we could just find a way to . . . filter them out from the bulk of the low-energy reactions, then concentrate them . . ." He sighed. "I'll be closer once we analyze the samples of wood and brick and steel that've been exposed to—"

"Uh, excuse me, Professor," Neale interrupted with a smile. "But we *are* in the middle of a goddamn desert, aren't we? Where're you going to get samples of that stuff around here?"

Cross twisted around and used an outstretched finger as a gunsight. "See on the horizon over there? That clump of blocky shapes?"

Neale saw it, barely, in the moonlight.

"That's what they call Atomic City. Four blocks of buildings constructed to see how they'd stand up to fission bomb blasts. They've got samples of just about any building material you can think of in there. It's, uh, pretty neat."

Neat, he said neat, she thought. She loved it. "Sounds . . . interesting," she said. "Is that where I'm going to be helping you and Dr. Kwong take samples?"

Cross shook his head. "We've already sampled that section of the target area. You're just going to be helping with the soil and vegetation samples. I don't know how Kwong expected just the two of us to do all the sampling work in the time we had."

Neale laughed. She had heard the student rumors about Kwong. "He was probably just trying to get you out into the desert by yourself, my dear."

Cross narrowed his eyes as if he didn't understand. Maybe he didn't, Neale decided, and smiled again at the innocence of youth.

"Too bad about the buildings, though," she said. "They look like they're a nice place for getting lost in." She kissed his shoulder again, tasting him, feeling an emotion grow inside her that she had always told herself would have to wait until she had graduated.

"Getting lost in together?" Cross asked.

"Mmm, hmm." She kissed his lips, lightly, teasingly.

"Maybe even disappear in?" he asked.

"Absolutely," she said, moving her hands from his chest and smiling at the stamina of youth. Three times and he was still hard.

"Then I'll take you there," he told her. He turned his eyes back to the stars, smiling at what she was doing.

"Promise?"

"Oh, yesss," he whispered. "Promise."

"When?"

"Does it matter?" he asked, gently moving his hand over her head, through her hair. "I don't think you and I . . . have to worry about time. I think we'll have . . . lots of time . . . together."

"How long?" she asked. She slipped her tongue across him, struggling against the sudden urgency she felt, the need to feel him in her once again. How could he possibly feel the way she felt? He was just a kid.

"Forever," he said, holding her to him.

"How're you going to manage that?"

"It's on the list," he said. "I'll figure it out."

And she didn't doubt it. She didn't doubt it for a moment.

FOUR

"*Förlåt mig,* Dr. Neale. Dr. Cross. I have a message for you."

Neale and Cross looked up from the green velvet banquettes on which they sat in a small alcove off the main hall, recovering from Cross's enthusiastic dancing. An aide from the Nobel foundation bowed obsequiously before them, his pink scalp gleaming through about five strands of white hair brushed carefully across his head.

Cross smiled at the man. *"Vad är det?"* Even Neale could tell that Cross's pronunciation was off, but the words had come quickly, without hesitation. Two months ago, he hadn't known a word of Swedish. But he had an eidetic memory and had decided to learn the language before arriving in Stockholm. It had taken him two weekends and three evenings.

The aide held his hands together apologetically. If the Nobel Prize ceremonies were like a national holiday to the Swedes, then Nobel Prize winners were like their gods. "Your fellow winners would like you to join them, Dr. Cross."

Cross took a sip of his mineral water. "Like for a group portrait, an interview or something?"

"No, no. Not *all* the winners. Dr. Kwong and Dr. Weinstein. They would like you to join them by the silver bar."

This is it, Neale thought as she got to her feet. *I hope I can get him through it. I have to get him through it.*

"Are they alone?" Cross asked as he balanced his glass on a narrow wooden ledge running behind the banquette.

"They are with the ambassador," the aide said.

Better play along, Neale thought, *as if I didn't already know what's been planned.* "Do you know which ambassador?" she asked the aide.

But Cross was the one who answered. "That'll be David Paine, the American ambassador." He took Neale's arm.

"You know him?" This wasn't right.

"Lee and Adam and I talked with him at the banquet. Interesting guy. He wants to meet you."

They stepped out into the Golden Hall again and began to make their way across the crowded room to one of the ten refreshment bars set up along the walls. Neale felt the cold of the Stockholm winter move through her. Cross wasn't supposed to have talked with the ambassador without her being present. Yet he seemed so calm. Was this what Kwong had meant when he said that things would be "better"? But how could such a drastic change in strategy be an improvement? And why wasn't Cross furious with what his partners had conspired to do to him and his work? Unless he didn't know yet. Or unless he knew something which Neale did not. She felt the panic of helplessness and loss of control and made it to the silver bar only because of Cross's strong grip, guiding her way.

"Mr. Ambassador," Cross said graciously as they joined the knot of tuxedoed men huddled in a corner behind the bar's serving tables, "may I present Charis Neale."

David Paine was a handsome man, with military short white hair capping an impressively sculpted and perfectly tanned face, quite an anomaly for Stockholm in December. Neale recognized the practiced, charming smile he offered as he extended his hand to her. It was as false as the ones she had given to all the nobodys and time-wasters she had met in the past five days.

"Dr. Neale, an honor to meet you."

Neale took the man's hand. "The honor's all mine, Mr. Ambassador," she replied, mimicking his smile and seeing the flicker of recognition in his eyes.

He nodded to her, a quick gesture of acknowledgment from one player to another. "Call me David, please," he said, and Neale sensed his effort to make his offer of goodwill genuine. He turned back to the tall man beside him, flanked by Weinstein and Kwong. Weinstein rocked uncertainly back and forth, a champagne glass in his hand threatening to spill at any moment. Kwong had a thick bandage on his hand. There was no sign of either Weinstein's wife or Kwong's student. This was a business meeting.

"Parnel," the ambassador said, addressing the tall man, "I believe you already know the youngest winner of the Nobel Prize in Physics."

The tall man shook hands with Cross. "The second-youngest winner, I believe that is. Sir Lawrence Bragg was twenty-five when he won it in 1915. X-ray crystal diffraction. Shared it with his father." The man was rail thin, cadaverous beneath an elegant formal suit that was perfectly tailored to his nonstandard form—at least six six but not more than one hundred and ninety pounds. He held out his hand to Neale, all bones and tendons, smiling with what seemed to be twice the normal number of teeth. "Dr. Neale," he said, "Charis, if I may, I'm Parnel Covington."

Neale took his hand. It was weak, surprisingly soft despite its appearance. "Are you with the embassy?" she asked.

The ambassador laughed. "Good God, don't I wish."

"Nothing so grand, I'm afraid," Covington said. "I'm with Shannon Industries. Just a businessman."

"Don't you believe him," the ambassador said. "Parnel *is* Shannon Industries. That makes him 'just a businessman' the way the President is 'just a politician.' "

"How interesting," Neale said politely. Shannon was a name that sounded as if it should be familiar to her, but she dismissed the man from her mind, not caring. She glanced at Cross, wondering how much of this he already knew. But she saw only his usual eagerness at experiencing something new.

She turned back to Covington, trying to determine the reason for his presence among them when there were other, more important things to discuss. "Tell me, Parnel, do you follow the prizes—as just a businessman—or did you just happen to be in town for the ceremonies?"

Covington's face was completely unreadable, as skilled as the ambassador, and Neale herself. "I've been following Anthony's work ever since he was a student and took part in that study on the unexpected effects of radiation at abandoned A-bomb test sites. Ground-breaking work."

"Yes, certainly," Weinstein slurred. "Helped set that project up. First time the three of us worked together. Saw the boy's promise even back then."

Kwong stared at Neale. "And I did the fieldwork with him. Long nights in Atomic City. Charis, I believe you showed up there, too. Toward the end."

Of course, Neale thought, remembering the hideous helicopter ride she had taken the day she had first met Cross. It was courtesy of Shannon Industries, Cross had said. Neale suddenly felt suspicious, wondering what other connections to Cross and Paine this Covington might have.

"And I have followed his work ever since, as a businessman *and* as an American," the tall man concluded.

"Patriotism? In science?" Neale tried to look appropriately innocent as she assembled a list of possible motives Covington might have for talking with Cross, especially since the American ambassador was about to take Kwong and Weinstein from Cross's life. Scientists divided much more readily along institutional lines, or in divisions between experimentalist and theoreticist approaches. Nationalism was usually far down any scientist's list of priorities, more a burden to communication and travel than an incentive for work.

But Covington looked serious. "A nation's wealth is no longer measured by its stores of gold, Charis, nor even, in these changing times, by its stockpile of weapons. We live in a technological age, for better or worse, and our wealth these days is our ideas. Of course I take pride as an American in Anthony's work, and the work of his teammates as well. This boy has helped change the course of particle physics and now the rest of the world has to look to him, and to America, for leadership."

"Until next year's prize ceremonies," Neale added realistically.

Covington laughed and sipped at his champagne. "I think that's unlikely." He smiled at Cross. "And I believe you think that's unlikely, too. You're in the lead to stay in the lead, aren't you, son?"

Cross's eyes were clear and unwavering. "Yes," he said, with more meaning and conviction than any speech Covington might give. "I am. That's why I was so intrigued when Ambassador Paine first mentioned your proposal."

To Neale, hearing those words was like feeling her heart stop. The only proposal supposed to have been made this night was the ambassador's, not a private businessman's. The understanding had already been reached months ago, as soon as the Nobel announcements had been made. Kwong and Weinstein were to leave Harvard for the Jet Propulsion Laboratory, to work for NASA on the design of particle physics test platforms for use in space. And Cross wasn't to be part of it. He was supposed to have finally been pulled away from Kwong and Weinstein and the chaos they inhabited, leaving him safe with Neale at Harvard. Where all conditions were known and under control.

Neale saw the expression on Kwong's face and realized that he knew everything. This was what he had been talking about: something had been planned behind her back. The assistant's back. "Oh, what proposal is that?" She tried to make the question sound casual.

But Covington wasn't fooled and Cross at least looked slightly uncomfortable. Neale was stunned. He had actually been trying to keep something from her.

"Parnel's company—group of companies, I suppose—wants to set up a private research facility," Cross said. He dug his hands a bit deeper into his pockets, rumpling his jacket and trousers.

Neale didn't see the point. "What type of research?" she asked. "Certainly not elementary particle physics?"

Covington was knowledgeable enough to laugh. "Not even the government appears able to afford that these days." He nodded to Cross. "Theoretical physics."

Neale blinked in surprise. "You're joking. A private facility for . . . for basic research . . . in *theoretical* physics?"

Covington shrugged. "Someone's got to do it."

"They're called universities."

"Underfunded, overburdened. Getting worse each year."

"But they *are* where all the important work is going on now."

"Because there are no alternatives, Charis. Now there will be."

Neale didn't like it. Whatever else universities were, they were safe. And why weren't Kwong and Weinstein saying anything? Unless they had already said all that they needed to say. "Why? There's no advantage to basic research for your company. For any company."

"Spoken like a scientist," Covington said matter-of-factly, avoiding any sense of paternalism. "But there are many advantages—private sector advantages, if you will—which someone from an academic environment might not be familiar with." He paused, but Neale did not interrupt. "First, of course, are the tax advantages. Every dollar my company spends on our proposed facility is another dollar and twenty-four cents that we don't have to give to the government for throwing away on its deficit. Then there are the public relations benefits. This is the team's first time in the public eye, but it won't be its last. You know the honor and prestige a Nobel Prize brings to your university, how it attracts the best and the brightest minds. Same thing applies for private companies like IBM. And it will apply for Shannon Industries when Anthony, Lee, and Adam win another."

Neale held up her hand to stop the man. "Anthony, Lee, and Adam? You want to talk all three of them into joining your . . . your private facility?"

Covington took a quick look at Kwong and Weinstein. "Well, Lee and Adam are already on board. I'm just trying to talk Anthony into joining now."

"They can't join. They're going to JPL. Paine is here to make the formal offer to them on behalf of NASA and—"

The ambassador shook his head. "That offer . . . fell through, Charis. I really think Anthony should give serious thought to what Parnel is offering."

Neale stared at Cross, but he made no sign of rebuking her for knowing about the JPL's offer for Kwong and Weinstein and not telling him about it. It was then she realized that he had not told her all that he knew, as well.

Covington began speaking again, taking advantage of the awkward silence. "And most important of all for Anthony to consider are the opportunities for developing the applications of his work."

That was going too far for Neale. "Applications! What possible applications can there be for equations that . . . that have no connection to our frame of everyday, classical, macro-reality?"

Covington allowed a look of concern to appear on his face. "I hate to say this, but that's a remarkably shortsighted question. What applications were apparent when Einstein first sketched out his special theory of relativity? Yet his work is the underpinning of the entire nuclear industry. And what applications could possibly have been expected to come from Heisenberg's and Bohr's work on quantum mechanics, which was so bizarre that not even Einstein wanted to accept it? Yet modern electronics wouldn't exist today without it. No transistors. No computers. No VCRs or microwave ovens. Who are any of us to say that Anthony's work will have no applications, just because we can't think of any . . . today?" Covington held his glass out to Cross in a salute. "Though personally, I'm hoping that someday this young man's work will give us artificial gravity." He laughed just before he sipped his champagne.

"Nonsense!" Neale felt her face flush. Who was this money-worshiping troublemaker? Science had its groupies like any other endeavor perceived by some to have prestige, but Covington didn't look the part. What was he doing here? Why would even Kwong and Weinstein listen to the man? "Artificial gravity is impossible!"

"For at least a hundred years or so," Cross said quietly.

"Maybe not that long," Covington interrupted. "The Higgs boson is, as far as we suspect, what gives particles mass. Mass warps spacetime. Warped spacetime is gravity. Once we find the Higgs boson—and the Cross Corollary has now made that a possibility with existing accelerators—who knows what we'll learn?"

"Your analysis is a bit simplistic," Neale said coldly, intending it as an insult. "We don't even know why particles have mass to begin with."

"Other things will probably come first," Cross agreed.

"See?" Covington gestured grandly. "He's thinking about applications, too."

"There's still an immense amount of theoretical ground to be covered," Neale insisted.

"Of course there is, Charis. And that's what the Shannon facility offers. The time and the money to cover that ground."

"Harvard provides time and money."

Covington shook his head. "How much time, Charis? Squeezed in between interminable classes and bureaucratic reports and artificial pressures to publish anything at all if you want some ridiculously small salary increase"—he held up a finger to stop her interruption—"*even* with tenure. And how much money? How many other departments and projects do you have to share time with on your preowned Cray computer? I'm offering Anthony his own Cray-Hitachi, latest model. How much time do you waste each year trying to decide for which conferences you'll apply for travel funds? How many opportunities do you miss each year because your teaching schedule and department budget won't permit you to attend those other conferences? I'm offering Anthony a blank check for travel. Any conference, anytime, anywhere."

Covington turned to Cross, the conviction of an evangelist in his eyes and voice. "Aren't you tired of all the time you waste worrying about paying the rent, taking the car in for repairs, finding department money at the end of the month to pay the fax bill because someone in Germany came up with a good idea and your long distance charges went overbudget? All that horribly mundane routine. Good God, think what you've already accomplished when you've only been able to devote . . . what, 20, maybe 30 percent of your time to the work you really want to do. Think what you can accomplish when you're able to devote 100 percent of your efforts to discovery and creative thought! Ten years' work accomplished in two! Even . . . artificial gravity in two decades instead of a century! That's what I'm offering!"

Cross's eyes were afire, embracing Covington's dream. Neale could feel Cross's intensity blanketing the celebration that still danced around them, muting it, banishing it. The American ambassador gazed at Cross as if seeing a religious vision.

"I've paid the rent the past seven years we've been together, Mr. Covington," Neale finally said into that silence. "I look after the car and the bills. I handle the department's budget for him. All the mundane routine."

"And look at how those tedious activities have affected your own work," Covington said bluntly. "Of all people you should know the advantages of the arrangement I'm offering."

"A university has other functions," Neale countered. "Anthony finds his students and his coworkers invigorating. They keep him on his toes."

"And that's precisely why my company extended its invitation to Anthony's coworkers to join him. *And* to any of his students whom he feels are sufficiently . . . invigorating. As well as to any other physicist in the world he might care to name." Covington smiled tightly, playing a final card. "And of course the invitation extends to you, Charis. I know how much you contributed to the work that brought the team here." He looked directly into her eyes. "If not for the archaic rule that says only three people may share a Nobel Prize, I have no doubt as to who the fourth physicist on that stage would have been today."

No matter how much she believed his words to be true, Neale refused to accept them. "At Harvard, a Nobel Prize does wonders for shaking extra money out of the budgets."

"I'm talking about never having to budget again."

That stopped her. Only for an instant, but it stopped her. The truth was that on the brink of the twenty-first century the pursuit of science was more rooted in checkbooks than in grand thoughts. Even theoretical physics, which once required no more than a piece of paper and a pencil, had grown dependent on multimillion-dollar computers able to model the birth of the universe in an afternoon. The rate of accumulation of knowledge in science, even of achieving break-throughs, was directly proportional to the amount of money made available to its practitioners. And Parnel Covington was now offering an unheard of opportunity: to lift those false barriers to the pursuit of the ultimate understanding. Unlimited funding could mean unlimited knowledge. It was within her grasp.

"Out of the question," she said. "The disruption in Anthony's work that would result from trying to set up—"

"Charis, it already is set up," Covington said. "Lee and Adam have been extremely helpful in that regard. What I'm offering Anthony, and you, is the key to a facility that's 90 percent in place now— SHARP: the Shannon Facility for Advanced Research in Physics. It's absolutely beautiful, in Malibu, overlooking the Pacific. If you saw it once you'd never leave. We just need the few final specifications for the computers and other equipment that Anthony has promised David he'd work out with us in New York in the next two days and—"

"Anthony will be in Sweden for the next *four* days, Mr. Covington. Then he'll be in Switzerland for the visit to CERN, then the lectures—"

"CERN!" Covington said it like a curse.

Neale blinked at the dismissal of such an important shrine of science. The European Laboratory for Particle Physics had been home to one of the world's most productive research accelerators for years and consequently one of the most important facilities in particle physics research. Nobel Prizes were born there almost as often as newly discovered particles.

"The team at CERN is the best placed to locate the Higgs boson in accordance with the Cross Corollary, without having to wait for the Superconducting Supercollider to finish its budget battles and come on line in Texas," Neale said. "And the leaders of the team that finds the Higgs boson are going to be the physicists up on the Concert Hall stage next year. Anthony must establish himself at CERN to become part of that team."

"Engineers," Covington said. "Clockmakers and mechanics." He studied Neale's incredulous expression. "Brilliant clockmakers and mechanics, I'll give you that, but even you must know that anything they do at CERN in response to the Cross Corollary is simply a mopping-up operation. They'll only be clinging to Anthony's coattails." Obviously Covington sided with the theorists and not the experimentalists.

Neale felt a shudder pass through her, of frustration or of fear she couldn't tell. The man was impossible to argue with; he understood nothing of what it meant to be a scientist. In their battle for Anthony Cross they had no common ground. And Kwong and Weinstein had apparently already given up the fight. Kwong stared at the floor, Weinstein at her gown, licking his lips drunkenly, eyes moving in and out of focus. Neither one of them seemed concerned about Covington focusing so much on Cross and the Cross Corollary, as if they, too, were no more than assistants. She almost enjoyed seeing them that way.

But it wasn't enough. "Mr. Covington, as intriguing and as generous as your offer is, I'm afraid that I cannot accept, and neither can Anthony. Basic research like this cannot be taken from an academic setting, *should* not be taken from an academic setting. Now, if your companies would be interested in setting up a funding program through . . ." And then she saw the look in Cross's eyes.

"I believe I will accept Parnel's offer," Cross said softly, without apology.

"Anthony . . . no." But Neale's words were no match for his youthful smile, the warm promise of his eyes. "You can't."

"He just has," Covington said, trying not to make it sound like a statement of victory.

"But . . . he can't. It's . . . impossible." She willed Cross to read the message in her eyes. He must leave Kwong and Weinstein. It was too dangerous to remain associated with them.

The American ambassador put his hand on her shoulder. "Why, Charis? Why can't Anthony accept this . . . magnificent offer?"

Neale couldn't speak. The reason was so obvious, yet so unspeakable. The brilliant work to which they had all contributed, and which had brought them all from Harvard to Stockholm to change the future of physics and, in time, the lives of all the people in the world, was founded on more than rigorous work, inspired insights, and incalculable hours of study.

It was founded on murder. Brutal, bloody, and insane.

And Neale knew that as long as the American Nobel Prize-winning team remained together, the madness would never end.

Never.

Los Angeles

ONE

T he coroner was out on the balcony throwing up when Detective Kate Duvall arrived at the scene. She thought about that situation for a moment at the doorway to the apartment, then decided she would go talk to the coroner first, before entering the kitchen to see what waited for her there. Eight years with the Los Angeles Police Department and her stomach was still as sensitive as that first time she had seen violent death.

The night air on the balcony was cool, more of the distant ocean than of Hollywood smog. But that would change in the next few weeks as July came and the summer took its relentless hold on the city. Duvall sniffed the air as she slid the glass balcony door shut behind her, cutting herself off from the forensic specialists inside, precisely measuring and recording the scene before Duvall came to take it apart. She had always liked the promise of summer, until she had started working Homicide. Now, too much heat meant too much work. And the stink of bodies.

"How're you doing, Ash?"

Ashraf File looked up from the balcony railing. A small whisker of liquid hung from his elegant Van Dyke. He wiped at it. He looked exhausted. "Oh, goodness. I'm thinking of starting a new diet," the doctor said hoarsely, smiling weakly. "The Beverly Hills Coroner's Diet. No special foods, no exercise. Just a book of photographs . . ." He leaned back over the side and dry-heaved, apparently empty.

Duvall glanced over the side, wondering if the doctor had managed to hit anything interesting, but saw only some jade shrubs five stories below, starkly side-lit by the light spilling from a first-floor apartment. On the street beside her dingy white VW Bug convertible, easy to spot because of its crumpled fenders, Duvall saw four unmarked cars, an ambulance, and three black-and-whites with slowly spinning cherry lights grouped around the building's entrance, their radios squawking with random chatter from the other police broadcasts of the evening. A plainclothes officer she couldn't recognize in the streetlight shadow was talking with a woman at the side of the ambulance. Other than that, all the action was up in the apartment with Duvall.

The detective looked back inside the apartment behind her and saw the forensic specialists milling like bees behind the glass. Her own reflection was superimposed over them by the double panes of the sliding door. She grimaced at herself, but the blackness of her skin was lost in the reflected shadows that fell across her face. All she saw was the indistinct form of a tired woman in old jeans and an LAPD Police Games sweatshirt, dressed for a long overdue weekend off. But her gold badge and ID hung in a plastic pouch around her neck like a child's necklace and that fabled weekend was going to be postponed again. The team inside were going to be her people now, just as the unseen body in the kitchen was. She sighed, not eager for the challenge, but happy for the comforting protection the immediacy of a new investigation would bring. For however long this one would take, she knew she would be justified in not letting anything from her real life intrude. This was her work and all the rest could wait.

"That bad, Ash?" Duvall asked when File came up for air again.

The doctor pulled a handkerchief from his suit jacket pocket and wiped at his beard. "I didn't even do this at my first autopsy as a student, but . . . maybe I'm getting the flu."

Duvall shrugged. "When you get used to it, you stop caring. I do it all the time," she lied, then leaned back on the balcony railing, watching the light from the photographer's flashgun strobe from the kitchen door. "What are we looking at here?"

File followed her gaze inside, shook his head. "Something bad," he said quietly. "Something quite, quite bad."

After a few moments in the kitchen, Duvall was surprised to find that her stomach wasn't threatening to rebel. The scene was too unreal. Surely what she looked at could never have been human.

"Female," File said, standing beside Duvall, handing her a pair of thin surgical gloves.

Duvall tightened her mouth. "Thanks for sharing that, Ash." The intact part of the body tied to the kitchen table before them wore a white micro-skirt over black leotards. The tight-stretched jersey above the skirt, original color unknown, was thin and soaked with the red sheen of new blood, still wet and shimmering in the bright light of the overhead fluorescents. According to the radio reports Duvall had heard, an unidentified caller who had distorted his or her voice had phoned in a tip fifty minutes ago. Less than two hundred minutes ago, Duvall estimated, this body had been alive.

File snapped his own gloves into place. "Male, female, in this neighborhood, who can be sure?"

They approached the body, File to the left, Duvall to the right, an audience of uniforms and technicians watching from the two doors into the kitchen. Everything in the crime scene had been photographed and charted for later analysis. Now it was time to look for the things not immediately apparent. The unseen.

The blood on the floor was still tacky under Duvall's Reeboks as she sidestepped the ringed footprints presumably left by the killer. The blood had dripped from the kitchen table, an inexpensive wood-grain melamine slab bolted to two pairs of black metal legs. Another source of blood at first appeared to be a bunched-up tablecloth hanging in a clump from beneath the body's head, but it was a rope of dangling long hair—once blond, now slick red—suspended from a flap of what seemed to be soft dripping leather.

Duvall looked away. Those details would come later. She squatted down to examine the ropes keeping the body in place on the table. Her left knee creaked noisily and she saw File give her a little grin. She was slim enough, she knew, and was still holding her own in the losing battle against gravity, but not eating was no longer enough for someone almost midway through her thirties. She promised herself, for the

fourth time that month, to get back to tennis again. She thought guiltily
of her unopened exercise bag in her car's trunk, then her eyes flashed
to the far corner of the room, onto the floor under the four-inch overhang of the built-ins. "We got some bloody tissues or something under
the cupboards over there by the fridge," she called out.

"I got 'em," the photographer answered from the door. "There's
another pile behind you, too."

Duvall glanced over her shoulder, placing one finger on the blood-
coated floor to steady her balance. There was a coarse weave to the
bloody tissues in the second pile, gauze pads probably, and underneath
them was something balled up, crumpled and thin like plastic. She
glanced down at her free hand, rubbed her fingers together, checking
the appearance of the rubber that protected them after its powder had
been cleaned off. Whatever was under the gauze pads looked just like a
discarded surgical glove. She filed the thought. Provided whoever had
worn them hadn't kept them on too long or sweated too profusely, there
was a better than even chance that fingerprints could be lifted from the
insides. She turned back to the body and the ropes.

"Looks like a regular Boy Scout," she said as she examined the
knots that had been tied in the white nylon cord. Behind her, she heard
some laughter. She knew no one thought she was funny. It was just that
in this job, if you didn't laugh, you cried. Or you drank. Or your
husband moved out.

"I'm going to cut these ropes so we can save the knots. Lewis?"

A short P-1 in uniform stepped through the kitchen door. "Yes sir,
ma'am, Detective."

Duvall held out her hand, thinking dark thoughts about rookies.
"How about a knife?"

Lewis looked around. A set of kitchen knives angled out of a block
of wood on the counter. "One of those okay?" he asked.

Duvall didn't believe it. "No, it's not *okay*. This is a murder
scene."

A forensic technician passed a utility knife to Lewis, who handed
it over to Duvall. "The perp didn't use the kitchen knives," Lewis said
in his defense. "We got two doctor's knives on the floor by the dish-
washer."

Duvall took the utility knife and looked under the table, past File's
legs. *"Doctor's* knives?"

File squatted down and looked at them, glittering in the shadow-less light of the kitchen. "Scalpels. A number-seven general purpose and a . . . Hagstrom probe? Goodness."

"What?" Duvall asked. She didn't like the doctor's tone.

File glanced at her under the table. "Look at this," he said, then stood up. Duvall followed.

"What do you see here?" File asked after a few seconds of study, gesturing to the ruin of the body's head. "What would you say happened?"

Duvall studied it, completely detached. It made no sense. So she fell back on what did, in this city of the angels, in this year of the Lord.

"I see a young woman, wrong side of thirty, realizing she's running out of time to be a starlet. Desperation sets in. She stops being as choosy when it comes to deciding who she's going to invite home. Tonight her judgment let her down completely. Some guy who said he was a friend of a friend of someone who worked at a studio said he could get her an audition, came home with her, offered to show her a few of his Boy Scout tricks, tied her up, raped her, then beat her head in with"—she looked around the kitchen for the proverbial blunt instrument, didn't find it—"something large that he apparently took with him."

"Why tie her up in the kitchen?" File asked. "Why not the bedroom?"

Duvall shrugged. She looked around again. What made a kitchen different from a bedroom? A refrigerator? Brighter lighting? "What's the bedroom like, Lewis?"

Lewis stammered. "Uh, there's a photo in there . . ."

"What kind of photo, Lewis?"

"I think of the . . . uh, victim."

Duvall called out for deliverance. "Joe!"

Detective Joe Seabrook, only three months on the homicide desk but first detective on the scene, stuck his head through a doorway, thin sandy hair framing the perfect bald sphere of his head. "Right here," he answered.

"What's the bedroom like, Joe?"

"A regular Playboy Mansion. Satin sheets, mirrors. Red lights. A 'boudoir' portrait of a young lady hanging over the bed."

"This young lady?"

Seabrook turned his palms up. "A reasonable assumption, but . . . ask me again tomorrow."

Duvall nodded. She understood. The face of the body on the table was too swollen, too covered in blood and gore for an identification to be made at the moment.

"Uh, Detective Duvall?"

"Yes, Lewis."

"Uh, the . . . woman in the photograph in the bedroom has a, uh, mole on her uh, left, uh breast." Lewis's cheeks were red. "If that's uh, any help."

"Thank you for sharing that with us, Lewis." Duvall wondered where they were finding rookies these days. She gestured to File. "That's your side, Ash."

File slipped a scalpel of his own from the small black case he carried, then slit the body's blood-soaked jersey along a side seam. He peeled it back from the torso, exposing a single pale breast mottled with blood in the pattern of the jersey's fabric. There was a small mole in the seven o'clock position, two inches from the nipple.

"That it, Lewis?" Duvall asked.

Lewis walked over, slipped a bit when he stepped in the thick blood, and swore. "I mean, yes, that looks to be the same as in the, uh, photo."

"Thank you, Lewis. Very observant of you. And take off your shoe before you track blood all over the place." Duvall turned back to the coroner as he carefully replaced the fabric over the exposed flesh, preserving dignity where no more could ever exist. "So, anything else?" she asked File.

The coroner turned to the photographer beyond the doorway. "Did you get lots of close-ups of her head?"

"Every angle, fully bracketed," the photographer answered.

"Good," File said, more to himself than to anyone else. "Look at this, Kate." With his scalpel and two fingers, File began to carefully push away at the semisolid matter that surrounded the immense wound on the body's head. Duvall had been in the LAPD long enough to recognize scattered brain tissue when she saw it, and she knew she was seeing it now. But there was something more beneath it on the body's forehead. Something that didn't push away.

"What's that?" she whispered, afraid that she knew the answer.

"Surgical gauze," File said. He reached across to Duvall's side of the head and moved away a thick clump of blood-soaked blond hair. "Held in place by surgical tape."

Duvall blew out a silent whistle. What she had thought to have been a bloody deformation of the body's crushed skull was instead a roll of thick fabric similar to the gauze wipes on the floor. "But . . . why?"

"And look at this," File said, using his fingers to wipe away the thick clumps of brain matter and other unidentifiable dark clots from the body's forehead. "See the break in the skin?"

Duvall's eyes widened. The skin hadn't been torn or ripped. The break in it was straight and clean.

File worked closer to the top of the head, or rather, to where the top of the head should have been. "And the cranium. See the opening in the cranium?"

"Oh, Jesus . . ." Duvall said, voice so soft it was no longer even a whisper. "It's . . . it's been . . . cut."

"And look at the cut line."

Duvall leaned closer, eyes straining to make sense of the mess that was once a head. "There are . . . scallops or something . . . the little indentations at the edge?"

"Drill marks." File pursed his lips, used his scalpel to smooth down a mass of tissue at the edge of the opening.

"*Drill* marks?"

"Standard procedure."

Duvall straightened up, angry. "What the hell is goddamned 'standard' about some asshole drilling into someone's skull?"

"Not some asshole, I'm afraid. This is a craniotomy."

"Craniotomy?"

"Surgical entrance into the head." File frowned as he pushed more clumps away from the wound. "Quite professional, too. Except for the trauma to the brain itself, of course."

From one of the doorways, Duvall heard someone softly swear.

"See, here?" File continued. "A ring of circular burr marks defines the area. Then a blade cut connects the drilled holes." He looked around the floor. "Someplace, there should be the piece of bone that was removed."

"Removed?" Duvall asked, still not wanting to accept the doctor's scenario. "Not bashed in?"

"Cut out, Kate. Quite deliberately. Quite, quite deliberately."

"Why?" Duvall heard herself ask, and was surprised. She had long ago given up asking the why of murder. The truth was, despite the public's fascination with the crime, despite the ongoing debate among ivory-tower criminologists eager to prove that all murderers were created by some combination of dysfunctional families or damaged genes, there was nothing special about the act of taking a human life. Certainly some murderers were "created" as the experts maintained, but on the street, cops knew that one person could kill another for the exact same reason that a different person might slam a door shut or lean on a car horn. Duvall was sure that some of the cynicism inherent in being a cop came from that: the knowledge that all people had it in them to be criminals of the worst kind, and that what divided honest civilians from degenerate criminals was usually no more than a stroke of luck, good or bad, a chance occurrence, or the temperature on a hot summer day. The truth was, most killers weren't any different from anyone else. But then, most killers didn't perform surgery on their victims. She shook her head. This was going to be something special. She knew it. "What makes someone kill a person and then cut into her head like that?"

"Oh no, Kate. It did not happen like that. Look at the blood flow, the swelling of the face. Oh no, this person was killed *by* the procedure. Not before it."

Duvall paused to play the doctor's words back in her mind to make sure she had actually understood what he had said. "Someone . . . did this to her, while she was still alive?" She put her hand on the side of the table, to feel something solid.

File nodded. "That would explain why her bonds are so tight. So she wouldn't be able to move during the . . . procedure."

"Jesus," Duvall whispered. "Tied down. Gauze. Drill." She looked at File. "How many times would it take to figure out the best way to do something like this? It looks too elaborate for a single killing."

"You think it's as bad as that?" File asked.

"I hope it's not, Ash," Duvall said. "I hope we find out this woman's boyfriend was a brain surgeon with an attitude. If this is the first of a new . . ." She couldn't bring herself to say the word.

"You ever investigate a pattern killer before?"

"This is one murder, Ash." She held up a rubber-encased finger, dotted with blood. "One. And I don't want to hear that term used, okay?"

"Kate, someone here you should see," Detective Seabrook called from a doorway.

File nodded grimly to Duvall as she turned and left. She stopped just inside the doorway to roll off her gloves and kick off her Reeboks. She walked into the living room in her socks. "Remember those shoes are mine, guys. No baggin' 'em as evidence. Like the last time."

In the tiny living room, Seabrook stood by the open door to the balcony and motioned to Duvall to join him. Duvall saw a woman in a crisp, summer white blouse and skirt, standing on the balcony, obviously the person Seabrook wanted her to meet. Maybe a witness from the apartments across the street, Duvall hoped, or a roommate, or the person who had phoned in the anonymous tip to check out this apartment in the first place.

But when Duvall stepped onto the balcony, she saw that this woman was not meant for a small one-bedroom off Sunset—an estate in Bel Air was more like it, with a chauffeur and maids. Duvall felt an unexpected knot of jealousy rise up in her. This woman on the balcony was perfect in a way that few could ever hope to be. Her skin was smooth and flawless, her shape full yet exquisitely honed by what was probably the attention of a personal trainer, and her blond hair, apparently natural, was long, gleaming, and stylishly cut. Duvall sighed, thinking of her own extravagant hair from the early days, before she reluctantly realized that long hair and forty-eight-hour shifts did not go together. Today, her curls were efficiently short, no longer a burden, and she knew that women who had long hair also had something else— time. More than the money the woman on the balcony obviously had, more than her physical perfection and the advantages that went with it, Duvall found that the woman's time was what she envied most. Time wasn't necessarily money. But it was freedom.

Seabrook introduced the women. "Detective Duvall, this is Dr. Neale."

Duvall kept her neutral expression frozen. Was it really going to be this easy? "Did you know the woman in the kitchen, Dr. Neale?"

Duvall felt Neale's eyes go over her as if the doctor were preparing for a dissection. *Please let it be this easy,* Duvall thought.

"I haven't seen the woman in the kitchen," Neale answered. Duvall heard the coolness in her voice, but also sensed a hesitation, an uncertainty. *Good.* There was nothing detectives liked better than talking to people who were nervous, because that meant they had something to hide.

"Then why are you here?" Duvall asked benignly, already organizing the information she wanted to obtain from Neale and the order in which she would ask her questions. She kept her ears tuned for the telltale flatness in Neale's voice that would tell a good listener she was lying. She watched to see which way Neale's eyes would flick, how often she would blink or nervously half-smile. All liars had a tell that would give them away; all good cops could spot that tell in minutes if not seconds. Then the trick was to prove with evidence what was already known by instinct.

"I was on my way to visit the woman who lives in this apartment," Neale said.

"And the woman who lives in this apartment is not the woman who's on the table in the kitchen?"

"I told you, Detective, I have not seen the woman on the table in the kitchen and so I am unable to tell you if it is the woman who lives, or lived, here."

Seabrook and Duvall exchanged a look and an unspoken assessment: Neale was being too precise, too evasive. Most definitely she had something to hide. It *was* going to be easy.

Duvall smiled tightly. "Would you like to see the woman on the table?"

Neale returned the smile in kind. "Would you like me to see her?"

Duvall's smile turned to a grin. "Joe, why not get that photo from the bedroom and bring it out here for the doctor to identify. The woman on the table is cut up pretty badly . . . but I suppose you're used to that in your line of work, aren't you, Dr. Neale?"

Neale blinked in puzzlement. "I beg your pardon?"

"You *are* a doctor, aren't you?" Duvall liked to see the look on a criminal's face when the realization of capture occurred.

"Yes, I am," Neale confirmed.

"And what's your specialty? Obstetrics? Neurosurgery?"

"I am an elementary particle physicist, Detective. A doctor of science, not medicine."

Duvall could see Neale register her flicker of surprise. She tried to keep her momentum going. "And are there any . . . medical applications to your work?"

Neale's smile made Duvall feel like a child being told that babies aren't really found under a cabbage leaf. "Detective, there are absolutely no applications to my work, medical or otherwise."

Duvall saw her easy arrest evaporate. She needed a few seconds to regroup. "Then why do it?"

"I would find that very difficult to explain."

Duvall heard the unspoken *to you* at the end of Neale's sentence and reluctantly let the insult pass. Above all else, she was a police officer, despite what some of the brass thought.

Seabrook returned to the balcony carrying a large color photograph, printed on paper embossed with a thick brush stroke pattern and held in an ornate antique gold frame that appeared to be made of thin plastic. The photograph showed a woman—the woman from the table according to the mole on her left breast—arched back on a thick white fur throw, wearing something black and lacy that anointed her body instead of covering it. The picture had been shot through softening filters, but the woman had looked directly into the camera and her face was clear though her expression was enigmatic.

Duvall watched Neale's face as the scientist looked at the photo. It was Neale's turn to show surprise.

"Is that the woman who lives in this apartment?" Duvall asked.

"Well, yes . . ." Neale stared at the photo.

"What's her name?"

"Cassie . . . Cassie Riley." Neale was distracted, eyes fixed on the picture.

"Is something wrong, Dr. Neale?"

"No, not at all."

"Have you seen this photograph before?"

"Never."

"How do you know Cassie?" Duvall asked.

"She . . . was one of the office assistants where I work."

"You seem a little surprised by this photo of her. Why's that?"

Neale shrugged, at last stopping her study of the image. "It just doesn't seem to be her style."

"In what way?"

"She seemed to be a very conservative girl. Quiet, soft-spoken. Not . . . not . . ."

"Not what, Dr. Neale?" Duvall was enjoying putting the other woman on the spot.

"Not as . . . adventurous as this photo would suggest."

"Adventurous," Duvall repeated. That was as good a euphemism for tramp as any she'd heard. "And why did you show up here tonight, Dr. Neale? Working late?"

"No, well, yes. In a way." She was still flustered by the photo. "I was going to tell Ms. Riley that she was . . . no longer needed at the facility."

"The facility?"

"SHARP. The Shannon Facility for Advanced Research in Physics."

"Is that where you work?"

"Yes."

"How long?"

"Three . . . three and a half years now."

"And why was Ms. Riley no longer needed at SHARP?"

"Missing too many days. Her . . . productivity was significantly less this past quarter."

To Duvall, Neale's last words sounded rehearsed. But perhaps they had been, in order to easily break the bad news to the person being fired. She turned to Seabrook.

"Joe, could you please take a statement from Dr. Neale. Time she arrived, Cassie's employment record, all the usual." Duvall turned back to Neale. "Doctor, it might be necessary for someone from my department to go to your office to check whatever files you have on Cassie. Just in case we see a pattern in the days she took off, that sort of thing. Would that be all right with you?"

Neale nodded. "Of course, but I don't think you'll find anything."

"Why's that?"

"I . . . I just don't think you'll find anything. Our personnel files aren't that extensive."

Duvall filed that comment, too, especially the way it had been said. No question but that Neale was lying about something, even if her lies had nothing to do with Cassie Riley—yet. "Well, we'll see. Never know what you're going to turn up on a good day."

Duvall slid back the balcony door. Behind her, she could hear Seabrook say to Neale, "Detective Duvall has a great eye for detail. She can find patterns where—" Then she was back in the confusion of the murder scene, hoping she had the murderer not more than ten feet away.

Fingerprint technicians were bagging some used dishes left on the coffee table in front of an old couch with a tattered arm that trailed stuffing. Duvall had seen that kind of damage before and knew what it meant. "Anybody seen a cat around?" she called.

A ragged chorus of no's came back. Lewis said there were two pet food dishes on the kitchen floor, one labeled "Misty," but no one had seen a cat. Duvall put the question aside and walked into the kitchen, expecting to find File waiting for her so he could prepare to move the body. But the coroner was gone. And so was the body of Cassie Riley.

Duvall wheeled in the doorway to the kitchen. *"Who moved the goddamn body?"* she demanded.

Lewis sheepishly pointed toward the open door to the hallway and Duvall stormed out. She was the detective in charge. Nothing could be moved from the scene without her permission. It was probably those rookies again. It was probably—

Lieutenant Maxwell Erhlenmeyer was in the corridor, talking with Ashraf File. Duvall almost stumbled when she saw him. The lieutenant snapped his head around.

"You all right, Detective?" Everything Erhlenmeyer said was like a cross examination from a defense attorney. He gave the perpetual impression that nothing anyone said to him could ever be the truth. He was a font of pure, undiluted, cop paranoia.

"Fine, Lieutenant," Duvall said, recovering from the twofold shock of seeing Erhlenmeyer somewhere other than his office and in something other than a suit. But even in his casual slacks and surprisingly loud Hawaiian shirt—obviously purchased on sale after everyone else in the city had turned it down—the lieutenant looked like a cop: big, beefy, crewcut, mean. The word was he had never had a successful undercover operation because he was always made as a cop within seconds. His promotion to lieutenant had been achieved not as a reward for brilliant policework, but by the department's seemingly insatiable need for getting additional anal-retentive administrators into the loop who could be counted upon to maintain the status quo. In Erhlenmeyer's case, both needs had been met.

"What are you staring at, Detective?" He always sounded as if his next sentence to Duvall was going to be an invitation to slug it out. Duvall didn't know if it was because she was black, a woman, or just a better cop than he could ever be. She suspected a combination of all three. But she didn't care. It wasn't anything she hadn't faced before. The important thing was that she knew she could take him. Anytime, anywhere.

"Not staring at anything, Lieutenant," Duvall said, keeping her tone civil at great cost. "Just surprised to see you at the scene of a run-of-mill homicide."

Erhlenmeyer's snort was like a bull's. "From what File says, this is anything but freaking run-of-the-mill."

"I don't know, looks like we might have the perp out on the balcony talking to Joe right now."

Erhlenmeyer's eyes clouded. "Who's out on the balcony?"

"Charis Neale, some scientist the victim used to work for."

"At the Shannon Facility for Advanced Research in Physics?" Erhlenmeyer spat out.

"Yeah," Duvall said, surprised again.

"Do you know what that is, Detective?"

Duvall kept her insults in check. "Suppose you tell me, Lieutenant."

"Suppose you find out for yourself, Detective. It'll give you something to fill up your spare time with." Erhlenmeyer turned back to File.

Duvall waited impatiently for a few seconds, not liking the subtext to what the lieutenant had just said.

"Excuse me, sir," she interrupted. Erhlenmeyer ignored her, discussing the scheduling of Cassie's autopsy with File. "Excuse me," she said again, louder, "but I don't know what you meant by what you just said."

Erhlenmeyer excused himself to File, then took Duvall aside. "This is your weekend off, Detective. Remember weekends? You got too many days saved up, you work too much, it's affecting your performance."

"*What!?*"

"This isn't your case."

Duvall slammed a fist backward into the hallway wall. "What is this bullshit? I'm the ranking detective on the scene. I don't have a caseload worth shit right now. I know this area—I live right across Sunset for God's sake. I—"

"You're on freaking vacation, Duvall. Now smarten up. You're a detective second and I'm a lieutenant. Your *supervisor* reports to me."

Duvall's rage was suffused with panic. "No, Lieutenant, come on! You can't take me off this one."

"You were never on it, Detective."

"But . . . this is my job!"

Erhlenmeyer leaned close, his voice a rough, threatening whisper. Duvall could smell scotch. "This never should have been your job, *Ms.* Duvall. Everyone knows the only reason you were made detective is so the affirmative action faggots get to see two checkmarks for the price of one." He counted off the two checkmarks on the fingers he held up in her face, whispering his hate to her. "That's one gold star for a nigger, that's two for a cunt."

Duvall felt her heart slam to a stop and her arms go cold. "You cocksucker," she spat at him.

"Funny," Erhlenmeyer snarled, "I heard that's how you got your promotion."

Duvall lost it. Her fist shot out and buried itself in Erhlenmeyer's spongy gut. He let out a woof of stale breath and took a startled step back. But his stomach was large and Duvall's fist was small and the damage she was able to inflict was inconsequential. He smirked at her, even as he fought to catch his breath. So she hit him on his jaw, brutally snapping his head around. He slammed into the floor with an even louder explosion of air.

Duvall was frozen on the spot. She glanced over at File, saw he was trying not to laugh, and immediately felt better. Two other cops appeared in the open doorway to the apartment and rushed to help the lieutenant up. Both managed to give Duvall an appreciative wide-eyed look. Duvall smiled, knowing she shouldn't, feeling her fist, elbow, and shoulder tingle. The first words Erhlenmeyer spoke when he sat up in the corridor were no surprise.

"You're . . . suspended." Then he broke into a fit of coughing.

"Yeah, but you're an asshole, and at least the union can get me a hearing." Duvall heard the suppressed chuckles of the uniforms and

File, and found herself laughing. Somehow, it was all worth it. At least for the moment.

Duvall left the apartment building's lobby and headed for her convertible. The ambulance was still parked outside, along with the three black-and-whites but only three unmarked cars. Someone had already left. Erhlenmeyer's black Lincoln was parked half on the sidewalk, half in a bed of impatiens. She walked past it, carrying her Reeboks in their evidence bag in one hand, dangling her key chain in her other, toying with the idea of keying Erhlenmeyer's door. But it would have been too obvious. Then again, she had never thought of herself as a subtle person.

She got to her car and through the open roof immediately caught a rich vanilla scent. She swore. The flickering red LEDs of her underdash police band scanner sparkled in the thick glossy puddle leaking out of a paper bag on the passenger seat. The Häagen-Dazs she had been taking home an hour ago when the first broadcast about the murder had come over the air was history. One way or another, summer heat was out to get her.

She got into her car, turned the key, heard the motor chug uselessly. *Here we go again,* she thought, but this time it took only two tries. She mentally added "get a tune-up" to "start tennis again" on her list of things to be done someday soon, then slipped her car into gear but kept her foot on the clutch. For a moment she paused, looked up, past the light streaming from the fifth-floor balcony, a solid luminous shaft in the moist night air, up to the glowing night sky of the city. No stars were visible. They never were, here. Maybe that's why she always felt lost in some way, as if she didn't know where to go without them. She sighed, thought of nothing more, then drove away, slowly.

Erhlenmeyer she could handle. The suspension, too. Even the twisted violence that had ended Cassie Riley's life. But now the real challenge was before her and she wondered how much longer she could face up to it. Alone, and with an empty weekend without work stretching blankly before her, Kate Duvall was afraid to go home.

TWO

C haris Neale sat at Cassie Riley's desk at SHARP, the image of the dead woman burning in her mind. Not surrounded by police as she had appeared in the last glimpse Neale had had of her through the kitchen door, tied to a table and butchered, but as she had appeared in the photo taken from her bedroom: almost naked, posing for her lover.

Neale had recognized the position Riley had assumed—legs parted, hands caressing her own breasts, and the black lace teddy she had worn. Neale had an almost identical photograph of herself. And the same underclothes. Both had been presents from and for Anthony Cross. Just for the bedroom he shared with Neale. Just for the two of them and no others.

"Is there anything I can help you with, Dr. Neale?" Beside the desk, Angelica Corkin waited patiently, her expression full of concern. She was one of eight office assistants employed by SHARP, seven now that Riley was dead, and Neale suspected the woman was excited by the sudden confusion her department had been visited with, not saddened as she tried to pretend.

"No, thank you." Neale placed her hands on the desktop before her, preparing herself for what she must do. "I'll just place everything into the box for her . . . parents, isn't it?"

"That's right. In Wisconsin. But . . . ?" Angelica screwed up her eyes.

"Yes?"

"Shouldn't the police be doing this? I mean, to look for clues or something?"

Thank God for television, Neale thought. *It makes everyone a legal expert.* "We'll keep the box here until the police come to look through it. But in the meantime, we'll need the desk for Cassie's replacement. Why don't you see if you can find a storage locker with room where we can lock these things up. For the police."

For an instant, a smile appeared on the office assistant's face, quickly erased by a studied expression of pious severity. "Certainly, Dr. Neale. Don't you worry. I'll arrange for that right away."

Neale watched the woman trot out of the small cubicle, then prepared herself to go through Riley's files and belongings. Alone, she could admit to herself that she was nervous. Desks were models of their owners—the tops of them the face presented to the outside world, their interiors a mirror of their inner selves. Neale was still shaken by the photograph and what it might mean. She was afraid that she was about to find something equally unsettling.

Riley's desktop was innocuous enough. In addition to a set of In and Out trays filled with various purchase orders and other ordinary paperwork, she had a framed picture of a house cat with the name "Misty" written beneath it, a Shannon Industries mug filled with a variety of pens and pencils, and a plastic-covered blotter beneath which an assortment of "Far Side" and "Cathy" cartoons had been placed. Neale glanced at them, failing to find their humor as she sought for some hidden message in the way they were arranged. But she found nothing.

The first drawer held office supplies, including what must have been a guilty collection of twisted paper clips. There was also a SHARP phone directory, well thumbed. Neale flipped through it. Cross's office extension was underlined and beside it, hand-printed in blue ink, was his private line's number as well.

Seeing that number, knowing that it could only have come from one person, made Neale feel as if a knife were moving through her stomach. But what had she expected? She knew that Cross had been involved with someone else in the past few months. Of course it was logical and efficient for him to have chosen that someone else from the facility. But why had he modeled her after Neale, even to the photograph and the costume? And who else had known about it?

A second drawer held nothing of interest. A third drawer contained reference books. Neale could understand an office worker having a pocket dictionary and a guide to writing business letters, but *The Penguin Dictionary of Physics* could only mean that the poor woman had been harboring some delusions of actually conversing with Cross, after he was finished fucking her. Neale knew that's all that Cassie Riley could ever have been to him. Not lovemaking, not passion. Just fucking.

But the fourth drawer dug the knife in deeper and twisted it. Neale pulled out a makeup bag, large enough to do double duty as an emergency overnight case. It was heavier than it should have been and Neale realized she had found the props that went along with the photos and the clothes. It had gotten that far.

She didn't recognize the largest vibrator from the case. It was larger than any of the ones Cross had preferred to see Neale use in the past—an anatomically incorrect sleek phallus of gleaming black plastic, studded with asymmetrical bumps that had not been designed for pleasure. She held it in her hands, looking for a manufacturer's name. The whole device seemed wrong, more like a homemade surgical tool than a sexual aid. She wondered why Cross had never shown it to her. Never asked to see her—

"Is this a private party or can two play?"

Neale's head jerked up and she felt her cheeks flush. But it was from anger and not embarrassment.

Parnel Covington stood in the open entrance to the cubicle, long arms stretching up over the tops of the gray-blue, fabric-covered partitions.

Neale laid the vibrator on the desk. She watched it rock back and forth for a moment before settling. She was beyond humiliation when it came to Covington. "Cross was seeing her, wasn't he?" she said coldly.

Covington widened his eyes. "Is that jealousy? I thought you had to have a heart to feel that."

Neale ignored him. "You knew, didn't you? You goddam knew and you didn't tell me!"

Covington stepped inside the cubicle and sat on the edge of the desk. "Would it have made any difference?"

"The girl is dead, Parnel."

Covington shrugged. He picked up the vibrator, hefting it like a bottle of fine wine. "So? There's nothing that can link her to SHARP."

"She *worked* here! She saw them all every day."

Covington held the vibrator out to her, narrowing his eyes. "What does this *feel* like, Charis? I mean do you push it in all at once? Or does *he* push it in? Or does he like to—"

Neale slapped the phallus from Covington's outstretched hand and the device thudded onto the floor's thin industrial carpeting.

Covington smiled and folded his arms over his chest. "If you had been looking after him the way you're supposed to, he wouldn't feel the need to go out with other women. Then none of this would have happened."

Neale gripped the edge of the desk. With anyone else, she'd be screaming at the top of her lungs. But her years with Covington had dulled that level of her emotional response to him. She felt only hatred, cold and dull. "Look after him . . . the way I'm supposed to . . . why don't you just say 'fuck him' the way I'm supposed to?"

"Fuck him. Suck him. Play his little games. Whatever it takes to keep him here and keep him happy. That was the deal, remember? You make Cross happy, I take care of Kwong and Weinstein. And money. And everything else."

Neale threw the makeup bag into the cardboard file box by her chair. She didn't need to see what else Riley had kept in it. She had her own. "There's only one thing that'll make Anthony happy these days."

"I know," Covington said calmly. "Finding the Beginning. Of everything. More power to him, I say." He flipped back the photo of Riley's cat to look at it. "Think he's going to be any closer with the demonstration he's running today?"

Neale began emptying all the other drawers into the cardboard box. She hated how Covington approached everything with such damnable calm. She was certain the man was a psychopath, completely incapable of any kind of emotional reaction. Maybe that's why he was such a successful businessman: He could lie, cheat, and steal without remorse or conscience. She wondered what else he might be capable of.

"Well . . . ?" Covington continued. *"Is* he up to some kind of breakthrough or what?"

Neale placed the photo of the cat on the top of the box. Cross said he liked cats but wouldn't let Neale keep one in the house. Too much trouble he had told her. Too many things to go wrong. "I don't know, Parnel. Anthony won't tell me. He says it's a surprise."

"You're the one person he's not supposed to be able to surprise, remember? You're his translator. His anchor."

Neale stood up and lifted the box to the desktop. "If he doesn't tell me what he's doing then I don't have anything to goddamn translate for you, do I?"

Covington placed his hands on the box to keep Neale from taking it away. "Is he not talking to you? At all?"

She wanted to say something in answer, anything. But all she could do was shake her head.

"Charis, you're the only one who can understand him. You're the only one who got him this far. Despite . . ."

"Kwong and Weinstein?" Neale asked bitterly.

"Despite everything."

Neale took a deep breath. Could Covington take the truth? She decided she didn't care. "I'm losing him, Parnel. It's not working anymore."

Covington got up from the desk and retrieved the vibrator. He stuck it down a corner of the file box. "Is it sex?"

Neale said nothing. She couldn't believe that he had asked the question, as if that were the only reason she might be having trouble with him.

"Look," Covington explained. "I know all about you scientists and sex. I've read the reports, okay? Half the researchers in the world are jerking off into their computers because they can't take the pressure of their work. One way or another, if they can't get something out of their minds they're going to damn well get it out of their bodies. Tension is tension. Am I right?"

"It's more than that, Parnel."

"There *is* nothing more than that. You call it acquisition of data. Cross calls it understanding. Scientific discovery or cold hard cash. Call them whatever you want, but they're still the same thing—power."

"Anthony is not that simple."

Covington shoved his hands in his pockets as if trying to keep them from doing something else, such as reaching out to her. "Jesus, Charis. You've seen Weinstein when he comes back from his Tijuana weekends. Once the hangover's gone he's twenty years younger. Recharged. Same for Kwong and half the staff he's got in his department."

"You know how I feel about them. You know how I've always felt about them and what they've done to Anthony. You can't compare them to him."

Covington came around to Neale's side of the desk. "Look at me, Charis. I know we can't compare Anthony to either of them. To anyone. Not his intellect, at least. But beyond that, maybe in spite of that, he's still a human being. And in that way he *is* the same as everyone else. Exactly the same."

Neale felt like running away from Covington, from SHARP, from everything. Except Cross. "The same as everyone else," she repeated. "Even you?"

Covington raised a hand to her face and brushed his fingers over her still reddened cheek.

"Especially me," he said. His hand dropped to her neck, the tips of his fingers brushing against the hollow between her collarbones before he took it away.

Neale refused to turn away from his gaze. "Anthony will be expecting us in the lab."

Covington's mouth twitched up into a smile. "And what are you expecting?" he asked.

Neale didn't answer. She didn't know.

THREE

"There will never be a TOE," Cross said offhandedly as he led the others through the wide, skylit corridors of SHARP.

Neale blinked in surprise, almost running to keep up with Cross's energetic strides. She looked over to Lee Kwong, white lab coat flapping as he, too, struggled to match Cross's lead. The other physicist looked shocked by Cross's unexpected announcement.

"I beg your pardon?" Covington asked cautiously, as if he thought he might be stumbling into a joke. He only had to increase his already long stride by inches in order to stay abreast of Cross and appeared as relaxed and as calm as ever. When he had greeted Neale by Cross's office, it was as if he had seen her for the first time in a week, their meeting in Cassie Riley's cubicle driven from memory.

Cross turned a corner and entered the facility's central courtyard. It was glassed-in at the roof, two stories up, and filled with a small encompassing forest of specimen palms and ficus. It had been specially designed, Covington once told Neale, for the day when momentous press conferences could be held there.

A handful of SHARP's hundred and twenty-five employees were sitting in the courtyard's multilevel conversation pits, either taking a break or furthering their work through heated discussion. Cross looked straight ahead as he passed them, ignoring a few half-offered greetings. "No full and complete unified theory," he said, nodding to himself. "No Theory of Everything." Neale had seen it before. His mind was thinking of one thing while his mouth carried on an independent conversation.

"A TOE is the Holy Grail of physics," Covington said. "Or have you just relegated sixty-odd years of science to the dumper because you've had an insight?"

"Yes," Cross answered simply. They left the courtyard for the long corridor leading north to Lab 2. Each of the four began fishing for their employee access cards to get through the large security doors ahead of them. "By the way, where's Adam?"

"Phoned in sick today," Covington said. "Apparently he had . . . a big night last night." His eyes never flickered.

"Forget that old fart. What in heaven's name are you talking about?" Kwong asked as Cross inserted his card, placed his palm on the glass plate of the reader, and impatiently waited for his identity to be confirmed.

"They're all wrong," Cross said as a green light glowed and the security doors slid open. He walked through and waited for the others to process their cards. Overhead, heat and motion sensors kept track of the number of people who passed through on each card.

"Are you suggesting the standard model should be trashed?" Neale asked, withdrawing her approved card from the reader. She was concerned, yet did not believe that Cross could possibly say yes. She hadn't even known he was moving ahead to develop a TOE. They had agreed that that work could wait until someone had actually found either the Higgs boson or the graviton as predicted by the Cross Corollary to Bell's Theorem. To proceed past the present point of confirmed findings without firm data was wasted effort. Even if they did happen to stumble upon the right answers, nothing could be accepted by the community without at least the possibility that an experiment or a set of possible observations could be described which would make their conclusions falsifiable.

"Of course the standard model shouldn't be trashed." Cross set the pace again down the white corridor. Behind him, Covington and Kwong cleared the security station and the doors slid silently shut. "No more than Newton's work, or Einstein's, should be trashed. It's just that the usefulness of their work all depends on the context it's to be used in."

"And that context is . . . ?" Covington prompted.

"Newton's work is pure mechanics. It adequately describes gravity as it's experienced in the everyday world. But it doesn't work at relativistic speeds. It's not wrong, just not universal. Einstein went the next step and his general theory of relativity described gravity at the extremes of mass and velocity that we might reasonably expect to observe —at the time he did his work. He didn't supersede Newton, he added to the earlier knowledge."

"Refinement, not replacement," Covington said. Neale could see him nervously glance at Cross, eyes echoing his confusion at what Cross was leading toward. She had not prepared him for it. Just as Cross had not prepared her.

Cross spun to Covington, smiling broadly. "Exactly! Refinement, not replacement. I like that, Parnel." He chuckled, seeming to forget all about the demonstration he had planned especially for the man who funded SHARP. "So the standard theory, imperfect as it is, that all of us work with to describe the universe at the quantum level of existence —beyond anything Newton could have imagined, and beyond anything Einstein *wanted* to imagine—is an additional refinement, and not replacement, to describe what goes on at the most extreme limits of reality, at the very smallest size and at the earliest instant of creation."

"And you've come up with another . . . refinement?" Covington asked. He glanced at Kwong and the scientist shook his head. Whatever Cross was leading to was a mystery to him, as well.

They arrived at the metal doors to Lab 2. Warning signs for laser light, radiation, high voltage, and explosive gases were mounted in permanent frames bolted to the door but Cross ignored them. It was his lab. There would be nothing going on inside it that was not under his control.

Just inside the doors was the main electrical supply panel. Cross lifted the clear plastic cover from it and threw the primary rockers as the others entered the lab. Overhead, the fixtures on the twenty-foot-high ceiling flickered into life and Neale could feel the rhythmic hum of the main generators starting up in the generator room next door.

"Listen, Anthony!" Kwong exploded after a few seconds of Cross's silent work.

Cross looked away from the electrical panel, baffled by the insistence in his coworker's tone.

"What?"

"What is it?"

"What?"

"The refinement?"

"Ah yes." Cross nodded. "Anyway, the standard theory now is able to describe electromagnetism, the strong nuclear force, and the weak nuclear force as three different aspects of the same basic phenomenon."

"Even I know that," Covington said. "GUT, a grand unified theory. Glashow, Salam, and Weinberg won the Nobel Prize for describing it in 1979, and Rubbia and Van der Meer won five years later for providing the experimental proof at CERN."

"Very good, Parnel," Cross said, holding up his finger to make a point. "And what they and everyone else are doing today is wasting enormous amounts of time and energy in trying to bring gravity into the equation, to describe gravity as a fourth aspect of the same force that gives us the two nuclear forces and electromagnetism." As he spoke, Cross led them along the forty-foot length of the left-hand tunnel branching from the monstrous eighty-foot doughnut of what was jokingly called the lab's mini-accelerator. Though compared with the fifty-three-mile diameter of the Superconducting Supercollider accelerator that had been under construction in Texas—in budget-related fits and starts—since '91, SHARP's machine was infinitesimal. The spotless apparatus, the first to be built solely to unlock the secrets of the Cross Corollary, looked like a string of silver milk truck tank trailers, joined together into a letter Q with an inordinately long tail. "And gravity is *not* a fourth aspect of the same force," he concluded.

"But it is!" Kwong sputtered.

"Is not!" Cross countered, falling into the rhythmic exchange shared by disagreeing researchers and arguing children. He sat down at a chair by the computer workstation control console, throwing back his white lab coat like a concert pianist adjusting the tails of his jacket.

Kwong swore in Chinese. "You *always* do this!" he exploded. "Yes, we are doing an experiment on electron mass that you still haven't adequately described to us, and you . . . you go off onto tangents . . . and waste time . . . and no one ever knows what you are talking about . . ." More Chinese mutterings. "Listen, Anthony, we have not published *anything* in almost two years! CERN cannot find our braided particles. Our work is being dismissed, uh huh. And you will not focus on the job at hand!"

Covington froze at Kwong's outburst. Neale began to move between the two scientists, though they were already separated by the table covered with computer equipment and video monitors. Of the four people in the lab, only Cross seemed composed. Neale enjoyed seeing Covington become nervous at last.

"Lee," Cross finally said calmly, typing commands on his keyboard. "Don't ever say I waste time. I took a drive last night. I looked at the lights in the city, and . . . and an idea just popped into my head. I can't stop having ideas, can I?"

"I talked with Adam last night," Kwong said, voice choking with anger. "He is very upset and I cannot blame him. He is talking about leaving us, publishing with Glashow. Listen, Harvard says there are flaws in . . . in our work."

Cross stopped typing. "In the corollary?"

"No, of course not," Kwong began. "The mathematics have been proven flawless time and time again."

"Good," Cross said and resumed his work as if the discussion had ended.

But Kwong hadn't finished. "Listen to me, Anthony. They say there are flaws in our *interpretation* of the corollary. They say that the reason CERN has not found our braided particles is because they cannot exist."

Cross shrugged. "They can't." He flicked on a video monitor.

Neale and Kwong exploded together. *"What!"*

Cross blinked. "It's obvious, isn't it? Actually, I'm surprised it took them this long to figure it out. I mean, the whole concept of braided particles was a mathematical construct to begin with. It was an easy way out for the problem of determining imaginary rest mass in relation to the Higgs field, but nature took a different way. Much more elegant, but not as apparent."

Neale leaned against a horizontal two-foot vacuum pipe joined to the accelerator's target chamber as she felt her world collapse around her. Cross had just said that the theoretical breakthrough for which he and Kwong and Weinstein had been awarded the Nobel Prize in Physics almost four years earlier was no longer valid, despite the near unanimous passion with which it had been embraced by physicists around the world, and despite the burgeoning numbers of papers it had spawned. But even in her despair, she saw a bright side. With funding for SHARP cut off by Parnel and Shannon Industries, she and Cross could go back to a university environment away from Kwong and Weinstein. A safer environment.

Covington stood by Cross, towering over him. "How long have you known this, Anthony?"

Cross seemed genuinely puzzled by everyone's reactions. "Over a year, I guess."

"A year!" Kwong cried. He shoved his hands into his crazed mass of gray hair.

"And why didn't you tell anyone?" Covington asked. Neale could hear the edge in his voice. She estimated Shannon had put more than thirty-eight million dollars into SHARP in the past three years, not counting the lease on the Cray-Hitachi.

"I had nothing to offer in its place," Cross said, and Neale began to sense a matching edge in his voice, too. She wouldn't want to see an outright confrontation between Cross and Covington. It could only end up one way—with Cross walking out.

"Do you have something to offer in its place now?" Covington asked, obviously reaching the same conclusion Neale had. He spoke as if his words were defusing a bomb.

"I haven't worked out all the math yet," Cross said simply, "but yes, I believe I have. Lee, could you check the nitrogen levels in the magnets?" Incredible, Neale thought. Through the entire conversation he was carrying on with business as usual and he was expecting everyone else to do the same.

But Kwong had had too much. "Here now, if you haven't done the math then how can you have *anything?*"

Cross looked at Kwong without comprehension. He held a finger to his temple. "Because . . . I've . . . *seen* it, Lee. I've . . . seen it." He clasped his hands together. "All I have to do now is get Charis to . . . fiddle with a few equations, a couple of symbols, so . . . so you can see it, too. Math is just a language of description. It doesn't change the reality of anything, you know."

Kwong's eyes glowed with his anger. "Math *is* reality, Anthony. And until you can show me a . . . a virtual photon, it will be the *only* reality I or anyone else will accept!" He stormed toward the lab doors, footsteps echoing against the metallic sides of the accelerator. The doors swung wide and he was gone.

Cross was completely unprepared for Kwong's reaction. "Now how are we supposed to run this experiment?"

"Maybe that's not the most important thing to think about right now," Covington suggested. "Maybe you should explain your latest . . . insights to me, instead."

Cross shook his head. "Parnel, you wouldn't understand. No offense."

"None taken. How about explaining them to Charis? I'll just listen."

Cross smiled blindingly as he turned to Neale. "I like explaining things to Charis," he said.

Anthony Cross sat on the desk where Covington and Neale had watched him prepare for the experiment and was delighted with the permutations that were in flux among the three of them, as mad and as complex as the phenomena coiled and waiting to be revealed in the accelerator beside them. The tension of the moment made Cross feel happy. Tension was something he was becoming more fond of as his days at SHARP went on. There were so many ways to deal with it here.

But, despite the tension, Cross remained ecstatic, knowing he was firmly at the center of his universe. SHARP was his—no matter what platitudes Covington tossed out to Kwong and Weinstein from time to time. Neale was his, whenever and however he wanted her. And so was Covington, even though the pompous financier wasn't yet aware of the fact.

The truth was that Covington was as transparent as vacuum to Cross, and Cross had known what the businessman was after from almost the first words of the first conversation he had had with the American ambassador at the Nobel Prize banquet more than three years earlier. Covington wanted power. Cross wanted knowledge. And each was planning on outdoing the other to achieve his dreams.

There was only one flaw in Covington's plan: Cross was a genius and Covington wasn't. There were still confusing things going on connected with SHARP and Kwong and Weinstein which Cross had not yet unraveled, but he knew that when the time came for all to be revealed, Covington would be found lacking, no matter what secrets he believed he held. So Cross was happy to appear to go along with Covington's plans, playing the court jester or the *idiot savant,* whatever Covington chose to believe. Cross didn't care which strategy he used or how he was perceived. All that was important was that his work to uncover the Beginning of all things would move forward more rapidly than it ever could at a university, and that, at the end of the game, Cross would win. And Covington would lose. Completely.

Cross smiled as he felt Covington and Neale watch him expectantly, waiting for the words of explanation to pour forth from him. It was almost like being back in front of a class once more. Almost like being a teacher all over again. He liked the feeling. He began.

"I start with the assumption made by some versions of the standard theory that the Higgs boson is the particle responsible for imparting mass to other particles. Acceptable?"

"For now," Neale said, very serious.

"Good," Cross said, amused at the look of intense concentration on Neale's face. She had to try so hard for such a simple level of understanding. He could also see that she was tempted to ask him to stop his preparations for the demonstration he had promised to Covington but that she had thought better of it at the last second. Therefore, knowing it was annoying to her, as he continued his explanation he kept turning his eyes back to his computer screen and typing in the preliminary commands to bring the accelerator on line. The resonating hum from the generators in the next room began to grow. "I then assume the original Einsteinian model of the effects of gravity being analogous to the warping of spacetime by the presence of a body possessing mass. The old metaphor of a ball bearing on a sheet of rubber. Acceptable?"

"Yes."

"I then acknowledge that no experimental evidence exists to confirm the detection of gravitons, the particles assumed by most versions of the standard theory to be responsible for mediating the effects of gravity. Also acceptable?"

"No," Neale said after a moment's reflection. "What about Pulsar 1913 +16?"

Cross shook his head and held up a finger. "No, no, no. Neither gravitons nor gravity waves nor whatever you want to call them have ever been detected radiating from that system. All we've observed is that the orbiting neutron stars of that system simply are *losing* energy at the same rate as predicted by theoretical descriptions of gravity waves. It's indirect evidence at best." Cross turned to Covington, letting him in on a private joke. "I'm not denying the *existence* of gravity here, Parnel, nor of any other gravitational phenomenon." He let go of a pen and laughed as it hit the floor.

"Then I don't see your point," Neale said.

"My point is that while we all agree that gravity exists, we have thus far been completely unsuccessful in finding the mechanism by which the force of gravity is transmitted. What I suggest is that our failure is not because our methods of detection are at fault, but because the mechanism we are searching for does not exist."

"You're saying gravity waves don't exist," Neale stated uncertainly.

"That's correct." Cross found the confusion in her face exciting.

"And that gravitons are not the mechanism for the exchange of the gravitational force," Neale continued.

"They are not," Cross agreed, smirking at his cleverness. "It's just intellectual inertia. The *tyranny* of virtual particles. Just because we've found that photons mediate electromagnetism, and massive vector bosons mediate the weak nuclear force, and gluons mediate the strong force, everyone else has been blindly expecting that yet another virtual particle will mediate the fourth force. But if that kind of particle—the graviton—did exist, the Cross Corollary showed how it could have been discovered with existing detectors, even Caltech's interferometer, with a much higher incidence than had previously been expected. It wasn't discovered, therefore it doesn't exist. Acceptable?"

"No," Neale said, but hesitantly.

"Why?" Cross demanded. "Where's the flaw? Where's the flaw?"

"I . . . I can't express it right now, but—"

"Because there is no flaw!" Cross jumped up from the console. "Admit it! Admit it!"

"Give me a moment here, Anthony!" Neale slapped her hand against the workbench beside her.

"All the time you want, but it won't help you," Cross gloated. "Because I'm right."

"And everyone else is wrong?" Covington asked skeptically.

Cross smiled. "Someone has to be the first, Parnel. This time, it's me." He turned back to the computer screen and saw that all systems were ready. "Now, you want to see something really neat?" He pretended not to notice the nervous looks Covington and Neale traded above him in an attempt to pass information without his knowledge.

But no matter how they tried to hide, Cross had already decided it was too late for Covington and Neale. SHARP had become a powerful learning experience for him. Their interaction had been observed, therefore their reality was confirmed, and as quickly, as predictably, and as pliantly as elementary particles speeding through an accelerator, he would adjust their paths to bring them to collision and reveal all their secrets, whatever they might be.

And then he'd really teach them something about high-energy physics.

FOUR

Katherine Duvall remained silent and still on the bed, eyes closed yet aware that the moment of victory had arrived. After watching the red numbers of her alarm cycle through each hour of the night, it was Monday morning. The long desert of the weekend was behind her and once again she had survived Jesse's ghost.

Plodding to the bathroom, tripping over Briggs as he weaved in and out of her legs, mewing for his breakfast, Duvall could still sense Jesse's presence. In the closet they had shared, the smell of his Brut aftershave and the chemical smell of a dry-cleaned suit he hadn't come by for still lingered. She supposed she should call him someday and tell him that the cleaners had found the suit, but after she had said those words, he would expect her to say something else, and she knew she couldn't, no matter how much they both thought everything had been her fault. Her job's fault.

She stood beneath the cleansing spray of the shower, remembering back to that last day, that last morning, when she had remained in bed, eyes closed, afraid to move even though she could sense him standing nearby, watching her. "I know you're awake," he had said after a while, an accusation. Then she had heard him move away from her, move away from their bed, out the door and into the real world. There had been a note on the kitchen table. He had only come back on those times she arranged to be out of the house, so he could collect his things, leaving all the rest of it to the lawyers, and to the long empty nights and endless weekends.

Duvall slowly turned down the hot water, chilling herself to morning alertness. Jesse had left almost four months ago and his absence still was fresh. She knew that she could make the call that he expected, say the words he needed to hear to bring him back, bring it all back, safety from the loneliness and the long nights and the endless weekends. But she turned off the hot tap completely, forcing the thought from her mind with the icy shock of blasting cold water. She and Jesse had had their moment and no matter how easy it would be to make that call and say she was sorry, so sorry, she knew in her heart it was time for the moment to pass, and for another to come her way.

When her front doorbell rang, Duvall was startled. She had been beguiled by the multiple shafts of sunlight shining through the wooden shutters of the window over the kitchen sink and falling in soft brilliant lines across the linoleum and the cat's dishes. She tried to remember when she had last seen late morning sun in her kitchen. She had seen it in other kitchens, other houses, usually with the outlines of bodies painted on a floor, bloodstains on a wall, dying breaths and violent protests still echoing in empty hallways. But there was none of that in her home, except a type of death of a slower and more subtle kind, a death of spirit not of body, and no criminal to arrest. Her house, in her solitude and its stillness, was alien to her at this time of day, as though its ownership passed to strangers during the hours of her work. She wondered if children might have made the difference. The doorbell rang again. It was time to find out how bad Erhlenmeyer was going to make it for her.

Opening the door, she recognized homicide detective Adam Nogura right away. He was five eight and looked as though he wouldn't weigh a hundred without rocks in his pockets. But he had a handsome face with the confident, easy smile of someone who knew he could throw a two-hundred-and-fifty-pound police fitness trainer across a gym. That was how he had qualified for immediate transfer into the LAPD after six years as an army MP. Nogura had been on the force for almost four years now, and since that most definitive response to the first and last time his size had been questioned, he had been "Nuke" Nogura forevermore.

But Duvall quickly saw this wasn't a homicide visit. With Nogura was Detective Hector Ramirez: dark, somber, Internal Affairs. The men waited patiently for Duvall to invite them in. The fact that they both wore lightweight summer suits with white shirts and single color ties— outfits that were as much standard uniforms for LAPD detectives as blues were for patrol officers—and the fact that both wore their IDs and badges clipped to their jacket pockets, meant that they weren't waiting for a social invitation, either. Duvall grimaced at them through the screen door. "What the hell did I do, kill the fat son of a bitch?"

Nogura cracked a smile but Ramirez's face was frozen. Word was he rubbed nerve-numbing hemorrhoid cream on his face to keep his perfectly dead expression motionless during interrogations, and the operative theory was that the cream didn't come from a tube. It rubbed off onto his face during his meetings with the division supervisor.

"Unfortunately, Katherine," Nogura said, "you didn't hit him that hard."

"But hard enough to bring in Internal Affairs." She smiled coldly at Ramirez.

"It's not as bad as you think," Nogura said. "How about letting us in?"

Duvall opened the door without comment. Being questioned by IAD wasn't one of her favorite experiences, but it was better than staring at sunbeams.

"First of all," Nogura began, stirring four spoonfuls of sugar into the mug of coffee Duvall had placed before him on the golden pine kitchen table, "no suspension."

"What?" Duvall came close to spilling the mug she passed to Ramirez.

"No suspension," Ramirez confirmed, sipping at the steaming coffee without appearing to mind its heat, almost as though his lips really were numb, Duvall thought.

"Not that I'm looking for any trouble, but I did drop Erhlenmeyer on his fat ass." Duvall had already concluded that her suspension

would be lifted only after she accepted a demotion and got kicked off
the homicide desk, probably to go back to being john bait in Vice.

"In front of several witnesses," Ramirez agreed.

"Who stated that you were responding to inexcusable and intolera-
ble provocation in the form of racial and other insults," Nogura said,
blowing on his coffee, "and the threat of physical violence. It was self-
defense, open and shut."

Duvall sat back in her chair at the table, folded her arms across
her chest, and looked from one detective to the other. Erhlenmeyer had
been a foul-mouthed bastard, but he hadn't tried to lay a hand on her.
Where had that story come from? Something wasn't right here, but she
didn't know how far she wanted to push it.

Nogura narrowed his eyes at her. "You got a problem with that,
Katherine?"

Duvall's mind raced through the various explanations for what the
detectives were saying to her—offering her, really. Her silence dragged
on, giving Ramirez, at last, an expression of discomfort.

"What's Erhlenmeyer say about this?" she finally asked.

Ramirez relaxed. "The lieutenant will be sending you a written
apology for his unfortunate comments."

"Max?" Duvall snorted with a laugh. "Apologize? Rub a lamp,
guys."

Nogura leaned forward, hands cradling his mug. "Look, I know
this seems . . . unlikely, but it's not the first time Max has been called
up on this sort of thing. You read the papers. You know the department's being pushed to clean itself up as far as . . . racially involved
incidents are concerned."

Duvall still didn't buy it. "No offense, guys, but as far as racially
involved incidents in the department go, what Erhlenmeyer said to me
was about a 1.1 on the old Richter Scale." She patted the table. "What
sort of bottom line are we talking about here? Erhlenmeyer apologizes
and I leave Homicide? Leave the department?"

Nogura waved his hands with a string of no's. "And I thought
undercover cops were paranoid. There are no strings here, Kate. Erhlenmeyer screwed up, stepped over the line in front of witnesses, unfairly suspended you. We're here to make it right. That's it, over and
out. You know?"

Even Ramirez joined in to help convince her. "Erhlenmeyer has had it coming to him for a long time."

Duvall thought for a moment about how her grammy had always told her that everyone had a guardian angel watching over her. Maybe hers had finally punched in. "So that's it? Suspension's over? I just waltz back into the office, pick up the Riley case, and . . ." She saw Nogura's eyes flicker. "Oh, Jesus, Nuke! I knew it! What's the goddamn catch? What?"

At least Nogura had the decency to look embarrassed. "It's not a catch. It's just that . . ."

"I'm not on the Riley case."

Nogura nodded. "You're not on the Riley case."

"Am I still in Homicide?"

"You're still in Homicide," Nogura said calmly. "And you're not on the Riley case because you're on vacation. Seriously," he quickly continued, stopping her protest, "you should look at your records for the past year. No time off, too much overtime. It's not good for you. And not good for the department. A bit of time off now would be best all around. Help cool things down, you know?"

Duvall rubbed at her face. Normally, the department rotated its detectives from desk to desk every eighteen months or so. But occasionally, when an outstanding detective shone in a given area, exceptions were made, which probably explained Nogura's unprecedented three-and-a-half-year homicide stint in divisions all over the city. For the past two years, Duvall had also been one of those exceptions and she had been led to believe that her career in Homicide was assured. She wanted that career because it was an area of policework where one person could still make a difference. She believed in that. She had to believe that. Or else, why bother with anything? "I know when I'm being jerked around, guys," she said.

Nogura snapped. "You're not being jerked around."

Ramirez cleared his throat. Duvall had almost forgotten he could speak. He delivered the most basic of the police officers' benedictions. "You're a good cop, Kate. A good detective."

Duvall glared at him. "Okay, Ramirez, you've set me up. Now give me the big 'but.' "

Ramirez pursed his lips and nodded thoughtfully. "You are an African-American, and you are a woman."

"Oh, for— Thank you for sharing that with us, Ramirez," Duvall said, dismissing him with a shake of her head.

"That makes you a role model for hundreds of other cops in the department," Ramirez snapped. "And maybe thousands of others who haven't joined yet, who think the department is God's gift to white redneck bigots who don't give a shit about your people or mine. People look to you, Kate. You're one of a handful. One of the first. And just because you have a goddamn fit with some asshole lieutenant who's retiring in two years is no bloody reason for you to blow it for the rest of us!" Ramirez's fist hit the table and the mugs jumped. So did Duvall.

"I don't want special treatment," she said. Her voice was tight and angry. "For any reason, understand?"

Nogura's tone was a match for hers. "Your career is important to a lot of people, Katherine. You should be glad . . . someone's watching out for you."

Duvall stood up. She could feel the same cold tingle in her arms that she had felt before she had slugged Erhlenmeyer. "I don't want anyone watching out for me. I want to know that I got to where I am because I'm good at what I do, not because some candy-ass bleeding heart took pity on me for being a po'—"

"Stop it!" Nogura shouted. "You got the chance to make detective ahead of anyone else in your class because you broke the Hill case in an afternoon when the rest of the department was sitting around with their thumbs up each others' asses. And you made second grade because every month for the next two years you proved the Hill thing wasn't a fluke. Everything you've achieved you've achieved on your own. Just the way you could have lost everything by slugging a superior officer on Friday night—all on your own.

"All that's happening now is that a few of your friends in the department are trying to give you the benefit of the doubt. They're saying, hey, maybe this cop's been working too hard for the past year. Maybe her judgment was just a little bit off on Friday night. Maybe we shouldn't hold that against her. They're trying to make sure one stupid mistake on your part doesn't screw up a good cop who'll do more for the city and the department in the next five years than anything Erhlenmeyer did in his whole twenty." Nogura jumped to his feet, nearly knocking over his chair. "And if you don't like that then just quit and give it all up because you *aren't* worth it."

Nogura stopped to catch his breath. He nodded at Ramirez. "Come on, Hec, let's get out of here." Ramirez fixed his eyes on her but said nothing. The two men walked out. The last thing Duvall heard was Nogura muttering, "Enjoy your vacation," and then they were out the door.

With the noisy company gone, her fat black-and-white cat waddled into the kitchen, tail up and feathery in the shafts of sunlight as she headed for his bowls by the cupboards. The sound of delicate crunching filled the room as Duvall watched the cat eat. "Hey, Briggs, how'd I ever get to be such an asshole?" she asked, but the cat was not inclined to answer.

A few seconds later, the doorbell rang again, followed by rapid knocking. Duvall got up and slowly went to the door, expecting that the way the morning was going so far, she was about to be told her house was on fire.

But it was Nogura again, this time alone and with his badge and ID no longer clipped to his suit jacket. On the street by the driveway, Duvall could see Ramirez sitting patiently in the unmarked. When Duvall opened the door, Nogura walked straight in. Duvall could sense that his anger had somehow turned to nervousness.

"I'm sorry," was the first thing he said to her.

"An official apology?" It was sarcastic and she knew it.

"No. An apology from me. Nuke. Okay?"

That was unexpected. "Okay."

But the apology hadn't been everything that Nogura had come back for. His hands grasped at empty air, his eyes jumped to hers, then flashed away. "Katherine, this is important." He took a breath and sped through the next sentence. "I don't know how to be nice to you, all right?"

"What?"

Nogura's face was screwed up, a mirror of his misgivings. "I'm not the only one, either." He held his hands up like a traffic cop's, though as far as Duvall knew, Nogura's prior experience as an MP had somehow exempted him from those basic duties in the department. "Let me finish. I mean, you *are* a good cop, Katherine. I don't know if you've made a lot of friends but a lot of people respect you. Probably more than you know. And the thing is, we don't know how to tell you that. Do you know what I mean?"

Duvall shook her head.

"I mean, the rest of us, all right . . . the *guys*, we can hit the bars after work, shoot the shit, complain about our wives and girl-friends, help each other out, that kind of thing. But . . ." He dropped his hands to his side, defeated. "We know things aren't going that well for you. I mean here, at home, since you and Jesse split. It gets kind of obvious after a while, you know? And the thing is, if you were . . . one of the guys, we could give you a hand. But, the problem, Kather-ine . . ." He made some sort of decision and lifted his head to look straight into her eyes. "How can I tell you that I understand, that I've been through it myself, and that I'd like to help . . . without it sound-ing like I'm coming on to you? You see what the problem is?"

Duvall found she couldn't hold his gaze, her turn to look away. "I guess I do," she said quietly. "Thank you, Nuke."

"This job is a killer, Katherine. Wives never understand it and I guess . . . I guess the same goes for husbands. People like us, we have a calling, a desire to do something . . . important. Is this making sense?"

Duvall smiled and nodded.

"Then take time off. Take a vacation. Go somewhere, meet some-one. It's the only thing that'll help. Really. I've been there."

In the silence that followed, Duvall felt her anger melt away. Nogura had opened himself up to her in a way she had never thought any of her male coworkers would ever risk. He had brought her into the fraternity, the brotherhood of cops, if only for a moment. She didn't understand why he had done it, what motives were really operating within him, but she wanted to thank him for the attempt. There was an awkward moment when almost automatically she started to move her arms to hug him. But she knew that would be wrong.

Nogura almost responded, just as automatically, pulling back after his arms had moved only an inch.

They stared at each other a moment longer, the uncertainty build-ing. Then Nogura smiled and slowly and deliberately punched Duvall on her shoulder, *mano a mano*. They both laughed.

"You give me a call if you need anything," Nogura said as he stepped out the door, then caught himself. "To talk or something," he quickly corrected himself, dismissing any suggestion of a double mean-ing to his words. "You know what I mean."

"Yeah, I know," Duvall said, and she meant it. "And thanks, Nuke. I really . . . appreciate what you said."

He faced her from the porch, arms extended, smiling. "Hey, just because they made me come over here with an IAD zombie, that doesn't make me a complete asshole, you know."

"Not a complete one, no," Duvall agreed, returning his smile. She waited by the door to wave as Nogura and Ramirez drove away, and realized that somehow the day seemed lighter.

She examined that new feeling as she returned to the kitchen and sat by the phone, mouth as dry and hands as damp as those few times as a teenager when she had actually dared to call a boy first. At last, after half an hour, she decided that she was wrong not to try and put Erhlenmeyer and the Riley case behind her—one more pompous lieutenant and one more dead body really didn't amount to much in the universe, as far as she could see. Her own sanity and peace of mind did, at least to her. Maybe it was time to stop trying to prove something. Maybe it was time to make life easy again.

But even as her finger punched out Jesse's number at the bank, she saw the ruined skull of Cassie Riley and wondered how it would have felt to put her arms around a man who knew none of her secrets and none of her fears. She listened to the phone ring on the other end, knowing that the next few days were going to be a struggle, especially since they had to begin with her saying she was sorry, so sorry to Jesse.

FIVE

A dam Weinstein had changed since the death of his wife three years ago. His dark hair, once full and curly and only sprinkled with gray, was now little more than a white fringe framing a mottled bald pate and, depending on the degradations of his weekend activities, a simple black yarmulke which he occasionally wore in a gesture of atonement. His skin was looser now, hanging in folds beneath his chin, even though his overall size had increased, and his eyes were too moist, the lower lids drooping enough to show a glint of red flesh beneath the eyeballs. But at this moment, the age seemed to drop from him as effortlessly as smoke as he smiled in a way that Neale had never seen him smile before.

"The little goddam fucker's really gone and done it this time, hasn't he?"

Weinstein stood in the midst of the disorder of Lab 2. The smell of smoke was strong, even though the sprinklers hadn't switched on in the aftermath of the near catastrophic failure of Cross's demonstration.

"Actually," Neale pointed out, "it was more Lee's fault than Anthony's."

Weinstein pulled on his thick lower lip, happily cataloguing the damaged equipment around him. "I heard Lee walked out before anything started."

"Exactly," Covington said. "He was supposed to run the magnets."

"Into the ground," Weinstein laughed. "Looks like the magnets ruptured."

"They did," Neale said. Four hours ago, thirty seconds before she and Covington were to have witnessed Cross's breakthrough, pressure seals failed on four of the sixteen liquid-nitrogen-cooled superconducting magnets which were installed around the accelerator. The freezing liquid had vented from the magnets' casings in thick white gusts of vapor and each affected magnet's controller circuit board had instantly erupted in gouts of electrical arcing. Cross had shut down the generators and walked out without speaking. Neale assumed he was still in his office. But she couldn't imagine anything else about what he might be feeling or doing at this moment. And she was glad for that.

"Why'd Lee walk out? Cross finally turn the little bugger down once too often?" He laughed again, poking at the blistered side panel of a destroyed magnet housing.

Covington stood beside the physicist, arms sternly folded. "Lee was quite upset about a conversation he had with you, Adam. Last night."

Weinstein turned away from the ruined equipment, nodding his head ponderously. "So he told you? That the braided particle theory is nonsense?"

"That's right."

"How'd the little smart ass take it?"

Neale stepped up beside Covington. "*Anthony* took it very well. He told us he had reached the same conclusion a year ago."

Weinstein snorted. "And he kept it to himself all this time? Man's a damned liar. Always said that. Never could take his word for anything. Won't take it this time, either."

Covington frowned. "Why weren't you on top of this, Adam?"

Weinstein pointed out the door. "I work on my side of the building. He works on his."

"That's not the arrangement and you know it."

Weinstein looked up defiantly at Covington. Neale could see the old man's body tremble, and not with fear.

"The arrangement doesn't mean shit anymore and *you* fucking know that! I came here to be a scientist. Not a goddamned monkey in a zoo, being watched all the time. You think I don't know that you're following me everywhere I go? Watching what I do? You and your fucking little Cathedral Three frien—"

Covington's hand lashed out like lightning and crushed Weinstein's shirt and jacket beneath his jowls. "You are never to mention that name in this facility." He shot his eyes to the lab's main doors, cautiously checking that Cross hadn't suddenly decided to reappear. *"Never."*

Weinstein's hands fumbled against Covington's fist and he tried to back away. But the tall man's grip was firm. "I'm . . . I'm sorry. It's just that . . ." Tears came to Weinstein's eyes. "I just hate him so goddamned much," he sobbed.

Covington watched Weinstein for a few moments, and then let go. "I don't want you talking with Glashow or anyone else outside this facility ever again. Do you understand? No more unauthorized collaborations."

Weinstein's eyes were empty, without protest.

"And I want you to prepare a full report on the flaws in the braided particle theory for Charis immediately. Do you understand?"

Weinstein's voice was a whisper. "Yes."

"And if you don't want to be followed anymore, then for God's sake stop doing anything that could reflect badly on SHARP."

"It's no one's business," Weinstein muttered.

"You *are* my business, Adam. You, and Lee, and Anthony. I bought you. I own you. And I don't want anyone fucking around with my business."

Weinstein ineffectually smoothed his collar. "May I go now?"

Covington stepped aside, leaving the physicist room to pass. Neale watched him walk slowly out. Broken. The lab doors swung shut behind him.

"You didn't have to treat him that way. He's an old man."

"He's a security risk."

"So suddenly the Cathedral Group has to worry about security?"

Covington looked at the doors again and rubbed the side of his head. "Not you, too?"

Neale stepped around to get into Covington's line of sight. "Look, Parnel, is there something going on here that I don't know about?"

"I was about to ask you the same thing. You say your arrangement with Anthony isn't working out. The braided particle theory is out the window. What else haven't you been telling me?"

Neale slipped her hands into the pocket of her lab coat. "I tell you everything that I know. It's just that . . . I don't know everything these days."

Covington moved closer to her. "And whose fault is that?"

"This is your show, Parnel. You tell me."

"Maybe someday I will. But until then . . . just take care of business. My business."

"Go to Anthony, you mean."

"He's alone in his office. Things haven't worked out. How do you think he's feeling? What do you think he's doing?"

Neale could see in Covington's eyes that he thought he knew the answers to the questions he asked.

"He's tense, Charis. Upset. Just like all those scientists we talked about this morning." Covington patted her arm. "Why don't you go to him, do what you're so good at doing. Make him . . . happy."

Neale knew what she was in Covington's eyes. She tried to reconcile it with what she felt in her own heart. But still, when he spelled it out, so brutally, she wanted to end her connection with Cross instantly. "And what if I don't?" she asked, goading him. "What if I say no."

Covington reached out to take the lapels of her lab coat, resting his hands against her as he slowly slid the coat open. "Why then, you can stay here, and make *me* happy."

Neale stepped back angrily and pulled her coat closed. "I'd rather burn in hell." She wheeled and stormed for the door.

"Don't forget Cathedral Three," Covington called after her. "That could be arranged."

SIX

"I thought you were on vacation."

"I am," Duvall called out as she waved and walked past Nogura's cubicle, one of a string of eight closet-sized rooms that the division chief insisted be called "offices." She continued on to her own cubicle at the end of the line, right by the emergency exit to the stairwell. It was a telling reminder of how some of the other officers in the department ranked her importance, despite her second-grade rank.

Duvall sat at her desk and fought the impulse to pick up her phone and start to work. She had lasted through her first day of vacation and told herself that Tuesday would be no different. Nogura appeared in the doorway of her office, tapping lightly on the dark wood frame.

"This is worse than when I quit smoking," Duvall said, waving him in.

"Work withdrawal?" Nogura asked, accepting her invitation and sitting in the scarred oak visitor's chair across from her desk. The chair didn't make a sound as he gracefully settled into it.

"It's terrible," Duvall continued. "I actually felt the urge to come in yesterday afternoon and reorganize my files. They're going to start thinking I'm a secretary. At least, those who don't already think that I am."

Nogura grimaced. "I hear they put crack in the coffee. Makes it impossible to stay away. But that's not why you're in today, is it?"

"No way," Duvall said emphatically. "I really am on vacation."

Nogura glanced around the room doubtfully. "And you're spending it here?"

"Hawaii," Duvall said, hardly believing the words were coming from her own mouth. "Thursday night." Should she tell him? Why not? "That's the earliest Jesse could get his days off."

"Jesse?" Nogura said. "As in ex-husband Jesse?"

Duvall looked away. "Yeah, so, maybe it's time to give it another shot. A week in Hawaii won't hurt. Could help." And she was too nervous to try and go with someone new, if there had been someone new. She watched Nogura's reaction and then decided she shouldn't have said anything after all. She felt embarrassed.

But Nogura was happy for her and as Duvall dug through an avalanche of paper on her desk, they talked about the relative merits of Oahu over Kauai and which volcanoes came closest to matching the air quality of Reseda on a windless August day. She pulled out her address book, a small makeup kit, three paperbacks she had lost track of, and sorted through her messages from the past four days, all of which she had already phoned in for. At last she stood up, still with a sense of unreality, preparing not to see her office or think of policework for another . . . twelve and a half days. But then she asked, "So who got the Riley case?"

"Seabrook," Nogura said.

Duvall was surprised. "I hope he's not listening but he doesn't have the experience for it." Duvall shoveled her rescued items into her battered brown satchel, a practical hand-me-down from Jesse's first days as chief teller. They had bought a new one when he had been promoted to assistant manager. She looked up and saw Nogura had a blank look. She felt her detective's sense for recognizing disruptions in order and pattern kick in. "Do *you* think he has the experience?"

Nogura shrugged. "The case seemed pretty standard to me."

"Is this some sort of cultural difference we're having here? You know, like you guys thinking raw fish is something people should eat?"

Duvall asked, not believing Nogura's comment. "A woman has her head cut open while she's alive and you think it's 'standard'?"

Nogura looked at her for a long moment, face frozen, as if making a decision. "She had her head what?"

"Cut open," Duvall said. "Alive."

Nogura tapped a finger against his lips. "I thought that it was a beating death."

Duvall shook her head. "That's what it looked like at first but . . . Ash was the coroner on the scene. He showed me the cut marks. Said a section of the skull had been removed with a drill and a saw."

Nogura looked up at the ceiling and whistled. "Tasty, even for this town. But I don't remember anyone saying anything like that about the case. I remember the bit about being tied to the table. They're calling it the Boy Scout murder."

"I guess I should write headlines," Duvall said. "That's what I said when I saw the knots. Is Seabrook in?"

"He was this morning," Nogura said, getting to his feet. "But I thought you were on vacation."

"Thursday," Duvall said, trying to sound unconcerned. But she could see by the look in Nogura's eyes that he didn't believe that any more than she did.

Seabrook's cubicle was empty and a uniform struggling with some two-finger typing at the desk outside said the detective was doing door-to-doors in the Riley woman's apartment building. Once again, normal procedure. But Duvall decided she'd check out Seabrook's board anyway. At least that would tell her why a decision apparently had been made to withhold the details of the cause of death even from other homicide detectives.

Case boards were a way of visually organizing information relating to a crime. Duvall drew intricate diagrams to link information on large sheets torn from an artist's drawing pad and thumbtacked them to her cubicle's walls. Seabrook's technique was to tape photographs and reports and lists to a beat-up, heavy wooden blackboard that he had rescued from an old schoolhouse. Then he added lines and squiggles and indecipherable comments in twelve different colors of chalk. It took Duvall a few minutes to check out all the material layered on

Seabrook's board before she realized that everything on it pertained to other ongoing investigations—gang hits, back alley knifings, the sort of homicide that no one holds out much hope for closing and which invariably got dumped on the new guy's desk. There was nothing on the Riley case.

"What is this bullshit?" Duvall muttered, turning around to look at the rest of Seabrook's office. There should have been material gathered together, displayed, and passed around within hours of the discovery of Riley's body. After the first twenty-four hours following a murder, the odds of finding the murderer dropped by about 10 percent per day. What was Seabrook up to, screwing around like—

There was a two-inch-thick cardboard file case in the middle of Seabrook's desk, a beige expandable case, perfect for adding material to during an ongoing investigation. Duvall stepped closer to the desk. The name "Riley" was scrawled across the case in red marker. Duvall scooped it up, hid it behind the satchel under her arm, and doubletimed back to her own cubicle. Nogura glanced up from his desk as she passed him again, but this time said nothing.

She started reading the material in the case from the beginning, starting with the detective-in-charge report form. It was handwritten, full of abbreviations for standard procedures that were followed, but nowhere did Duvall see her name listed as one of the officers at the scene. She checked again, slowly. Erhlenmeyer's name was missing, too. The reasonable side of her said that IAD had arranged the omissions so that nothing official would remain to remind anyone of her encounter with the lieutenant that night, but the cop side of her wasn't buying. She turned to the coroner's report.

The cause of death was neatly typed out: "Sev trau/hd, csd hvy shrp instr. vis machete, sword, eqiv."

"Bullshit," Duvall said to herself.

"What is?" Nogura asked from the door. Duvall looked up as suddenly as if she had been caught in the evidence cage without a pass. "Desk just said Seabrook called in. He's heading back. Should be here in ten minutes or so. Thought you might appreciate the time to get that stuff back to his office."

"That obvious?"

"You make a great detective, but a lousy thief." Nogura glanced over his shoulder, down the row of cubicles, then leaned against the doorframe. "So what's bullshit?"

"This cause of death," Duvall said, snapping her finger against the flimsy NCR form from the coroner's office. "Severe trauma to the head caused by a heavy sharp instrument. A machete or sword or equivalent."

"You said Ash told you her head had been cut open."

"By a scalpel, and a drill and saw." Duvall flipped through the stack of material until she came to a set of photographs. "Look at this," she said, spreading a sheaf of color eight-by-tens across her desk. Each showed a different view of the Riley woman's ruined head. Nogura moaned as he studied them.

"Okay," Duvall said, speaking as if she were arguing with the other detective. "I'll admit that a machete would leave a clean cut in the skin, not a tear. And if it was sharp enough, it would even cut through the skull without splintering. But if you were going to take a section out of somebody's head with a big bladed weapon, you'd be cutting a . . . a wedge out of it, like from a cheese wheel or an orange or something."

"God, I love this job."

"No, I mean it. Look at the wound on her head. That's a rectangle. How are you going to cut a rectangle of bone out of someone's head by swinging a machete?"

Nogura grimaced. "May my ancestors forgive me, but how about some sort of ninja weapon? Shiruken? Something like that."

"Those are small blades. Ash says here that it was a *heavy*, sharp instru—hold on." Duvall lifted the coroner's form from her desk. "This isn't Ash's signature."

"He's booked off sick. Bad flu or something. He can't do all of the autopsies anyway, you know."

Duvall sat back in her chair. That was two anomalies to the case: Seabrook and the coroner's report. And each existed because someone else had been taken from the case: herself, and Ashraf File.

"He would have done this one," Duvall said. Then added quickly, "And there were scallops on the edge of the bone cut. Ash said they were the marks from the drill. The saw was used to cut between the holes that were drilled."

"Both versions agree, Katherine. The bone *was* cut. Maybe the coroner who did the autop—"

"A machete wouldn't leave scallops on the edge of the bone, Nuke." She started to flip through the other reports piled in front of her, quickly scanning the filing title on each official form.

"Go back to the idea of an ornamental weapon," Nogura tried. "The scallops could be left by carving or scrollwork or something like that on the blade."

Duvall slammed the paperwork down on her desk, ignoring the man. "And where's the report on the prints?"

"They got prints?" Nogura asked in surprise almost verging on panic.

"They better have," Duvall threatened, then shoved all of the photos and forms back into the file case without bothering to line them up. Nogura winced as he saw the papers get crushed. "They damn well better have."

"Prints from what, for God's sake?" Seabrook asked. He was dripping in sweat from being stuck in traffic on Santa Monica without air conditioning. His ten-minute trip back from Cassie Riley's apartment building had taken half an hour and the temperature was on its way to breaking an unseasonable one hundred. He was in no mood for questions. "Except for the woman's, and a bunch of stupid paw prints from her invisible cat, the place was clean."

"I'm not talking about the apartment, Joe. I'm talking about the gloves." Duvall shifted from one foot to the other, waving the file case in her hand.

Seabrook took a wad of Kleenex from a box on his desk and wiped his face and gleaming scalp. "What gloves, Kate?"

"The surgical gloves wadded up with some bloody gauze pads under the cupboards."

Seabrook was suddenly aware of what Duvall had in her hand. "Is that my case file? Aw, Kate, what have you done to it?" He stepped forward, heavily, as if each foot fought against mud, but Duvall swung the case back out of reach, holding it hostage.

"The gloves, Joe. They should have gone to ID for dusting or laser fluorescing. What happened to them?"

Seabrook gave up and leaned back against his desk. On his wrinkled white shirt, dark circles of sweat grew under each arm and traced the path of the straps of his shoulder holster. "Kate, it's too hot to argue. There were no gloves. Bloody gauze pads, yes. Gloves of any kind, no."

"I saw them, Joe. Right behind me when I was by the body."

"Then they're going to be in the photographs, Kate." He looked at the wrinkled corners of yellow, pink, and white forms sticking from the file case and shook his head.

"Okay, okay," Duvall said. She pulled the photos out of the file case and spread them out on the desk beside Seabrook. She found the photo she wanted. "Here!"

Seabrook only glanced at the photo for a second. It was one of the gridded close-ups of the floor in the kitchen. "That's a wad of gauze pads, Kate."

"That's where I saw the gloves, like they had been rolled up together with the pads."

Seabrook sighed and took another look at the photo. He read out the number. "Look up twenty-seven on the evidence list. For the kitchen."

Duvall passed over the yellow form after checking it for herself.

"Item twenty-seven C, bag thirty-one. Gauze pads," Seabrook read. "Sample to Gas Chromatography for typing." He looked at Duvall, tired and hot. "No gloves."

"I saw them. They were rubber, shiny, like the kind we use."

"You saw a specular from wet blood. You *thought* you saw something rubber."

"They were there."

Seabrook sighed. "Kate, why would anyone want to take the murderer's gloves from the scene? And more importantly, *how* could anyone take them. There were twelve guys there at least. A photographer covering everything before and after the body was moved. Look at the before and after photos for yourself. Everything's intact. Nothing was tampered with."

Duvall thought her response out carefully. "They were there," she repeated.

Seabrook's head slumped down, chin to his chest. "Aren't you supposed to be on vacation?" he asked, a desperate man.

"Thursday," Duvall answered, glancing at her watch and calculating that given an 8:30 P.M. departure time, she still had just over forty-eight hours to straighten everything out.

Even if it was on her own time, it felt good to be back at work.

SEVEN

Charis Neale stood by the mirrored door of the large closet in the bedroom she shared with Cross, studying herself in her bathrobe, peering intently for the evidence of how she had changed since she had come here, to the house that SHARP had provided for them in the Malibu hills. She didn't like what she saw, the faint wrinkles that flickered on the edge of her vision, the suspicion of sag that lurked under her eyes and along her jaw. But the changes in her body were like the changes in her beliefs. Day after day, thousands of small alterations built up unnoticeably, and then a small line became a furrow in the forehead, and the decision to passively ignore some things led to the decision to actively pursue them. But precisely how and when those changes happened, she didn't know. *People weren't quantum phenomena,* she thought. *Too many gradations, too many shades of gray.*

She heard a knock outside the half-open bedroom door, an unfamiliar sound in this house, where genius ruled and nothing was forbidden or barred to him. She was slow in turning. It was Covington, drink in hand. "May I come in?"

"Where is he?" Neale asked, no elaboration necessary. Her hand pulled shut her robe around her neck.

"Still on the deck. Watching the sun go down. What is it about him and the sun?"

"Not here," Neale said. She knew she and Covington still had things other than the sun to talk about, away from Cross. But the last place she wanted Cross to find her and Covington discussing him was the bedroom.

But it was too late. Covington had stepped inside and had seen the photograph framed and hanging across from the bed.

Neale didn't feel ashamed as he stared at the picture of her—just like that woman's. Cross had been with Neale the day it had been taken. He had arranged the teddy on her, so that it enhanced but did not cover her. He had directed her as the photographer had worked. He had told her where to place her hands, what to do with them. It was supposed to be a picture just for *them.* And now Covington's mouth was open as he stared at it, an intruder. She expected him to start drooling any second.

"Get out, Parnel. Get out now."

He turned away from the photograph, staring at her and seeing her as she was in the picture. "Have you two got any other hobbies I should know about?"

"What do you care? It's just my job, remember?"

Covington leered at her. "It was your job long before I came along, Dr. Neale. Don't forget that." He looked at the photo again, reached out to it, and trailed his fingers across it. Across her. "Looks like there's enough to go around."

"If you don't leave now, I will call for him." She didn't have to ask if Covington knew what that would mean.

"I'll see you in the living room." He left her.

Neale went to the door and closed it, her hand shaking on the latch. Then she returned to the closet and chose something fragile to wear beneath her dress. Cross was always more urgent, more insistent after he had met with Covington. Neale had long ago understood what Covington had told her about the passions of scientists. She knew the deep connection between the demands of Cross's mind and his body, both sets of passions relentless, both tethered to the same all-consuming quest for more, whether knowledge or experience. And both her own mind and body succumbed to those passions, were lost within the flame and the brilliance of a mind that could see further into nature than any who had gone before, within the fire and heat of a lover who could touch her heart and her soul as if she were spread among the stars for all to see, transparent and eternal, without care or weight. He had that power over her and she no longer tried to fight it.

But still there were practical matters to consider, which was why she chose something fragile. After Cross had talked with Covington and his mind had worked itself into a frenzy of creative thought, his body would demand that whatever she wore should be torn from her. And something fragile was faster and less painful. Not that she minded, she realized with surprising sadness as she dressed again, not that she minded anything at all that he did to her anymore.

She paused in her preparations, stopped by her sudden comprehension. How far was she willing to go to understand him? How far was she willing to go to be like him?

She frowned at herself as she slid the closet door shut and watched her reflection dress. She had always known that eventually all their shades of gray would have to be resolved down to that final choice, that decision, that moment. All or nothing. When the time came, she was afraid to know what her choice might be.

"Come on, Anthony, it's not like they were big explosions or anything," Covington said as Neale found him in the open living room leading to the deck overlooking the sea.

"They ruined the magnets!" Cross shouted. He looked up at Covington like a defiant child, then suddenly pushed the tall man's drink out of his hand. "Four of them! All of them! It doesn't matter."

Cross stormed out to the deck as Covington's glass bounced across the bleached oak floor, scattering scotch and ice cubes.

"I was just trying to calm him down," Covington said.

"You're doing a fine job," Neale said, checked that Cross was only standing on the deck and not about to do something foolish, then went to retrieve the glass.

"I'll get that," Covington said, annoyed. "You're not my goddamn keeper."

"Oh, of course," Neale answered, handing over the empty glass. "I'm Anthony's. That is, unless Cathedral Three has updated my job description." She smiled as she saw Covington panic at her mention of the unspeakable word.

"I don't like this new attitude toward security, Charis. Alone in the lab is one thing, but here? With him out there . . ."

Neale shook her head as his voice trailed off. "And I've never liked the *old* attitude toward security, Parnel. You think Anthony would have any more of an idea about what Cathedral is than I had before you . . . brought me here with him? Are you in that much awe of him that you think a single word would be enough to tip him off?"

"Let's not find out, shall we?"

Covington looked annoyed but to Neale he was the man who had stared at her in the photograph she had submitted to for her lover. She wasn't inspired to let him off easy. "I mean it. So what if he finds out? Your goddamn consortium has already got new technology out of him. Shannon's cornered the particle probe business. You said yourself the royalties you'll get from metal fabricators will more than pay for the initial investment in SHARP. You've got what you wanted, Parnel. Why be so paranoid?"

Covington looked down at his empty glass. "Let's just say there are a few other applications that the . . . consortium feels can come out of Anthony's work."

"Like what?" Neale demanded.

Covington shrugged.

"Come on, Parnel, where's the mad vision and infectious enthusiasm you had in Stockholm? After you had purchased Anthony for the low, low price of taking on Lee and Adam and me? Remember that meeting, Parnel? After the party? When we discussed *all* the details?"

Covington glanced out to the balcony, making sure Cross was still in place. "For what it's worth, Dr. Neale, there is no record of that meeting. Nothing of your involvement with Cathedral Three has been recorded."

"Am I to take that as a threat, Parnel?"

Covington turned back to her. "Yes."

Neale felt an odd moment of relief, now that battle lines had finally been established in the open. This wasn't about sexual tension any longer. This wasn't about physical superiority. This was war, clean and simple. "All right, then, I will. But in the meantime, you remember this: Cathedral Three might have been formed just to get its hands on the applications of Anthony's work, no matter what other baggage came along with them, but I'm the only one working for you who can deliver those applications. If it wasn't for me, Parnel, Anthony would be off in a dreamworld, going from idea to idea without stopping to record his procedures or his math. Without me to keep him in line, he's useless to you. And you can take that as a threat, too." Then she walked out to join Cross before Covington could say anything else.

On the deck, Cross talked to himself, hands clenching the soft wood of the unpainted railing, nails picking at cracks and splinters. For almost a mile beyond him and the hillside house SHARP had purchased on his instructions, the dry scrub of rolling hills fell away to a set of smaller houses closer to the Pacific Coast Highway, and then past the highway to the beach and the Pacific, dotted with small white sails, getting ready to swallow the sun.

Neale came up behind him and ran her hand along his back, feeling the hard knots of his shoulder muscles bunching as he squeezed the wood. At her touch, they relaxed, and Neale tensed at the instant change, knowing that Cross had descended into one of his moods. He would be as volatile and mercurial as an ocean storm. But he would be nothing that she hadn't handled before.

Cross turned to her and smiled, the face from *Time*, and now *Discover*, and *Newsweek*, and dozens of other magazines around the world: the clear eyes and handsome features of the boy genius who was going to hand the ultimate understanding of the beginning of the universe to the world. The new Prometheus.

"It's that motherfucking chink cocksucker's fault."

Neale didn't react, already prepared. "You mean Lee?"

He asked her who else she thought he might mean, calling her foul names no other man could speak without feeling her hand slap across his face or seeing her walk away.

"Why do you think it's Lee's fault?" she asked calmly. The names were just as ugly and as shocking coming from Cross as they would have been coming from anyone else, but dealing with these rantings was just another part of the price that Neale had learned to pay.

Spittle flew from Cross's lips as he began his tirade. "Because he's a fucking moron, no brains, a chink asshole who lay down and took it up the ass for that cocksucking kike Weinstein and sucked his way into my Nobel Prize. *My* fucking prize, and they both tried to steal it from me. Goddamn fucking morons, lucky to have one brain between the two

of them, one asshole, no balls, and why don't you know any of this or
are you just a dried-up old empty withered ga—"

Not knowing how far she could push him, Neale held her fingers to
his lips and whispered, "Shhhh," to him, a mother quieting her babe.
"Shhhh."

Cross spit on her hand and pushed it away. Called her a name.

"You're better than Lee is, Anthony," she whispered to him, willing him to be calm. "Better than Adam, better than anyone. You can
show them."

"I can show them." His eyes were fixed on the setting sun.

"Whatever Lee did to the magnets," *if he did anything at all,* she
thought, "you can fix. You can make it work better than before. Show
Parnel, show everyone."

"Everyone." Another internal switch was thrown and now his
voice was calm and even.

"What did Lee do to the equipment?" Neale asked, still moving
her hand across his shoulders.

"The fucking chink cock—"

"Shhh. How can you fix it? How can you show him that he's no
match for you?"

"The timing coils," Cross said.

"What happened to the timing coils?"

"They went out of phase. Overloaded."

"How did that happen?" Neale glanced behind her. The shifting
red ball of the setting sun glowed in the windows of the living room, a
pulsing ball of fire engulfing their reflections, pulling them inside its
brilliance. She was caught by the image. Off to the far corner, back in
the living room, Covington waited, fresh drink in hand. Watching his
business.

"At 99.9999 lightspeed, the electrons in the accelerator gain forty
thousand times their mass." Cross trembled. She could see his mind
working feverishly, holding all the equations in some unseen space
before him, oblivious to the real world surrounding him.

"Shhh," she whispered, guiding him, steering him. "I know that.
But how does that affect the timing coils?" She remembered his delu-
sion. "How did *Lee* make that affect the timing coils?"

"The relativistic frame of reference gets dragged around . . ."

Cross said softly, peering out to the horizon as if trying to read some distant sign.

"Shhh," she whispered. "I know that."

"No . . . no . . ." He held out his hand, reaching for something Neale couldn't see. "Each electron . . ." His eyes widened, unfocused. "I can see them . . . yes . . . each electron moves at a different speed . . . see them? There and there? A different speed, so small, so tiny, on the order of Planck length . . ."

"We can't measure anything that small with our equipment, love. The effect must be negli—"

His voice was cold as starless space, all his anger wound deep within it. "I can *see* it," he said. "The effect *is* there and it is *cumulative.*"

Neale moved her hands from his back, reaching around in front of him, pushing against the straining hardness of him. "Tell me about it . . . the Planck length . . . the cumulative effect . . ." Her hands opened his belt and his pants, letting him free.

Cross's eyes darted from place to place, watching the electrons orbit a kiss away from lightspeed through the accelerator in Lab 2. His words were fast now, barely keeping pace with his thoughts. "Each electron's relativistic frame is dragged at a minutely different velocity . . . the time dilation factor in each frame interferes on the boundary edge of each impinging frame . . . see? Over there? It's like a picture out of focus. That's why the timing coils in the magnets overloaded. There was no coherent signal to detect. Only chaos. Only chaos."

Neale licked her hand to smoothly slip across his penis, back and forth, slowing his breathing to match the timing of her strokes. "How can you create a signal, love?" He was like iron, resonating to some deep inner signal that pulsed to the surface.

"Focus the electrons. See? Like this." He gestured to the sun half sunk behind the far Pacific, a maestro conducting the interplay of all nature, his hips moving with the rhythm of her hands upon him. "Bring them all into perfect phase, all within the precise velocity, matched and bound to ten to the minus thirty-three . . . their frames will be in step, will stop their destructive interference . . . they'll reinforce each other . . . gravity will be the only force that matters . . ."

"How can we measure that small a distance?" Her voice soothed, her hands tightened and relaxed around him. She could see the direction his mind was going but how did he know there were answers there? How could he be sure? She could feel the direction his body was going, the quake that was coming in him. She felt the release building in his body and his mind.

"We don't have to measure it . . . the electrons will know . . . it's fundamental to them . . . to everything . . . we just have to kick them toward that synchronization of velocity, then their relativistic frames will match, the timing coils will detect their signal, and . . . the experiment will work." He exploded into her hands with sudden heat. He squeezed his hands against the wooden railing as Neale squeezed against him, draining him, bringing it all to the surface with his drawn-out groan. And after a moment, Cross breathed again and jerked his head like a hypnotist's subject awakening.

He turned to her as the last red smear of the sun succumbed to the sea, the white sails now dark smudges above twinkling running lights as the distant boats passed into the night. He closed his hands over hers, smearing them both with what she had called forth. "You see it now, don't you?" He made no other acknowledgment of what they had done.

Neale did see, quite clearly, with only one small problem. "How do you kick the electrons into that kind of synchronization? You're talking a power requirement of something on the order of"—she did the calculation—"twenty *teravolts?* Maybe the Supercollider could handle that when it's finished, Anthony. If it ever is. *Maybe.* But our accelerator's only good to ten gigavolts." Feeling the heat of him in her hands, her heart raced as his had calmed. She forced herself to concentrate on his words and not on her need of him.

Cross held his damp hand to Neale's face, painting a lover's caress across her cheek and to her lips. "The pattern and the rhythm of that synchronization is already there. It exists in nature already. We don't have to have the power to *create* it, Charis, we just have to make sure all those madly vibrating electrons fall into that one single groove and vibrate and respond to the accelerator's fields at the precise, exact time. Their natural resonance will force them into the pattern I need." He brought his other hand to her face, cradled her head between them. She licked her lips to taste him. She wanted him to stop talking, but knew he couldn't. "We don't have to know how to generate gravity to extract mechanical power from falling water, do we? And we don't have to create gravity-bound sustained fusion to be able to extract chemical power from the radiation produced by the sun. We just have to take advantage of an already existing phenomenon." He looked out to the darkening sea, lit only by the soft sparkle of lights on unseen hulls. "For the experiment to work, all we have to build is a sail, a sail for the quantum sea." He laughed, cold and maniacal, his hands squeezing into the sides of Neale's head. "And it will take us anywhere we want to go. Anywhere."

"You're hurting me," Neale said gently, feeling the power in his hands.

Cross smiled at her, *the* smile. "But you like that, don't you? The pain. And the hurt." He squeezed harder, his dark eyes showing the change inside the man, new personalities and priorities emerging and sinking like something seething and boiling in a mad foam. "It's your punishment for being smart enough to know what I do, but never smart enough to know it first."

She felt the pressure of each finger at her temples like a sudden migraine, heartbeats of agony. "Please, Anthony, you're right." And he released her.

"A sail for the quantum sea," he whispered like a love poem in her ear, then held her and kissed her as though they had been apart for years.

His hand slid up her leg, bunching her dress to expose her nakedness, hidden only by a fragile band of lace. "I like that," he whispered, moving his fingers beneath the delicate fabric. "Ah, and I like that . . ." He sighed as he slipped his fingers easily inside her.

But Neale pulled down on her dress and pushed his hand away, fearful for his reaction. Keeping up with his sudden swings and unpredictable moods left her exhausted. "Parnel will see us." At least Cross had been hidden as she had caressed him. But she couldn't stand to let Covington have anything more of her.

Cross eased his hand away, stepped back from her. She forced herself to look up to his face, to see the hateful expression of rage that surely must be growing in his eyes. But he was smiling at her, playful, the young boy returned.

"Parnel is blind. He can't see anything. He can't see what I can see. He can't see what *we* can see." He shook his head as gently as the cooling night breeze and kissed the fingers he had drawn from her. "Not Parnel."

Neale smoothed her dress again, afraid to look back at him, completely lost in understanding the thoughts that Cross had just experienced, but excited by the concepts he had unlocked. What if what he suggested *were* possible? The possibilities were . . . infinite, unthinkable. Her mind raced in confusion for him. Her body ached for him.

"A quantum sail."

She relaxed. He was back to work, to normal, what passed for normal at least. "Intriguing, if we . . . if you can determine the technique for . . . building it." Now she must work to understand him, no matter what it took.

"The technique," he said, nodding as he puffed out his lips in thought. Without looking, he closed his pants, and fastened his belt. "The technique is . . . is . . ." He turned suddenly and waved toward the living room. "Helloooo, Parnelll!" Laughed again. Then he slapped Neale playfully on her backside, gave her a quick kiss on the forehead, and said, "You keep Parnel company for a while. I think I'm going for a drive." He winked at her. "To look at the lights. Get my thoughts in order. I think this might be it." He walked off to the stairs at the side of the deck, leading to the carport.

Neale watched him warily, waiting for him to turn suddenly and catch her in midflight, but he left without turning back. Even so, she waited till she heard his Mercedes start.

Covington was on the phone when she walked into the living room from the deck, forcing herself to remain calm and unhurried. She took a moment to pour a drink for herself while she readied herself for what she knew she must do, now that Cross had left her again.

"What was all that about?" Covington asked when he had hung up.

"He's going for a drive," Neale said lightly. "To get his thoughts in order."

Covington tapped his finger against his lips. "What do you think he's really going to do?"

"Does it matter?" Neale put her empty glass down. She felt a warm wave of security and purpose sweep through her. Her battle with Covington could wait. She knew what she had to do and it was time to go.

The night waited for her, full of inspiration.

EIGHT

T he motels off that stretch of Hollywood Boule-
vard were way stations. Sometimes between arriving in the city with dreams grander than any
that Vegas could offer and leaving as anonymous as the gray tatters of
paper that melted against the curb, and sometimes, Katherine Duvall
knew, between life and death. She had been to these way stations
before. This Wednesday night was nothing new.

She found the motel identified in the chatter on her Volkswagen's
scanner by the two black-and-whites parked on the street in front of it.
The sign attached to the second-story wall of the office and manager's
suite simply said "Motel" in flickering green neon. Somewhere beneath
that word, above the Vacancy No Vacancy notice, other words, as pale
and faded as the cracked pink paint on the wall, spelled out the motel's
name. But Duvall couldn't read it as she parked her car on the curb
beneath it, and she knew the name had never been important to anyone
who had stayed here before. It was just a place to pause, not even to
rest, before moving on. For those who could move on.

Duvall hung her ID and badge around her neck, then pulled her
service revolver out of the glove compartment and replaced it with her
small shoulder bag. She slipped the gun into the holster in the small of

her back under her jacket, got out of the car, and walked into the motel's central parking lot.

The motel was built on two U-shaped levels surrounding the lot's cracked and rippling pavement. Civilian cars were parked against the edges of the building but the center of the lot was jammed with emergency vehicles. Duvall looked around to see which unit they converged on, and saw that the doors on the ambulance outside Unit Eight on the first level were open and the gurney was gone from inside. One of the uniforms standing by the door to Unit Eight was a familiar face and she went to him first.

"Hello, Lewis."

"Hi, Detective Duvall." Then the P-1 blinked, just remembering something.

"I go on vacation Thursday," Duvall explained. She nodded toward the door. "Is this like the one we found last Friday?"

Lewis shrugged. "I haven't seen it, but, uh, yeah, sounds like it. The girl's been tied down on the, uh, bed."

"Head wound?"

Lewis nodded.

"Who's in charge? Erhlenmeyer?"

"No, sir, ah, ma'am. He left already. Detective Seabrook's in there now."

Duvall studied Lewis's wonderfully open and unmarked face and wondered for a moment if the rookie had even started to shave. Then she thanked him and went into Unit Eight.

The small room was an efficiency with peeling yellow wallpaper and a corner kitchen consisting of a built-in double burner hotplate and a tiny cube of a refrigerator. It stank of old mildew and the fresh sweat of the ten investigators crowded within, bagging anything of interest, peering at all the grimy surfaces, disassembling the room like beetles stripping a corpse. But the real corpse of the room, encased in the shimmering liquid-black plastic of a body bag, was just being lifted to the wheeled stretcher.

Beside the stretcher, a double bed, still made up with its bedspread in place as far as Duvall could tell, was sopping with blood. Something flat and hard, about the size of a small desktop, lay sideways across the bed, edge to edge. A tubular metal kitchen chair, tagged as evidence, remained in place facing the bed at one end of the flat object.

Beside the bed and the chair, a small table held three lamps, shades removed, positioned to add light to the area in front of the chair. Above the bed, two faded color photographs of smiling children and happy puppies, cut from a twenty-year-old calendar, were screwed to the wall in cheap black wooden frames. Both pictures were crooked.

Duvall stepped around a man crawling across the flattened orange and brown shag broadloom, gathering dirt, hair, and fiber samples with squares of adhesive paper. She walked over to the ambulance attendants by the stretcher. She couldn't see Seabrook anywhere.

"Hold on," Duvall said, "I want to see that."

The attendants, indistinguishable from each other in wrinkled and dirty whites, and both two days past a shave, were used to cops. They didn't change their expressions as the one closer to the body's head grabbed a large zipper tab and pulled down, spreading the two sides of the thick plastic bag apart.

The first thing Duvall saw reminded her of the training videos that the department showed from time to time, where ATF agents fired AK-47s into watermelons. The head inside the bag looked as if it had exploded just as thoroughly. She felt her stomach tightening, but forced herself to look past the clotted lumps, red-black and shiny, and concentrate on finding the lines of the face as it once had been. She found the curve of a cheekbone, the central ridge of the nose, then overlaid in her mind the order and pattern of a real face on the pulped destruction gleaming in the folds of black.

She found what she had expected to find. Dear God, she realized, what she had hoped to find. All that was scattered and strewn of the woman's head had erupted from a roughly rectangular opening high up on her forehead, framed by a blood-matted nest of long blond hair.

"Okay?" the attendant asked, annoyed with the delay.

"Yeah," Duvall said, feeling the word catch and disappear in her suddenly dry throat. She coughed. "Yeah," she repeated. Blond hair. "No, wait."

"Jesus, lady, we got a schedule." The attendant zipped up the bag. A tuft of the victim's blond hair stuck out at the top of the bag, caught in the zipper's teeth.

"Open it up," Duvall said. The attendant hesitated. Duvall held her badge up. The attendant sighed and pulled down on the zipper once more. It jammed on the hair. He swore again, asked his partner for help. The partner leaned over and held the top of the bag in a double fistful as the attendant used both hands to yank on the zipper tab. The hair tore and the zipper opened, revealing the ruined face again. But that wasn't what Duvall wanted this time.

"Keep going," she said.

The zipper ripped farther down and the bag parted over the victim's torso. She wore a tight top, like a Danskin, under a loose, open shirt. Duvall reached in to move a side of the shirt away.

"Kate! What the hell are you doing here?"

Duvall looked away from the body to Detective Seabrook, approaching her from the unit's bathroom. Part of his fringe of thin hair stuck out over one ear, his eyes were shadowed, and he wore scruffy, off-duty clothes. He held four plastic evidence bags in his hands.

"Just driving by, Joe," she said, withdrawing her hand from the bag. Then told the attendant to open it up the rest of the way. A mini-skirt over fishnet stockings, and the stockings seemed undisturbed. There was a stench of feces. "That's okay," she said to the attendants, then stepped away as the body was swallowed by blackness again.

Seabrook passed his evidence bags to a plainclothes, took Duvall by the arm and led her to the other side of the bed, out of the path of the wheeled stretcher. Duvall looked more closely at the flat slab on the bed as she circled it. In between the smears and puddles of blood on its surface, she could see an exaggerated wood-grain pattern. From underneath the slab, the cut ends of bloodstained nylon ropes emerged, like white worms, bleeding.

"Don't give me that crap," Seabrook said, inexplicably dropping his voice to a whisper. "Tell me what you're doing here."

"She was stacked," Duvall said. "I mean, that is how you guys put it down in the old locker room, isn't it?"

Seabrook looked furtively around. "Okay, okay, like Cassie Riley." He glared at Duvall. "You're not the only detective in the world, Kate. Built like Cassie Riley, blond like Cassie Riley, clothes like Cassie Riley, what else did you want to spring on me that you think I don't already know?"

Duvall felt embarrassed. With all the anomalies in the Riley murder and its investigation, she had been thinking that perhaps some details might have been overlooked, perhaps even on purpose. But the feeling only lasted a moment. On duty or off, she was still a detective. There was a job to do. "Any sign of rape?"

Seabrook's mouth twitched nervously, or in anger. "Won't know for sure until the coroner's report, but there's no sign of violence. Her clothes are intact. No obvious marks or bruises other than the ones left by the ropes and the . . . head wound. For now, we're assuming no rape. Just like Cassie Riley, okay?" he added.

"Why are you getting mad at *me*, Joe?"

Seabrook's voice became even softer, more urgent. "C'mon, Kate, we got two victims, almost identical in appearance, killed the same sick way. It's a pattern killer. The big time. And it's *my* case, okay?"

Then Duvall understood his urgency. "And you don't know why they assigned you to it, right? Three months in Homicide and you get a big one that'll probably be in the hands of a thirty-man task force by the morning news, and you think there's a chance they're going to let you stay in charge? Catch fire, Joe."

"I *am* in charge of the task force."

Duvall choked. "What task force? When?"

"Erhlenmeyer gave me the go-ahead twenty minutes ago. I've got twenty-four men to begin with, more—"

"That's bullshit, Joe."

Seabrook put a hand on Duvall's shoulder as if to force her down into a secret huddle. "Don't say that. I can do it. But I don't need you—"

Duvall was incensed. "You *can't* do it!" She yelled it out and everything in the motel room came to a stop.

Seabrook straightened up, saw the reaction of the cops and the technicians around him. "Get out of here," he told Duvall. "I got twenty-four guys and you're not one of them. So just get the hell out of here."

But Duvall wasn't going to give up, though she kept her voice a whisper, trying not to provoke him again. "This case stinks, Joe. They don't give a pattern-killer task force to a three-month second-grade fresh from Robbery. Think it through."

Seabrook's teeth were clenched, his eyes burned. "I've been after something like this for a long time, Duvall. I didn't have anything goddamn handed to me on a goddamn silver platter like some people in

the department. I can do this and you're not going to screw it up for
me."

In the silence that followed, Duvall was surprised to learn that her
first reaction was sadness. Was it always going to come down to this? No
matter how many times she came *this* close to believing that at last her
skin and her sex had disappeared and that they were finally only seeing
her badge, when it came down to the bottom line, would they always
dredge a little bit of Erhlenmeyer out of the slime and throw it in her
face?

"Now do you leave? Or do I have you escorted out?"

Duvall glanced over Seabrook's shoulder. Everyone in the room
was still watching. A hundred different arguments ran through her
mind. For an instant, she even felt like flattening him the way she had
decked Erhlenmeyer. But the sense of sadness, and of betrayal, still
remained. She wondered when she was going to smarten up.

"I always thought you were different, Joe."

"I always thought you were smart."

Duvall left quietly.

Lewis was still outside, leaning against the hood of his black-and-white,
writing something on a clipboard, tongue quivering at the side of his
lips.

"Whatcha doing, Lewis?" Duvall kept it light, kept herself under
control. She still needed some information.

Lewis's head popped up as if he had heard a disembodied voice
whisper in his ear. He looked around with such a blank expression that
Duvall wondered if in his concentration the kid had forgotten where he
was. But when he saw Duvall, he greeted her happily. He hadn't heard
anything of the encounter inside Unit Eight.

"It's a list of those people," Lewis said about the clipboard, then
pointed up to the handful of people staring over the second-floor balcony railing that overlooked the parking lot. Some were shirtless, one in
a bathrobe, a couple with beers in their hands. Four uniforms were up
there with them, taking preliminary statements. Most other times, the
sight of a police officer conducting interviews would be enough to make
everyone escape behind locked doors and Do Not Disturb signs. It was
obviously a slow night for television.

"Any of them see anything?" Duvall asked idly.

"Not so far."

"How'd this one get called in?"

Lewis thought for a moment, making the decision to give up writing on his clipboard while he was engaged in conversation. Probably didn't chew gum when he was on duty, either, Duvall thought, so he wouldn't get confused. "Anonymous call like before, I think."

"Nine-one-one?" If the call had been placed to the emergency number, a recording of the tipster's voice would have been automatically made and the location instantly traced.

But Lewis shook his head. "Local station call from a pay phone. Told 'em to check this place out. That's all."

Duvall nodded noncommittally, keeping her tone even and, she hoped, casual. She leaned against the unit's hood, sat beside Lewis, then snapped her fingers. "Gosh, Lewis, I forgot to ask who the coroner was. Darn, I'll need that for my report. Was it Dr. File?" She smiled at the rookie.

"Nope, it was somebody else. I don't know all of 'em yet." There was a flash of what Duvall recognized as suspicion in the rookie's eyes. She tried to ease it.

"That's okay." She smiled again, friendly and winning. "I don't know them all yet, either." She patted him on the shoulder. But Lewis only seemed to tighten up even more.

"Uh, Detective Duvall, ma'am," Lewis said carefully. His eyes dropped down to the hood of the car, where he and Duvall were separated by almost a foot. "Um, I'm . . . I'm a married man," he blurted, then scooted away from her and the hand on his shoulder.

"*Lewis*, I . . ." Duvall let her hand fall to the hood of the car. Lewis watched her as if he expected her to bite him. "I was just *talking* with you," Duvall said, wondering which of them was the bigger asshole at the moment. "Cop to cop, you know?"

"I got two kids," Lewis said, "and I promised Dorothy—"

"Two kids?" The kid shaved after all.

"Arlene and George," Lewis said proudly.

"How old are you, Lewis?" Couldn't be more than twenty, Duvall thought.

"Twenty-seven," Lewis said, slipping back into his suspicious expression.

Duvall had a terrible sense that something important had just passed her by. Somehow, she felt out of touch with Lewis and all the other cops around her. What other stories and details had she missed, or worse, taken for granted about them? Lewis's revelations were like the first break in a case, the first detail that leads to the slow unraveling of all the others. She hadn't even been able to guess how old he was. So how could she be sure of Seabrook's motives? His qualifications? Or even the reasons behind Erhlenmeyer assigning Seabrook the case?

A horribly long moment of doubt engulfed her, sitting there in the parking lot, removed from Lewis—the slow rookie who was really somebody other than she had expected—removed from the body being loaded into the ambulance twenty feet away. She remembered being a P-1 herself, still on first-year probation, the uniform cut wrong, pants too short, stiff blue shirt too hot, standing in Marjorie Hill's bedroom, waiting for the coroner, waiting for the coroner, watching the body and seeing the one tuft of hair snagged in the bracelet, like the thin blond strands jammed in the zipper of the body bag.

There had been doubt then. Incredible doubt like a huge thick wave of suffocating mud in the silence of that bedroom, the body of the old lady sprawled and stiffening on the floor, waiting and waiting for the coroner. Waiting for the coroner was one of the worst duties a uniform could pull, traditionally awarded to the greenest rookie. The detectives had come and gone. The unmarked body of a wizened old lady, collapsed on the floor of a bedroom untouched by disarray, on the hottest day of the year, had not encouraged them to stay. There were murders waiting for them elsewhere in the city, bad guys and criminals, and that's what detectives investigated, not the natural end of a long life.

But Marjorie Hill had not been under a doctor's care and her body couldn't be moved until the coroner arrived. So the radio call had gone out and Katherine Duvall, four months on the force, heavy black shoes spit-shined and long hair painfully pinned up flat under her cap with enough barrettes to set off a metal detector, got the job. The detectives had laughed at her earnestness and told her she could call in for relief if the coroner hadn't arrived within, oh, say, eight hours or so. Then they were off to fight crime and Officer Duvall stood watch over the dead woman. And saw the small tuft of hair snagged in the bracelet. And had time to think it through, just as her instructors had told her to do.

When the coroner came six hours later, Duvall fought through the wave of doubt she had wrestled with all afternoon and told him not to move the body yet because Marjorie Hill had been murdered and the detectives had to be called back. The coroner had laughed at first, like the detectives. Duvall was a rookie, as eager to find an imaginary crime and break a nonexistent case as first-year med students were to diagnose rare tropical diseases stewing in their own guts. But it was his last call of the day and the coroner remembered what he had been like as a first-year med student and he gave her a minute to explain herself and she had.

It was all in the details. Marjorie Hill's hair was dark brown, dyed in a woman her age, Duvall knew. The tuft of hair, which she had examined on her knees by the dead woman's outstretched hand, using a pencil tip to gently separate the strands from the clasp on the costume jewelry bracelet, was auburn. A subtle difference, but she had had an hour to watch the sun move across the body after the detectives had warned her not to cover it so the coroner wouldn't report her for interfering with the body—more jerking around for the rookie to go with the order not to leave the body for any reason. So Duvall had seen that the highlights in the hair on the bracelet were red. The highlights in the woman's dyed hair were not.

Details. The webs that connected them. There were pictures all over the walls of Marjorie Hill's bedroom, some hanging in their own frames, others slipped into the molding of the dressing table mirror or the other photos' frames. Duvall had studied them, wondering what to do about the hair in the bracelet—perhaps it had been left over from an earlier dye job—struggling against her doubt and wondering how she could dare see something that experienced detectives had not been concerned about.

There were faded black and white portraits of unsmiling, wide-eyed, stiff people in antique clothes. Holiday snaps of men and women and children in the baggy clothes and swimsuits of the forties, and blurry color shots of anonymous people with party hats sitting around tables decorated with a succession of birthday cakes, Christmas turkeys, and Easter hams. In three of those blurry color shots, and one instant photo in a small frame on the bedside table, Duvall had seen different aged versions of Marjorie Hill with the same person as a teenager and as a young man. He had red hair.

Certain she would be able to hear the door when the coroner arrived, Duvall had gathered her courage and stepped outside the bedroom to the hallway, defying the detectives' mock orders. There were two other bedrooms on the floor, full of old furniture and the smell of an old woman's powder. But one room wasn't quite as precisely neat as the other, didn't smell quite like the others, and there were small commas of red hair on the sheets that Duvall pulled down on the bed in that room. Details.

Three days later they caught Marjorie Hill's nephew in Utah, trying to sell some of her jewelry and with more than four thousand dollars in small bills taken from a dress box in her closet. He confessed to smothering her, though the coroner concluded that her heart had stopped before she had suffocated. Duvall had received the first of her six commendations and a personal promise from the division supervisor that she would be given a chance at her detective's exams at her first eligibility. Eight years later, her eye for detail was still legendary. And all it had taken was getting over that initial wall of smothering doubt to attempt something new. To make a difference.

But in the parking lot, beside Lewis, the doubt Duvall now felt did not come from inexperience. Maybe from too much experience, she thought. Maybe she had become blinded by detail and nuance, become incapable of seeing the whole. Like using a magnifying glass to study the glowing dots of phosphor on a television screen, she could see each color but had no conception of the picture they described. Lewis was a father. Seabrook knew the pattern of the killer's victims. Duvall had missed those details.

"You okay?" Lewis asked. "I . . . I didn't mean nothing."

Duvall stood up, breathed in the air, heard salsa playing from one of the units behind her, tinny with an echo.

"Just thinking about Hawaii," she said, thinking she was jumping to too many conclusions.

"Thursday, right?" Lewis said, trying to be encouraging.

"I'm going with my husband." Duvall smiled as she saw the look of relief on Lewis's face. She said good night to him and headed back to the street and her car, swapping her gun for her bag once again. Ex-husband, husband, what did it matter?

The Bug was being balky again and after five tries Duvall had flooded it, so she resigned herself to sitting patiently for a minute before trying again. The minute passed and she flooded the car after three tries. And this time the sound of the engine cranking began to noticeably slow. She swore. The last thing she needed tonight was to go back and ask one of Seabrook's guys for a boost. She took a deep breath and to give the battery time to rest began to organize what she was going to pack for Hawaii. The way she had avoided that task in the past few days, it was almost as if she hadn't really believed she'd be going.

Suddenly, Duvall was blinded by the flashing red and white lights of the ambulance as it pulled out to the street in front of her. The attendants were eager to keep their schedule, she assumed, and didn't want to wait for an opening in both directions on Hollywood. The traffic slowed to give the ambulance right of way and it screeched out, the driver not concerned about giving his passenger a smooth ride. Two black-and-whites, using the same trick to keep the traffic open, followed. Duvall followed their spinning lights as they swept the road like miniature searchlights. Then she stopped thinking about her trip or her car. There was an almost embarrassingly obvious car thief across the six lanes of the street, standing in the shadow of a nearby street lamp, watching the police cars drive away. A late model blue Plymouth was street-parked about ten feet away from the figure, and when the black-and-whites were gone, the slime ball headed straight for it.

On duty or off, Duvall thought, *this is my job.* She sighed and slouched down in her car, watching as the figure crossed behind the Plymouth to go to the driver's side door. It was a woman, Duvall saw in the light from the street lamp. Obviously one of the 12 percent of car thieves who gave women a bad name. She wore black slacks and a black jacket, with a black cap pulled down low over her head, being far too conspicuous about trying not to be noticed.

Duvall knew she couldn't get any worthwhile theft charges to stick if she confronted the perp before the Plymouth had been taken, so she waited for the car to pull away so she could see its plates and then put out a five-oh-three on it. At least this unexpected diversion beat trying to start her own car again. It would be somehow comforting to have the chance to write up an ordinary stolen car report again.

The Plymouth started up smoothly, the headlights came on, and Duvall saw the backup lights flash as the perp put the car into gear. The perp pulled off her cap and looked over her shoulder to check for traffic, turning her face directly into the light from the street lamp as she pulled out and away. It was then that Duvall felt the familiar cold tingle envelop her, and she didn't know if it was from excitement, or fear.

Quite clearly in the light from the street lamp, the driver of the Plymouth was Charis Neale. And she wasn't just stealing a car.

As far as Duvall was concerned, she was present at the scene of a murder.

Again.

NINE

Anthony Cross stepped out of his shower, through his bathroom, and into his office, leaving dark footprints in the light gray carpet. The windows that looked onto his private terrace and the ocean were covered with matching gray vertical blinds. It was still night outside, but the SHARP facility knew no time constraints. Every hour of every day, it served its master.

Cross folded a thick white towel around his waist and used the smaller towel around his shoulders to dry his hair. He felt awake and alive. Driving along deserted roads, high in the hills, seeing the lights of the city spread out before him—it always made him feel inspired. "How long?" he asked enthusiastically.

Rich Daystrom looked up from the four pages of notes and pictures arranged on Cross's desk and rubbed at his eyes, still half-closed and full of sleep. His usually rich black skin had taken on a chalky undertone. Cross recognized it as a sign of exhaustion, something he had seen in most of the workers at the facility from time to time. But Daystrom was young and the infirmary had doses of B-12 and smelling salts, even amphetamines if they became necessary to meet a deadline, so Cross didn't worry about pushing the man. Besides, Daystrom was a programmer. He had a còt in his office. He was used to the hours.

Daystrom glanced at the notes again: ballpoint pen, scrawled down so rapidly that it seemed only the first half of each word or string of numbers had been inscribed before the next had begun. "I could breadboard it in a day or so—"

"How many hours?" Cross asked. "We've got the D-RAMs in stock. I checked. How many hours to put it together?"

Daystrom frowned at the diagrams. "Eight, maybe ten."

"But . . . ?" Cross prompted, hearing the unspoken word in Daystrom's answer. Why couldn't anyone here ever have a simple conversation, give a simple answer?

"Well first," Daystrom answered, tapping out his points with one of the many pens from his stuffed breast pocket, "I could simulate this chip array on the Cray in about half that time. And second, it won't work."

Cross's mouth tightened. Daystrom's eyes widened.

"Sorry, Dr. Cross, that came out the wrong way," he said rapidly, holding his hands up in apology. "I meant to say I'm not quite sure exactly what this array is supposed to accomplish."

"It's all there on the diagrams," Cross said icily.

"Right, right," Daystrom said in defeat. He looked back at the half-formed sketches, talking himself through some understanding of what Cross's concept was. "It's a timing array, I can see that. An elegant one, too. Very efficient layout. Cascaded parallel processors, each level subdividing the internal clock signal of the one above it."

"So what's the problem, Rich?" Cross leaned across his desk, supporting himself on tented fingers. His nails were perfectly clean, even arcs of pure white at each tip, contrasting starkly with the black leather surface of the desk. Other than the four sheets of paper, a high-intensity lamp, and a scattering of perfect hemispheres of liquid dripping from Cross's wet hair, there was nothing on the desk. He kept all of his notes in his head. Neale was the one with the gift for handling details.

"I don't have a problem with it, Doc," Daystrom said. "It's just that at about the fourth level of subdivision of the time signal here, I believe these specs exceed the operational capabilities of the computer chips we have in stores. Or, uh . . ."

"Go on."

"Or the capabilities of any chip currently being manufactured," Daystrom concluded, looking away.

Cross laughed and the programmer jumped.

"Is that all it is, Rich? Boy, oh boy, I thought I had gone and done something dumb the way you were moping over those plans." Cross made up his mind to fire Daystrom as head of computer operations as soon as Covington could locate a replacement. SHARP needed people with vision. People who could see beyond.

Cross came around the desk and stood beside Daystrom. "Look at page three, Rich. Second diagram."

Daystrom ran his finger along it. "Oh yeah, the offset. I think I'm going to have to work around this somehow because it will probably set up interference across this band here and—"

Cross successfully fought to control his rage, displayed no outside evidence. "Rich, it's *supposed* to create interference. That's why the alternating levels are offset. Each chip will double the resolution of the timing signal from the one above."

Daystrom was hesitant. "Well, yeah, in theory the math will work out. You'll keep doubling the sensitivity and all. But really, Dr. Cross, these chips can't operate faster than 80 megahertz. I can wire them up this way, have them feed signals to each other this way, but it'll be like blowing up a photograph past the resolution of the grain. By this level here, when the operational capabilities of the chips are exceeded, you'll just be generating noise."

Cross took a deep breath. "Rich, the operating capabilities of these chips are determined from testing averages, aren't they?" Daystrom nodded. "And that means some chips operate at a slightly lower efficiency, and some at a slightly higher efficiency—"

"Yeah, but the burned-in software determines the precise clock rate of each chip. That's an industry standard."

Cross stepped back from the desk, afraid to remain within arms' reach of the programmer as the rage inside him grew. "This is an *advanced* research facility, Rich. We're not interested in 'standard' here. We're interested in going beyond the standard. We're interested in exceeding *everything* that's gone before. Isn't that right, Rich?"

"Well, yes, sir, but—" Rich began to turn around to look at Cross.

"Stay where you are, Rich." Cross's words were a command. The man was being an obstinate fool. A moron. A mindless nigger shit cocksucking . . . "Look at the diagrams, Rich. Carefully, carefully. And understand them. Understand that I wouldn't ask you to do anything foolish with your time . . ." Clouds of blood erupted before Cross's vision. He saw the scalpel enter the cat's stomach, the fur and skin and muscle layers peeling back as the creature screeched and struggled against the wire, spraying blood, joining the pattern, caught in the transition. "You are a valuable member of the team here, Rich." He saw the blood spurt from Daystrom's eyes as his fingers gouged into them, teaching the interfering ape-faced shitsucker his lesson, *the* lesson of all time. "And I think that you'll see if you just wire everything up the way I . . . suggest there, then the type of signal the array will produce will be fairly obvious and guess what, Rich, that's exactly the kind of signal I want it to produce." Cross added a small happy chuckle, tasting the flesh of the programmer in his vision, seeing the copper twist and bind and . . .

"But you won't get any sort of coherent signal at all," Daystrom protested.

The programmer turned his head a fraction of an inch and heard Cross make a sound like a small, high-pitched groan. Something in that sound alone stopped Daystrom from turning all the way around. He turned back to look at the diagrams.

With a sigh, Cross said, "The diagrams, Rich, please just look at the diagrams. And believe me when I say that of all the billions of offsets and timing interference signals that array will produce each second, on average, *on average,* Rich, one or two of them will succeed. One or two absolutely precise timing signals every couple of seconds of operation, Rich, that's all I need. On average."

"Well, okay," Daystrom said. "I can see how this might work like that—"

Cross sighed, so deeply, so gratefully. "Oh, thank you, Rich. Thank you for saying that."

Daystrom continued, confused but not knowing what else to do. "Yeah, okay, but, even if it does generate those absolutely precise signals every second or two like you want, there's still no way that you can get those signals out again. They might be there, they might not be, but there's no way to be sure." Daystrom tapped the desk with his knuckles as he had a realization. "Like Heisenberg's Uncertainty Principle, you can't know for sure."

"Thank you, Rich. I am familiar with the concept. Now will you build it for me?" The decision had already been made as far as Cross was concerned. One more provocation on Daystrom's part and he would be taken apart and laid out like a grandfather clock, each shining well-oiled part and gear in precise alignment, skin stretched out over spikes and hooks and a web of the finest copper with which to encase his body and—

"Oh, I can build it for you, Doc. I don't have any problem with that."

Cross sighed and stepped back to the desk. "I'm glad to hear you say that, Rich. For a few seconds there, you made me feel as if I were asking you to do something insane."

"Oh, not you, Dr. Cross."

"No, Rich. Not me."

"So," Daystrom said, standing up and gathering the handwritten pages together, "eight to ten hours?"

"That would be most helpful, Rich. I've got an experiment in Lab 2 waiting for this."

Daystrom nodded, checked page two of the sheets. "You going to be plugging it into the control computer down there?"

Cross's hands tightened on the towel around his shoulder. He looked down to the carpet where his footprints had almost dried and disappeared. A transitory phenomenon. Most things were. "Do you have a problem with that, Rich?"

"No, sir. Just wondering what sort of interface you'll need, and what kind of power supply it'll run on."

"Page four, Rich. I already have special batteries made up for it, and I'll add the interface myself."

"Batteries?" Daystrom asked, flipping through to the final page as he walked toward the door. He paused as though to say something more, but then thought better of it. "A portable, huh? Going to take it with you someplace?"

"Someplace," Cross said, hoping the imbecile would get out of his office before the night was ruined entirely.

But Daystrom stopped in the doorway, turned around, gestured with the papers.

"You know, Doc, might help me a bit if you told me what you were going to be using this for. Might be able to suggest a few different strategies, a workaround or two."

Cross took a long breath and adjusted the towel around his waist. "It's not important, Rich. Just build it as you see it there. Exactly as you see it there."

Daystrom accepted that final instruction, earned the right to his paycheck for another day. "Just another crazy idea, huh, Doc?" He laughed, used to Cross's crazy ideas, as was everyone else at SHARP.

Cross smiled, the moment passed for now.

"A sudden inspiration, Rich. You never know when they'll come."

"I know what you mean, Doc."

Anthony Cross smiled again, and said nothing. He still had lots to do in his private workshop. It was time to go back to work.

TEN

A large white paw reached up past the side of the table, landed on the bloody mass of Cassie Riley's face, then slowly started to drag it over the edge. At the last second, Detective Nogura placed a finger on the photo and kept it from slipping off to the floor. The paw stayed in place for a moment, then two pointed black ears and a spray of thick white eyebrow whiskers appeared above the table, followed by two curious green eyes.

Nogura smiled evilly. "Boo!"

The cat's ears flattened and it hit the kitchen floor with a thud that rattled dishes on the counter. Duvall turned away from her coffeemaker by the sink. "What was all that about?"

Nogura settled back in his chair, going eye to eye with the black-and-white cat as it glared at him from under the dining room table in the next room. "Your cat wants to get involved in policework."

Duvall laughed, pouring fresh coffee into two mugs. "Briggs just wants to lick the emulsion on photographs."

"Briggs?"

"Hey, he's as close as I figure I'll get to Mel Gibson in this life-time," Duvall said wistfully as she returned to the table that was covered with the paperwork and photographs generated by the murders of Cassie Riley and Amanda Frost, the just-identified sometime hooker found in Unit Eight. Duvall cleared two spaces to put down the mugs she carried. The silence after the laughter lasted a few seconds too long.

"Nuke . . ."

"Yeah, I know. 'Thank you for sharing this with me.' "

"Catch fire, Nuke."

Nogura smiled. "That was my second guess. But really, don't worry about it." Then his expression became unreadable, the expression detectives practiced for use during interrogations, when they couldn't risk giving up any information to their prisoners, however subtle. "I've been thinking, though, maybe we should be partners. I don't think Erhlenmeyer would mind putting it through."

Duvall was puzzled. Nogura didn't have partners except on a case-by-case basis. Probably made it easier for him to be transferred between divisions like he was some kind of private task force, Duvall thought.

"Come on, Katherine, you're still in the department, remember? This is just an enforced holiday, not a suspension. You're going to need a partner sooner or later."

Duvall shook her head, arranging the photos of the two bodies side by side, matching content and angles. Seen quickly, the two sets of photographs might be mistaken as being images of the same victim. "I gave up asking about a new partner two months ago. Guess Erhlenmeyer won't do anything more about it until I'm officially back from my 'vacation.' "

Nogura cleared away some typewritten forms, giving Duvall extra room for her comparison of the photographs. "Heard you turned down a couple that he offered."

"It wasn't like that," Duvall said. Though it had been. But what else could she say? That the department had wanted to pair her with one or the other of two detectives who had reps for getting "involved" with their female partners? Erhlenmeyer had stopped both assignments when she had informally indicated she might feel incompatible with either choice. As far as Erhlenmeyer was concerned, the longer Duvall went without a partner, the harder hit her arrest record would be and the more oppressive her caseload would become. So what?

But even if the lieutenant had cared and asked what Duvall's problem had been, then she would have had to lie. There was no way she was telling anyone that the reason she didn't want to be paired with either of the two—single, available, no complications—was because she didn't want to be in a position of feeling vulnerable.

Because Nogura had been right. This job was a killer and only another cop could understand what it was a cop had to do, had to put up with. Only another cop could offer solace and escape and absolution. Duvall wanted to avoid the risk of that solace, until she had accepted for certain that that ordinary part of her life was over: her life with Jesse. She wondered what it would take, what sort of a brick wall she wanted to be slammed into.

"So, what about it?" Nogura asked, breaking her out of her reverie. "You and me?"

Duvall considered the proposition. Nogura didn't carry around any stories of colossal screw-ups. Definitely good in a fight. And though Duvall was sorry she had to make it part of her overall judgment, Nogura did have his girlfriend's photo prominently displayed in his office. Maybe he'd be safe.

"What's taking so long?" Nogura protested her silence. "I mean, look at this stuff here." He gestured to the table and the grotesque material upon it. "We're practically partners on this one, aren't we? Even if you have been ordered off it. Even if I am on my own time." He played a final card. "I could've got into a shitpot of trouble if Seabrook or Erhlenmeyer had caught me taking this stuff."

"I know, Nuke. And I appreciate it." She also wanted to know why he had risked it, but was afraid what his answer might be. Because he had almost taken her into his arms in the front hall, because she had found herself wondering what it would feel like to be held by someone who didn't know the dull secrets of her life. Because she was vulnerable and she suspected that Nogura might be, too.

Nogura shook his head in frustration. "Look, I'll try you again when you're back from Hawaii. Maybe you'll be in a better mood."

Duvall decided it was time to say it out loud, the decision she had made driving home from the motel last night. The decision she hadn't been able to tell to Jesse when he had called this morning, happy and eager with suggestions for their plans for Hawaii. With this new case, even if it wasn't official, the panic of the empty days had fled, and so had her need for reconcilement.

"I'm not going to Hawaii, Nuke." Saying it had made it real and she felt better. She waited to see if his reaction would betray his feelings. There was something cautious about the way he was dealing with her. Vulnerability, she thought.

"Why not?" But Nogura read the answer in her eyes though his own eyes gave up nothing. "Because of this?"

Duvall nodded, more determined than ever. "You just spent the last hour going over this stuff, too. What would you do?"

"Go to Seabrook. Tell him what you think's going on." Nogura was actually angry.

"And what if he's part of it?" There, that had made that element of her suspicions real, too.

Nogura's eyes widened. *"Joe!* Taking evidence from the scene? Not his style. Forget it." Then he regarded her almost with suspicion. "Unless, of course, you feel you have a strong reason to suspect that a member of the department is involved in some kind of a . . . cover-up."

Duvall dug through the photos again. "Nobody's taking evidence from the scene, Nuke. That's what makes all of this so bad. Somebody's taking it *after* it's tagged and bagged. See here?" She pointed to photo twenty-seven from the Riley kitchen.

For an awkward moment, Nogura watched her intently, then seemed to relax. He looked at the photo. "Yeah, yeah," he conceded. "The surgical gloves you say you saw."

"Did see. And they were rolled up in this mess of bloody pads."

"I know. And the pads are in an evidence bag."

"And the gloves aren't. Somebody opened the bag up, pulled out the gloves, sealed it up again. After everything was admitted into custody."

Nogura sighed. "I thought this sort of conspiracy shit went out in the seventies."

"I'm not saying it has to be a conspiracy, Nuke. Could just be one guy paying off a mob connection or something. Who knows? But even if it is one guy, that guy . . . or woman . . . is a cop. Has to be to have access to evidence."

Nogura pushed aside the Riley photos and pointed to the gridded placement shots from the motel room. "But you can't say that anything's missing from these shots of the second murder, can you? Seabrook had all sorts of close-ups done. Sort of like he listened to what you said about the gloves and made sure it couldn't happen again. *If* it had happened in the first place. Seabrook's covering every angle. If he's guilty, why's he being so careful?"

"Throw us off track?" Duvall was reaching and she knew it.

Nogura knew it, too. "Try again, Katherine."

"Okay, but look at the evidence list from the motel room. Compare it to the list from the Riley apartment." She pushed both out in front of Nogura. The Riley list was longer.

"Yeah, so?" Nogura said coolly.

"Yeah, so," Duvall said, running her fingers along both lists, reading them upside down though she already knew what each said. "At the Riley apartment, we found scalpels, a half-used roll of adhesive tape, the empty box the gauze pads came from, surgical scissors and . . . those brain probe things, a jar of surgical sealant. Even a squeeze bottle to hose down the blood. You get it? These are the killer's tools. Throwaway stuff. Probably untraceable. But in the motel room, we got none of it except for some gauze pads. Somebody had already gone in and cleaned it up before forensics arrived."

Nogura didn't seem impressed. "Sorry, Kate. We've seen that kind of thing before. In the Riley apartment, the killer got spooked. Had to leave before he could clean up. But in the motel, he had time and was able to take everything with him."

Duvall's words started coming faster as her excitement built. The details all fit if only Nogura would open his eyes. Why was he being so stubborn? She pulled out other forms, spread them over the staring emptied heads of Riley and Frost. "Look at the time of death versus time of the anonymous calls for both women. At least two hours' difference. The killer had the same amount of time in each place. In fact, the two-hour delay before calling in a tip might be part of the pattern. Maybe the killer lives two hours away from the areas where the murders were committed. Maybe—"

Nogura reached across the table and took Duvall's hands to stop her from digging out even more forms and sheets and photos. "Pull back, Katherine. You're jumping too far ahead. Stay with what we can know." He let go and sat back again.

Duvall nodded. She sat back and took a deep breath. Maybe it was time to go all the way.

"How do you draw the line?" she asked. "When you're making a conclusion. Combining two facts to make a supposition. How do you know the difference between a . . . logical inference and a . . . leap of faith?"

"Why do you think that there's a difference?" Nogura slumped in his chair, resting his chin in his hand.

"If the facts are correct, then the inference is usually right. The other can be wrong."

"A good detective's leap of faith *is* a logical inference. Experience makes the difference." He smiled at her, wary. "This shit is too philosophical for cops, Katherine. What're you getting at?"

"What we know," Duvall answered enigmatically, then decided it was time.

Nogura looked thoughtful, finding the meaning behind her words. "You mean that you know something that isn't in these reports? Not like the gloves, but something definite?"

Duvall smiled as she nodded. Maybe he'd end up being her partner after all. "Do you remember the name Charis Neale in all of this?" She gestured to the material on the table.

Nogura closed his eyes and his face returned to a neutral expression. "Riley's boss, right? Showed up at the apartment the night of the murder." He opened his eyes again. "It's in Seabrook's first report and then there was a follow-up interview at her place of business. What about it?"

Duvall heard the tension creeping into her own voice, despite herself. "So, was it a coincidence that Neale showed up at Riley's apartment that night?"

Nogura's sudden change of expression showed he could see she was building to something but that he didn't know what. "Seabrook put in his report that Riley had missed a few days at work and that Neale was coming by to fire her. Sounds sort of reasonable, doesn't it?"

"Sure," Duvall agreed. "Now why do you suppose Neale was outside the motel last night when Amanda Frost's body was found?"

Nogura frowned. "You saw her there?"

"Right across the street from the driveway entrance. She was waiting for the cops to go before she moved into the street to get her car. I got a perfect picture of her right here." Duvall tapped the side of her head. The legendary eye.

"Be real. If she did have anything at all to do with the murders, why would she be stupid enough to hang around outside the motel for three hours?"

"Why did she go back to Riley's apartment? Maybe she gets a kick out of watching the police come to investigate. Maybe she wants to see if she's left any loose ends around. Who knows?"

"Did you tell anyone you saw her there?" The wary look came back to Nogura's face.

"Seabrook had already shut me out and . . . right then . . . I didn't know how far I could push anything." She settled back in her chair. "I mean, what if there *is* a conspiracy? Christ, Nuke, maybe I shouldn't even be telling *you* all this shit." There, everything was on the table, now.

Nogura smiled. "If you really believed that, Kate, I wouldn't be here right now, would I?" The smile left. "So, what do you know about Neale?" He was finally taking Duvall seriously. He looked worried.

"She was at both scenes. She was Riley's boss. That's it."

"Where was it they worked?" Nogura started flipping through the forms, looking for Charis Neale's interview record.

"Some company out by Pepperdine in Malibu," Duvall said. "A research company. Science stuff."

Nogura didn't look up, still digging. "The Hughes aerospace setup?" he suggested.

"No." Duvall stared up at the ceiling, trying to call up the name of the place Neale worked.

"Here it is," Nogura said, pulling out the pale pink interview report with Neale's name on the top. He skimmed through it. "Not Hughes, Shannon Industries." He rolled his eyes sarcastically. "As if there's a difference. The Shannon Facility for Advanced Research in Physics. Yawn."

"SHARP," Duvall said suddenly, remembering at last.

"That's what it says here," Nogura confirmed. "I never heard of it." He looked over at Duvall and the strange expression on her face. "What is it now?"

"I'd never heard of it, either," she said slowly. "But Erhlenmeyer had. He mentioned the whole name in the hallway outside Riley's apartment."

"When?"

"Right before I decked him."

"So he watches PBS," Nogura said. He skimmed through the rest of the report. "This confirms Riley's employment record. Real spotty over the past three months. Caution notes in her file. Her severance check was drawn up that afternoon for Neale to hand deliver. It all checks out."

"I wonder what kind of a story she'd come up with to explain what she was doing outside the motel?" Duvall asked. "Was she going to fire the hooker?"

Nogura put the interview report back on the table. "Guess there's one way to find out."

"But is it a logical inference or a leap of faith?" Duvall felt a sensation of calm envelop her. She had a strategy, now, a way to act, something to *do*. Work.

"What does it matter?" Nogura said, sensing her change of attitude, her quickening pace. "As long as you're right?"

"Do *you* think I'm right?"

Nogura's face was set again, impassive, giving up nothing. "I'm not your partner."

"Do you still want to be?" Duvall asked, trying to understand why she felt Nogura pulling back.

"Talk to me after you come back from this SHARP place."

"You think my going there is a bad idea?"

Nogura assembled all the sheets and photographs into separate piles, like straightening a table full of mixed-up cards. "I think that if you'd take a minute to join up all the details, it's probably a dangerous idea," he said. "And if you go there without telling Seabrook what you've come up with, well . . . whatever you do, whatever you find out . . ." He reached out and took her hand—the gesture of a friend, Duvall hoped. "Just promise that you'll come to me first. Otherwise, you're on your own."

Duvall thought about that and then said the only thing she could say, the words that made it real.

"I know."

ELEVEN

For the moment, standing on the terrace outside his office at SHARP, Anthony Cross banished all the complexity of the modern world from his mind and concentrated on the combined force of what the ancient Greeks had called the four basic elements of nature. The Water of the Pacific pounded relentlessly at the cliff beneath him—patiently wearing away at the strong Earth that gave him its support. The Air of an onrushing high-pressure cell swept past him, all its power easily parting around him, cooling him from the assault of the Fire of the California sun.

Cross laughed, poised and balanced between the ancients' forces, attacked and protected equally by all. Scissors cut paper wraps stone dulls scissors. The worm ouroboros, eating its tail at the same rate as it grew. The gutted cat in death, swelling with the gases of the bacteria still living within. The winding of the copper for the special equipment and batteries he constructed in the private workshop attached to his office. All the kaleidoscopic images of his childhood games and favorite stories flowed through him, random connections forming with each alignment of an unseen prism, leaving Cross's consciousness as the only arbiter of which was incoherent, which logical, which held the key. The answer.

More images formed before his eyes, as fast as his racing pulse, obscuring the realtime sensations of his realworld senses with visual and aural and kinesthetic illusions that became to him a heightened reality. All the disparate aspects of his personality coalesced as he became whole, and sensed *more* than any other ever had.

Anthony Cross was not like the cowering cretin Einstein, who was forced to imagine himself an observer on a photon. Cross had to *imagine* nothing. He rode those photons in actual fact. Traveled with them and moved among them and was able to experience all the other sensations available to him in that mode of luminal existence. He *was* more than any other ever was.

Time dilation was real to him. In his visions, he heard the slowing thuds of his accelerated heart. He felt the acquisition of mass brought on by his relativistic velocity, observed the foreshortening of his dimensions in the direction of travel, yet sensed implicitly how his four-dimensional volume remained constant as he reached lightspeed with infinite mass and infinite energy and became *all*, bringing singularity within reach.

Those who had gone before him were dreamers, madmen, and morons. Except for Cross, who alone of all of them knew the reality of what lay beyond their inadequate equations. He could feel that ultimate reality, warm and pulsing as he passed through its folds and fissures. He could taste it, smell it, feel the heat and the life of it, hold all the secrets of all existence in his two hands as he pushed deeper, deeper . . .

He held up his multidimensional fist and called forth the seething rage of the Water, commanded the Earth to hold its ground, caused the Air to move between them, brought down the Fire of the sun to fuel all life, creating the universe entire with his act of will. And through it all, the echo of his laughter rang, filling all of spacetime with the enormity of the joke he had seen: three thousand years after the Greeks and their four basic elements, the modern world had come to this, to this—the same four basic forces.

Three thousand years to go from four to four. Cross's mind reeled with the absurdity. Why had no one seen it before? He held the Fire of the ancients in one hand, matched by the radioactive fire of the Weak

Nuclear Force in the other. He cupped the Water in one hand, and the ebb and flow of Electromagnetism in the other. His one fist closed on the solidity of the Earth, his other felt the binding strength of the Strong Nuclear Force.

And he juggled everything in the all-encompassing Air—the absolute context in which the other three elements existed for the ancients.

And he juggled everything in the all-encompassing Gravity—he saw it clearly now—the absolute context in which the other three forces existed for all time.

He saw each element and each force enmeshed in one another, their connections webbed like intricate tracings of copper wire pulled over flesh and into the cat's living organs. The concept was so simple, so trivial. The secret of the grinning green monster. Enclose the object to be the focus and then all the forces would be rejoined in the ultimate fusion.

Of the Beginning.

The laughter of Anthony Cross split the heavens, moved the stars, shattered time. The answer was so clear. So obvious. How could anyone else ever have missed the simple secret that he knew now?

He rubbed his hands across his face, wiping away the tears and the visions. The roar of the ocean came back to his ears, the gentle pressure of the wind through his hair, the heat of the sun on his skin, the solidity of the tiled terrace beneath his feet. He looked out to the ocean where a storm was growing. The real world returned to him but his vision of the secret was still as clear and apparent as the shimmering, moist, and pulsing surfaces of the naked, living brains he had entered. Each of them. All of them. To wrest from the moments of their destruction the ultimate understanding of everything.

"God," he whispered.

There was someone behind him.

By any normal definition of the word, Charis Neale knew, Anthony Cross was not sane. She had suspected it in their first year together, after they had returned from the desert, and she had seen her suspicions brutally confirmed in their second year. But by then, it had been too late for her. By then she knew that of all the paths of discovery she might follow as a scientist, Cross's path alone was the one that held the promise of success. In those early years, she had spent uncounted sleep-

less nights wondering how she was different from the stagnant professors she had once feared would try to unfairly attach themselves to
Cross's work.

Now, coping with his work and with the bewildering range of his
many personalities—so similar, yet so different—was a small price to
pay, and a justifiable one, given the benefits. After all, the way society
worked, as an individual's worth increased so did the degree of his
departure from normalcy that would be tolerated by those around him.
Thus movie stars could drink and drive, Fortune 500 executives could
commit minor embezzlements through their expense accounts,
televangelists could sin, and senators could kill. But Anthony Cross was
creating new frontiers of departure with each day. So far, at least, his
worth had increased at the same rate.

"Hello, Charis."

"Shouldn't you be wearing something?"

Cross faced her from the edge of the private terrace that was
attached to his office—a glass-walled refuge protectively sheltered in an
angle of the elongated white arc and sweep of the SHARP main building. The terrace was finished in large, sand-colored ceramic tiles, fur-
nished with canvas and wooden chairs, lounges, and tables, and ringed
by a low, rough stone wall that would not block the view of the ocean
from Cross's desk.

Cross was naked before her. Drops of sweat slipped from his slen-
der body to splash onto then quickly evaporate from the hot tiles.

"Shouldn't you be wearing nothing?" He grinned. "It seems we
only got halfway through the program out on the deck last night."
Neale felt a familiar flutter within. What she thought of as the "real"
Cross was with her: that part of him which could deal almost rationally
with the ordinary world.

She smiled back without meaning to. "I don't think so. The replacement magnets are on line. Parnel is anxious to see you try that
demonstration again."

Cross walked up to her and crushed her in his arms. She drank in
the musty scent of his sweat, was painfully aware that the terrace was
protected and sheltered and could not be seen by anyone else at the
facility. Cross's office and private workshop were always off-limits to the
staff.

"I know what Parnel is anxious to see," he whispered into her ear.

"We showed him some of it last night, didn't we? He saw me come all over you. He wants to do that himself, you know. He wants to see you come the way that only I can make you." She felt him grow hard against her.

"We can't," she said in what she hoped would sound like a normal and professional voice.

But he wasn't fooled. He pushed against her, digging into the fabric of her dress. "I don't believe you," he whispered again, then kissed her, hard and deep. "I felt you last night. I tasted you."

Neale came to her senses and pushed him away. "Stop it, Anthony." She couldn't help but laugh at the expression of surprise he affected.

"But I can't stop, Doctor." He spit in his hand. "This is your creation and only you can save me!" He laughed. Then standing in the open air, only feet away, he began to masturbate himself, still grinning.

Neale stared in shock. She felt a laugh build within her, felt anger, and to her despair, felt an overwhelming rush of passion flood through her. The innocence of those clear eyes peering out from beneath the shock of dark hair, never moving from her own, the easy grace of his muscles flexing rhythmically beneath his smooth skin, the slick shine of his swollen penis as it disappeared and reappeared within his fist as it had in hers only hours ago. She opened her mouth to say something more to stop him, but her lips were dry, the words lost in the ache of her heart. She went to him.

"No," she said softly. One hand caressed his face. "Not like that," she whispered. One hand moved his own hand away, replaced his grip. "Over here," she said gently as she squeezed him, feeling the pulse of life within him, this time unconnected from the confused questioning of his mind. She kissed him lightly, tasting him as she moved him back to a lounge chair beside a small table.

Effortlessly he slipped down into it. Without sense of movement she was beside him. "Like this," she said and her voice trembled. It had been a long time since he had been this open with her, this playful, this normal.

She tasted the length of his naked skin, trailed down his chest to take him in her mouth. Then everything else fell away from her but Anthony Cross, the real Anthony Cross, and the demands of her heart.

When the world returned, she looked to him and his face was turned away, up toward the sky.

"Anthony?"

He turned at the sound of her voice, but his eyes didn't find hers. She saw his pupils had contracted to pinpoints. He had been staring at the sun again. Probably for the whole time.

"What were you doing?" Exasperation and heartache in her voice.

"Looking for neutrinos." Still the same joke: the sun did not produce enough neutrinos according to the latest theories, but the way his eyes moved blindly around, he had taken it too far as usual. "They're in there somewhere."

She moved up to caress his head, kiss his face. "What am I going to do with you?"

Cross suddenly took her head in his hands, squeezed tightly as he held her immobile in front of him, fingers pressing hard against her temples. "You've already done it to me. The question is . . . what am I going to do with you?"

With those words, that look, everything she had worked so hard for in her life became shambles. She had no will, no strength, no self-determinacy. The weakness was back in her voice, the weakness she had fought against all her life. "What do you want to do with me?" she asked, giving up everything, wanting to be with him forever, praying that he would feel the same.

He whispered his answer into her ear and moved his hand to slide under her dress, crushing the fabric as he forced it up along her legs. Neale's hands tore at her blouse, ripping at the buttons, pulling her bra up and uncomfortably out of the way so she could feel the weight of him on her.

Cross moved fluidly, sliding down beside her, then lifting her up to the chair, then freeing her legs, then driving into her, filling her, making the world go away again.

She stretched her arms around him, pulling him tighter and closer and deeper, never wanting him to pull away. She looked up at him, moving above her, looking for his eyes, his mad dark brilliant little boy's eyes.

But Neale saw Anthony Cross's face was turned upward once more. Turned to the sun, seeing things within its brilliance that she knew she would never see, never imagine, until he told her what was there.

She held him closer, trying to make him a part of her, trying to pull him completely within, always together, never apart, a fusion, a joining forever in the heat of his sun.

"Please," she called out as she felt her climax building. "Please," she called out, so happy that he was finally back with her, the others scorned, her heart returned.

But Anthony Cross still looked up, seeing alone what she could not.

Whatever part of Anthony Cross was present that day did not look up at the sun.

The physical part of him worked like a machine following a brilliant program, each thrust, each hesitation, perfectly matching the catalog of Neale's preferences that he had compiled over the years. To do this to her, despite what she so pitifully thought, no longer required his thoughts or awareness. He left it to another part of himself as his real consciousness dealt with other, more important, more intriguing efforts. Occasionally, like a flat stone skipping over the ocean, Cross would return to watch his progress with her, to feel her moving beneath and around him, to compare the timing of her breaths, the intensity of her pleas, with all the other responses she had made during all their other interactions, which he perfectly remembered, which he perfectly could replay at any time.

Cross skipped back to her. Allowing for the time of day and relative discomfort of the unpadded lounge chair, Neale was progressing well within her usual response curve, which she did 83 percent of the time. He undertook a brief analysis and calculated she would climax within thirty-seven seconds. He skipped away, looked up not to the sun but to visions of creation contained in infinite coils of wire. There were answers in there, if only he could see far and deep enough.

At thirty-one seconds, Neale arched up against Cross, her words trailing into a drawn-out, meaningless syllable. Cross kept his eyes on the sharp cutting wire, skipped back to Neale, and allowed his autonomic process to proceed with Neale's as his mind ran wild with thoughts of flesh and wire, meat and machines, knowing that everything could be taken apart and understood and that in his workshop everything could be reassembled again.

They came together, the way Neale preferred it. She shuddered against him, then sank back to the chair, muscles limp. Cross sank with her, eyes looking up to where the lustrous copper flowed like space and time and blood.

Cross smiled and looked down at Neale. She smiled back, thinking his expression was for her. Cross kissed her, reviewing the procedures for his new demonstration that afternoon. Neale would be easier to handle now. But he still needed some time to himself to organize his thoughts so, still hard, he moved again within Neale, expertly propelling her past the threshold of refraction, making her reach out to him again. Then he skipped out and returned to his Work, thinking of the copper and the cat and the soft yielding flesh.

And how they all pointed the way to the Beginning.

Of everything.

TWELVE

Anthony Cross grinned as the hum of the generators feeding the accelerator in Lab 2 set up a
standing wave in Parnel Covington's cold mug
of coffee sitting beside Cross's computer.

Covington pointed to the circular ripples moving across the dark
liquid. "Isn't that vibration going to throw off the laser optics?" His
hollow face was even tighter than usual.

Cross shook his finger at the man. "Now, Parnel, don't go changing the subject. Tell the truth. You are annoyed with me, aren't you?"

Covington tried to smile but it was false.

"Nothing's exploded yet today." Cross could close his eyes and see
Covington on the end of a fishing line of copper, being played in and
out, back and forth.

"There's still time," Covington said. "And you're right, I am annoyed."

Cross pouted, inwardly delighted. "Tell me why," he asked, already knowing the answer. Covington was like the half-life of pluto-
nium, completely predictable.

The tall man looked around the lab to be certain that the others
couldn't overhear what he had to say. Half the lab away, Charis Neale

was adjusting the field strength readings on the magnet circuits. Beside her, Rich Daystrom fiddled with a thick and awkward-looking jury-rigged circuitry breadboard by the main control console, and Lee Kwong, still frowning and talking to himself, read through a thick sheaf of printout paper, sending a cascade of white to absently trail on the floor behind him as he paced. Weinstein was home again. His early morning phone call pleading illness had been almost incomprehensible. It was another normal workday in Lab 2.

"We didn't set up many rules for you when we asked you to head this facility," Covington began, leaning over Cross, one hand on the back of the physicist's chair. "In fact, we tried not to set up *any*, other than you just keep us informed of what you're doing. I would think that's a small price to pay for complete freedom of research."

"I never thought of that as a price, Parnel. I always thought of that as a sign of my respect for you and Shannon Industries, for all that you've given me here." Cross smirked inwardly at the look of surprise that came to Covington's face. That statement had thrown him.

"I . . . I appreciate the sentiment, Anthony. But still . . ."

"Still, you don't know exactly what I'm going to demonstrate to you today, do you?"

Covington shook his head. "Except demonstrating how to spend two and a half million dollars. Of my money."

"You can take a better guess than that."

Covington glanced over at the gleaming metal bulk of the accelerator and thought for a few seconds. "Most of the breakthroughs you've given us in the past year or so have been related to getting higher energy levels out of existing accelerators. Shannon Industries has developed two new sources of inexpensive X-ray emitters for our metallurgy subsidiaries and, using your techniques, the Stanford Linear Accelerator is finally doing some useful work for a change."

"But those are all outgrowths of the Cross Corollary to Bell's Theorem. That's old news now. High schools will be building these things in metal shops in the next five years."

"Your corollary isn't all that old."

Cross was suddenly taken with the urge to actually explain something to Covington. For this aspect of him, as for most scientists, the important thing in science was finding out something that no one else had ever known before. The next important thing was being able to tell others what he had done, so they would understand his genius.

"The corollary as formalized in the published equations isn't all that old, no. But, as an idea, as a solution I saw, it's a decade old." For a moment, Cross allowed an expression of wistfulness to come to his eyes. Covington would like that, he knew. "It took me that long to translate what I *knew* to be true into the proper scientific description that others would be able to understand. Einstein had his vision of gravity all at once, sitting at his desk in the Swiss patent office, and then had to spend the next ten years formalizing the concept so that others could accept it."

Covington straightened up, the slow pressure of excitement building in him. "What you're going to demonstrate for me today . . . it's going to work this time, isn't it? No explosions."

Cross slowly nodded. He had no doubt.

"How long have you been working on it? I mean, how long has it been since you . . . *saw* it? Whatever it's going to be."

"I first understood it the night we talked at the reception in Stockholm, after the Nobel ceremonies. But I didn't complete the technical details until just the other night." Cross pointed over to Daystrom. The head of computer operations was peering intently through a thin thread of smoke rising up from his soldering iron at the side of the control console. "Rich is just installing the final bit of control circuitry now."

Covington's mood had changed. He looked happy again. "What *did* we talk about back then, other than SHARP? I can't remember."

"I remember every word, exactly as each was said."

"But you're not going to tell me?" Covington asked after a silent wait.

"I'm going to show you," Cross said serenely. "I'm going to show you all."

Neale joined the two men, carrying a blue binder with procedure checklist sheets. "Everything's within operational tolerances," she announced. "Except for that new timing circuit you've got Rich installing. He says it doesn't have any operational tolerances." She closed the binder and passed it to Cross.

"What he means to say, is that he doesn't understand the tolerances." Cross turned to Covington. "I'll want him fired as soon as you can get me a replacement."

"So now what happens?" Covington asked, referring to the experiment in progress. Both he and Neale knew better than to comment on Cross's decision to fire Daystrom. Many lessons had been learned in the past three and a half years.

Cross checked a readout on the computer screen in front of him. "In about five more minutes we'll be over the threshold." He stood up and shouted across the lab to Kwong. "Lee! Bring the laser on line!"

Kwong waved tersely and dropped his sheaf of printouts to the floor. Cross had personally talked Kwong into staying. He needed someone around with whom he could at least pretend there was a chance for an intelligent conversation. Kwong was almost good enough for that, even if he was a useless parasitical chink faggot who—

"Will we need goggles for the laser?" Covington asked.

"The beam's virtually microscopic and completely contained," Neale answered. "We'll have to use monitors to see it hit the target zone at all."

"Miss the target zone, actually," Cross added, but didn't explain any further. "Four more minutes. Time to close down the doors." His eyes sparkled as he winked at Covington. "Can't be too careful about security, can we?"

Cross picked up the phone by his screen and punched the code for the front desk. "Dr. Cross here," he told the guard who answered. "Could you close down the security doors to Lab 2 for the next half hour, please." And then the guard had said something delightful.

"Yes, of course Dr. Neale is here," Cross said, making no move to pass the phone receiver over. "No, no, no. She should never have been kept waiting all that time. Of *course* Dr. Neale is in. Of *course* she may interview her. Send her down right away. Very well, then *escort* her down immediately. Oh, and if she's carrying a gun—I think they all carry guns, don't they?—that much metal could interfere with the experiment so please have her leave it with you. Thank you, too." Cross hung up.

Neale and Covington both were frozen in place, neither daring to ask what the conversation had been about. But Cross told them anyway, delighting in the new variable thrown into the equation.

"We have a visitor," he said, "and apparently someone told the guard at reception to tell her that you weren't in yet, Charis. The poor woman's been sitting there for more than two hours waiting to speak with you." He shook his head, smiling at the look on Neale's face. Then he checked his screen. "But she won't have to wait much longer."

Katherine Duvall spotted Charis Neale about thirty feet away, even before the security guard beside her had finished opening the doors to the laboratory. Neale's long hair was tied back, probably to keep it out of the way, and her white lab coat was little different from the white clothes she had worn the night she and Duvall had talked on Cassie Riley's balcony. Duvall felt vindicated. Despite what the guard had been telling her all morning, Duvall had seen the blue Plymouth in the staff parking lot and knew the woman must be in the building. Then Neale spotted Duvall and for a moment, the detective thought the pulse of the machinery around her came from Neale's eyes.

Neale turned to speak to the almost shockingly tall and thin man beside her, but because of the distance and the hum, Duvall couldn't hear what she said. Beside the detective, the security guard finally found the person he had been looking for, and waved.

Then it was almost as if the sound of the lab's equipment disappeared. The man who approached Duvall was that striking, that compelling. She recognized the grace with which he walked, the ease in the gentle smile he wore, the image he created of a warm pocket of peace and calm in the midst of the hurry and confusion of the lab. Duvall had seen it a handful of times before and it told her a great deal about the man who came closer.

First of all, she decided, he must be rich, because she had seen that same confidence in the people she had sometimes met in her job, people who never had to worry about where the next car payment was coming from, or how much anything in a supermarket cost. There was a special kind of worry that came from just trying to get through the ordinary tasks of everyday life, and this man, she could tell, was a stranger to it, unaffected by the commonplace.

But though Duvall knew little of science, it stuck in her mind that scientists were like teachers or cops, they weren't supposed to be rich, couldn't be rich unless the Lotto paid off, or relatives did. So she saw another reason for this man's peaceful stillness. Fundamentalist Christian or Orthodox Jew, whichever this man was, he was devout and at peace with his beliefs. Duvall had also experienced that zone of tranquility radiating from some of the ministers she had known, an aunt she remembered from her childhood, all people who had faced the battle of understanding their lives and who had won, securely and absolutely.

That was what, in the end, was focused so tightly within this man, his smile, strong features, with hair like a child of twelve might wear. He was someone who had all the answers, knew all the truths. Duvall felt drawn to him as if falling down a gently sloping tunnel, with that man at the center, drawing everyone and everything near. The sensation was exhilarating. And welcome.

"Anthony Cross." The man had somehow appeared in front of her. Duvall realized that she had lost track, just for a moment, of where she was, what she was doing. But the moment passed and she recovered.

"Detective Katherine Duvall, LAPD," she said, taking his offered hand as she held up her badge case and ID. The man's skin was smooth, the pressure of his hand just perfect, neither challenge nor retreat. She held it an instant too long, surprised at her reaction.

Cross smiled at her, waving away her ID, and she could see some happy thought working away behind his large dark eyes. "I bet you're a Kate, aren't you?"

"Why, yes."

Cross suddenly looked alarmed. "But of course, just to your friends. I'm sorry, I didn't mean—"

"No, that's fine," Duvall said, trying to allay his apparent fear of having been too familiar, bemused by the sudden switch in their roles. "Please, call me Kate. That's okay."

He looked relieved, such charm in his awkwardness. "But I'm afraid I'm a full-blown Anthony. We've got too many other Tonys working here." He winked at her, friendly, with no hidden meanings.

"Detective Duvall, isn't it?"

Duvall was startled. Neale had come up alongside Cross without her noticing. "That's right," Duvall said, trying to bring her mind back to her work.

"We talked at Cassie's apartment the night she was murdered."

"Yes."

"And I then talked with a Detective Seabrook. Here. On two other occasions."

"Correct."

"Can there really be anything more for you people to ask me?"

Before Duvall could reply, Cross interrupted. "I didn't know you went to Cassie's that night." Duvall heard the inflection he placed on the woman's name and instantly knew there was some connection between the two.

"It wasn't important," Neale said to Cross. "You have other things to worry about."

Cross seemed saddened, but bravely trying to hide his change in mood. He turned to Duvall. "Cassie was an asset to this place. She . . . had her troubles, but . . . is that why you're here . . . Kate?"

"Yes, sir."

"Well, certainly. Of course, it is. Anything I or any of my staff can do to help you"—Duvall was intrigued to realize that Cross was in charge—"all you have to do is ask. Anything at all."

"Anthony," Neale interrupted again. "We *do* have an experiment to run here." She smiled at Duvall, coldly, unconvincingly. "Perhaps if you'd like to come back another time . . . ?"

Cross brightened, ignoring Neale. "Say, Kate, if you have a few minutes, would you like to see a neat experiment? Actually, it's more of a demonstration because I already know how it's going to turn out, but . . . you'll be able to tell your grandchildren. And you'll want to, believe me."

Duvall couldn't quite believe it. Cross, evidently the person for whom this entire facility was provided, spoke like a twelve-year-old about to do a backflip off his skateboard.

"Sure," she said. "I'm not in a hurry." She wanted more time around Neale, and she found Cross fascinating. "Perhaps I could talk to Dr. Neale when it's finished."

"Anthony," Neale protested. "This . . . this is confidential work. It's . . . not ready to be . . . demonstrated for the public."

Cross gave a quick sidelong glance to Duvall, sharing a joke. "How about if I have Kate promise not to tell the Russians, the Chinese, the French, the Germans, Dan Rather, and the Hughes people down the road?" He turned back to Duvall. "Promise, Kate?"

"Dan and I aren't talking these days." She was surprised to feel herself becoming excited over the prospect of the demonstration Cross had mentioned. It sounded like it might be something that might make it to the news. And she was somehow pleased that a guy as nice as Cross obviously was didn't let himself get pushed around.

Neale protested again, obviously intending to bring out the big guns. "Parnel will not allow it." Duvall concluded Parnel was somebody who might be more important than Cross.

But Cross didn't act as if he shared Neale's impression of the man. "Kate is my guest." The way he said it meant that he was no longer willing to permit discussion. Cross told the guard who had escorted Duvall through the security doors that he could leave, then brought the detective to the master control console.

A young, exhausted black man was doing something complicated with what appeared to be the insides of a computer. If Duvall had seen anyone on the street looking that strung out, she would have smelled a dope bust. But Cross and Neale didn't seem concerned by the man's appearance so Duvall decided it must be normal for him.

"Are we connected, Rich?" Cross asked. For the first time Duvall heard something other than warm friendliness in Cross's voice.

"Connected, Doc," the man answered with a sigh. He seemed to want to say more but instead packed up his tools: a soldering iron and several tiny screwdrivers. No scalpels, Duvall noted.

Cross called out several more questions and commands to the oriental man in a creased and crinkled white coat standing impatiently by a wall bank of lights and controls amid a cloudlike pile of computer printouts. The cadaverously tall and thin man, whom Duvall realized must be Parnel, came by to join Cross and Neale. His strides were long and slow and he reminded Duvall of a mantis walking.

Cross introduced the tall man to Duvall and she sensed the same coldness in him that she had felt coming from Neale. She decided she wouldn't be surprised to learn the two were involved with each other. Certainly, unspoken messages of some sort were passing between them even though Cross seemed to be oblivious to what they were doing.

At last, all the flurry in the lab came to an end. Everyone was in place and stayed put. Everyone looked to Cross. Duvall had not the slightest idea what to expect, but she was happy just watching Cross work at his keyboard and computer screens. He reminded her of how Jesse had worked in the garden or on some woodworking project in the garage, shirt off, sweat defining each plane and muscle. The scientist was totally absorbed in what he was doing, giving it his full concentration, all his powers, like a lover. Uncharacteristically, Duvall wondered what it would be like to have someone concentrate on her that way.

Duvall felt that Cross's excitement and enthusiasm were contagious. She could even feel them infecting Neale and Covington. She wondered if they could also feel the sexual undercurrent to what Cross did, the almost primitive intensity he brought to his work. But most likely they didn't, Duvall decided. After a while, they would probably get used to Cross's energy, then ignore it. It seemed to happen that way every place else in life, why not in a lab?

"All right," Cross finally announced, adjusting the color balance on a large color video monitor built into the control console. "Lee, give us a reference firing. Laser only."

Duvall heard a sudden deep tone followed by a sharp "pop" sound, like a gunshot heard far off in a field with no echo. A small circle of red light pulsed on the video monitor, perfectly centered between a set of rough-edged cross hairs and precisely in the middle of a series of concentric circles. Then, just as the light faded, it was replaced with a superimposed choppy black outline that marked the light's position.

"Bull's eye," Duvall said. Targets were targets and, as far as she could see, the little red light had hit dead-on. But Neale gave her a look as if the detective had just gone after a fingerbowl with a soup spoon. Cross came to her rescue.

"Actually, it couldn't help but be anything other than a bull's eye," he said, reminding Duvall of the grade school teachers she had had, the nice ones. "That little red dot you saw was a pulsed microlaser, about ten to the minus . . ." He smiled at Duvall. "About one one-thousandth of an inch across. That's how big the target is, too." He pointed over to the long tail that branched off from the circular accelerator like the tail of a Q. "It's installed at the end of that big tunnel over there, in a vacuum chamber."

"Sounds hard to hit," Duvall said, ignoring Neale's patronizing sigh. She didn't care what Neale thought of her comments. Cross gave her the impression that anything she might say was worthy of consideration.

"Hard to miss," Cross said kindly, glancing at his screen. "All the equipment is locked into place, perfectly focused and aligned."

"Then what's the point?" Duvall asked.

"Exactly," Covington added impatiently. "What is the point, Anthony?"

"That was just a test firing, to ensure that the alignment was still fixed. Now we'll fire the laser again, but this time, we'll be creating a small vortex of electrons right next to its path . . ." He paused and smiled again at Duvall.

"This big doughnut machine here is technically called a betatron, but we just call it an accelerator," he explained. "Right now, there are two different streams of a couple of hundred thousand electrons each circling inside, driven by alternating magnetic fields." He narrowed his eyes at her, reading her noncomprehension. "Have you ever seen any footage of those levitating trains from Japan, where the whole shebang floats on a magnetic cushion?"

Duvall nodded. She had seen and even, she thought, understood those news stories. But what kind of a person used the word "shebang" these days?

"Well, that's somewhat similar to what's going on inside the accelerator."

"Anthony," Neale said. "I can give her the Shannon publicity handouts. Parnel has a plane to catch."

Cross smiled tightly, annoyed at being interrupted. "This might give Parnel a whole new way to catch a plane," he snapped, then turned back to Duvall.

"Anyway, electrons have what we call a negative electric charge, so when they're in a magnetic field, they're attracted toward the positive pole of the field and repelled by the negative one. What that accelerator does is use a whole series of supercooled magnets to keep a pattern of alternating magnetic fields circling through the insides of the doughnut and aligned to pull the electrons ahead from the front and push them along from behind. That gets them going faster and faster, almost to the speed of light. The trick is to keep the fields turning off and on at the proper time intervals to keep the electrons accelerating faster and faster. At a critical speed, the electromagnets can't switch off and on fast enough and the computers just can't operate quickly enough to keep track of where the electrons are inside, anyway."

Neale sighed again and Cross ignored her. He was making Duvall feel as if she were the most important person in the room.

"Now, labs all around the world do this sort of thing all the time so it's no big deal, up to the critical speed that is. About 99.9999 the speed of light. But what we're about to do here is combine the two streams that are circling so that one stream of electrons will pass some of their energy to the other set, the way a space probe will pick up energy by swinging close to a planet. Make sense?"

Duvall nodded, ignoring Neale's impatient shifting. Obviously, whatever was going to happen here was of great importance to Cross. She wanted to understand it. She wanted him to know her interest.

But Neale interrupted again. "Anthony, this is a very inefficient technique for upping power levels in this type of an accelerator. You're just going to end up scattering both electron streams. Surely this isn't what you've been leading up to for the past five months."

Cross continued as if Neale hadn't said anything. "Of course, I'm using a new technique to combine the electrons." He glanced aside to Neale, his voice becoming tight. "Look at the tolerances on the beam widths, Charis. *Now*, do you understand?" He tapped the computer screen, then turned back to Duvall, back to normal.

"Einstein tells us, and it has been confirmed by scores of experiments, that the faster an object goes, even an electron, the more mass it gains. In the case of this—"

"The tolerance on the beams is too fine, Anthony. You'll never control them that way. Can't be done." Neale spoke like a judge delivering a death sentence as she looked up from reading the computer screen. Duvall felt like telling the woman to shut up and stop interrupting Cross, but the scientist beat her to it. Duvall was surprised to see such anger emerge from the man, as if it had been there all along, silently building. But Neale had been provocative, and the lab was hot and noisy.

"*I* can't control them, Charis," he snapped, "but *that* can." He pointed to the messy block of circuitry Rich had connected to a flat, rainbow-colored ribbon of wires at the side of the console. "Just watch. Just you watch." Cross shouted out to the oriental man again. "Now, Lee. Trigger the vortex and fire."

Once again Duvall heard the sudden deep tone of the laser building, but before the pop sound, she heard a grating crackle and a booming echo that came from inside the accelerator.

"No," Neale whispered.

Duvall followed the woman's gaze to the video monitor. The red pulse of the laser was just fading and being replaced by the superimposed outline. It was two beam widths off the bull's eye.

"Do it again, Lee!" Cross cried out. He sat on the edge of his chair as though he were ready to fly up from it.

The tone, the crackle, and the booming echo followed. The red pulse missed its target again.

"What's deflecting the laser beam?" Covington asked. His tone was urgent, his body stiff.

"You tell me, Parnel. Or Charis. You tell me what deflects photons traveling through a vacuum in the target chamber. You tell me what has to change to change the path of light in the absence of reflective or refractive mediums." Cross literally burned with passion. Whatever had just happened, Duvall thought, she was going to remember this day. But what *had* happened?

Duvall stepped back in silence as Neale peppered Cross with questions about torr ratings and gauss readings and all manner of other things that were a foreign language to Duvall. But she could see that Cross was enjoying the slow growth of what almost might have been panic blossoming within Neale and the dark brooding thoughtfulness of Covington.

At last it was Covington who broke the tirade of Neale's questions. "Stop for a moment, Charis. Let's just give Anthony the benefit of the doubt and assume that he's managed to rule out every possible normal explanation for what we've just seen."

"Which I have," Cross said with merriment. "Everything."

Covington took a deep breath. "Gravity," he said flatly. "Gravity deflects photons in a vacuum."

"Very good, Parnel. Though curved spacetime is a better way of describing it." Cross turned back to Duvall, winked again. "That's Einstein again. He tells us that the effects of gravity can also be described by thinking of space as being curved." He turned back to Covington. "Gee, Parnel, you seem to have trouble with that."

"Are you claiming you changed the value of gravity inside the test chamber?" the tall man asked. Duvall had heard hostage negotiators speak in the same careful way, when each word might be misinterpreted and mean instant death.

"In a very small part of the test chamber . . . just around the electron vortex . . . yes." Cross folded his arms.

"Jesus," Neale said softly.

"That's . . ." Covington whispered without knowing what to say.

"Exactly," Cross said. "But why the surprise, Parnel? That *is* what we talked about that night at the reception. Remember now? Artificial gravity? In twenty years instead of a hundred? Would you believe it's yours in three?" He laughed. "And in five years, high schools will be building this in metal shops."

Covington reached out for a tabletop to steady himself. Neale looked pale. Even Rich, who had hung back from them during the demonstration, looked wide awake now. Duvall gathered that what Cross had just done was impressive.

After many long moments of silence, Duvall couldn't hold herself back any longer.

"Uh, excuse me, but what just happened here?"

They all turned to her, Cross beaming, everyone else just stunned.

"The old world just came to an end," Neale said, speaking as if in a dream.

"No," Covington said very softly, a rich deep smile forming on his lips. "A new one's just begun."

Duvall didn't understand, but the way Cross smiled at her, she didn't care. This man had somehow just changed the world, and he had made Duvall a witness, shared his triumph with her.

Duvall's heart raced as she returned the look he gave her, suddenly devastated that she would have no grandchildren to tell this story to, no one to share this with who would understand.

Except for the man who gazed at her with peaceful eyes and a smile that held all the answers. The face of an angel and a genius. A face that made Duvall feel . . . vulnerable.

THIRTEEN

Duvall didn't like Charis Neale. She had known that from the first moment of their meeting on the balcony of Cassie Riley's apartment. Now, in Neale's office at SHARP, the feeling was even stronger.

"Will twenty minutes be sufficient?" Neale asked as she sat behind her desk. "Or let me put that another way: twenty minutes is all you're going to get."

"That'll do, for now," Duvall answered, then sat in the black leather chair Neale indicated. The scientist seemed hurried and distracted, but Duvall couldn't tell if it was because she was nervous about another police interview or because she was still reacting to the results of Cross's experiment. Either way, Duvall concluded, as long as Neale was distracted, there was a good chance that she would make a mistake.

Duvall pulled out a notebook and pen. "Just to go over some background, Dr. Neale, how long have you worked here?"

Neale tapped her finger against the golden oak surface of her desk. There was a small laptop computer open on it, four In baskets, and several towering stacks of file folders. One wall of the office was floor-to-ceiling filing cabinets. Another wall was glass, overlooking the ocean.

"I've already answered that question. I've already given background to you, and Detective Seabrook."

Duvall slipped smoothly into her role of sympathetic cop—the type of authority figure criminals were compelled to confess to, usually. "We just have to make sure all our facts are accurate, Doctor. Other people can make mistakes and usually everything still works out, but police—"

"Oh, get on with it," Neale interrupted, annoyed. "I don't have time for games. If you want to know something new, ask me now. If you don't, leave."

"Of course," Duvall said, smiling. "Something new." She made a show of flipping through her notebook, feeling Neale's impatience growing with each second. "You know, I'm still not sure why you went to Cassie Riley's apartment personally to tell her she was being fired."

"She hadn't been coming into work."

"But still, I mean, it looks like you have a lot of work to do around here. Isn't there a personnel manager who could have done that?"

In her notebook, Duvall drew a small star for herself when she saw Neale check her watch. The scientist was stalling. That meant she didn't have a ready answer or, at least, an answer she wanted to share with a cop.

"I like to keep a personal touch in all my interactions with the staff here," Neale said.

"Even when you fire them?"

"Especially then. Anything else?"

Duvall looked at a wall where a number of diplomas and certificates hung. She could read "Harvard" on one of them. "What kind of car do you drive, Dr. Neale?"

Duvall turned back in time to see Neale's half-smile. "Some type of BMW, I believe."

"You don't know?"

"It's provided by SHARP. Apparently it's a nice car, but . . . I really don't pay attention to it. Why do you ask?"

Duvall judged the answer to be truthful, if peculiar. But it hadn't been the answer she wanted so she told the lie she had prepared. "Someone at Cassie Riley's apartment building thought you drove away that night in a blue Plymouth."

That's it, Duvall thought. There was a definite reaction to the car.

"I might have," Neale said slowly, looking down at her desk. "The pool cars are Plymouths, I believe—"

"Pool cars?"

"The facility has some extra cars we can use if our own need servicing, or if we have visitors. Spares I suppose you'd call them. I might have been driving one that Friday night, but I really don't remember. Is that important for any reason?"

According to the look in your eyes, it is, Duvall thought. "Just trying to double-check everyone who was present at the building the night of the murder."

Neale checked her watch again. "Do you have any idea who might have done it?" she asked, trying to make it sound like an idle inquiry.

Duvall waited for a few seconds before answering. "Yes," she said, prepared to wait some more.

"Good," Neale replied. "I hope you will keep us informed with your progress." She rose.

Duvall was impressed with the scientist's coolness. "Aren't you interested in knowing anything more?"

Neale acted surprised. "Should I be?"

So much for the personal touch, Duvall thought. "You're very busy, Dr. Neale. Perhaps I should be going."

"Yes, you should be." Neale walked around to the front of her desk.

Duvall closed her notebook and stood up. "That experiment we just saw, is it important?"

"In what sense, Detective?"

"I don't know. Like the Wright Brothers? Or the first atomic bomb, or something?" Duvall saw Neale relax now that the subject had been changed, not realizing that she was being set up.

"No," Neale said, walking with Duvall to the main door of her office. "Perhaps someday, fifty or a hundred years from now, there will be a breakthrough of some sort and a historian will say it all began years ago with an insignificant experiment at SHARP, but that's all."

How interesting, Duvall thought. That had been a lie, too.

"Well, it was interesting to see," she said, reaching out to shake Neale's hand.

"Yes, I suppose it was." Neale took her hand politely.

"Where were you last Wednesday night?"

With perfect, rehearsed timing, Neale answered, "Dining with Parnel Covington. The entire evening." She started to withdraw her hand but Duvall kept it firmly in her grip.

"Did you kill Cassie Riley?" Duvall asked.

"How dare you!" Neale's face turned white as her cheeks flushed. She yanked her hand away.

Duvall smiled. "But you know who did, don't you?" It was her final gamble.

Neale's hand swung for Duvall's face but the detective grabbed her by the wrist, easily.

"Thank you for answering my questions, Dr. Neale." Duvall dropped the scientist's arm and stepped out the door. "I'll be sure to keep you informed of my progress."

Charis Neale's hand shook as she took the glass Covington offered her. The crystal produced delicate clinking notes, soft music, the Brownian motion of ice cubes. But Neale didn't know if she was reacting more to Cross's astounding demonstration, or the interview she had just had with Detective Duvall. Both seemed equally likely to drastically reorder her life.

"How did it go?" Covington asked, sitting on the side of his desk. Like all the furniture in his SHARP office, it was teak and oversize, making his height appear almost normal.

"Terribly. She thinks that either I killed Riley or that I know who did."

"I didn't mean the detective," Covington said. "I meant your analysis of Anthony's little demonstration. Has he done it or what?"

"Parnel, did you hear what I said?"

"Yes, I heard what you said, and no, you don't have to be worried. You know police involvement was anticipated long ago. We're all covered. Have been since the beginning. Don't even think about it."

"She was just in my office and *accused* me of—"

"Forget her! Just tell me about Anthony's work."

Neale gulped at her scotch and felt it burn its way down her throat. "All right, all right. *Theoretically*, it makes some sort of sense. But technically, I still don't know how he managed it."

Covington was in a straight business mood. His words were fast and clipped, a computer seeking input. "How is it right? And how is it wrong?"

Neale sat down on an angular, buttery brown leather sofa, feeling as if she should be in shock. A square of striped sunlight fell at her feet through the partially opened venetian blinds that shut off the view of the ocean. A gentle, air-conditioned breeze flowed lightly over her. She didn't want to talk about Cross's work right now. She wanted to think it through for herself first. She wanted to understand the threat Duvall presented.

"Charis, forget the detective. You're the closest to Anthony," Covington urged. "That's what's important right now. You're the closest to understanding how his mind works." He looked to the closed door of his office. "What did Anthony just do in Lab 2?"

Neale sighed. "What he *says* he did is impossible." She shivered without knowing why. "He claims he was able to bring a stream of electrons so close to the speed of light that their mass gain rose to something on the order of several thousand tonnes in a very small volume of space."

"How small?"

The words were distasteful to her. "He hasn't given me his calculations yet but . . . it's on the order of a singularity."

Covington blinked slowly, as if translating her sentence into another language. Then he smiled, almost drunkenly.

"A black hole? Are you saying Anthony Cross generated a black hole in a *laboratory?*" All his teeth showed, dazzling.

"Close to it," Neale conceded uncomfortably, trying to put a damper on Covington's enthusiasm. How could Cross have come so far without even giving her a hint of what he was up to? "He's still a couple of orders of magnitude off, but if he's broken the back of the technical processes, then I imagine it's just a matter of time."

Covington's eyes fluttered around the room, seeing futures and possibilities that Neale didn't even want to contemplate. "And in five years they'll be doing it in high schools," he whispered. Then he calmed, momentarily. "But you're not convinced?"

"I don't know what to say. We saw the laser beam deflect. If anyone else had shown me that demonstration, I would distrust it instantly. But Anthony has no reason to lie to us." She looked at Covington. "Has he?" Cross had said that Covington wanted her. She wondered what else he knew, or thought he knew, of their relationship.

"Anthony just wants to be first," Covington said. "The same frailty shared by all scientists." He held her gaze. "What are the technical problems you have with accepting what he's done?"

"Anthony says the laser beam was deflected when it traveled past a vortex of electrons of immensely increased mass. The increased mass of the electrons created a . . . warp, I guess is the word, in space, analogous to a very small but very powerful point source of gravity. The photons making up the laser beam were caught in that gravitational field for the brief time it existed—about ten to the minus nine seconds according to the computer—and curved through it, the way light from other stars curves through the gravitational field of the sun. The curve was enough to deflect the beam from the target.

"The technical problem I have with that is how did he manage to accelerate the electrons to such an incredible fraction of lightspeed that their relativistic gain in mass was so high? That's why nothing can ever travel exactly at the speed of light. The faster an object goes, the more mass it gains and therefore the more energy it requires to be accelerated even faster. Mass and power requirements continue to climb until at the speed of light, both are infinite. And that's an impossibility. There wasn't nearly enough power going into the equipment to come anywhere close to the performance we saw."

Covington nodded. "But the most common application of his theoretical work to date is to get higher energy levels out of existing accelerators."

"More *efficient* energy levels. Better use of existing power is a lot different from getting more power out of a process than you put in."

"Is Anthony somehow using the accelerator to *generate* power, like a fusion reactor?"

"I don't see how that's possible. What he seems to be claiming is that he somehow managed to completely transfer the kinetic energy of one stream of electrons to the other stream, but . . ."

"What's wrong with that?"

Neale frowned. "The idea of it makes a dismal sort of sense. In a bullwhip, say, kinetic energy is transferred along the length of the whip until it all collects in the very tip and the tip is then able to accelerate so quickly it breaks the sound barrier and gives off a little sonic boom. But there's no way to 'snap the whip' of a stream of electrons. I mean, as soon as the two streams came close to each other, they'd destructively interfere with each other. Sure, some particles would gain speed just by chance, but most would lose. And besides, the accelerator in Lab 2 isn't equipped to handle a stream of electrons on a particle by particle basis. This isn't CERN."

"How about that new timing circuitry Anthony had Rich make up? Would that change the control characteristics of the equipment?"

Neale drained her glass but didn't feel any of the tension leave her. The patch of sunlight had moved to warm her feet. "Rich said he didn't understand it. Didn't know how it was supposed to work. I'll have to take a closer look at it."

Covington looked at the floor. "Can you handle that?"

To Neale, the words were like a slap. "There's nothing Anthony can do that I can't."

Covington held her gaze, long and hard. "Except be first," he said softly. Then, "I'm sorry. I didn't mean that."

Neale stood up. "You'd better hope you didn't." She went over to the refrigerator built into the office's teak wall unit and poured another drink.

"I meant the computer circuitry part, Charis." Covington sounded almost apologetic. "I know you're the equal of Anthony. More than an equal." He stood beside her. "What good is it for Anthony to be first if the rest of the world doesn't know what he's done? The scientific method, right? A scientist has to be able to describe his results to others. Anthony can't do that. Not without you."

Neale didn't look up from the glass on the counter. Anger had overwhelmed anything else she might be feeling about Cross or Duvall. "Anthony couldn't do anything without me. And neither could you. And neither could Cathedral. Just don't forget that." She reached for her glass.

But then she felt the surprisingly light pressure of Covington's hand on her shoulder. "I think it's time to remind you of a few things that *you* shouldn't forget," he said.

"I forget *nothing!*" Neale shouted at him, twisting away from his grip. "Haven't you figured that out yet? Haven't you realized that there's nothing you have said to me in the past three and a half years that I don't remember? Don't you know there's nothing that Anthony has done to me that I haven't forgotten? I know exactly what's going on around here, Parnel. I know what it's costing."

"I don't think you do, Charis," Covington said calmly, stepping back from her. "You don't know everything there is to know about the Cathedral project."

Neale rubbed at the tears that were coming to her eyes. "I'm not talking about your goddamned consortium of fat cat industrialists, Parnel. I'm talking about what this is costing me. What it's costing Anthony."

"Anthony was what he is long before there was Cathedral and SHARP, Charis. You were there."

"Damn right." She struggled not to cry in front of Covington. She couldn't cry in front of Covington. He had too much power over her already. She had a war to win against him.

"You're still upset about that detective, aren't you?"

"Christ, Parnel, what do you think? I've been covering up for Anthony for almost ten years and now . . ."

"And I've been helping you cover up since Stockholm." He went back to her and this time when he placed his hand on her shoulder she didn't pull away. "You're not alone in this anymore, Charis. You haven't been for a long time. The stakes and the payoffs are too high for a few petty worries about a few missing people more or less in this world."

Neale hung her head, unable to look at him. "We've seen what's been coming, Parnel. Anthony must know by now that someone is covering up for him. He's getting sloppier about leaving prints and equipment to be cleaned up after at the scene. He's phoning in to the police in less time than before. Christ, Parnel, the detective asked me about the blue Plymouth. The car that Anthony left outside the motel. Someone must have seen me. I thought I waited until the police had all gone, but . . . she *knows*, Parnel. She can ruin everything."

"Oh no, she can't," Covington said gently. "Not the slightest chance. I told you that police involvement was anticipated. Cathedral has its own people in the department. How do you think we've managed to keep Anthony's other little 'inspirations' covered up so well? Cathedral looks after its own, Charis. You have nothing to worry about."

"But what about the detective? She's so close now. What if she manages to put it together?"

"If she does manage that, it won't do her any good," Covington said in a voice of absolute logic and control, "because she'll be dead."

He smiled at Neale. "There, see how easy it is?"

FOURTEEN

When her Volkswagen engine had cranked for the third time without turning over, Katherine Duvall was not concerned. She was used to its obstinacy by now. But by the fifth try, she felt annoyed, and turned her anger toward the car and not herself for not taking it in for a long-delayed servicing.

By the eighth try, the chugging of the engine had noticeably slowed again as the battery was drained. She hit the steering wheel and swore just as a deep horn sounded behind her in the SHARP parking lot. For a moment she thought it had been her own horn that had sounded and stared at the dashboard, wondering what had happened to her car.

Then, in the rearview mirror she saw Anthony Cross waving at her from his own white, German convertible: a Mercedes 760 SL. "I can give you a lift," he called. His smile was exquisite, a perfect match for the blinding Pacific sun.

"No, thank you," Duvall answered reflexively, but Cross got out of his car anyway. He offered her a small cellular phone, about the size of the pocket calculator Jesse had always carried in his suit jacket.

"I can make a call. There's a gas station about a mile up the PCH.

It's so reputable that I think it's going to be declared a historical monument."

Duvall smiled but shook her head. She didn't want to even guess what the service charge would be from a garage used to answering calls for the Jensens and Ferraris of Malibu. "But if you've got the time," she asked instead, "I've got some jumper cables."

"Time is relative," Cross said with a laugh. "I'll pull up my car."

"Battery's under the back seat," Duvall called after him, watching him walk away in the rearview mirror. She wondered if he had ever been a dancer.

She got out and opened the trunk up front, pushing aside an oily stack of yellowed newspapers and her neglected red sports bag, which she didn't want to even think about opening because the clothes in it dated back at least three months to the last time she had played tennis. Beneath the bag, she had to sort through the strewed contents of one or two tool kits until she came up with the brass-colored clips of her jumper cables and pulled them out like a recalcitrant black-and-red snake. When she closed the trunk, Cross's Mercedes was backed up next to the Bug and the physicist was crouched down, peering into the engine compartment at the back of her car.

Duvall smiled as she walked around to him. *What a rocket scientist,* she thought. "Looking for the battery?"

Cross nodded. There were smudges of grease on his fingers from where he had been prodding around.

"Back seat."

"Oh," Cross said as he stood up. *"That's* what you said. I've never understood cars." He shut the engine hood and took the cables from her. For a moment, he seemed distracted by something he saw or felt on the braided copper wires exposed between the clips and the insulation. But he quickly went on to connect the batteries.

Drawing current from the Mercedes, the Volkswagen's motor cranked more energetically but still wouldn't catch.

"Try one more time," Cross suggested, standing back, hands in his pockets, one foot resting on its outer edge. He looked as though he was going to say "Aw, shucks" at any moment.

"Then both cars will be stuck here," Duvall said.

"That's not a problem," Cross encouraged. "It's a company car. There're a bunch of others we can use. See those over there?" He pointed to another section of the parking lot where six different colored Plymouths were parked, including the blue one Duvall had seen Neale drive away from the motel. All the pieces were assembled, she felt, it was just a question of putting them together in the proper pattern.

Cross's smile tempted her, but, "Thanks anyway. I'll have to call that station for a tow."

"I'll drive you. They give SHARP a special rate. We can encourage them to think that you're a new employee." His dark eyes sparkled. "That's not illegal, is it?"

"Better not be," Duvall said as she started to close up her car, "or we'll both be in a lot of trouble."

"That sounds like it could be fun," Cross said.

The Mercedes hummed down the highway. Somehow, the sensation of the wind through her hair and the sun on her face felt different in this convertible from the way it did in her own. Improved engineering, she thought. Or an improved driver.

From the corner of her eye, Duvall saw Cross do a thorough check in all three mirrors, then the car suddenly, though smoothly, slowed, cut across the empty oncoming lanes, and slipped into a lot beside a large, natural-wood-finished restaurant. Cross waved to a parking attendant, who obviously recognized him, then swung down in front of the building, parking beneath a large wooden deck looking out to the sea.

When she realized that his maneuver had not been a shortcut to a gas station, Duvall felt the first intimation of alarm rise up within her. Automatically, she pushed her back further into the seat and felt the reassuring pressure of her service revolver.

"There," Cross said as he turned the key in the ignition, cutting the steady vibration of the motor so only the crash of the waves could be heard. "We can't be seen from the road."

Duvall's right hand moved to her door handle, the other poised just above the seatbelt release. "Why is that important?"

"I want to ask what you and Charis talked about. I want to know about Cassie Riley." Cross's face had taken on a new, more serious expression, almost of hurt. "I don't know how police conduct investigations, but you may already know that I often visited Cassie."

Duvall hadn't known. There was nothing about it in any of the files Nogura had gathered for her. Nothing had turned up in any of the door-to-door interviews with anyone else at Riley's apartment building. Could that have been one of the facts that Neale was trying to keep hidden? "Was she your . . . girlfriend?" Duvall asked, trying not to display any of the sudden urgency she felt.

Cross looked away, both hands still on the steering wheel. A line of narrow sunlight, slicing through a crack in the wooden balcony above, fell across his eyes. He seemed to look directly into it. He didn't blink. "I liked her," he said quietly, his voice almost lost among the waves. "SHARP keeps me very busy. I . . . find it hard to meet people."

Duvall filed it, every word, pressed on. "Did you visit Cassie last Friday night?"

"No."

"Did she ever tell you of anyone who might be trying to hurt her? Anything about threatening phone calls? People following her? That sort of thing?"

Cross shook his head, but kept his eyes fixed on the band of light.

"Do you know why she'd been missing work? Any trouble with anyone at SHARP?"

"She wasn't happy with her job anymore. She felt she'd been a receptionist too long. She wanted to advance and was going to other interviews."

"Do you know where?" Duvall asked, then instantly regretted having done so. It was a cop's knee-jerk reaction to find a source of confirmation for Cross's statement, even though she had no reason to doubt him.

"No, I don't." He turned to face her. His pupils had contracted to tiny dark dots, making his irises unnervingly appear solid black, moist and glittering. "She didn't tell me everything. We weren't . . . lovers or anything." He acted embarrassed to use the word. Duvall felt oddly relieved.

"I liked her," Cross continued. "Wanted to help her. She was a nice person."

"Was she seeing someone else? Do you know if she did have a lover?"

"No. I don't know that."

Duvall was baffled by the man. Such competence in the lab, such helplessness in the world.

They talked longer under that balcony. The band of sunlight moved past Cross's eyes and he finally ignored it. They talked of what it was like for him to work at the SHARP facility and Duvall learned she had been right in her supposition: it had been created exclusively for Cross and his work, though she had not the slightest idea what his work entailed, other than it excited the rest of the staff at the facility and every other word seemed to be "quantum."

"What's so special about *quantum* physics?" she finally had to ask.

"It's just a name," Cross said, not minding the question. "It's left over from over ninety years ago when Planck demonstrated that electrons didn't continually lose energy in their orbit around atomic nuclei the way that planets lose energy circling the sun."

"Yeah, so?" Duvall said. His words had meant nothing.

Cross laughed. "Well, as the Earth orbits the sun, it's constantly slowing down and moving closer in—losing energy on a very slow but continual basis. What Planck discovered was that if electrons behaved like little planets, they would have to lose their energy so quickly that they'd fall into the nuclei of atoms almost immediately and, therefore, atoms couldn't exist. Since atoms do exist, there had to be a new mechanism to account for how energy was transferred at the atomic level.

"What Planck showed was that under the new mechanism, an electron could only gain or lose energy in discrete amounts, which he called quanta. That meant that the subatomic world didn't work in a smoothly continuous manner. There were no half-states, no fractions. It was either all or nothing, with no in-betweens. It was quite a profound discovery."

"I'll take your word for it," Duvall said. It seemed the wise thing to do.

During their talk, Duvall also came to realize that Cross was brilliant. The deference shown him by the others in the lab demonstration, the way they had hung on to every word he had spoken, had conveyed that to Duvall though she hadn't understood what had happened. And, she could see now, Cross knew he was smart, not in any boastful or snickering way, but in a quiet, self-conscious, almost deprecating manner. It was as if he felt it wasn't his fault he had been cursed with whatever gifts he had. More than anything else, she sensed from him, he wanted to be an ordinary person, just as so many who were ordinary wanted to be special.

Duvall could understand that wish, because from it came such sadness and loneliness that she was almost overwhelmed. Cross was like a little lost child calling out without realizing it, especially now that Cassie, perhaps his only friend, had been taken from him. And under it all, in multiple currents and rhythms she couldn't yet fully understand, there was something else to him, something unsettled. Something that called to her, from the sadness, and the loneliness, and the common wish to be something else.

"Why did you want to talk to Charis again?" Cross asked. He watched the waves now, building and crashing.

Duvall considered her answer carefully. She wondered what might happen if Cross were able to turn his intellect to the mystery she faced: the two murders with missing evidence and Charis Neale's involvement in both, and her involvement with Covington. But Duvall's training and her instinct said not yet, no matter how much her heart said now. The hardest thing for a cop to give was trust and Cross worked with Neale every day.

"I had to double-check some of the things that she told the other detectives," Duvall said, lying easily. "Standard procedure."

"Verification of results," Cross said lightly. "A proper application of the scientific method. That's what they're all going to be doing back there for the next month." He laughed, obviously meaning the people at SHARP.

"Verifying that demonstration you did?" Duvall was pleased to get off the subject of murder. It didn't seem right for a person like Cross to worry about darker matters.

The man nodded. A new streak of sunlight was creeping up the hood of his car and his eyes fixed on it as it approached.

"This might seem like a stupid question," Duvall said, hoping it wasn't quite as asinine as she thought it was going to be, "but what *did* you do back there that got them all so excited?"

Cross looked away from the light and studied Duvall intensely. But his expression and manner were so open and unthreatening that she held his gaze, returned it, feeling as if she were being judged.

"You really mustn't tell anyone," he said sincerely.

Duvall felt a thrill of excitement in her chest when he spoke. She

had known that Neale had lied to her about the experiment's importance. Could she actually have been present when something important
had happened? Important in the broad real sense, not like getting a
raise or finding an honest garage, but something that would actually
have meaning to the world.

"Who could I tell?" Duvall asked. She suddenly realized that a
part of her life *was* over. There was a time when she had told Jesse
everything.

"I created a region of gravity independent of mass," Cross said
cautiously, as if revealing the greatest secret of all time.

Duvall was embarrassed. She understood each word, but not their
combination. "I'm sorry, I don't know what that means."

Cross kept his steady probing eyes on her. She felt her cheeks heat
up. Then he laughed, loudly, ecstatically. "Neither do they!" He held
onto the wheel of the car, taking deep breaths. "But, you see, they're
pretending they do. Oh, how they're pretending!" Unexpectedly, he
reached out and took her hand, brushing the side of her leg. He was
warm, smooth, perfect. "And only you have the honesty to admit that
your ignorance is the same as mine." He smiled at her, brilliant as the
band of sunlight, almost as if he were suddenly someone else. "You see,
I don't know what it means either." That smile melted into her. "We're
much the same, aren't we."

"No." She almost stammered.

"It's true. Seekers of truth. Of knowledge. Each in our way."

"I doubt it."

"There's no doubt, Kate. No uncertainty. At the smallest levels, at
the finest resolution in the world of the quantum, a thing is, or it is not.
No doubt. Only possibilities." He let go of her hand, slowly, lightly,
sweeping his fingers across her skin until all that was left was the
memory of his touch. "And everything is possible. Everything."

The memory of that touch burned for hours.

Like a ghost forming whole and sudden from the air, Anthony Cross
was in the doorway to Covington's office. Neale looked at him dully, still
grim from her discussion with Covington. But even from where she sat
on the leather couch, she could smell the sun and the ocean on Cross.
Even from the hollowness of her feelings, her heart ached for him. In
her eyes, he was flawless.

"Where have you been?" Covington asked. It was the voice of a father, determined to discipline, yet knowing his son had surpassed his parent's capabilities.

"The detective's car wouldn't start. I gave her a ride to Smokey's." His eyes twinkled. Neale could see the provocation in them. He was looking for a fight, probably just so Covington would have to apologize and Cross's net would then be that much stronger. She was finally coming to understand that at least some of his personality changes were deliberate, to force inappropriate actions out of others. Perhaps there was only one personality at work in him, the rest only illusions by which he manipulated those around him. She wouldn't be surprised, or frightened, by anything she found out about him now. She was well past that.

"You were supposed to be here," Covington continued, "pulling together the calculations for your demonstration."

"Smokey couldn't get to the detective's car until tomorrow," Cross explained, ignoring Covington. "So I gave her the keys to one of the pool cars. The blue Plymouth." He smiled again, glanced at Neale. Was he doing it on purpose? "Will there be a problem with insurance?"

Covington folded his hands on his desktop, sitting up straight, composed. "When will I have those calculations?"

"You couldn't understand them, Parnel."

Covington nodded. "When will Charis have those calculations?"

Cross sat down on the opposite end of the couch and spread out comfortably. He bobbed his knee up and down impatiently. "You saw the demonstration," he said to her. "You should be able to reconstruct from that."

Neale looked away. As much as she cared for Cross, she was happy to let Covington deal with him when he was like this.

"Anthony, why are you acting this way?" Covington remained calm.

"My time is valuable. Charis doesn't need me to write up tedious equations she can do herself."

"If your time is so valuable," Neale said, "why waste it on that detective?"

Cross's eyes half-closed. His attention seemed to slip from the room, leaving only a shell behind. "Cassie was an asset to this facility.

It seems only right to help the police in their investigation of her horrible death."

Neale saw Covington signal her with his eyes, but what was the use? She understood Cross's moods well enough. He wasn't going to be cooperative until he had been calmed down enough. She knew what that would take. In a way, she didn't mind.

"I need some sort of explanation from you, Anthony," she said, delaying the inevitable.

"I created a region of gravity independent of mass. Do you understand?"

"I understand," Neale said pointedly. "I just don't believe it."

Cross was unperturbed. "Parnel, I have no motive for lying to you. You ensured that my contract with SHARP wouldn't place any performance pressures on me. I don't understand how you can suggest that I might have conducted a false demonstration."

Covington had not moved. "Your demonstration went so far beyond anything in physics today that it is only reasonable for us to ask for confirmation. If true, what you have accomplished is quite remarkable. Astounding, actually."

"That is what you wanted when you brought me here."

"Yes."

"You seem upset that I've given you what you wanted." Cross stood up. "We all know there are no secrets between the three of us." Neale heard the silence of his pause and was chilled by it. What was his hidden meaning? "It doesn't take a genius to understand the applications of what I demonstrated."

"No," Covington agreed. "It does not."

Cross's eyes opened fully. He had returned. The taunting look left his eyes. "You have a mighty, international industrial complex to run, Parnel."

"I find SHARP the most interesting this week."

"Wait until next week," Cross said enigmatically.

Neale realized that it might have been a threat. "What do you mean, Anthony?"

"I'm going to give you another demonstration." He walked back to the open doorway.

"Of what?" Covington remained unmoving, though Neale could

see that his folded hands worked against each other. "Artificial gravity again?"

Cross shook his head, in an attitude of pitying them. "You missed the point as usual, Parnel. Gravity was not important to my demonstration. The technique by which it was generated, that was the real purpose."

Neale stood, smoothed down her skirt, went to him. "What was the technique, Anthony? I want to know."

"A sail," Cross said in the voice of a poet reciting his most stirring work. "A sail for the quantum sea." He put his hand on the doorframe, like a parachutist preparing to plunge into empty space. "Think about that, Parnel. Think about the applications *that* would have."

"Shall we go to the house?" Neale asked, stopping at Cross's side. There she would find the real Cross beneath all his layers and troubles. There she would reclaim him, bring him back to the ordinary world, if only for a little while.

"No," Cross said, sadness in his eyes, as if he knew the cost of his refusal. "I have a lot of work to do now. I have to get ready."

"To do what?" Neale trembled. How could he say no to her? Especially now that Cassie was gone. Unless, *dear God,* she thought, unless he now had someone else to replace the girl.

"To show you," Cross said quietly. He nodded good-bye to Covington. "To show you all." And he was gone, just as he had arrived, the power of his presence flowing back into the empty vacuum.

Covington was up instantly. He closed the door to his office, stood inches away from Neale. "Give me the context of that," he demanded, voice like steel. " 'A sail for the quantum sea.' He said it as if you knew what it meant."

Neale felt exhausted. Her whole life was spent trying to keep up with Cross and now, it seemed, she must keep up with Covington's machinations, too.

"He said it on the balcony, two nights ago. After he knocked your drink from your hand. We talked on the balcony about why the timing coils overloaded, about synchronizing the electrons. I said the power requirements were too great and he said—he implied—that he didn't have to produce all that energy. He said he could take advantage of an existing phenomenon."

"Your . . . talk on the balcony," Covington said so that Neale knew he had seen everything that had happened that night. His tone was worse than the way he had stared at the photograph of her. "I understand. A sailboat does not have to create the wind, only exploit it." He held Neale's shoulders. "Then he . . . went for his drive. Then he had Daystrom build the new timing circuitry. His new inspiration."

"Yes."

Covington's fingers dug in, but Neale could see that this time it was unconscious on his part. She felt the tension vibrate through him, like holding Cross in her hands.

"Did he create a gravitational field in the accelerator today? No equivocation. I don't care if you understand *how* he did it. But, *did* he do it?"

Neale could see where Covington was going with this. All the safety nets were being cut away now. "Anthony was right. He has no motive to lie to us." She thought about that. "At least, not about his work. He doesn't have to."

"Did he do it?"

"Yes. I believe he did."

The clenched hands on her shoulders relaxed. A new look came into Covington's eyes.

"Three and a half years," he said. "Three and a half years."

"That's faster than anyone thought."

Covington's eyes were cold. "He's insane."

"He's the most staggering intellect our world has seen." It wasn't an argument. "He understands what he's doing intuitively. The insights that others labor years for, just . . . just come to him naturally. He's a new class of mind, Parnel. A new class of human."

"I'm going to call them in, now," Covington said. "The rest of the team." Neale sensed more than three years of waiting and frustration behind those words. He let go of her completely, walked back to his desk, reached for his phone.

"As soon as he finds out about Cathedral, you'll lose him." It wasn't a threat. It was the truth.

"He can't exist on his own, Charis. Whatever class of mind or person he is, he can't function in a vacuum. He needs us, if only as an audience to his brilliance." He lifted the receiver, punched in a string of numbers, longer than any normal long distance call or service.

Covington was wrong in his assessment of Cross. Neale knew that, but saw little point in arguing. How could she justify her knowledge of him? Insane, brilliant? What rules applied? What system of measurement could be brought to bear on one so clearly beyond any concept of what had been previously quantified?

There was only one standard that could be used, one standard that transcended the limits of the real world as easily and as smoothly as Anthony Cross transcended the limits of humanity. And Charis Neale was the only one who could wield that standard, the only one who could hold it to the flame of Anthony Cross and withstand his fire and comprehend his innermost needs, his innermost core, to see what truly lay beneath the brilliance, the insanity, and all the other useless, meaningless words incapable of describing that which could not be imagined.

Because Charis Neale had a power that went beyond the quantum, surpassed space and time, confounded logic and chaos both. Charis Neale *loved* Anthony Cross, and with that love came the knowledge and conviction that they would be bound together, forever, eternally, throughout all time. In this, her understanding and acceptance lay. She could not imagine her life without him. Or her death.

"This is Cathedral Three," Covington said slowly, carefully pronouncing each word for the benefit of the recorders that Neale presumed were now on the end of the line, awakened amid an untraceable tangle of wires and circuitry, three and a half years dormant.

Covington smiled as he gave the rest of his signal, delivering a sign hidden for years, waiting for this day which Neale could see only as the beginning of a long, cold night.

"Morning has broken," Covington said.

The real work of SHARP was about to begin.

FIFTEEN

S ingularity. The point of infinite density and infinite mass at which physics broke down. Cloaked by an event horizon from beyond which no information could pass, no knowledge could be obtained. The end point of relativity and reality and time. The embarrassment of the quantum. Anthony Cross laughed at the simplicity of the singularity as he wove his copper strands in the dim light of his private workshop. It was all so obvious now.

His hands moved as precisely and as deftly as a surgeon's wielding a scalpel, testimony to his years of concentrated practice. Number-ten copper wire, uninsulated, smooth and molten in his fingers, just thick enough so that it wouldn't cut into bare flesh, unless pulled tightly, ever so tightly across soft flesh, easy skin. It flashed and twisted as he created his form, as intricate as the system of nerves and capillaries found in the living brain.

His hands created the shape and the interconnections of the wire as if they operated independently of his eyes and his mind, so quickly did they move in and out of the range of his vision. His eyes were half-closed, his head nodded with the irregular beat of the reaching and stretching of his hands and arms. He thought of the singularity. Of copper-wrapped motors in green plastic monsters. Of cats uncoiled. Infinite mass and infinite energy.

His eyes saw the house. Not the beach house, but another one. The first one. Leaning against the window of his room, watching a far-off summer storm roll past, dissipating. The distant instant tangles of lightning like the sparks he could cause to jump between his finger and the doorknob. The boy estimated the length of the lightning. (Once he had read a book that gave the average height of different clouds. He closed his eyes and saw that page again, comparing the paintings of the clouds with the real ones on the horizon, found the corresponding picture, read off the altitude figure given below. That told him the average distance the lightning must travel and, therefore, its average length.)

The boy gazed at his fingertips, moving them closer together, farther apart, and calculated the distance he could make a spark jump from the doorknob after rubbing his sock feet on the carpet. The numbers wheeled into position before his eyes as easily as a migrating flock of birds changed leaders in the sky. The lightning was 506,880 times larger than the spark.

Once he had put his feet into the shoes his mother's friend had left in the hall when they had gone upstairs and told him to play in the basement. He had gone back up to the ground floor of the house when he had heard his mother's cries. He waited in the hallway, beside the stairs, frightened of the basement, frightened of the sounds his mother made, frightened that if he ran upstairs to her that she would hit him again, or that her friend would do the worse thing. He knew exactly all the things of which he should be frightened. They had all happened before and he remembered them with absolute precision, laid out in his memory like dead beetles mounted on sharp tiny pins in neatly labeled drawers at the museum. (He had read a book once that showed him such things.)

So he stayed in the hallway, trapped by his fears, and placed his small feet in the shoes his mother's friend had left in the hallway. He remembered that moment as he thought of lightning and 506,880. Not the fear. That was long gone. Not the hitting. He didn't feel that anymore when they did it to him; it was easier to just go away and come back when the pain had stopped. But he remembered the slippery feeling of his feet in the shoes, his narrow ankles rocking back and forth as he clumped up and down the hall carpet, trying to balance the shoes on his feet without having them fall off. After a while his mother no longer cried upstairs and instead he heard laughter, coarse and rough, and he remembered that the soles of the shoes had been approximately twice the area of his feet, though the shoes themselves had been about four times the volume. (There were a lot of curves so he couldn't be sure. He hadn't yet read a book about topology.) And when he concentrated on those measurements, as precise and as exact as they could be under the circumstances, he couldn't hear anything at all that could frighten him, and that was good.

So he watched the lightning and saw the numbers dance and they said 506,880 of his feet, which, when the measurements of the man's shoes were taken into account, meant 253,440 grown-up feet, which meant 126,720 grown-ups because everybody had two feet. (Though he had seen some people with only one leg and realized that he would have to find out what percentage of the population had only one foot so he could adjust his calculation to allow for it. There would have to be a book about that, someplace.)

He closed his eyes again with the number 126,720 buzzing before him in black dots like midges at sunset. The sound of the number was more high-pitched than the low buzzing of 506,880. The sound of 126,720 was like the crackling of wires on dry days, tart and vanilla at the same time. It was a familiar sensation, and he knew he had experienced something like it before. He looked for it, without knowing how, and found it, without knowing where: the same sound, the same taste and smell, almost the same black swarm of the midges.

It was the population of the Andaman and Nicobar Islands, a political subdivision of the Republic of India, located at 12° N, 92° E, which was 127,000. (He had read a book once and he could still see the numbers written on the page, black on white, humming like wires, vanilla and lemon, permanently etched . . . somewhere.)

Anthony Cross smiled as he leaned against his window, watching the lightning, secure in the knowledge that if everyone in the Andaman and Nicobar Islands took off his shoes and shuffled his feet against the carpet and reached out to a large enough doorknob at the very same time, there would be a spark as big as a bolt of lightning. And the sudden snap of a spark on that scale would be thunder. It was just that simple. Most things were.

The boy was three years old. The complete chain of calculation about sparks and shoes and lightning had taken him six seconds. It brought him the same feeling of warmth and safety and control that weaving his copper did so many years later.

The form on the workbench before him had taken on an organic shape by now, multiple strands taking on a three-dimensional shape which followed lines of pattern and force perceived only by its creator.

Anthony Cross smiled as he worked out the new calculations, the taste and the shape and the feel of the singularity. What morons they all were. Einstein and Kwong and Weinstein and Hawking and all of them who thought that singularities were the end when it was so obvious, so painfully blatantly embarrassingly obvious, that the singularity was the beginning.

His hands flew over the indistinct form, trailing streaks of copper wire like lightning, twisting and molding and shaping. They'd see soon enough, the boy thought happily to himself, enmeshed in his calculations and his understanding, feeling and hearing and seeing nothing but what he could create for himself. He'd teach them all a lesson that they'd never forget. Just as he had been taught, so many times, so long ago.

It was just that simple. So many things were.

SIXTEEN

T he phone was ringing as Katherine Duvall fumbled with her keys at the front door of her house. Her hands were shaking and, in the front porch light, she couldn't tell the difference between the silver deadbolt key and the brass doorknob key. It might be Jesse. But she knew it wouldn't be.

The worst had been when he hadn't argued with her. She had expected a huge blowup when she finally told him that she wouldn't be going to Hawaii. The memory of Anthony Cross's hand still scorched her skin. She was prepared for the catharsis of raised voices and fast words, of tears and finally of regret. She needed to cleanse herself, for things done, for things half-imagined. But Jesse wouldn't let her.

Instead, the excitement she had felt building in him the past few days since her unexpected apologetic phone call, had evaporated, almost as if he had expected it to. Quietly, resignedly, he had asked her about her current status with the department. She had given him the answer he already had known, the confirmation he had wanted. She was on vacation leave, but a case had come up, and she was pursuing it on her own. And he had said, "I see." That was all, no other reaction. She might have been telling him of a bus accident in Italy, meaningless TV news on a slow Sunday night.

The expectation in those moments of his silent waiting had been terrible for her. She wanted him to rage at her, even, with the memory of Cross lingering upon her hand, to accuse her of having an affair, someone new in her life, and that she was tormenting him only because other things weren't working out for her. But he hadn't, and Duvall had realized that perhaps Jesse had always known she had such an affair—her badge and her job, her refuge from the rest of the world.

After the damned reasonableness of his reaction, the sickening civility of it, Duvall had not been surprised when he announced that he would go on his own. He had pulled strings to arrange the holiday time, he had explained, asked for favors. It would not look proper if he did not go now, after causing others at the bank to rearrange their schedules. It had been the bland acceptance of a stranger, someone no longer affected, someone who no longer cared.

Hands shaking as she fumbled with her keys, fearing the urgency of the ringing phone, Duvall felt tears come to her eyes as at last she realized that within herself was that same acceptance, that same civil blandness, and she didn't know where either had come. What lies had she been living with for these past few months? Or had she always been living those same lies in all her time with Jesse?

She answered the phone on what she thought was the eighteenth ring. Very urgent, she thought. She glanced at the kitchen clock. Eight forty-five. Perhaps he was calling from the plane. But what more could possibly be said?

"It's Nuke."

It took a moment for Duvall to cycle back to the here and now.

"Kate? Are you there?"

Could he hear her tears? "Yeah, I'm here."

"You okay?"

"What's up, Nuke?"

She heard him hesitate, just like Jesse. She felt his decision, just like Jesse: it wasn't his problem.

"Two things. One: I got hold of a copy of that records search Seabrook ran. No other dissection deaths reported anywhere. He even ran it through Interpol."

Duvall's detective's mind pulled itself out of the morass of her emotions. "Did you see the records search before or after Seabrook got hold of it?" Other evidence had gone missing before.

"I got it raw. There was *nada.*"

"Which would mean that the Boy Scout's just starting up now. And I don't believe it." Duvall was convinced that the detail and preciseness with which the murders had been carried out indicated the killer had had some practice, some experience. "What was the basis of the search?"

"Seabrook's task force requested a search of any unsolved murders involving dissection, with a flag on dissection trauma as cause of death. And there was nothing similar to the Riley and the Frost murders."

"So, did you manage the computer search *I* wanted?"

"Bludgeoning deaths where the victim was immobilized. With a flag on head trauma as cause of. Just like the Riley case was presented to the media." For all the good that had done, Duvall thought. In this city, it seemed, the threshold for mass murderers was five victims. Any less and a case couldn't make it past the competition for page one.

But Duvall could hear Nogura's results in his voice. Her hand was fused to the phone, everything focused on what he would say next.

"How many?" she asked.

"Seventeen. In the U.S. alone over the past ten years."

Duvall closed her eyes, ignoring the stickiness of her tears. *Seventeen* previous murders! Now, with Riley and Foster, she had a chance. Nobody could be perfect nineteen times.

"Where, Nuke?"

"All over the U.S. Both coasts, Midwest, you name it. No obvious geographical pattern or main location. Plus another three in Canada and one in Europe. All victims bound in various ways—"

"Describe them." Blond, she wanted to hear blond.

"Jesus, Kate, I just got the printouts five minutes ago and I'm going to have to wait for faxes of the case sheets."

"Okay, okay. What else?"

"Let's see, all victims bound or otherwise immobilized, dead of massive head wounds, all cases open, you should pardon the expression." He didn't let her interrupt again. "I'll get the package over to you as soon as the rest of the stuff comes in. Morning at the latest. You know which one to go for first, right?"

Duvall nodded. Go for the oddball, the anomaly, the break in the pattern. "The singleton in Europe."

"Stockholm. Three and a half years ago. December. Student. Female. There'll be more on the case sheet when it comes."

"Thanks, Nuke. I really appreciate it. You going to give this to Seabrook?" She could hear Nogura sigh on the other end. It was odd to sense his reluctance. "You have to, you know."

"I know," Nogura conceded. "But if I plunk it on his desk without warning, he's going to wonder how and why I came up with it."

"Why not just drop a few hints to one of the guys on the task force and let them come up with the idea to do this sort of check on their own? Shouldn't be hard to get their attention. They can't have all that much to go on for themselves."

"You want me to do it right now?" Nogura asked.

"How long would it take them to get moving on it?"

"An easy forty-eight hours before Seabrook will know what to do with it and report."

"A lot can happen to evidence in forty-eight hours, Nuke." *As in disappear, like the evidence in the Riley case,* she thought. "Any idea who Seabrook's reporting to on this?"

Nogura took his time replying. "If you mean within the department, he reports directly to Erhlenmeyer. If you're suggesting that someone else might be involved . . . I have no idea. Honestly, Kate. Things may be slow and sloppy down here, but that's SOP. There's no big conspiracy, just screwed-up cops."

"I hope so."

"Believe me, Kate, by the time this is over you're going to wish you went to Hawaii after all, you know?"

But Duvall already wished she had. "Thanks, Nuke. I'll be here in the morning."

"You're sure?" Nogura asked. "No midnight sleuthing out on your own?" He sounded serious.

"We've got a deal, Nuke. As long as I'm officially off the case, I do everything through you. Does that make you happy?"

"It makes me feel safe," Nogura said. "See you in the morning." He clicked off.

Duvall felt a familiar pressure hit her feet. She looked down at her cat, rolling on his back, looking for his supper. Duvall knelt down and scratched the cat's stomach. "Beats a holiday at the kennel, huh, Briggs?" Her voice was hollow and loud in the empty house. Didn't belong.

The cat instantly brought all four paws up to grip and disembowel Duvall's hand, all in the spirit of good clean carnivore fun. The small claws playfully scratched her skin. "Feels like it's time for a trim," Duvall said, pulling away and standing up. The gentle clawing had left faint white lines on the back of her hand. She looked at them and suddenly saw the tattered arm of Cassie Riley's couch as she had seen it that Friday night, almost a week ago. A cat had used it as a scratching post. She remembered asking if anyone had seen the cat. She wondered if anyone had found it. She would have to ask Nuke tomorrow. The doorbell rang. From some hidden reflex, a habit buried but not forgotten, the first thought to come to her mind was *Jesse.*

But it was Seabrook and Erhlenmeyer. Her affair was over. They had come for her badge and her gun.

"What?" Nogura said, the sound of a man being strangled. "Why? What the hell do they think you did?"

Duvall shut her front door behind the detective. Her eyes were puffed, bloodshot. Once again, she had seen all the hours flash by on her bedside alarm, and with each hour, the bed had grown emptier.

"It's not what they *think* I did, it's what I *did* do," Duvall said. "I went back to talk to Charis Neale at the SHARP place. She complained about . . . some of the things I said, and it got back to Seabrook."

"You talked to her with a rubber hose or something? Or just wire her up to a car battery?" Nogura looked like a stage comic, arms flapping at his sides. A larger man might have banged against the walls, dislodged something from a shelf or shifted a picture, but Nogura's movements fit perfectly within the narrow hallway. Somehow, though, his reaction seemed excessive, as if he were trying to make a point he didn't believe in.

"What can I say?" Duvall asked, eyes going to the fat manila envelope Nogura waved with his right hand. "You laid it out for me yourself. The department dropped my suspension in trade for me being off the Riley case and taking vacation time. Well, I'm still in town and I'm still on the Riley case. So big surprise. I'm suspended again."

"Is it worth it, Katherine?"

"Yes." And she believed it.

Nogura shook his head and handed over his package, then followed Duvall into the kitchen as she ripped the side of the envelope open. "The case sheet from Interpol is on the top," he said. "There's a picture, too."

Duvall spread everything out on the pine table, just as she had before. The graduation picture of the student killed in Stockholm was what she had hoped for. Blond, curvy, an open fresh look to her face. Just like Cassie Riley and Amanda Frost. She showed it to Nogura. She wondered what that open fresh face had seen. Whom she had seen.

"It's the same guy," Duvall said. "He keeps killing the same person. Textbook pattern killer."

Nogura wasn't impressed. He poured himself a cup of coffee. "This is raw data, Kate. Look at some of the others before you get too excited about a pattern."

She sorted them by date, starting ten years earlier, and saw what Nogura meant. The first six were all men with dark curly hair, thick features, burly physiques. The killer must have been a giant to subdue them. One victim had been wrapped in packing tape. Two had been held down by heavy chains. One had been found in a chair. Another on a bed. Only one had been tied with nylon cord and tied to a table: number five.

"What was the hard thing, like a plank or something, on the bed in the motel room where they found Amanda Frost?" Duvall asked, reading the cold, detached details of the six murdered men.

"Coffee table top," Nogura said, peering into the refrigerator. "The legs had been unscrewed."

"Was she tied to the tabletop or to the bed?"

"Tabletop," Nogura said. "Can I have one of these?" He held out half a pack of supermarket danishes. Duvall nodded. The cellophane crinkled. "But there were a couple of ropes holding the tabletop to the bed."

"A rigid board so she wouldn't move," Duvall said, full of understanding. "With a light shining right on her head. That's why Cassie was tied up in her kitchen and not in her bedroom. The killer needs lots of light to see what's going on." Duvall moved onto the next group of victims, still in chronological order. Three were male, two female, but all were Asian, slight, thin, middle-aged. Three of the five had been tied to tables with ropes. "He's been perfecting his technique," Duvall said, pleased that her hunch had been right. The way in which Riley and Frost had been killed was too practiced to have been first efforts. The killer had been honing his skills for years.

The next four were men again, back to Caucasians, but darker than the first set. Thick dark hair with varying degrees of baldness, older, rounder shapes. Maybe the killer was losing strength, or had been injured. "Over this two-year period he went after weaker victims," she said. "Maybe he was sick, broke an arm or something." All four had been tied to flat surfaces with a combination of ropes and belts.

"Kate, the same guy can't be responsible for all of these." Nogura swung a kitchen chair around, straddled its back, a raspberry danish in one hand. "The guy going after the blond women, sure, that's a standard pattern cluster. But the three other sets of victims are so different, so distinct, no way it can be the same guy."

"It's the same method. Massive head wounds. Victim tied."

"Massive head wounds are one thing," Nogura protested, "but your victims were cut open, right?"

Duvall frowned at Nogura's use of "your." He was distancing himself from the case. Or maybe he had never felt committed to it. She wondered what other motive he might have for risking Erhlenmeyer's wrath to help her. Could it be his way of getting to know her?

"Look at the morgue shots of the other victims," Nogura continued. "Some of them look like they had cinder blocks dumped on 'em from a tenth-floor roof. Those aren't the same kinds of wounds."

Duvall had seen the phrase used once in one of the background reading kits the department sent around. "It's a learning curve, Nuke. See how the earliest victims were tied up all sorts of different ways? Eventually, by the time he moved up to blond women, he figured out the best way to hold his victim down while he dug in. Same way with cutting into the skull. Maybe he started out by taking off the whole top of the head—"

"Jesus, Kate." Nogura grimaced at his half-eaten danish, but he bit into the raspberry filling again.

"And he kept doing each victim a different way until he figured out the best way to open them up."

"The best way for what?"

"How should I know? Maybe he's eating their brains or something." She looked at the morgue photos again, blocky and contrasty from the fax. "Christ, maybe he's looking for something inside them."

"His car keys?"

"Catch fire, Nuke."

Nogura popped the last of his danish into his mouth and sucked on his fingers. "I still say you wouldn't get a psychologist to agree that one pattern killer could choose four different groups of victims so cleanly. Completely random killings, sure. That happens. A single cluster of similar victims broken up by one or two oddballs, sometimes. But not this. Male and female. Asian, Caucasian. It's not random enough but there's no pattern to it."

Duvall felt a quick rush of impatience. "Nuke, records pulled up all of these cases together. That means there's a definite pattern."

Nogura shook his head. "It's the pattern you and I created when we asked for the search, Kate. I could ask records to pull up all the open cases of people shot with a .38 in the left temple between ten and twelve P.M. on odd-numbered days and we'd get a hundred hits. It might look like a pattern but that's only because there are only a certain number of ways for people to die and so many people die that there're bound to be random clusters when every record is searched."

Duvall thought it through. Patterns didn't have to be static. A change in pattern could be a pattern in itself, like traffickers who dealt a couple of lids of grass, then bought up to crack, then started moving a couple of keys of cocaine. They learned the system and progressed with it. Growth and change could be a valid pattern. These murders could be following that type of pattern, too. "You're not convincing me, Nuke."

"Okay, smartass, if it's a pattern killer, where's your goddamned pattern? Answer that." He folded his hands together on the back of the chair and rested his chin on them.

Duvall said the first thing that came to mind, free-associating. "Multiple personality. And each personality's a killer but with a different victim fix."

"If you believe that you're so full of shit you should be a lieutenant."

"More than one killer, then," Duvall tried. "A cult or something."

Nogura thought about that for a few seconds. "Doubtful. Cult crimes tend to be absolutely identical. And cults that kill have never been stable over such a long period of time."

"And they leave identifying marks," Duvall continued for him.

"But better than multiple personality," Nogura said. He reached forward and shuffled the pictures around. "We'll use your trick." He arranged them side by side, as Duvall had matched the shots of Riley and Frost, trying different combinations and groupings, like arranging a jigsaw puzzle at random, searching for connections.

Duvall watched him work at his side of the table. She tracked the photos as they moved around, upside down, letting her mind wander to find connections, like Briggs's scratches and the arm of Cassie Riley's couch.

"Hey, did they ever find a cat in Riley's apartment?"

"You mean Misty?" Nogura asked, peering at the photos through half-closed eyes. "They figure it ran away." He shuffled the photos again, moving the blond women beside the Asian women. Duvall concentrated on the upside-down photo of Cassie Riley, head destroyed from the eyebrows up. The same for Amanda Foster. Only the Interpol photo of the Stockholm victim was different; whole, intact, blond, and perfect, long hair that would take forever to wash and style . . .

"That's it," Duvall said. Nogura looked up, eyes questioning. Duvall reached across the table and grabbed the three shots of the blondes.

"What?" Nogura asked.

"She looks like Charis Neale," Duvall said, dropping the photo of the Stockholm victim on the table. "I saw her on Friday night, at Cassie Riley's building."

"We've been through that," Nogura said, swinging the picture around for another look. "She was there to fire Riley."

"No, no," Duvall said, the picture suddenly forming before her eyes, called up like a slide in a computer bank. She had looked over the balcony railing to see if Ash File had thrown up on anything interesting. She had seen a plainclothes officer she hadn't recognized talking with a woman beside the ambulance. A blond woman. Charis Neale. The physicist had been downstairs long before she had come up and been questioned by Duvall. "I need the original reports of the Riley investigation."

"I gave 'em to you," Nogura said. He used his hand to block out the tops of the photos of Riley and Frost, comparing them with the Stockholm photo.

"No, those were the official forms, the ones that didn't mention that I was there and got into the fight with Erhlenmeyer. The forms were changed."

"What do you need the originals for?"

"There was another plainclothes at the scene. I didn't recognize him. He was talking to Neale before she came up. But *he* didn't come up." She closed her eyes, seeking, searching. "I knew everyone else in the apartment."

"You remember all that?" Nogura asked skeptically.

Duvall pointed to her eyes, still puffed and bloodshot. "Eye for detail, remember? I even remember when you came on the force and were so happy to be out of the Army that you grew that pitiful beard."

"Tried to grow it," Nogura said with a grimace. "But anyway, what's the big deal? A plainclothes from some other division was driving home, heard the call and showed up to see if there was anything he could do. That's how you showed up that night."

"Yeah, but I hung around."

"So, the guy saw everything was under control and took off. We all do it on a slow night."

Duvall got up, too much energy building in her to let her sit in one place. "But he talked to someone who might have been a witness. He got involved. He should have at least come up and reported to the officer in charge. Charis Neale might have arrived earlier than she said she did." She paced, wondering how far she should go in revealing her suspicions to Nogura. "Hell, for all the plainclothes knew, he might have *seen* the murderer."

Duvall froze. She looked at Nogura and it was as if he could read her thoughts.

"No way," Nogura said. "It absolutely can't be her."

"She was at the scene of Amanda Frost's murder, too," Duvall said. "Dressed in black. Driving away in a SHARP company car after the police left."

Nogura snapped his fingers at her. "Wake up, Kate. Women don't commit pattern murders. Don't you read your background papers?"

"I do read them. Women commit 15 percent of serial murders, Nuke. She was at both scenes. She is evasive under questioning. And there are three chances in twenty that the murderer is female. I'd say that's a good start until someone better comes along."

"Then what's her motive?" Nogura asked. "And I don't like that look in your eyes."

"That Professor Leyton's work on serial killers says that most of them kill people who belong to a sociological group which they themselves want to belong to, but can't for whatever reason. Maybe Neale's uncertain about herself as a . . . I don't know . . . an attractive blonde or something?"

Nogura held his nose. "And before that, she was uncertain of herself as what? An oriental female? An overweight male? Come on, Katherine. That doesn't make any sense at all."

"Nuke, if she's a pattern killer, we shouldn't expect her motive to make any sense to anyone except her." Duvall remembered what Cross had told her about Riley and about SHARP. "Though maybe in Cassie Riley's case, it was jealousy. She didn't want the receptionist involved with the number-one scientist at SHARP."

"And the hooker in the motel?"

Duvall had a guess but was uncomfortable saying it. "Maybe the scientist was seeing her. On a professional basis. There's no other link between the two victims. Maybe the scientist is it."

"Who's the scientist?"

"Anthony Cross."

Nogura shrugged. "Never heard of him."

"Sweet guy. A real absent-minded-professor type. SHARP was set up just for him by some big money bags. Parnel Covington." Duvall stopped dead as another pattern emerged. She had seen Neale and Covington exchanging some kind of signal when she had been in the lab with them. At the time, she had only noticed that something was going on between them that they were trying to keep hidden from Cross . . .

"So, what are you going to do now? Go back to the woman who complained about you questioning her and arrest her for being the killer?"

"Catch fire, Nuke." Duvall held her hands together, mind racing. Neale and Covington. Two people with a secret. Two people stronger than one. Two murderers. The details were all in place. It was time to see how they would resolve into a final picture. She smiled at Nogura. He frowned back.

"I'm serious, Kate. You can't go back to SHARP. There's only so much I can drop onto the task force for them to look into without some of them getting a bit curious about where everything's coming from. And without another witness to put Neale at the motel when you saw her, you've got nothing against her." He stood up so he wouldn't have to keep looking up at her as she crossed the kitchen floor, back and forth, like something caged.

Duvall stretched her arms in front of her. She felt better than she had all week. Maybe this was the catharsis she had needed. "Can you track down the original reports from last Friday?" she asked.

"Yeah, I can probably do that," Nogura conceded. "But that's about all I can do." He reached out a hand to her arm. "Will you stop that for a second?"

Duvall stopped her pacing.

"Do you realize how serious this is for you?" Nogura asked. "I mean, you're off the case, suspended from the department, with no support and no one you can go to for any kind of help."

Duvall smiled and patted Nogura's hand. "Yes, yes, yes, and no."

Nogura narrowed his eyes at her. "There *is* someone you can go to?"

Duvall's path was clear, the decisions made. She was not alone. She knew exactly to whom she could turn to for help, assistance, and total understanding—someone who knew and worked with Neale and Covington, someone who was smart and as open and honest as a child. Someone whose touch still lingered on her hand.

"Come on, who?" Nogura asked.

Duvall shook her head. Despite the intuition of her heart, cop paranoia demanded she not give up anything. For now, if only to spare herself a knee-jerk sermon from Nogura warning her that everyone at SHARP should be a suspect at this stage, she decided to let Anthony Cross remain her secret.

Everything would probably be a lot easier and safer that way.

SEVENTEEN

Duvall found her car in the lot behind Smokey's garage off the PCH. The little Bug was sandwiched among the other vehicles Smokey wasn't keen to show off out front: two late-model Cadillacs, a Corvette, and two Volvos. In the lot out front, visible from the road, were a powder blue Rolls, two Ferraris, a Vector, and something else so low and sleek that Duvall didn't know how a driver could sit in it. The station attendant who walked her around to the back was quite pleased to tell her that the stainless-steel Delorean up on the hoist was Johnny Carson's.

The attendant passed over the keys to the Bug. "Starts up fine, now." His hair was blond, skin a golden brown. *Probably star in his own series after he fixes the right person's car at this place,* Duvall thought. Then she prepared for the worst of it.

"What's the charge?"

"Hey," the attendant said, "no charge for SHARP. They have a service contract."

It was tempting but Duvall was incapable of accepting it. She had even felt guilty when the clerks at Pollo Loco had thrown in a free coffee when she used to eat lunch there in uniform.

"Thanks, but I have to pay for this one myself. I . . . wasn't using the car on business for SHARP."

"Hey, really, it's cool," the attendant said. "It was just the cotter pin on the carburetor. No big deal. It's like a fifty-cent part and Smokey didn't even have to put it on the hoist." He opened the engine hood of the car. "Here, I'll show you. Next time it happens you can fix this with a hairpin or something. Look."

He showed her a small cotter pin that worked as a hinge linking the accelerator pedal cord to a valve arm on the carburetor. Without the pin, no gas could get to the engine. "A dude couldn't even hot wire it. Better than an alarm in your high crime areas."

Duvall wiggled the pin for herself. It seemed permanently installed. "Would this have had anything to do with the car taking a couple of tries to start?"

"No way," the attendant said. "Either the pin's in or it's not. It works or it doesn't. That's all." He looked at her quite seriously. "The reason your car won't start is because it hasn't had a tune-up for mucho too long. Oh yeah, Smokey wants to know if you want an estimate on those fenders."

"No, thanks. What makes the pin come out?"

"Who knows, like? Metal fatigue or something. They just crack and it's game over. Shit happens, you know?"

"That I know," Duvall said. "So, not even ten bucks?" She clanged the engine hood closed.

"Costs more than that to write up a work order around here," the attendant said. "Hey, I got to get back and polish the Delorean, you know? You have a real good day, now, okay?"

"Oh, I will," Duvall promised. She opened both doors on the car then popped and folded the roof, losing two nails in the struggle with the cover. She swore.

"You'll have to say it louder," a familiar voice said over her shoulder. "I don't think the car heard you."

Duvall turned around, a reflex smile on her face. Anthony Cross stood in the brilliance of the sun, a pale pink shirt tucked into white pants, hair and clothes fluttering in the breeze from the beach, eyes and smile as dazzling as the silver smear of sunlight on the ocean. He moved around to fasten the other side of the roof cover.

"Everything fixed?" he asked.

"Even the bill." She got the silly grin off her face, she hoped, leaving something that at least looked friendly, but nothing more.

"Was it bad?" Cross asked, real concern in his voice.

"It was nonexistent."

Their hands brushed together on the final snap. "Something for nothing? Sounds like the violation of a natural law. Someone should be arrested."

Duvall drew her hands back. "That's all right. Sometimes cops look the other way."

Cross's face became serious. "I think that's not true. I think you're not the type of person to look the other way." His eyes were dark and bright at the same time. Riveting. "I think you always look ahead, carefully, precisely, seeing things that no one else sees. And that you know what to do with your knowledge."

His words had captured her as thoroughly as his appearance. Her witticisms trailed off into wisps of random thought. He demanded sincerity. "Why do you say that?"

"That's what *I* do."

"You mean, that's what scientists do. I'm a cop."

He smiled at her, just for her it seemed. "I told you, both are seekers of the truth. Would you have dinner with me some night?" He stuck the last sentence on as if he was trying to sneak it past her, the strategy of a nervous teenager asking for a date.

Duvall thought it was charming. And a relief. She had been trying to work up her nerve to ask him the same thing. So she could discuss her suspicions about Neale and Covington. And Cross, too, she reminded herself. "How about tonight?"

Cross was surprised and he looked it. Duvall found it a marvel, so refreshing that a man could be freely open to interpretation, so uncomplicated.

"You mean it?" he asked.

"Why wouldn't I?"

"I don't know. Sometimes . . ." He shrugged, suddenly clumsy with words again.

But the awkward moment passed and they quickly and decisively went through the mechanics of choosing a place and a time as efficiently as a computer sorting punchcards. Neither of them was a person to waste time.

Maybe in that way they were alike, Duvall thought, as she drove out through Smokey's front lot. But only in that one characteristic. She waved to Cross, waiting in his own car by the station's pumps. His wave in return was exuberant and energetic, real joy in his expression and movements. In contrast, Duvall felt tired and old and exhausted. *Who was she trying to fool?* she thought. How could she think that they could ever be alike? He was too smart, too kind, too nice a person.

Duvall was sure that she could never measure up to his standards and, thinking about the upcoming dinner, that thought made her feel inexplicably safe.

Cross signed the chit the attendant brought him showing the total for the gas pumped into the Mercedes. Everything here was charged to SHARP. In the rearview mirror, he watched Duvall's Volkswagen accelerate down the PCH, heading back to the city. He found her stimulating, one of a handful of such people he had met in his life.

Weinstein had been the first Cross had decided he had really wanted to understand, after the mysteries of his own life had been dealt with and he had turned himself to science. In his time, Weinstein had been a gifted physicist. Not too adventurous in his own work, but quick to understand other's accomplishments, pointing out errors without emotion, swiftly seeing relevant innovation and supporting it. He had been Cross's most important instructor at Harvard, instrumental in bringing him on staff at such a young age. He had also been instrumental in assigning Cross to the first research project in which the student's intellect had had a chance to be noticed in the world community: the remeasurement and reevaluation of the radiation yields of early atomic weapons conducted on the old test sites in New Mexico, long before any other physicist had suspected that the original studies of the forties and fifties had been as incomplete as they were now known to be. That was when Cross had first realized what powerful reactions were lurking within the quantum, hidden by others more mundane.

As he swung his car out from Smokey's for the drive back to SHARP, Cross lost himself in the memories of those early days of his Work. It had taken him six tries to finally peer inside the inner workings of Weinstein and actually come to believe he knew the man, could *be* the man. Six tries, the first since the earlier mysteries of his mother and her friend, and the quick disposal of his foster parents once they had fulfilled their use to him. Those early attempts had been ungraceful, messy, details not quite right. But in the end, he had been inspired to come up with the basis of the Cross Corollary and reached a thorough understanding of Weinstein. Thorough enough for Cross to know that he had surpassed his teacher, become more. So, Weinstein had been left behind, no longer a challenge to Cross's intellect.

Kwong had been the next mystery. The most arcane and elegant mathematics bloomed from his mind without conscious thought. His graduate students claimed his brain was wired like a Cray. Cross had been in awe of the man's abilities and decided that Kwong deserved the same study and devotion he had given to Weinstein. But Kwong had had an unanticipated surprise in store for Cross. It had taken three unsuccessful tries before Cross had learned that the innuendos and rumors were true and that Kwong was gay. Cross, an associate professor on a fast track to tenure at the time, had railed against the waste of time and effort that delayed realization had cost him. But then, in only two more tries past that, women this time, he had succeeded in understanding that like Weinstein, Kwong, too, had been surpassed by his student, and that student had *become* Kwong. It was then that Cross had been sufficiently inspired to understand that time didn't flow, it proceeded in discrete increments, like the jumping liquid crystal image of the second hand on his watch. Once again, Cross's Work had succeeded and he had become more.

Then there had been Neale. From their first night in the desert, Cross had seen something in her that had not been in any of the other scientists he worked with. She had a scientist's mind, of that there was no doubt. Rigid and well trained, capable of understanding his work if not furthering it on her own. But somewhere, hidden in the depths of her, there was something more, something baffling, echoes of strange memories from his childhood. An attraction, perhaps, that went beyond the logic of science. Sometimes, he thought it might be love. Though for Cross, since love could not be quantified or measured, it was to be ignored. Yet there was that elusive element to her that led him finally to look within her for inspiration. To try to understand her as thoroughly and completely as he had delved into Weinstein and Kwong and the earlier mysteries.

His first try had been inconclusive and had provided no insight, no moment of transition. Women were different from men he had decided, in more than the flesh. But the second try in Stockholm, that *had* been a success. In that moment of lucidity, of final understanding, he had at last glimpsed the true structure of spacetime, saw it devoid of the fiction of gravity waves and fixed instead by its web of dark matter. And he had touched the soul of Charis Neale on the final leg of his quest for the Beginning.

For more than three years, that first insight and two more had carried him, and carried SHARP. But it was only recently, in the pressure to bring the massless gravity experiment on line, that he had realized there was still so much to learn about Neale, so much of the quantum left to probe. He had had to try again.

Cassie Riley, pliant and impressionable, had allowed herself to be molded and shaped into a perfect duplicate of Neale—a precise model of an existing system for an even more precise experiment in perfect accordance with the Scientific Method. And she had, in the end, shown him how copper was the way to twist into the manifold intricacies of multidimensional space, and touch the soul of Charis Neale.

Amanda Foster, brusque and professional, had been a quick confirmation of results—an experimental control. For the appropriate amount of money, she had spoken and acted like Neale. And she had, in the end, shown him how to capture the Planck time in the circuits of macro-reality computer chips which were generations too primitive for such fine calculations, and touch the soul of Charis Neale.

And now Neale was like Weinstein, and Kwong, and the earlier mysteries. She was understood and surpassed, holding no more secrets. Once more the Work had succeeded, Cross was more, and it was time to move on to other goals, other mysteries, to go deeper into the quantum, to bring the world the lessons it needed so badly, just like the lessons given to Cross so long ago. In the Beginning.

The Work. It was so satisfying in the way that it progressed. To set a goal, achieve it, then move on. The steady and relentless progression of true science. Cross felt filled with purpose, filled with the explorer's spirit, the adventurer's quest. He had chosen those things that must be understood for his life to make sense, and he had succeeded each time. The toy, the cats, his mother and her friend, Weinstein, Kwong, and Neale. Each task had been successful, each had brought him closer to the ultimate understanding, the final knowledge that would unite relativity with the quantum and reveal at last the universe's beginning.

Driving into the parking lot at SHARP, noticing that both Neale's and Covington's cars were gone, Cross knew he was closer now than he had ever been before in his life. A few more insights, one, perhaps two more inspirations, and he would know it all, the final secrets, the ultimate knowledge.

All that remained was to choose a final accomplishment, a goal whose completion would be the entrance to a completely new existence for himself. And for everyone in the world. To penetrate the quantum, he had to choose one final mystery, one final person to totally, completely understand. One final inspiration for his Work. And he had made his choice.

Tonight he would dine with Katherine Duvall and soon, very soon, he was confident he would touch her soul. And change the world.

EIGHTEEN

Lee Kwong and Adam Weinstein sat in the hotel suite without talking and Charis Neale couldn't blame them. Almost four years earlier, with Anthony Cross as their pedestal, they had been elevated to the top of their profession without fully understanding that science was a pursuit as unforgiving, as critical, and as arbitrarily judgmental as any in the worlds of modern art or fashion. For the legendary fifteen-minute interval, they had shared the fame of a Nobel Prize, been photographed, asked their opinions, and then the next year's crop of scientists had eclipsed them by going that extra step farther—science progressing like a squad of soldiers storming a beach, each given a chance to be first, to gain an extra foot of sand, before falling on the barbed wire to be used as a stepping-stone by the next in line.

Occasionally there might be one worker whose star shone a bit brighter than the others', a Feynman or an Oppenheimer or an Einstein, who would be remembered with kindness and respect, in public. But privately, when no one not of the inner club could overhear, the other sage and noble practitioners of modern science were as caustic and as cruel as any high school clique. Kwong was an experimental physicist, Weinstein a theoretical physicist. So great was the division between them, Neale was surprised the two men hadn't drawn pistols and shot each other by now.

"Anthony will wonder where we are," Kwong said, breaking the silence of the past few minutes in the suite's main room. He sat in an overstuffed white chair, hands folded between his knees, far from the matching couch where Weinstein nestled, clutching a crystal tumbler of scotch. Both men avoided looking at each other.

Neale walked across the soft broadloom to the windows overlooking the sea. From the roof of the Malibu hotel, she knew that the remote white streak of SHARP could just be seen to the north. But Cross had never shown an interest in this hotel so Covington had concluded it would be both convenient and safe for the team to assemble here.

"It won't be much longer," Neale said, checking her watch. But Kwong was right. The last thing any of them needed to do was alarm or disturb Cross. She wondered what was keeping Covington, or who.

Neale had never been let in on the full membership of the Cathedral team or the identities of its backers. There were Kwong and Weinstein, of course, who had first brought Cross to Covington's attention even as Neale had tried to shelter the scientist within the anonymity of his Harvard professorship. There were herself and Covington, and at least three others of whom she had no idea. Plus however many there were in the LAPD responsible for distancing Cross from his crimes. Covington maintained it was safer that not all of Cathedral's organizational details be shared in order to limit possible testimony in the future. In establishing the grounds for such strict secrecy, he always emphasized that the industrial consortium that had created the Cathedral Three project was operating in complete violation of several antiquated antitrust laws. In any event, that secrecy would evaporate as soon as they all assembled to begin the next phase of the project.

The door chime sang out the first fifteen notes of "Ode to Joy." It was Covington and a fifth member of Cathedral. Though Neale had not expected to recognize any other member of the team, she knew who the man with Covington was and she could see Covington read with enjoyment the shock on her face.

"I believe you've already met," Covington said as he closed the door behind him, the furtive movement of a man with too many secrets. "Charis Neale, David Paine."

"Which branch of the government are you with now?" Neale

asked sharply, seeing new layers of subterfuge appear behind all of Covington's actions since SHARP was founded. But she did not extend her hand to Paine as she had the night they had first met, at the reception after the prize ceremonies. That night, David Paine had been the American ambassador to Sweden, so eager and anxious to help her believe that Covington's offer to Cross was worthwhile.

Paine's reply was as unexpected as his presence. "I left public service three years ago, Dr. Neale. I'm a consultant, now. Under contract to Shannon Industries, among others." He kept his own hand extended. "I believe that means we're working together on this."

Neale turned away. "And what is 'this,' Parnel? I get the sudden feeling that your altruistic interest in science has expanded into other areas."

"Such as?" Covington asked.

"Him!" Neale said angrily. Paine was still as white-haired and handsome and tanned as he had been at their first meeting in Stockholm, but she saw him now as the revelation of an almost four-year-old lie. How had she managed to convince herself that Covington's interest in physics and in Cross's work had been legitimate, that Cathedral was a combined *industry* R&D program? Had she been that desperate for escape and security? Perhaps, for Cross's sake, she had to be.

"What's the problem, Dr. Neale?" Paine was not wasting any of his graceful manners on her this time.

"You are, Mr. Ambassador."

"I told you, I withdrew from—"

"That's right, you're a consultant. For what? The Pentagon? CIA? OCI?"

Covington took on the same tone and manner as Paine.

Christ, Neale thought, *how long have they been in this together?"*

"I can see what you're getting at, Charis, but you're wrong. David is completely free of any government connections. At least in this matter. I can't be sure about his other clients or projects."

"Oh, spare me. After all the garbage we've been through and now you're telling me Anthony's so protected he could just as well have gone up into a bell tower with an Uzi and—"

"Charis!" Covington's shout was like a gunshot in the room. "We are here to discuss Anthony's *work*. Not Anthony." Neale glimpsed a

rage in his eyes that she had never seen before. Never even suspected. What other secrets was he hiding?

There was a rasping of fabric from the couch as Weinstein shifted his position. "Could someone tell me what the hell you people are blathering about?"

Covington looked relieved by the interruption. "David, may I introduce Adam Weinstein. He works with us at SHARP."

"Yes, of course," Paine said smoothly, slipping into his ambassadorial guise. "We met in Stockholm."

Weinstein kept his hands wrapped on his now empty glass, following Neale's lead in not shaking hands. "And you're part of Cathedral as well?"

"See how obvious it makes everything, Adam?" Neale broke in. "SHARP has been a setup from day one. Just so the government can get direct access to the military applications of Anthony's work."

Weinstein nodded. "Should be a lot of them."

"Oh, really? Such as what?" Paine asked, wide-eyed with all the innocence of a hungry shark.

Covington gripped Neale's forearm tightly as he stood beside her, silently warning her not to interfere. She reluctantly decided that whatever this sudden escalation of interest in Cross's work meant, it had gone beyond her ability to control it, for now.

"Well," Weinstein said, scratching at a pendulous earlobe, "are you talking tactical or strategic?"

Paine glanced at Covington. Covington nodded in encouragement. "Suppose you start with whatever's more likely," Paine said.

"Defensive systems first, I suppose," Weinstein began. "With gravity generators scattered across the country, even other parts of the world, you could alter the gravitational landscape." He saw Paine blink at him, not really understanding. "The force of gravity varies all over the planet. You'd probably weigh a half pound less at the equator than you would at either pole because at the equator you're farther away from the center of the earth. And it's stronger over islands, weaker over the oceans. Different land formations, mineral deposits, all that sort of thing affects it locally."

"And how do those conditions lend themselves to a gravity generator being a defensive system?" Paine asked.

Weinstein appeared annoyed by the man's ignorance. He spoke

quickly, getting through unpleasant history before turning to his more exciting creative thoughts. "Incoming missiles and bombers have maps built into them so they can recognize significant local gravity anomalies which help them know they're on course. Put a few unexpected gravity fluctuations under their flight paths and they'll lose track of where they are. Fly blind. Our birds would self-destruct if they couldn't find their target."

Neale groaned in frustration and ignored the way Covington squeezed her arm. "Excuse me, gentlemen, but isn't the cold war over? Where's the market for a system like that?"

Paine smiled condescendingly. "The cold war is over for now, Dr. Neale. But some of us must look to the future. In the next five years, perhaps Libya or Iraq will have perfected the delivery systems for their nuclear stockpiles. In the next ten years, perhaps the Russian Republic will collapse to be followed by a return to a more belligerent stance. In twenty years, it could be China. In thirty, perhaps even Japan. To stay at peace, we must prepare for war."

Neale was astounded. How could Covington say that the government wasn't connected to this?

"Course, bombers could still get through on visual sightings," Weinstein continued, staring up at the ceiling as if talking to himself.

"And enemy missiles could lock onto one of our own NavStar satellites, determine their exact location from the NavStar's positional signal, and then locate their target independent of onboard maps," Kwong added enthusiastically. Neale felt Covington's grip tighten even more as she began to protest Kwong's entry into the discussion. Kwong and Weinstein, like so many others in their profession, didn't realize that this was suddenly more than an intellectual challenge or a "what-if" game.

"I read a lucid paper about targeting algorithms," Kwong began, but Weinstein cut him off.

"We're talking about hardware, Lee. Things we can do with Anthony's gizmo." He chewed his lip. "Gravity bomb would be good."

"How would that work?" Paine asked.

"Depends how big you built it. It would destroy itself, of course, like the satellite X-ray lasers pumped by a nuclear warhead, but I imagine a gravity bomb would just suck everything into itself, like an implosion."

Kwong jumped up from his chair, hands shaking with creative excitement. "But you'd have to make sure you didn't form a singularity," he said urgently. "There would have to be strict operational restraints."

"Of course, of course," Weinstein agreed.

Neale felt trapped in a slow-motion dream. Weinstein and Kwong acted as if no one else were in the room, as if they were discussing energy levels in electron shells or the merits of different brands of tires.

"What would happen if a singularity formed?" Paine eagerly kept the conversation alive, consumed by fascination.

Weinstein laughed. "Oh ho. Then you've got a black hole. It would keep sucking matter in even after the generator was destroyed. Self-sustaining. At least over the short term if Hawking's right."

Kwong nodded rapidly. "Fall straight through to the center of the earth."

"Swallow up the core," Weinstein agreed.

"Planetary destruction in about . . ." Kwong looked at Weinstein. "How big would the black hole be?"

Weinstein rubbed at his nose in thought. "Say, ten to the minus ten centimeters? That would be reasonable for a piece of equipment patterned after the lab's accelerator and that you could transport in a plane."

"In that case . . . the planet would start to break up in about four years," Kwong said happily.

Paine's eyes were wide with amusement and something else Neale couldn't quite identify. Something that looked frighteningly like the sexual hunger that had once consumed Weinstein.

"This is insane," Neale blurted, despite Covington's armhold. "How can you even think of telling *him* something like *that?*"

Kwong was startled by the question. "It's just an extrapolation, Charis. There is no upper limit on the hydrogen fusion bomb, after all. Both theoretically and technically it is possible to build one large enough to also annihilate the planet. But so far no one has suggested building one that size."

"So far," she repeated, amazed at how matter-of-factly he stated it.

Then Weinstein laughed again. "What am I saying? Transport in a plane? Good God, you could build a gravity generator bomb any size, stick a few smaller generators above it, nullify its mass." He slapped

Paine's knee as he worked the thought out. "Hell, the payload wouldn't weigh anything!"

"It would still have inertia, Adam," Kwong cautioned.

"Then you could accelerate it through a . . . a . . . linear accelerator which used gravitational fields instead of electromagnetic ones, like the way electrons are accelerated in the . . ." His eyes popped wide, his mouth opened.

Paine leaned over in concern. "What is it?"

"No limit," Weinstein said.

"You'd have to build it in space," Kwong added.

"Wouldn't cost anything to get the parts up there," Weinstein said.

Paine smiled, bemused by the rapid conversation. The two physicists responded to each other as if they read each other's mind. But it was just the logic of science, unfettered by the demands of morality. "What are you talking about, gentlemen?"

"A gravity accelerator," Weinstein said. "Get a ship to near light-speed." He shook his head. "Wonder how you'd stop it?"

Kwong sat down on the couch on the other side of Paine. "You wouldn't need a gravity bomb then, no."

Paine turned to the younger of the two. "Why's that?"

Kwong smiled, eyes dancing with delight. "Build a smaller gravity accelerator that would work in the atmosphere. At even a fraction of lightspeed, a BB pellet would have enough kinetic energy to bring down a missile."

Weinstein tapped Paine's knee again and the man turned back to him. "Yes, but, build a gravity accelerator in space and a ten-kilo rock could take out a city."

"Atmospheric friction?" Kwong asked.

"At half-lightspeed, it would only be in the atmosphere for . . . ten times three to the minus four seconds," Weinstein replied.

"Longer than that if the trajectory's angled, but you could always clear a path with a powerful enough laser," Kwong conceded. He patted Paine's other knee to get the man's attention again. "If Anthony's device works, generating power for such things will not be a problem. There will never again be an energy crisis."

Paine smiled grandly at that and put his hands on both physicists' shoulders. "I have to hand it to you two gentlemen. When you came to Parnel ten years ago and told him that Cross was someone to watch out for, who could have known how true those words would become and how magnificently his promise would be fulfilled. I can't help but feel that all of the success we are on the brink of achieving today, is all, in the end, because of you two forward-thinking men. I think you can count on everyone involved with Cathedral being properly appreciative in the days ahead."

"If Anthony's device works," Weinstein said, unconvinced.

"Well, that's what we're here to find out, aren't we, gentlemen?" Paine stood up, obviously hoping to forestall any more discussion between the two.

Throughout the calmly surreal exchange of planetary destruction and almost inconceivably powerful technologies, Neale had come to realize that despite all he had done for her and Cross, Covington had used them in the worst way possible. Neale's dream of complete anonymity was lost forever to her now. She could live with that, but she knew that Cross could not.

"What about it, Parnel?" Paine asked as he left the couch. "When do we actually get to see this forerunner of quantum technology?"

Neale finally pulled away from Covington's relaxed grip. "You bastards! You even gave it a name. How long ago? Ten years ago when Anthony was just a kid in the desert? Or longer? How long have you been looking for someone like Anthony. Good God, how many others do you have who are like him?"

Covington's eyes were like ice. "Charis, none of this has been undertaken lightly. The world—this country, is filled with psychopaths who kill believing that some grand work is being pursued with each death and that eventually some miraculous conclusion or . . . transformation will take place. And for the most part, few of those psychopaths can function normally in the ordinary world. But Cross doesn't function in the ordinary world to begin with—he functions in quantum physics and mathematics and . . . other dimensions, other modes of existence. His . . . problem . . . does not appear to affect his work in those areas."

"Problem . . . ?" Neale whispered in disgust.

"Indeed, it seems not to be a problem to him. It seems to help focus his mind. Help him concentrate, as if the acts he commits work like drugs or something similar for him."

"His . . . inspiration." Neale began to feel herself tremble. Covington was twisted and sick and . . . no different from Cross. And, dear God, she was part of it, too. Just as much a part of it.

Covington tried to reach out to her but she pulled away. "So in Anthony's case, perhaps for the first time in history, we have a classic psychopathic murderer who truly *is* progressing in a great work. And he is on a breakthrough that literally could transform the world. Believe me, Charis. There is only one Anthony Cross. And I just thank God that he's on our side."

Neale could say nothing. Covington turned to Paine. "And to answer *your* question, David: early tomorrow morning, when we know that Anthony has left the facility, that's when we'll be able to run a demonstration for you."

Paine looked at Neale. "I am not with the government, Dr. Neale, no matter how much you want to believe that I am. And while there are many possible applications of Anthony's work that might be of interest to the government—"

"Try, 'the military,' " Neale said softly.

Paine accepted her comment. "Obviously, the military. I can certainly concede that gravity bombs sound like something they'd be interested in." He turned to acknowledge Kwong. "Provided they're built small enough, of course."

That set Kwong off again. "Small enough or incredibly large," he said quickly. "Yes, you see, small enough and the singularity is not self-sustaining. At the critical size range, it *is* self-sustaining. And then, if you exceed that range . . ."

"Nonsense," Weinstein said grumpily, reading his coworker's mind again.

"Guth at MIT has prepared a whole series of elegant papers—"

"With no possibility of experimental confirmation."

Paine smiled. They were at it again. But he didn't necessarily want to hear them go on any longer.

"Excuse me, please," he said serenely, a parent breaking up his children's squabble. "Tell me, Lee, what happens if the critical range is exceeded?"

"The spacetime curve becomes so great that the black hole cuts itself off from all possible dimensions in the universe and . . . pops out someplace else," Kwong said. "In fact, Guth has conjectured that it might be possible to actually use the process to re-create the first moments of the universe's beginning—"

"And destroy this one in the process," Weinstein muttered.

"*Without* destroying this one because the newly created envelope of spacetime couldn't exist in our continuum. It would literally expand into directions which don't exist in our universe so it would . . . appear in some other manifestation of superspace and . . . create a brand-new, completely independent universe of its own. With enough mass compressed into a volume small enough and hot enough, theoretically it is possible."

"Multidimensionalist nonsense!"

Paine held up his hand. His diplomatic ploy hadn't worked. "Adam, please. Let's complete the discussion after we've seen Anthony's experiment. Until then, all this talk about . . . creating new universes, well, it's all pretty much hypothetical, isn't it?"

"It's not hypothetical," Weinstein said tersely. "It's nonsense. Is now and will be later."

"Is not," Kwong grumbled.

"It *is.*"

Covington stepped into it. "Lee, Adam, let it go. We've got too much work to do in the here and now." He went over to the bar. "Let's have a drink," he suggested. "A toast."

"He poured scotch all around. Neale refused, sticking with Evian, still dreading how she would have to face Cross after all this. He'd know something had gone wrong just by looking at her. And she knew she couldn't stand up to his questioning. She couldn't resist doing anything he asked of her.

Covington held his glass up. "Gentlemen, Charis, to the dawn of a true new age. Of science and not of superstition."

"To quantum technology," Paine added.

Neale held up her own glass. "To Anthony Cross," she said.

She found their sudden hesitation gratifying.

NINETEEN

"Chaos," Cross said. He pointed to the rippling arcs of light playing across the tabletop. They came from a flickering candle flame, dancing erratically in a small red glass set at the side of the table he shared with Duvall.

"It appears to be a very simple system," Cross continued, the shifting light reflected in his eyes. "A wick, the wax, combustion with atmospheric oxygen, resulting light modulated by passage through the glass of the candle holder, yet it's inherently unpredictable. The best computer in the world, the best computer imaginable, could not predict the pattern this light will take from moment to moment." He smiled at Duvall, as warm as the candlelight. "It's the secret of the universe."

"Sounds messy," Duvall said. She might have been isolated on a mountain with Cross, alone in the desert. His presence overwhelmed everything else; the restaurant, the other diners, the things she had yet to talk to him about.

"But it's what makes the universe so full of possibilities, gives us what free will we have, or at least lets us think that we have it." He leaned forward over the table. His plate of vegetables had long gone.

Only his water glass and Duvall's glass of wine and cup of coffee remained. "Do you know about Isaac Newton?"

"The apple on the head guy? Discovered gravity."

Cross smiled again. "Fair enough." Duvall had lost any inhibitions about displaying her ignorance about his field. He never once through the evening had shown impatience with how little she knew. "He did write once that his thoughts on gravity were 'occasioned by the fall of an apple.' And he didn't technically discover gravity because it was here all along. But he was the first to describe it mathematically, to reduce its gross effects to equations. Anyway, the thing about Newton's work is that at the time it seemed to confirm what some philosophers had believed anyway, that the universe was as predictable as a piece of clockwork. With Newton's equations as a guiding light, some people thought that in time the entire universe would be seen to be completely deterministic."

Duvall shook her head.

"That everything in the universe, from the movements of the planets to the smallest decisions of each individual person could be predicted," Cross explained. "That each of us was trapped in a specific mode of action as surely as a cannonball must follow its trajectory."

"And you think we're not trapped?"

"By convention and society, of course. By laws, certainly." He looked at the candle flame the way Duvall had seen him stare into the sunlight beneath the wooden balcony. She wondered what he saw. "Some of us, at least. But in the final analysis, we're not important. What is important is that at its most fundamental level the universe is not predictable. Cannot be predictable." He turned back to Duvall, eyes solid with blackness, glittering with light. "And that's what saves us."

"How?"

"By giving us mystery, which we may explore. Must explore. Otherwise, what meaning is there to our lives?"

Duvall said nothing. That question had rolled through her mind in various guises all the long nights she had watched the red numbers on the bedside clock, listening to the slow gentle breathing of her cat beside her, untroubled by his feeder's dark thoughts. Duvall's answer was her belief that one person could make a difference in the world: a belief which she clung to, desperately at times, as a shield against all the mind-numbing despair and irrational violence that policework exposed her to. But in the end, her one small, personal answer brought only other questions. Endless questions it seemed. As long as the night.

"What happens if we explore that mystery," she asked quietly, "only to find that its solution is that everything is predictable after all?"

Cross pulled his chair closer, face alive with intelligence and excitement. Duvall had never met anyone so interested in discussing ideas. Was he like this with everyone, or could it be something which she alone brought out in him, as if she had some special worth?

"You've asked the right person that question," Cross said. "Because modern physics has answered it absolutely."

"I thought there weren't supposed to be any absolutes in science."

"Not in science," Cross agreed. "But nature is full of them. Absolute zero, the speed of light, Planck time and Planck length. All of them irreducible . . . in their appropriate contexts. Science is just a description of nature. An interpretation subject to change. But nature, the universe, is the ultimate absolute of them all. Something, instead of nothing."

His words flowed over Duvall like the unexpected warm streams she had felt while swimming in a cool mountain lake. She didn't know where they had come from or what had caused them to be, but they felt comforting, soothing, and new.

"So what's the answer you scientists have figured out?" she asked. "About why things can't be predictable even if we don't know all there is to know yet."

"There *is* a limit to how far we can see into the fundamental structure of existence." He tapped the table gently with his knuckles. His hands were sculpted by the candlelight. She wondered how they would feel, moving on more than just the skin of her own hands. She wondered about the heat of them, gentle and warm as a candle. "Everything around us is made up of atoms. Atoms were supposed to be indivisible but they're made up of electrons orbiting protons and neutrons. Protons and neutrons are made up of quarks. Over the past seventy years we've gone deeper and deeper, smaller and smaller, but we've finally found that there is a limit. Not because of the equipment we use, but because of the inherent nature of what we call reality. Have you heard of Heisenberg's Uncertainty Principle?"

"I'm not sure," Duvall said and they laughed together, sharing a moment, unique and of themselves. She had a strong sense of belonging. Something she hadn't felt in a long time.

"It's a concept fundamental to modern physics yet very misunderstood. The thing is—and it's been proven a thousand times over by experiment—that at a certain level, we can't know everything there is to know about the characteristics of the constituent parts of matter and energy. Not because they're too difficult to deal with or because we haven't yet invented the technology that can do it, but because at that fundamental level of subatomic particles, what humans call reality is seen to be an illusion. At that fundamental level, the constituent parts of matter and energy don't exist as solid particles or as waves of energy."

"What's left?"

"Probability," Cross said, eyes ablaze like a fire and brimstone preacher's. "Possibility. A chance that something might exist here"—he tapped a finger against the table—"or here"—another tap—"or here. There is demonstrably no way to say *where* a particle is and *what* it is doing at the same time. So what is left, for physicists at least, is what we call the probability wave—a representation of the area of space and time where nothing exists, but where we might find something if we look. Like Schrödinger's cat."

"Who's Schrödinger?"

Cross smiled again. "I sometimes get in trouble for telling this one, so remember it's just a *thought* experiment, all right? No one actually did this."

"I don't think I'm going to like this."

Cross became very serious. "That's the point about science, Kate. It doesn't matter whether you like it or not. Its principles are independent of human thoughts or feelings. At least, they're supposed to be." He held her eyes for a moment, then continued. "Anyway, Schrödinger described an experiment in which a cat is placed in a closed box with a radioactive particle and a sealed glass bulb of poison gas."

"I'm positive I'm not going to like this."

"Inside the box is a device like a Geiger counter which can detect the decay of the radioactive particle, if and when it does decay. If the decay is detected, the device will break the glass bulb and the poison gas will be released. Now, the experiment is allowed to go on until, according to the nature of the radioactive particle, there is a fifty-fifty chance that it has decayed."

"What's the point of this?"

"Finding answers to a fundamental question. After the required amount of time has passed, what do you think is the condition of the cat?"

Duvall had no idea where Cross was going with this one. "Well, if there's a fifty-fifty chance that the gas has been released, then I'd say there's a fifty-fifty chance that the cat is dead."

"That's a logical assumption but, according to some interpretations of quantum physics, wrong."

"What else is there?"

"Probability again," Cross said. "The cat is said to exist as a probability wave, neither fully alive nor fully dead. It only becomes one or the other when the experimenter opens the closed box and looks inside. At the precise instant of that observation, that's when the probability wave collapses and the cat is instantaneously transformed into one or the other. Dead or alive. Brings new meaning to the old song, doesn't it? 'The Cat Came Back.' " Cross smiled like a magician about to open the box to reveal that the elephant had vanished. "According to quantum theory, by the very act of looking, we create that which we look for."

"But that was only a thought experiment, right? I mean, no one's actually done anything like that, have they?"

"Not with a cat," Cross said, excited and enthralled. "Though what a miracle that would be to see. But the principle of observer-created reality has been shown to possess some merit. Look, the smallest bit of light that can exist is called a photon. Early on, the question arose, is the photon a particle, like a baseball being thrown against a wall, or is it a wave of energy, nonphysical, like the ripple of water caused when a stone is dropped into a lake? It was a good question. Fortunately, good experiments could be set up to answer it." He paused.

"And . . ." Duvall prompted. "What was the answer?"

"When an experiment was set up to find out if a photon was like a particle, the absolute, consistent answer returned each and every time was that, yes, the photon was a particle. But when an experiment was set up to find out if the photon was like a wave, the absolute consistent answer returned each and every time was that, yes, the photon was a wave. Whatever was looked for was what was found."

"And a particle and a wave are supposed to be completely different, right?"

"The difference between a sculpture of marble and a hologram of light," Cross agreed.

"Then how can one thing be both? It doesn't make sense."

Cross reached across the table and took Duvall's hands in his. *Too involved in his conversation to know what he's doing,* Duvall thought, *surely nothing more.*

"It is not the photon that doesn't make sense," Cross said, the warmth of his powerful enfolding hands matched by the warmth in his voice. "It's that our conception of reality is at fault. We're used to this" —he squeezed her hands together in his, crushing them, softly—"the macro world of flesh and blood, solid matter, cause and effect." His eyes burned into hers, candlelight flaring to the sun's intensity.

"And this isn't real?" she asked. Her hands wouldn't come free.

"For us, it is, of course," Cross said. "This is very real. But it is built upon the collapse of billions and billions of probability waves, by blind interactions between waves, or even, as Schrödinger and his cat would say, by the simple act of observation by an aware observer." He released her hands. She held them in place, imprinted. "We are real, we are likely, we are . . . full of possibilities."

"And what makes those possibilities into reality?" she asked, slowly lowering her hands to the table, not moving her eyes from his.

"Proper observation," Cross said. "How we choose to observe nature is what determines what we see. What we choose to see determines how we understand nature. And how we choose to understand nature is how we can control it. We must understand the mystery, become the mystery, then become . . . more."

Her heart was racing, trembling, perhaps, with uncertainty, fueled not by his words but by the passion behind them. "Do you understand that mystery?" she asked.

He reached a gentle hand to her face, caressed her, touched his probing fingers to her temple, as if feeling for her pulse, searching for her secret rhythms.

"Soon," he said. "Very soon."

Afterward, they walked along Melrose, beneath the chaos of its brilliant neon, the ebb and flow of other pedestrians, the overlaying mix of music from the passing cars and the open doors of stores and restaurants. At Martel, the clerk at a newsstand played guitar just for himself. Duvall still hadn't brought up what she had wanted to talk about.

"You understand more about physics than you thought you could, don't you?" Cross asked.

His words were like his touch, unexpected and comforting. He knew exactly what she had been thinking. "Were you ever a teacher?" she asked.

"At Harvard," he said. "Before I came out to SHARP. I taught a few introductory courses and had a few graduate students."

"Do you miss it now?"

"Oh, I still find time to be a teacher, now and then." He smiled at her, matched her step, took her arm.

At that she pulled away. His action had not been hidden behind another topic. He questioned her with his eyes. She couldn't answer with her own. But it was as if he read her mind again.

"What do you want to ask me now?" he said.

Duvall walked on for a few steps in silence. Was she that easy to understand? That predictable?

"Cassie Riley?" he asked.

"Cassie Riley," she answered, impressed by his insight, reminding herself that she must not reveal too much to him, yet. "The case." She walked on.

"How is it proceeding?"

She took a breath. She had decided she would tell the truth in response to every question he asked, to hold nothing back, to ask for his help.

"Officially, I don't know. I'm not on it." He said nothing. "I was suspended from the department for coming to SHARP and questioning Dr. Neale. I wasn't authorized to do that."

"I was barred from the labs at Harvard many times for carrying out . . . unauthorized experiments, misappropriating computer time. Sounds like neither one of us can help ourselves when we have an idea."

Again, his reaction had been like nothing she had expected. Perhaps at his level, the normal rules of propriety weren't important. The important thing was to *act* on ideas.

"Aren't you curious about why I came to talk to Dr. Neale? About why I was suspended?"

"I'm curious about everything. And I anticipate that you're going to tell me. Would you like some ice cream?"

Whatever the true nature of reality was, Duvall decided, it couldn't be more unpredictable than this man. They crossed the street to an ice cream store. Cross didn't drink coffee or alcohol, didn't smoke, she suspected he had no sex life to speak of, and at dinner he had asked for a plain vegetarian plate, so she wasn't surprised when he decided not to have ice cream for himself. Though he seemed to enjoy watching her eat it as much as if it had been his own.

"Cassie Riley was not an isolated murder," Duvall said as they sat at a small table on the street, both leaning back against the glass of the store as she ate her sundae. She watched his eyes, straining for a flicker of surprise or fear, anything that might reveal he already knew as much as she did, that he was lying just as Charis Neale had. "Have you heard about it on the news?"

"I don't often listen to the news." A simple statement of fact.

"They're calling him the Boy Scout killer."

"Him?"

"The one who killed Cassie and a hooker in a Hollywood motel."

"Two?"

"As far as the department knows."

Cross pulled away from the window and sat facing Duvall. "And what do *you* know?"

"Nineteen."

Cross didn't react except to look thoughtful. She found no trace of hesitation, no masking. "How do you account for the discrepancy between your figure and your department's?" he asked.

Then Duvall understood. Anthony Cross was too removed from everyday life. Murder wasn't something he could understand easily. Probably he had never been faced with anything so catastrophic in his life. He was treating it only as some sort of mathematical equation, a scientific problem. She wondered how far he would get with it that way.

"Information's being withheld," Duvall said, studying him, judging, searching, aching.

"Is that a usual procedure?"

"Yes and no."

"Indeterminacy," Cross said with a smile. "Heisenberg would be pleased."

Duvall continued. "It is usual for investigators to withhold some pertinent details about a murder so that when and if a suspect is arrested or comes in to confess, the withheld facts can be used to corroborate or insubstantiate the claims made either by the police or the suspect."

"That's a true scientist's technique," Cross commented. "Very sound."

"Except that the various law enforcement agencies are supposed to share their information among themselves. It appears that some of the pertinent details about the Boy Scout's victims have been withheld and are not being circulated. And it also appears as if that's happened in all the other cases as well, which is why none of them are coming up in computer searches."

"What details are being withheld? Or are you allowed to tell me?"

No, Duvall thought, *I'm not.* But she decided she could still tell some of the truth without compromising the investigation. "The actual details aren't important. The fact that they're being withheld is."

"Therefore, you see a pattern developing among the nineteen murders, correct?"

"Yes."

"So you must establish a hypothesis to account for that pattern and then test it." He put his elbow on the small table and rested his head on his hand, a tired boy after a big day. "That's the scientific method."

"That's standard police procedure."

"I know. Police and scientists . . ."

"Seekers of the truth." She licked the last of her ice cream from the white plastic spoon.

"Your mouth will be cold," Cross said, a comment coming out at random.

"It'll warm up," Duvall said, puzzled by the sudden change in topic.

"Yes, I know it will." Cross didn't move his head from his hand, staring intently at Duvall's lips.

She was flustered for a moment, but went on. "So how's this for using the scientific method? Out of nineteen similar murders, only one took place outside North America. A singleton."

"An anomalous datum."

"What would a scientist do with that one?"

Cross laughed. "Most would ignore it, I'm afraid. Attribute it to improper recording techniques. A statistical fluke."

"This one isn't," Duvall said, and meant it. The young woman in Stockholm had looked just like Cassie Riley and Amanda Foster. Just like Charis Neale. She was definitely part of the pattern. "No question about it belonging with the others."

Cross sat up, becoming more serious. "Then that's the one to be studied first, to see if it exhibits any other unique characteristics which might lead to the hypothesis being confirmed or rejected." He paused for a moment, considering his next words. "What *is* your hypothesis?"

She hesitated, wondering how far to go, deciding to hold back. "I'd say one person is responsible for all nineteen murders." Or two people are involved in a cover-up.

"That's self-evident," Cross said evenly. "Can you refine your hypothesis to a single individual?"

"I don't know yet," Duvall said, deciding that the time had come to draw Cross in completely, for better or for worse. She fixed her eyes on his. "I was thinking that maybe you could help me."

"How?" He gave no reaction.

"The way you're helping me now. Asking questions I might not think of. Looking at things in a different way."

The fire returned to his eyes. "It would be my pleasure, Kate. However I can help you, whatever I can do for you, I'm yours completely."

She tried to ignore the undercurrent to his words, tried to keep him at a distance, but his words were not those of a guilty man. She felt her professional barriers crumbling. She thought of vulnerability. She began talking too quickly, revealing her true reaction. "I've only looked at the two local murders closely. Of the seventeen others, I want to focus on the one outside North America."

"A question first. Why are you doing this and your department isn't?"

"When we find out who the murderer is, maybe I'll be able to answer that."

"Ah," Cross said, eyes widening. "You suspect a conspiracy."

"That hypothesis hasn't been drawn yet." Duvall didn't want him to know that she had thought that far ahead. Cross worked with Covington and Neale. Even if he wasn't part of it now, he might choose to be later, however inadvertently.

"All right, then." Cross folded his hands on the table, settling in for a long discussion. "What is the significance of the one foreign murder?"

"Okay. I have . . . one suspect we'll say, that I can place at the scene of both recent murders here. I can . . . hypothesize a motive for one of the murders as well. What I would like to do is see if there is any way I can connect the foreign murder with the same suspect, probably by first establishing that the suspect was out of the States at the time."

"Tell me about the foreign murder. Where did it take place?"

"Stockholm, Sweden."

Cross pursed his lips and nodded. "Americans need passports to enter that country so there will be a record of arrival and departure. When did it take place?"

"Three years ago last December. Almost four years, now."

Cross wrinkled his brow. "What date?"

"December 10."

His mouth opened.

"What's wrong, Anthony?" This time she reached out to him to touch his folded hands.

"That's the anniversary of Alfred Nobel's death."

Another random comment, Duvall wondered, or was it important? "As in the Nobel Prize guy?"

Cross nodded, looking stunned. "I won it."

Duvall felt a twinge of excitement run through her, a twinge of danger. All she knew was that the prize was given to the best and the smartest and that he had just bought her ice cream.

"Three years ago December, almost four years ago, *I* was in Stockholm."

She froze. Dear God, she hadn't expected that. Now Cross was connected to two of the murders as well. She took her hands away from his.

"Anthony, this is important. How long have you been associated with Dr. Neale at SHARP?"

"At SHARP? Just about . . . four years," Cross said, uncertain, unsure.

"Was she in Stockholm with you, Anthony? Was she?"

Cross nodded, face blank.

Duvall sat back in her chair, filled with relief. "How about Parnel Covington? Was he there, too?"

"It's where we met," Cross said. "Why is that important, Kate? What does it mean?" He stared hard at her suddenly, as if making the connection. "You're not suggesting that Charis or Parnel is somehow involved in this? Are you?"

Duvall saw a flash of pain pass through him. He was so innocent, so unprepared. "I'm sorry, Anthony."

Cross stared at the table, he rocked in his chair. "Well, then, you have to suspect me as well, don't you? I mean, that is the rational thing to do. I was in Stockholm. I knew Cassie." He looked up at her, eyes full of confusion, of loss, of tears.

"Are you the murderer, Anthony?" She had never spoken so carefully in her life.

"Of course not," he said, still upset. "But how can you know that? How can you believe me?"

Duvall's heart ached for him. Blessed and cursed by his genius, what did he know of the real world?

"I'm sorry," he said. "I . . . it's just that . . ."

She squeezed tightly on his hands to let him know she was there for him. "What, Anthony? You can tell me." Her voice was low and soothing, the comfort of a lover.

"It would explain so much . . ." Cross whispered. "About Charis. And Parnel."

Duvall hated herself for what she had done. For all the grief she had seen Neale hand out to Cross at SHARP, who knew what he really thought of her? Perhaps he thought she was some type of friend because he had so few. Perhaps, now, he had none. And what more had she unleashed?

"What does it explain, Anthony? Do you feel . . . do you feel you might be in any danger?"

He intertwined his hands with hers, held on as though to be kept from being swept away in dark currents and storm-shattered waves. He clung to her, pulled himself closer, she did not resist, and then there was calm in his eyes once more.

"Not now," he said, his skin fusing with hers in what Duvall finally, explicitly recognized was the first slow movement toward an inevitable joining of them both. "I'm not in any danger at all, any more."

Innocent, she decided as she looked into his eyes and saw only the details, and not the scene.

TWENTY

Anthony Cross remained at absolute rest, perfectly motionless at the center of the universe. The galaxy pinwheeled about him at 630,000 miles an hour, the sun coursed through empty space above him at 43,200 miles per hour, and the California coastline blurred past him at eighty miles per hour as the gleaming white ramparts of SHARP rushed ever closer to him. Relativity. All of Einstein's work. So trivial and simple.

Cross laughed into the morning air streaming by him through the open roof of his speeding car. He knew it now, could see it now: there were no blind interactions of chance and circumstance, the universe existed because *he* observed it, and how he chose to observe it would define it exactly, mold it to become precisely what he wished it to be, just as he had manipulated Duvall, such a complex person, such a simple person.

She suspected Neale *and* Covington, Duvall had told him in all seriousness. Cross howled. "Are you in any danger?" she had asked with concern. Cross screamed into the dawn, banshee wails of glee. And she only knew of *nineteen* murders! *Nineteen!* How dismal the police were. How full of nonsense, how easy to lead. How trivial and simple.

The painfully obvious secret was to know how to observe, to see everything at once, interconnected, a single particle in a single dimension, twisted and folded through infinity, given time by gravity's curve and the illusion of entropy, gathered together in one man's mind, a singularity without bounds, infinity in a finite volume. And Anthony Cross felt that secret closing in on him as he remained motionless, felt its hot breath scorching him, peeling back his blackened blistered skin, exposing him to the final ultimate knowledge of the Beginning as fiery and magnificent as the brilliance of the sun's interior, birthplace of neutrinos.

There were no absolutes in science. But he had surpassed science. What he saw was no longer a description. It was nature herself. He would experience her. He would *be* her.

Nature. The universe. All existence. The ultimate absolute. He, Anthony Cross, would become more than anyone had ever been before. Become all those things. Become everything. An he knew now that Katherine Duvall held for him the key.

He had kissed her as they had parted at their cars the night before, held her close in the awkward fumbling manner that worked for so many others whom he had lured to forgotten places to help him in his Work. He had kissed her gently, hesitantly, showing neither force nor fear, letting her impose whatever feelings, whatever motives suited her. Male and female, he had chosen them because they had chosen themselves, coming with him of their own free will. Until the ropes and restraints appeared. But by then it was too late.

Duvall had been like all the others. She had wanted his embrace. Yet he had felt her muscles tighten as his arms moved around her. She had wanted his kiss, but she had pulled back, uncertain. Simple desires, complex reactions. Perhaps she really did still suspect him. Ah well, when he understood her, he would understand everything. She would become his final inspiration, and it would happen soon.

Cross thrummed with the tension of creation as he pulled into the SHARP parking lot; he felt the excitement pulse through him, the hyper beating of a relativistic heart. Nothing could spoil his plan for him now. Nothing could interfere with his Work.

Except for the cars he saw parked where none should be this early. He drove by them slowly, on the way to his parking spot, reading their license plates to be sure, matching each to the list in his memory of every SHARP vehicle's license. Covington was here, and Neale, and Kwong and Weinstein, even the facility's white limo was parked outside with their cars, not in the garage. SHARP had company.

Cross turned around in the lot and parked his Mercedes on the grass by the main entrance, ready for a fast departure. He knew where they would be, he knew what they would be doing, but whoever they were, whatever they intended, the Work was almost finished.

They were too late.

The pulse of the generators in the next room resonated through Lab 2, bringing the circling electrons within the accelerator closer and closer to the impossible velocity of light.

"Two more minutes," Kwong announced, sitting at the master control console, studying the computer screens. The magnified target of circles and cross hairs was steady on the monitor above him.

Weinstein stood nearby, leafing through a sheaf of printouts, muttering to himself. "This is nonsense," he announced. "Even at four decimal places each electron would gain only enough mass to barely equal the mass of a proton. To go beyond that threshold, even to the point of a *gram* per electron, would require more power than . . . a thousand of these accelerators." He slammed the printouts to the table beside the console. "The little prick bastard's lying to you. You've all been had."

David Paine turned to Covington and Neale. "Is Adam right?"

"That was my reaction at first, too," Neale said. "And it would be right if this accelerator were standard. But Anthony has made modifications to the timing circuits, added some sort of special equipment to the target chamber—"

"Where do the electrons get their energy?" Weinstein angrily interrupted. The old man was agitated, Neale knew, not by what he concluded was faulty science but by what he saw as Cross's disrespectful manipulation of it and the attention it had nonetheless won him. "This is a ten-gigavolt accelerator. It can't produce enough energy for these velocities. And you can't get energy from nothing!"

"Well, not so far," Neale conceded.

Paine smiled. "That sounds intriguing."

"I suppose you'd think so," Neale said.

"And you're not going to explain it?" Paine waited expectantly, but Neale shrugged. She wasn't.

"Vacuum fluctuations," Kwong offered after a moment, looking away from the computer screens. "The foam on the quantum sea."

"Please, go on," Paine said, walking over to stand beside Kwong.

"It's simple," Kwong continued. "It happens all the time. Everywhere. You *can* get energy out of nothing."

Weinstein sputtered. "Certainly you can, for all of ten to the minus twenty-one seconds!" He glared at Paine. "That's one billionth of a trillionth of a second to you."

"It sounds like . . . an exceedingly short period of time," Paine said. Neale could see how he played the scientists like children. They never seemed to realize how he stroked them, alternating his interest and his signals of approval, leading one to continue against the other.

"It's short, but it's a start," Kwong said. "Listen, at submicroscopic levels Heisenberg's principle of indeterminism prevents us from knowing precisely what is going on. Simply put, the inverse of that is that *everything* is going on. Matter and energy are created spontaneously out of nothing at the quantum level, all the time."

Weinstein rolled his eyes in exasperation. "And then vanishing again, Lee. You're not explaining it correctly."

"I'm getting to it."

"You are not."

"I am—"

"Gentlemen," Paine interrupted again. "One at a time please. I find this most fascinating."

Kwong smirked. "This isn't guesswork. It's been recorded in laboratories. Yes, further proof that quantum theory is correct, even though it doesn't seem logical. The fact is that at the quantum level, paired electrons and positrons spontaneously appear out of nothing"—he frowned at Weinstein—"and then, within a billionth of a trillionth of a second later, as Adam has so properly pointed out, they combine again, matter and antimatter, and completely cancel each other out. The net effect is that nothing has happened, but for that brief instant of time, energy *has* been created out of nothing." He tapped the computer console. "You see, I *think* that what Anthony has come up with here is a way to interrupt that process in the middle. That is, he's figured out some way to . . . harvest that spontaneous energy before it can be swallowed back into the quantum sea." He smiled at Paine, ignoring Weinstein. "Yes, according to the few notes Anthony has left around, I believe it's all in the timing. This circuitry right here." He tapped the bare circuit board Daystrom had assembled, studded with a confusing array of large oblong chips and connected to the control computer by its wide ribbon of multicolored wire.

Paine nodded thoughtfully, then turned to Weinstein. "All right, Adam, what have you to add to what Lee has said?"

Weinstein waved his hands as if he didn't know where to begin. "In theory, perhaps that might be a way of generating, or at least obtaining energy, sometime in the future. The *distant* future, Lee. But for now, there is no conceivable way that any technology could operate quickly enough, finely enough, to search at the quantum level for vacuum fluctuations, then harvest them before they collapsed again. It cannot be." He folded his arms, a final punctuation.

"Still," Kwong said softly. "Anthony's experiment works. If not for the reason he has put forward, then for some other, equally unique, and no doubt progressive one."

Weinstein pointed at the printouts on the table. "I say that according to those figures, this experiment can't work."

Kwong muttered something unintelligible and turned away from Weinstein. "Charis, Mr. Covington, you were here. Did the experiment work or not?"

Neale spoke for them both. "We saw the laser beam deflect in a vacuum, Adam. And it deflected the proper amount for the size of the gravitational field that Anthony said was formed by the electron vortex, independent of mass, other than the electrons' relativistic gain."

Weinstein pursed his lips. "Prove it." That was all he said.

"Power levels are over the threshold," Kwong announced.

"Why don't we begin?" Covington said.

Kwong got up and crossed the lab to the large control panel that monitored the microlaser's status. "I'll handle the laser again, Charis," he said. "Anytime you're ready."

"Give us the reference shot," Neale called out. "Now."

The laser drew power and a low rich tone intermingled with the pulse of the generators. Then there was the distinctive pop of the laser as it discharged. Neale pointed to the computer-drawn circle that ap-

peared on the monitor around the quickly fading red glow of the laser
beam, dead center in the target's cross hairs.

"The laser assembly is fixed in position in the vacuum target
chamber," she explained to Paine and Weinstein. "All the optics are
bolted into place. Now, the next time the laser fires, as the beam is in
transit from the emitter to the target site, the streams of electrons will
be brought together, their energy levels transferred"—she looked at
Weinstein—"*somehow,* and concentrated into one stream in a small vortex configuration which should lead to the creation of a point source
gravitational field strong enough to deflect the laser by two beam
widths."

"Ha," Weinstein said under his breath.

Neale typed the key command into the computer, then called out
to Kwong. "All right, Lee. We're set."

The deep tone of the laser getting ready to fire grew louder, but
just as it popped this time, a rough electric crackle echoed from the
metal walls of the accelerator.

The laser beam hit dead center, once again.

"A very subtle result," Weinstein said, not bothering to disguise
his amusement.

Covington leaned over Neale's chair. "What went wrong?"

Neale scanned the computer outputs on the screen. "Nothing, according to this." She called up two more analysis screens, then sighed.
"The only thing I can think of is that Daystrom's circuit board is at
fault. He threw it together in an awful hurry and timing *is* critical to the
experiment. The vortex *must* form while the laser beam is in transit."

Covington looked closely at the exposed circuit board. "Can you
test it?"

Neale shook her head. "Daystrom told me he's not sure what the
operational tolerances are. I wouldn't know where to start."

"Can we call him in this early?"

"Sure," Neale said. "He usually spends weeknights in his office
anyway."

Weinstein stepped forward, grinning happily. "Did you just say
that this experiment depends on a circuit board for which there are no
operational tolerances? Anthony's attention to protocols seems to have
become even worse than when he was at Harvard. You can't take any of
this seriously, can you? He's making fools of you all."

"It worked before, Adam." Neale slipped a small SHARP phone booklet out from beneath the console.

"I'll tell you why it worked," Weinstein said. "It worked because Anthony Cross is an arrogant son of a bitch. It worked because he set up this whole show with a powerful pulse laser. You heard the bang. You felt the echo off the metal walls. Why does the experiment require that? Why not use an off-the-shelf low-level constant output survey laser? Just switch it on, then create the electron 'vortex' whenever you want. If a point source gravity field is created, the beam will deflect for as long as the field exists, and then it will swing back into position. But this pulse laser . . ." He shook his head sadly. "The vibration from the capacitors caused the bolted-down optics to shift. If you had had a constant laser beam, you would have seen it. I thought this might happen someday. Anthony's gone off the deep end. He's bamboozled you, the little lying prick son of a bitch."

Neale kept her response professional. "You don't know Anthony. He would never do something like this in his work. There is no reason for him to try to lie to us. His funding is not related to results."

"Maybe that's the problem," Weinstein said. "You've kept him insulated from pressure and, by the same token, you've kept him insulated from incentive. Why should he lie to you? Why shouldn't he? You've put him in a meaningless situation."

Paine was frowning almost angry. Covington stepped forward. "Anthony has his own incentive, Adam. He wants to be first. That's more important than anything we could offer him in money or perks."

"Besides," Kwong added, "consider this. If vibration caused the laser to deflect, then why did the reference beam hit the target in the first shot? All was the same except for the vortex."

"Lee's right," Neale said to Covington. "This morning's failure could just be equipment error."

"Or experimenter's error," Anthony Cross said.

They all jumped. Hidden by the sound of the generators, Cross had entered the lab unheard and unseen. Neale could sense the cold rage burning in him. His lab was strictly off limits to everyone, yet he had arrived in the middle of a visitors' convention. She realized it would be up to her to contain the damage.

"Hello, Anthony," she said, going to him. "We didn't know where you were going to be this morning and we had—"

Cross ignored her and turned to Paine. "Well, Mr. Ambassador, what can you be doing here? Has California suddenly become a sovereign nation?"

"He's a private consultant to Shannon," Covington said, reacting with the same urgency Neale felt. "To further develop your breakthrough here, you're going to need more than what SHARP can provide. I brought in David to explore other options for funding, serious funding, Anthony. A consortium of industry if we can get it past the antitrust provisions. David is still connected in Washington. He can—"

"Parnel, please," Cross said, a strange mixture of savage restraint. "What breakthrough are you talking about? Adam, you never set foot in this lab. You don't think there's been a breakthrough here, do you?"

"Of course not."

Cross held his hands up empty. "There you go again. The man's a Nobel Laureate. The man is on the cutting edge of modern science." He hissed at Covington like a snake. "The man's so fucking senile he wears diapers and drools and wouldn't understand gravity if a rock fell on his shriveled balls."

Cross's hand shot out and shoved the thick pile of printouts from the table, sent them fluttering across the floor. "Damn you, Parnel. If you want to understand my work, come to *me*. Don't . . . don't soil yourself with Lee and Adam. Maybe, just maybe, they've got one brain between them. But they can't comprehend what I've done here. They can't possibly understand—"

"It didn't work!" Weinstein shouted. "You're a fraud! Always have been! One lucky thought you had! One mathematical synthesis that we all shared but that you published on your own to make sure it became *your* corollary and not ours. You're a cheat and a fraud. An imbecile full of . . . of . . . nonsense!"

Neale felt cold. Cross was on runaway, an unstoppable chain reaction. His explosion would be foul, horrendous, and she was incapable of stopping him. She turned to Covington and saw the same fearful desperation in his eyes.

Then Cross chuckled. He nodded his head like a man finally understanding a complex joke. He went over to Weinstein.

"Adam, Adam, Adam . . ." he said, extending his arm to wrap it around Weinstein's shoulders. The old man tried to slip away but Cross was too young and too strong for him. His arm clamped onto the old physicist like an electromagnet binding to iron. "What a way with words you have. What a way." He chuckled again. Neale tensed as though at any moment Cross might try to rip out Weinstein's throat and drink his blood. She could still see that rage in him.

Cross released Weinstein with a grand gesture. The old man stumbled back. "Tell you what," Cross said lightly. "Why don't I just run this experiment for you the *right* way—no offense, Charis and Lee—and then, after you've seen what it can do, we can discuss it as . . . colleagues. Fair enough?"

Weinstein nodded, his tremor more pronounced, his face white.

"Sure," Covington said. "Whatever you say goes, Anthony."

Cross's eyes were cold, unreadable. "That's exactly right, Parnel. Whatever I say goes. And whatever I *see.*" He turned to Kwong. "Lee, may I ask you to run the laser, please? Exactly as you did before." He smiled at Charis. "I believe your little problem was at the control console. Some of the command lines have been changed to account for the extra equipment in the target chamber. I . . . never got around to documenting them." He smiled at Covington. "My apologies."

Covington nodded without meeting Cross's eyes. "Whatever you say."

"Charis, may I?" Cross asked, gesturing to the chair by the control console. Then he went to it, sat down, and began to type faster than Neale could follow. After a few screens had come up and cycled away, Cross looked up at Covington. "Do you think we might dispense with the reference shot? I think you've already demonstrated that the optics are aligned."

Covington glanced at Weinstein and Neale. "Certainly," he agreed.

"Good," Cross said. He turned back to the console. "Now, I've made a few more refinements in the experiment which I believe should take care of Adam's concerns about vibration caused by the pulse laser." He lifted his face to the ceiling and shouted. "Lee! We'll be firing a continuously lased pulse this time!"

Neale was confused. "The circuits aren't set up for that . . . ," she said just as Kwong called back, "What?"

"Just fire when I tell you to," Cross shouted. Then he explained to Neale and the others, "All he has to do is turn it on as he has before. It'll run continuously now."

"How?" Neale asked. The entire laser system would have to be replaced to give it that capability.

Cross tapped the bare circuit board at the side of the console. "This will take care of it. Trust me." He shouted to the ceiling again. "Now, Lee!"

The low tone of the laser came on more suddenly than before, louder than before. Covington looked to Neale but she had no explanation to offer.

The laser tone grew stronger, rising in strength and pitch until it drowned out the generators, turning into a shriek that made Neale's lungs vibrate in time. Weinstein, Paine, and Covington placed their hands over their ears. Neale grabbed at Cross's shoulders.

"Anthony! What have you done to the system?" She had to scream to make her voice heard over the rising whine. She saw him mouth the word, "Nothing," and then the laser fired.

It was the roar of demons, gut wrenching, the sound of all earthquakes ever. Weinstein lurched to the floor, hands and arms wrapped around his head and ears. Neale looked at Paine and Covington. They were blurred as if her head rested on the sill of a car window, picking up the vibration of rough road. Their mouths opened but she could hear nothing over the sound that Cross had called forth. And it *was* continuous, not a pulse.

Neale looked at the computer, forcing herself to resolve the numbers and images dancing on its screen. The power graph was climbing. A warning alert flashed. The simple point source of gravity formed by the electron vortex was increasing, beyond the scale of the computer to measure. Then the rising shriek exceeded the ability of her ears to hear, leaving only a coarse rumbling vibration in her chest.

Something exploded behind her. She wheeled with the others to see a blinding red beam erupt from the upper metal surface of the accelerator target chamber. *The laser beam deflecting?* Neale thought in wonder. *So small we shouldn't even be able to see it?"*

The beam cut through the gleaming metal skin, producing cascades of sparks that were instantly sucked back inside as the vacuum chamber lost integrity and sought equalization. The beam arced across the high ceiling, torching through the metal supports and light fixtures. Gouts of sparks from heat and shorted wires rained down in radiant fountains.

Back and forth the beam raced, like the mad whipping of an out-of-control high-pressure hose, incinerating everything it touched. Lab 2 filled with smoke shot through with the glowing shafts of warning lights and fires. Neale could hear Weinstein screaming. Kwong was gone. But Anthony Cross laughed, and his laughter resonated with the roar of the laser.

She heard the shriek of metal rending. The long gleaming silver tube of the accelerator's target chamber suddenly buckled near its end. Another section popped inward, and another, sudden sunken shadows forming. She heard the sound of metal ripping. Saw brilliant beams of blue light streak out from the holes and rips of the chamber, all radiating through the smoke from the same central point within.

The gravity source, she suddenly realized. Still growing. Self-sustaining.

"Dear God, no," she whispered, with only one thought forming in her mind as her body felt a lightness, felt like floating, felt like falling into a long tunnel leading to the center of the chamber. The center of everything.

Singularity.

TWENTY-ONE

E ven in scratched and blocky black and white, Anthony Cross was compelling. Kwong, on his left, and Weinstein, on his right, were shadows by comparison, insubstantial, barely distinguishable from each other. But Cross . . .

Duvall stared into those dark eyes on the microfilmed copy of the cover of *Time* magazine, remembering what they had looked like real and in person, on the street off Melrose, when he had kissed her the night before. She couldn't recall Jesse ever having kissed her that way, no matter how much she tried to, no matter how much she wanted to believe that he had, once. There had to be more than that spark, that thrill of electricity and passing current, that bound two people to each other, but Duvall couldn't remember what it was supposed to be. *You're vulnerable, girl,* she warned herself. *That's all it is.* The hole in her heart was opening up to new feelings, new experiences, no matter how much she wanted to remain safe, and unaffected, and predictable.

Chaos, she decided, that's what love was, or at least what attraction was. Two people, a simple system, but beyond the capacity of the human mind to predict. She pressed the advance button on the microfilm reader and the image of Cross streaked away in black and white smears, like her cat chasing dust in sunbeams. She stopped on the contents page, found the cover story's page number, then advanced the film again.

Halfway through reading the article on the team that was to bring Harvard and the nation into the science of the twenty-first century, Duvall felt a hand on her shoulder. She spun, twisted, unthinkingly tried to pull away. But reality quickly returned. She was in the public library on San Vicente and it was only Nogura. He had got her message to join her here.

She apologized for her jumpiness as everyone else in the row of microfilm reader carrels watched her suspiciously.

"That's okay," Nogura whispered. "Coffee withdrawal. I told you they put something in it at the office." He slid a chair over from a reading desk and sat beside her. "So what have you got?"

"I'm positive it's her," Duvall said. She pointed to another high-contrast photograph on the reader. Charis Neale stood in the background beside three blackboards that carried the complex mathematical hieroglyphics of the first part of the Cross Corollary. Neale was four years younger in the photo, but her hair, her shape, and her white outfit were unmistakable. "She's either the killer herself or working with Covington. But she is the key."

Nogura was serious, he kept his voice a whisper. "Is that your conclusion because you worked it out on your own or because you went to . . . whoever it was you decided could help you?"

Duvall nodded, keeping her voice subdued as well. "I had help. An informant. The informant confirmed my suspicions."

"And the informant is . . . ?"

"An anonymous source," Duvall said. "Sorry, but it has to be that way."

Nogura frowned and massaged the bridge of his nose. "I did some checking on my own, Kate. All about the SHARP place. Neale is big time. Two doctorates, widely respected in her field. International reputation."

"So?"

"So, we're not going to be able to bring her down on the say-so of an anonymous source. She's not a receptionist. She's not a Hollywood hooker. She's connected. The task force is going to need—"

Duvall spoke out loud. "The task force?" She felt the stares of everyone else in the row.

Nogura whispered urgently, hunched over his chair. "You can't do this on your own anymore. It's become more than just running down an oddball lead on your own time."

"You believe me, then?"

Nogura sighed. "I believe you have a strong lead that deserves to be followed up to the best of the department's ability."

Duvall nodded. "Okay, that's fair. Now what?"

Nogura studied the picture on the reader's screen. "I've got to take everything you've got to the task force—Seabrook and Erhlenmeyer. Everything."

"What do you mean, *you've* got to take it? Nuke, it's my investigation." Duvall wasn't going to let go of this one easily. She wasn't going to let go of this one at all.

Nogura turned away from the reader and looked down at the floor, seemingly embarrassed by what he felt he had to say, though Duvall couldn't understand why.

"Be real, Kate. You're suspended. Erhlenmeyer hates you. Seabrook thinks you're a pain. They won't listen to you."

Duvall could feel the anger rising in her. Too many people had stood in her way too many times. There had to be a limit, an absolute, and she was reaching hers. She grabbed Nogura's jacket. "Listen to me, Nuke. I've been shit on for being black, for being a woman, even for being a fast-track detective, and I have had it. There is no way in hell I'm going to sit down and be shit on for being smarter than Erhlenmeyer." An old woman in a pink track suit sitting at a reader two seats down sighed loudly as Duvall's words climbed out of the range of a whisper.

"Kate, if you go in there with your Neale and Covington theory, Erhlenmeyer's going to put it at the bottom of the pile just for spite."

Duvall spoke through clenched teeth. "Then at least it will be in the goddamn pile. They'll have to get to it eventually."

Whatever Nogura felt, he kept it expertly hidden. Duvall couldn't read him at all. "You're not thinking. You say evidence is being tampered with. You think someone in the department might be in on it. If that's true, how much damage is going to be done if Neale and Covington are named as suspects but then nobody follows up on them? Do you have any idea how much evidence can disappear in a week? What if they're warned? If you're right about this, and the task force doesn't jump on it ASAP, then Neale and Covington as good as walk." Nogura pulled Duvall's hand off his jacket. "And all because you're so hung up on sticking it to Erhlenmeyer."

The old woman two seats over shushed them loudly. Someone else, said, "Yeah, keep it down."

Duvall attempted to whisper again, but unsuccessfully. "So how the hell are you going to make the task force go after Neale and Covington right away? Or does Erhlenmeyer just automatically listen to anyone with a dick?"

The old woman in the pink track suit finally spoke. "Young lady, will you please keep your foul mouth closed!" Someone else chorused in with, "Yeah, asshole."

"Let's get out of here," Nogura suggested.

"I'm not finished," Duvall said. Maybe if she kept Nogura uncomfortable, he'd be more likely to change his mind in order to avoid confrontation.

Nogura rubbed at his face. "This is how it works. If I take everything you've got to Seabrook, and I mean everything, I can say that I put it together after I got a call from a snitch. I'll tell Seabrook I had some time, the snitch had delivered before, so I took a flier. My name's on all those computer search requests anyway so it'll look good. I'll tell him I put a couple of things together and came up with this couple at SHARP. Seabrook's desperate for some good leads, so he'll follow up on it right away. If it starts to pan out, then he'll come back and ask for more info, and that's when I'll bring you in."

"And Seabrook will listen to me then?" Duvall asked skeptically.

"He'll have to," Nogura said. "He'll have committed the task force. Even Erhlenmeyer won't be able to call it off."

Duvall stared at the screen. Neale stared back from the photo. Arrogant and contemptuous. And dangerous. *I can't make this personal,* Duvall thought. But Neale and Covington could be dangerous to Cross and that did make it personal. But Nogura was right and no one would listen to her in the department. But Jesse was gone. But Cross had kissed her. But, but, but . . . she hated it. She had had enough.

"Oh, fuck it!" Her fist slammed into the side of the reader and the machine clanged as its bulb flickered.

"Young lady, I have had enough!" the old woman snapped. She stood up, drawing the attention of everyone in the row and all the others in the reading area of the library. Other people muttered their support.

Then Nogura stood up, facing the old woman, opened his coat to show his revolver in its holster. The old woman blanched.

"You're interfering in a police investigation," Nogura told her, flashing his badge case. All the other heads in the area popped down to their carrels again.

"Oh, just shoot her," Duvall said.

"Think I should?" Nogura fell into the patter effortlessly. No matter that they were involved in an argument. First of all, they were cops, and they always stood together.

Duvall smiled at the woman. "I'll be your witness, Nuke. You'll definitely be shooting in self-defense."

The old woman sat down. "I . . . I'm sorry, Officer."

"Just don't let it happen again." Nogura glared at her, then settled back in his chair. "So," he said to Duvall, whispering, "you were about to say?"

Duvall sighed. It felt like one of those days when they were all out to get her. "I was about to say that you're right. I don't like it, but there you go."

Nogura put his hand on her arm. "Hey, I don't like it either. But you know this job, half of it's paperwork, half of it's politics."

"And half of it's bullshit."

"I think I already said that." Nogura seemed more relaxed now that agreement had been reached.

"So," Nogura said. "I can pick up all your files and notes at your place?"

"Yeah, why not?"

"And . . . ?"

"And what, Nuke?"

Nogura glanced at the screen again. "Your anonymous source," he said. "The one who confirmed your suspicions about Neale."

Duvall frowned. "I can't."

"You have to. I need everything."

Duvall shook her head. It would be like betraying a child. Cross wouldn't understand. It would be too confusing for him.

"Look, Kate, I need a name. I have to give the task force something they can attribute the lead to."

Duvall knew Nogura was right, knew his request was logical, but she wanted to keep Cross out of this, had to keep him out of it. *Or the department's conflict regulations say I won't be able to talk to him again until the investigation is closed,* she thought. Was that it? Was that her reason? She wanted to see him again?

"What if they kill again? How are you going to feel then, knowing you might have stopped them, saved their next victim?"

And what if they kill Cross? No matter what she thought of her motives, no matter how much she wanted to see him again, Duvall couldn't risk Cross's safety.

"Okay," she said, and she whispered her words without thinking.

"Do I know him? Or her?" Nogura asked, leaning forward.

Duvall nodded her head. "Anthony Cross." Even his name made her ache.

"Jesus Christ! Didn't you say he was the number-one guy there? How the fuck did you come up with him?"

Duvall gestured emptily. "I've talked with him. I've questioned him. He's not the one."

Nogura was incensed. "You *told* him about Neale and Covington? The people he works with every fucking day?"

"I led up to it, yeah. Look, Nuke, it's not Cross. I don't get that . . . feeling from him." It sounded lame and she knew it. But she knew she was right. She had to be.

"Don't get that feeling from him," Nogura muttered. "Ever hear of Ted Bundy? Ever hear of sociopaths? No emotions. No feelings. Can act like they're one thing when they're really another. Sociopaths make good murderers, Kate. No guilt. No remorse. Nothing to hang a feeling on. And you're telling me you never once thought that about him?"

Duvall hadn't thought that. She didn't want to think that. Cross was a child, not a sociopath. He was a brilliant scientist, not a brutal killer. It was a quantum distinction.

She didn't explain that to Nogura. She sat back and said nothing, trying to figure out why he had gotten so upset all of a sudden. But whatever Nogura felt, whatever he thought, once again he kept his reaction expertly hidden, and for the first time, Duvall found herself wondering what else he hid.

TWENTY-TWO

C haris Neale awoke to rain and darkness. She brought her hand to her face and felt cold drops splatter about her fingers. For a moment, she became confused by memories of childhood fantasies and thought she had been sucked through the black hole in the target chamber and been miraculously transported to another world, another universe.

What are the equations for that nonsense? a more conscious part of her insisted. She opened her eyes. The other world was the ruin of Lab 2: the other universe the whimpering of Adam Weinstein and Lee Kwong, bloody and cowering beneath the contorted metal shell of the destroyed accelerator, hiding from the cold shower of the overhead automatic sprinklers.

Neale sat up. She felt a sudden sharp pain in her left arm, glanced down, saw jagged shards of glass from a broken monitor screen embedded in her flesh. Her blood flowed to the concrete floor of the lab, mixing with the water. Covington was sprawled across an overturned desk. She couldn't see Paine or Cross.

Over the hiss of the artificial rain, she heard footsteps approaching from behind her. She turned. A security guard picked his way carefully through the rubble of the lab. He hurried when he saw her.

"Dr. Cross said there'd been a malfunction," the guard said dully. Cross had apparently not informed him of the "malfunction's" scope.

"When did you talk to him?" Neale demanded, pulling herself up from the debris around her, almost slipping on the soaking floor.

The guard waved vaguely toward the door, still looking around the lab in shock. "Just a minute ago. I heard the explosion . . . saw the fireboard light up . . . and then Dr. Cross came barreling out saying there had been . . . what exploded?"

Neale didn't bother with the man's question. "Help him," she said, pointing to Covington. "Was Dr. Cross alone?" The guard nodded. "Then there's someone else missing in here." She shivered, a reaction to the cold or the blood loss or both. *Singularity,* she thought. How close had Cross come to creating one? How powerful had his point source of gravity been? How close had Paine been standing to the target chamber when it imploded? Would she find him in there, compressed into a bloody ball of condensed flesh and crumbled bone?

"Charis, are you all right?" Paine asked. He emerged from behind a curved section of metal wall which had torn loose from the doughnut of the accelerator. Blood streamed down from his white hair. His tanned skin was pale.

Neale shook her head, heard Covington moan as the guard helped him to his feet. "I think we're all all right." Even Weinstein and Kwong were rising from their sheltered position.

"What happened?" Paine stared at the place where the target chamber used to be. The metal of the chamber resembled a large ball of crumpled foil. Water drops splattered on it from the sprinklers in a cascade that sounded like rain on empty oil drums.

"Obviously, Anthony managed to increase the power output of his artificial gravity field," Neale said dryly.

"By how much?" Paine asked, not taking his eyes off the remnants of the chamber.

Neale shook her head. "A factor of a hundred, a thousand . . . I'll have to check the computer data, if they make any sense."

Paine looked to the floor of the lab. There were bits of computer strewn all about. "I don't think the computer's going to tell you much."

"All the data is dumped directly into the central system and the main core is on the other side of the building. It will have readings on everything up to the moment the network connections were severed."

"Are we going to be able to duplicate this?" Paine sounded eager, a child in a toy store.

Neale had had enough. "Duplicate this? Duplicate this? Do you have any conception what almost happened here? Cross created a singularity in there! A black hole! You heard what Lee said back at the hotel. If it had become self-sustaining it would have fallen through to the center of the earth! It would have consumed the planet! And you want to duplicate it?"

Paine looked at her, apparently puzzled by her reaction. "Under controlled conditions, of course, Doctor. I—"

Neale turned from him. She couldn't hear anymore. She picked her way through the rubble and left the lab, ignoring Covington calling behind her.

The skylights of the corridor were blindingly bright after the emergency battery lighting of the lab. Neale had to stop and shade her eyes. Her left arm stung as she moved it. Away from the rush of the sprinklers she realized her ears were ringing. Her clothes were soaked. Her body ached. She stumbled to the wall, leaned back against it, slid down to the floor. But she would not give in to tears.

When Covington came out from the lab, she had twisted her left arm around and was pulling the largest pieces of glass out, one by one, in deep concentration. Covington sat down on the floor against the opposite wall, breathing deeply. He shook his head, trying to clear water from his ears, or the sound of the explosion, still echoing. Down the corridor, where the security doors were open, Neale could see a milling group of early employees being kept back by another security guard. Far in the distance, she thought she could hear fire sirens.

"I'm sorry," Covington said, then coughed. "About Paine. He's an ass. But Anthony . . ." He laughed weakly. "The boy's a bloody genius, isn't he?"

Neale pushed a thick strand of wet hair off her forehead. The lab was in ruins, the equipment destroyed. They were all lucky to be alive. What could she do but laugh herself?

"Any idea how he managed to pull that off?" Covington asked, still coughing, still laughing, mostly from shock and exhaustion.

Neale lowered her left arm beside her, gently dropping it to the floor. "Has to be some sort of equivalent to fission or fusion. He got far more energy out of the equipment than those generators put into it. He's tapped into something new."

"Vacuum fluctuations? The quantum foam?"

"We know that energy is there," Neale said. "It's just a question of the techniques and the technology to get it out."

"And he's done it?"

"I think so." Neale leaned her head against the wall, shut her eyes. "And now you're going to give it to Paine to turn into vacuum bombs and God knows what other horrors."

"Paine won't do that."

"Then his bosses will. The Army, or the Air Force, or the whole Pentagon."

Covington's voice was tired. "Paine is a consultant. *I'm* his boss. He has contacts in Washington, which is why I brought him in two days ago. Look at me, Charis. I'm sorry I did bring him in."

Neale opened her eyes again and stared at Covington across the corridor. The fire sirens were louder. "Paine isn't part of the Cathedral Three?"

"How many times do I have to tell you? Cathedral is an industry consortium. It's just the people who are needed to keep Anthony Cross happy and working. On the science end, there's you and Lee and Adam, and on the . . . other end . . . well, it's probably better for you not to know. That boy leaves a lot of loose ends lying around."

"But not Paine? Not the government?"

"Jesus, Charis. My bottom line is the thing you hate about me, remember? I'm a businessman. I want to make money. If Anthony was doing any of this for the government, he wouldn't even be able to patent it because of military restrictions. None of this could be published."

"Published?" Neale asked in disbelief. "Parnel, if Anthony had formed a self-sustaining black hole in there . . ."

"I know, I know. But there's got to be something in all of this we can share with the world. A new energy source. New communications. Cheap transportation. Something." His voice became stronger, stirring. "This is going to change the world, Charis. This is what we all hoped for when we saw the direction Anthony's work was taking. I won't let it be locked up by Washington, and I won't let it stay hidden because it has a downside."

Neale's sudden cackle echoed in the hall. "Planetary destruction! A downside?"

"You know what I mean," Covington said sharply.

The doors to the lab swung open again. Paine and the security guard came out. The blood from Paine's head wound made half his face a grotesque mask, but he ignored it. Something else was more important. He went to Neale, then spoke to the guard.

"Describe what you saw Dr. Cross carrying."

The guard was still unnerved. He spoke hesitantly. "It was, like, about the size of a big book, but thinner." He sketched a shape in the air with his hands. "A green board with all these black rectangles, like, stuck on it. And it had this ribbon thing coming off one side, all different colors—"

"That's the timing circuit Rich built," Neale said.

"Thought so," Paine agreed. He thanked the guard and told him to go and get a first aid kit. "We couldn't find it in there. That must be the secret to what Anthony has done. All in the timing. And he's made off with it."

"It was built by the head of SHARP's computer division," Covington said, pulling himself up with a sigh. "We can make another."

"Good, good," Paine said. He looked down at Neale. "How soon before you can start to analyze the computer data?"

"Depends," Neale said bitterly. "You need it before or after I bleed to death?" She lifted her arm, glossy with dark blood. She felt light-headed and so cold.

Paine was instantly down beside her, making a tourniquet with his tie. "Scientists," he complained. "Never know when to stop when something interesting is going on, do you?"

Neale couldn't say anything. She felt too tired.

"Charis?" Covington asked gently, kneeling beside her. "We don't need to rush on the computer data." Neale saw him exchange an unspoken communication with Paine. "But I have to ask: is there any way Anthony could have modified any other part of the equipment other than the new timing circuit he had Rich build? Power leads, wiring, anything?"

Neale shook her head. "He usually fiddles around with everything in the lab, but I'm sure he hasn't been in there in the past few days without either me or Lee being with him. The only thing that's been added since the first round of experiments was the new timing circuit. That has to be it."

"Okay, okay," Covington said gently. "Just so we know there're no more surprises waiting for us in there. It would be hard to tell by now, anyway."

Neale tried moving her arm against the pressure of Paine's tourniquet, but she couldn't. Her muscles felt numb. "Where are Lee and Adam?" she asked. "I thought I saw them in there." She suddenly found herself feeling very tired.

"They're in there," Paine said. "I've got them going through the wreckage."

"For what?"

"Just in case there was anything in there that they didn't know about. Just trying to cover all the bases."

Neale wanted to spit in the man's face but her mouth was too dry. "Parnel, why don't you tell this—"

The lab doors burst open again. Lee Kwong stood there, long hair plastered to his face by the rain from the sprinklers still operating inside.

"What is it?" Paine asked.

Kwong looked stunned. Part of his face was stippled with blood from a wide scrape. "We . . . we found something," he said. His voice sounded odd.

"What?" Paine asked. "Nonstandard equipment?"

Kwong nodded. "Nonstandard equipment," he repeated. "Yes, I think . . . I think you have to see for yourself." He just stood there.

"Well, okay," Paine said impatiently. "Parnel? Charis?"

Covington reached down to Neale. "I think you'd better come see. You're probably going to lose a day or two to rest and recuperation. The lab'll be all cleaned up by then."

Neale grimaced but knew he was right. She let him help her up. For a moment, until her blood pressure equalized, she felt the corridor lurch beneath her, spinning.

"Okay?" Parnel asked.

"Yeah, sure," Neale said. She went through the doors into the lab.

Twenty feet away, she could see a flashlight beam glittering against the wet, twisted metal of the target chamber. She saw Weinstein look up, flashlight in hand. Even at that distance, Neale could tell his face was death white and she felt the first warning thrill of fear. What nonstandard piece of equipment had Cross left behind?

She pulled away from Covington's supporting arm and forced her legs to move faster. When she was beside Weinstein, she could see his hands shaking, the flashlight he held strobing over something in the shadowed ruins of the equipment at his chest.

"It's . . . it's wired into the circuitry . . ." the old man said. His breaths were short and shallow, close to panic.

"What is?" Neale demanded, trying to push by a fallen section of light fixture supports to get around to Weinstein's side. Covington and Paine stayed behind her. She could hear them whispering to Kwong.

"And the wires are . . ." Weinstein looked back into the shadows in the clump of metal before him. "I think they're supposed to be some sort of capacitor . . . I mean, they do have a pattern . . . dear God." There were tears in his eyes. "I mean, there is a pattern in that." He pulled away suddenly, vomiting on the wet concrete floor.

Neale grabbed the flashlight from the heaving man. She thrust it into the gap in the metal, looking into a small section of the targeting chamber still relatively intact. The light from the flashlight hit home. Neale stared at the nonstandard equipment within, seeing it all at once in perfect illumination, but not understanding it, not comprehending it, except in its pieces.

First was the wire, copper, uninsulated, twisted and woven into an intricate half-sphere. Weinstein had been right; the twists and interconnections weren't random, there was some pattern apparent, maybe a capacitor if the proper transistors were in line. But Neale saw only bare copper wire, golden in the beam of her flashlight. On one side, a hundred ends were braided together and spliced into a power cable attached to a metal support post. In the middle of the half-sphere, reaching into the object suspended in its center like a spider in its web, a hundred spikes of gleaming copper reached and snaked and twisted through . . . through . . . what? Neale asked, seeing without comprehension. What?

It was red in places, wet and moist and dark as her arm had been dark, glistening with blood. It was white in places, fragile and delicate splinters, lifted like winter bare trees through a dense ground cover.

She saw teeth, small, fine, and pointed, tiny jaws wrenched open in a silent cry. She saw an eye, sunken, green, inhuman. She saw fur, split down the center, pulled back by the wire, opening the body within to the intricate snakings of wires, interconnections, a pattern.

She saw a band of leather around a small neck, a gleam of a metal other than copper. Neale leaned her head in, smelled the stench of rotting flesh in the crisp surround of modern science. She peered at the metal disk on the leather band, suspended above the yawning cavern of the opened body, each tiny organ intact and connected to the wires, to the wires, and the pattern.

There were letters on the disk, and Neale suddenly knew what she was looking at. There were words on the disk, and Neale suddenly knew that all safety had fled. The probability wave had collapsed completely. The atrocity that was Anthony Cross was revealed to the world.

"What do you see?" Covington asked her. His voice echoed in the confines of the opening in which the mad pattern of flesh and wire hung.

"A cat," Neale said quietly, all emotion gone from her voice and from her.

The words on the disk said, "MISTY RILEY."

Once Cassie Riley's missing cat. Now part of the Work of Anthony Cross.

TWENTY-THREE

I t was over and in a way, Kate Duvall decided, she felt relieved. The case was out of her hands, beyond her control. Nogura had all her files, soon the task force would have her leads, and perhaps she would finally have piece of mind.

"Whaddya say, Briggs?" she asked the fat cat on her lap as she scratched at a tufted ear. "Are we having fun yet?" The cat stretched and turned his head so his other ear came within range of Duvall's fingers. "I forgot," Duvall said, "you're always having fun." She reached over for the beer bottle beside her chair and took the last swallow. It was her third but she didn't care. It was Saturday night and she was finally on vacation.

She burped unexpectedly, then laughed. The cat twisted around, instantly awake, staring at Duvall with flattened ears. "Excuuuse me," Duvall apologized, but too late. The cat jumped off her lap and scooted out of the den. Duvall stared at the empty doorway through which the cat had run. She tried to picture Jesse standing there, dark and beautiful, smiling at her, taking her upstairs to bed, the way things had been a thousand years ago. But all she saw was an empty door, just like the empty bedroom and its empty bed.

She aimed the remote control at the TV set and shut it off. "Catch fire, VHS 1," she said. The easy-listening video station always made her feel old and tired, as if the best years of her life had been ten years ago and there was nothing new, nothing more left for her. She went into the kitchen, brushing Doritos crumbs off her sweatshirt and jeans. The crumbs dug into her bare feet on the tile floor. One more beer, she decided, then she'd have no trouble at all falling asleep. Maybe she wouldn't even dream.

The doorbell rang just as she took another Sapporo out of the refrigerator. She looked up at the wall clock. Eleven twenty-five, Saturday night. Jesse would never have anything to say to her for the rest of her life. Nogura had already been by. One of the neighbors might be in trouble, that had happened before. But she took her personal revolver from the cupboard by the refrigerator and carried it behind her back as she walked through the front hall to answer the door. Screw the world and everyone in it, no matter what else she was, she was a woman at home alone and there were crazies out there, horrible crazies. She pushed the safety off, opened the door, standing to the side, finger on the trigger.

It was Anthony Cross.

He looked windswept, glowing, just off a sailboat in a glorious summer sea. His smile was dazzling. But even through the filter of three beers she could see that there was something more in his eyes than just a friendly greeting. There was something hurt and painful. Or maybe she saw it *because* of the three beers.

"What are you doing here?" she asked, excited and afraid at the same time.

He looked left and right from the porch, at the other small houses crowded together on the steep street. His smile flickered, something else breaking through. "May I come in?" he asked.

Duvall couldn't help herself.

"Thank you," Cross said, pushing the door shut behind him.

"How did you know where I live?" Duvall asked. She felt compelled to drive something between them. The case was still open. All her police instincts came to her defense. What would his answer be?

Cross shrugged apologetically. "Your car license plate."

Duvall tensed. He was lying. "The DMV doesn't give out the addresses of police officers or judges, Anthony."

Cross grinned. "You look so serious, Kate. I didn't ask the DMV. SHARP has an eight-million-dollar computer and some talented programmers. I just asked them to call up the DMV and search the database."

Duvall felt the weight of her gun, still hidden behind her. Why would he lie to her anyway? "That was definitely illegal."

He held out his hands, crossed at the wrist. "Get your cuffs," he said. He held her eyes. "I'm yours."

Duvall broke away from the awkwardness of the moment. "Is there something I can do for you?" Wrong question. "Anything the matter?"

Cross looked over her shoulder. "Am I . . . are we . . . ?"

Duvall took a breath. It hadn't come up at their dinner. She felt like she was stepping through the door of an airplane, an untested parachute on her back. "I live alone. Separated."

"Oh," Cross said, as though innocently realizing that the logistics of the evening had just changed. Duvall was curious about his reaction. Could it mean that he had a reason for coming over other than just to see her? "Maybe I should come back another time." He stepped back toward the door.

"No," Duvall said quickly. She didn't want him to leave. She admitted that to herself. How could he have dangerous intentions if he had expected her to be with someone? She reached out without thinking to take his arm. She still had her gun in her hand.

Cross felt the hard metal brush his arm. He looked down, frowned. "Who were you expecting?" he asked.

"I . . . don't know," Duvall said, slipping the revolver's safety catch back into place.

Cross reached out his hand to her arm, touched her. "I understand," he said. "I'm afraid, too."

They sat on either end of the couch in the den. Cross drank a glass of ice water. Duvall deliberately chose to drink her fourth beer. She wanted her nervousness to go away. Maybe, she told herself, she wanted an excuse, to ignore what she knew she shouldn't.

Cross looked at his glass as he spoke, telling Duvall about Charis Neale's strange behavior over the past few days. And Covington's.

"And there was an accident at SHARP this morning," he said, at last looking up.

"Serious?" Duvall asked, thinking that even in such an ordinary setting, an ordinary house with ordinary furniture, Cross was an extraordinary man.

"Might have been," Cross said. "That big lab you were in, number 2, the accelerator and the laser setup, it's all destroyed."

"How?"

"Explosion."

"Oh, God, that's terrible," Duvall said, meaning it. The experiment she had seen had been important, whatever it had been. Something to tell her grandchildren. "Was anyone hurt?"

Cross shook his head. "Minor stuff. Two associates got a few cuts." He smiled at her. "My ears are still ringing a bit."

"You were there?" She saw Cross in the midst of a fiery explosion, danger and destruction all around. She leaned forward and took his hand, worried for his safety. He must be protected at all cost.

"What?" Cross said, looking at her hand on his.

"I . . . I don't want anything to happen to you." It was what she felt, unedited by good sense or professional caution, released by the alcohol in her system, or by the late hour, or by her heart.

Cross moved his other hand to hers, turning on the couch. "Nothing will happen to me," he said with conviction. "At least, nothing that I don't want to happen."

"Good," Duvall said.

"Good," Cross agreed.

"Was the explosion an accident?" she asked. "Or . . . ?"

"They're investigating now," Cross said. "I think it was. I hope it was. But . . . I didn't want to be on my own."

"I know the feeling," Duvall said, and she did. "So, what happens now?" She saw the puzzlement in his eyes. "With your work?" She smiled. Somehow, she felt that now there would be no more misunderstandings between them. Their words would be their words, their meanings their meanings. It was just a matter of time, and it was already so late.

"My work will go on," Cross said, "to its conclusion."

"What is that?" His hands burned. She looked at them. They were pink and glowing as if freshly scrubbed, immaculately clean.

"To answer the ultimate question."

"The ultimate question?" Her own question punctuated by the pressure of her hands.

"The Beginning. The creation of the universe. All matter, all energy, all stars, all life. The Beginning of everything."

Duvall shook her head in wonder at the man. How could a sociopath have such dreams? How could she consider Nogura's theory even for a second? "How can you find that out? How can anyone? The universe is so . . ."

"Big?" he asked.

She nodded, feeling warmed by his presence. So comfortable, so dreamlike. The things he knew, the things he could explain. She would ask him about anything just to hear the comfort of his voice, the security of his words spoken just to her. She ignored her vulnerability.

"The universe is expanding," Cross said. "Have you heard that?" He shifted in the couch again, brought one leg up, his knee brushed their hands held together. No awkwardness now.

"Yes," she said.

"So tomorrow it will be bigger than it is today. And last year it was smaller than it is today. And a million years ago it was smaller still. So we extrapolate. We run it back, further and further back in time to a point when everything in the universe was condensed together into one place at one time."

"How far back?"

"Mmmm, maybe fifteen billion years ago."

"That's a long time."

Cross nodded, so perfect, so at ease. Her private teacher. "The earth's only about four and a half billion years old. And all the atoms that make up the sun and all the planets around it, and everything on earth including you and me, were formed in the fusion reactions of another sun maybe ten billion years earlier. That sun exploded and some of the matter from it all came together and formed us."

"We were born in a star?" The things he knew.

"And we'll die in one, too. At least, all our atoms will be consumed in the fire of our own sun when it expands into a red giant, maybe five billion years from now."

The room was still and silent as she thought about that. But the concepts were beyond her, the numbers too large. "I can't hold that in my mind," she said. "It's too much."

Cross leaned forward to whisper a secret. "No one can."

She whispered in return. "Not even you?"

He shook his head. "I can . . . see it, but . . . I can't explain it. That's my work, you see, to figure out some way of explaining it so I can use it."

"Is that why you became a scientist?"

He nodded. "To find out things no one has ever known before." His eyes eclipsed the room, the house, the memories of Jesse. "Why did you become a police officer?"

"To help people," she said. "To try to make a difference."

"But how do you do that . . . ?" He leaned closer, as if the secret was growing like the universe, to be spoken in ever softer whispers.

She saw what he meant. "By finding out things that no one knows," she said quietly.

"Scientists and cops. Seekers of truth."

There was something wrong in his analogy but she couldn't stop to think about it now. Things were moving past the time for thought. She could smell him now, his breath, sweet and warm, the musk of his body.

"What do you see?" she asked. "All those billions of years ago. The beginning of everything. Tell me what you know."

A moment passed. "Come here," he said. She slipped across the couch, not knowing what would happen. He moved so that she leaned back against him, her head against his broad chest and shoulder, his arms across her chest, the weight of them crossing over her breasts. He held her hands together in his. She felt him breathe. His voice was like the sound of waves on a night beach, wind through forest leaves. She wanted to know. She wanted to forget. She was tired of fighting. She wanted someone to just *tell* her what she was looking for, what she should do.

"There are four forces in the universe today," Cross said. She felt his head dip to her head, felt his chest move as he inhaled the fragrance of her hair. "Electromagnetism, which is the basis of electricity and magnetism, but—"

"I probably could have figured that one out," Duvall said, laughing gently, slipping one hand free and holding her arm over his. He hugged her, an experiment.

"You probably could have," he agreed. "But what's important about it to scientists is that electromagnetism keeps electrons in their places around the nuclei of atoms."

"Even if you can't say exactly where those places are, right? The uncertainty guy."

"You've got the idea." His breath was warm on her ear, down her neck. "Then there's the strong nuclear force, and that holds together the protons and neutrons that form the nucleus of an atom. And there's the weak nuclear force, which is responsible for radioactivity. And finally there's gravity, which anyone can describe but which nobody can explain."

But Duvall had seen the first experiment in Lab 2. "Except you, you mean."

"Except me, that's right." She felt his arms close around her. "Now, have you ever heard Einstein's equation, $E = mc^2$?" Duvall nodded. "Know what it means?" She shook her head. "It means that matter and energy are equivalent, different forms of the same thing. Think of liquid water and solid ice. Both are made of the same type of molecule, but under different conditions, the molecules form into different states of matter. Same for energy and matter: it's the same stuff in two different states."

"Got it," Duvall said. She relaxed further into him. She felt as if she were floating and she knew it wasn't the beer. "You make a fine teacher, Anthony."

"I know," he said. "Now, just as Einstein proved the equivalency of matter and energy, other workers have also proved the equivalency of three of the basic forces: electromagnetism, and the two nuclear forces. The way it works is that during the very earliest moments of the universe's initial expansion, conditions were so hot, matter and energy so densely crammed together, there was only one force operating on anything. But as the universe expanded and cooled off, conditions changed. And, simply put, just as water molecules can form themselves into steam, or ice, or liquid, the fundamental force broke down and formed into the different forces we see today."

"How early are the earliest moments?" Duvall closed her eyes, not caring if she understood another word. It was enough to be held. It was enough not to think. Just for the moment.

She felt Cross sigh behind her, felt him move so she could lean back against even more of him. "When the universe was about three minutes old, it became cool enough for the strong force to be able to form protons and neutrons into atomic nuclei for the first time."

"And there was light," Duvall said, caught by the concept of a universe only minutes old.

"Not exactly," Cross corrected. "The conditions of the early universe were such that light didn't exist until it was about a hundred thousand *years* old. Then there was light."

"Do they know how big it was back then, at three minutes?"

"Thirty-three, thirty-four million miles across. Wouldn't even reach halfway to the Earth from the sun." His lips brushed her head. She felt safe, melting, wanted him to keep talking so she wouldn't be able to think about what she was feeling, about anything else in her life except the here and the now.

"What was it like when it was one-second old?" she asked.

"It would take up just over half the distance between here and the moon."

"A tenth of a second?"

"Less than twice the size of the earth."

"A hundredth of a second?" The way her lips felt, it was hard to pronounce.

Cross laughed. "I'd say about a diameter the same as the distance from . . . here to Detroit."

"You could keep going, couldn't you?"

"To the size of a grapefruit," he said, and she heard wonder in his voice. "At about ten to the minus thirty-two seconds."

"What's that in real seconds? A billionth? A trillionth? Something like that?"

Cross laughed again. "I told you, no one can keep this sort of thing straight with just words. That's why we need math to keep it all manageable." He stretched his neck so her head fell into the curve beneath his jaw. "That's a decimal with thirty-one zeroes in it which makes it . . . ten trillionths of a quintillionth of a second. Does that make it any easier?"

Duvall laughed. "No."

"Well, add four more zeroes. Ten to the minus thirty-five seconds."

"How big is the universe?"

"Depends whose theory is correct. Could be smaller than a proton. But it's at this time that the three forces other than gravity are all the same force."

"How can anyone, even you," she said, hugging his arms, "know that?"

"We accelerate particles in equipment like you saw at my lab. By causing high-velocity collisions between particles like electrons and protons we can create energy levels similar to those that existed when the universe was up to a billionth of a second old."

"But you created gravity in yours, didn't you?"

He held her very tightly. "Gravity is an illusion, Kate. The others say that at Planck time, five point four times ten to the minus forty-three seconds, that gravity was joined with the other forces, that it was the dominant force of the universe. But they're wrong. Gravity is only a side effect of quantified space. It's the only explanation that makes sense. Otherwise, to explain the influence that gravity has on the structure of galaxies and the universe, there's not enough matter to go around. We have to make up theoretical explanations, like dark matter."

Duvall smiled. "Sort of like me?"

She could feel Cross's laugh move through her and he slowly drew a fingertip along the inside of her forearm, barely touching her skin. "Oh no. You're very real, Kate. Very noticeable. Dark matter is all the mass in the universe which we can't see. Unlit by stars, shadowy, ghost-like. Completely undetectable, except for its actions on the luminous matter that we *can* see. But where dark matter is and what it's made of, no one can say. So I say that it isn't important. I say that gravity is a condition of existence independent of the other three forces. The other forces move within it but they are not part of it."

"How can you know this?"

"I see it."

"And the others can't? No one?"

She felt his arms move over her chest and shocks traveled through her. She never knew she could be so sensitive to a gentle caress. He brought his hands to her head, ran his fingers through her hair, pressed his fingertips against her, pushing, stroking.

"You could, Kate. You could see it."

"No," she said. He felt so good against her. So powerful, so protective.

"I could show you. Teach you. Take you to that first moment. To the Beginning."

She sat up from him, turned to him, heart pounding, body vibrating with a rhythmic harmony to what she felt in him.

"Into the quantum, Kate." His hands moved over her face. She tasted his fingers, not thinking, not wanting to think ever. "Into the reality that underlies it all." His hands touched her breasts, as lightly as soft wind, gentle water. "Into the Planck time, into the instant of transition. From nothing, to something."

She kissed him, hungry for him. Their lips slipped smoothly, tongues tasting, intimations of sharing. "Into the quantum," he whispered, against her neck, his breath moving through the collar of her sweatshirt, over her breasts as his hands moved behind her, holding her, kneading her.

"Yes," she said, knowing no other words were possible. Knowing no other choice, no other possibility than the one she had always known, the one she had never admitted, the one she had always wanted from the first moment she had seen him, beyond all reason.

On the floor of the den, cushioned by the comforter her grammy had hooked while she spoke of guardian angels, Duvall and Cross were uncertain no more.

Cross moved within her, not skipping out, not cataloging and comparing, but enthralled by her, entranced by her, giving himself to the moment of her.

Duvall did not know him, did not know his work, had nothing to gain from her attachment to him, except what she wanted for herself. He had never known that attention or desire, divorced from his abilities and notoriety. It was baffling, a mystery, something which he must understand.

They lay together afterward, quietly, comforting, the contrast of their skin remarkable to him, the luster of the sweat on her body glistening, shifting, reminding him of so many other things wet and organic.

"When did you know?" she asked.

"What's that?" He kissed her neck. Licked her skin. Felt her pulse subsiding within the powerful artery there.

"That you wanted to be a scientist. That you could see things. Know things that others couldn't know."

He stared at the ceiling of her den, rough plaster in a chaotic pattern. Unlike the regular winding coils of copper wire.

"I had a toy once," he answered. "A big ugly green thing that rolled around on huge feet with hidden wheels. It could move forward and backward, bend at the waist, move its arms back and forth like a seal." He could see it in front of his eyes as he spoke, the image unbidden, just there. A dragon's crest of spikes over the head. An imp's grimace, green scales, leopard skin kilt, green plastic driven by two C cells. A plastic medallion around its neck. The Great Garloo it was called, he remembered. By Marx.

"It had about three feet of wire coming out the back with a remote control. The control had buttons for all the movements and a steering wheel for making it turn." Duvall ran a finger across his chest, touched his nipple, exploring his new pale body.

"One day it didn't work. It wouldn't roll forward or back anymore. We couldn't take it anywhere to get it fixed. I was . . . furious." He saw himself running at his mother, running at his mother's friend, screaming at them, with more troubling him than just the loss of a toy. His mother's friend started to hit him and Cross had to go away, to leave the punishment to another part of him. When he came back, his legs were mottled with yellow-blue bruises and he was determined to fix his toy himself.

He rolled over on his side, propped himself up on his elbow. It was important that Duvall know this. "I took it apart. It was glued together, the plastic parts, so it wasn't supposed to be opened up ever. But I used a very sharp knife, scraped at it very slowly. It came apart."

His eyes stared past her as he saw the Garloo split open in front of him. The surprise he had felt, and the power, being able to look within something which was supposed to stay hidden. "It did those three different things: rolled, bent, moved its arms. But when I opened it up, there were three motors in it, and the motors were all the same." Three different actions from the same three motors. He had stared at the insides of the toy for an afternoon, still whimpering with the pain of his beaten legs. There was something important to what he saw.

"I used the controls to make the arm and waist motors move. I watched how they worked, both the same. Then I disconnected all three motors, put them beside each other, started taking them apart piece by piece." They all looked the same, but one was different: it didn't work. He could find out why one was different from the others by comparing it.

"They were electric motors so they had armatures wrapped with thin copper wire." Spun gold, he had thought as a boy. He had found a secret treasure trove that no one else knew about. He could buy his way to freedom with all the gold hidden in the secret depths of his toy. "On the motor that didn't work, there was a little black spot. Some wires had fused together. I unwrapped it to that point." His small hands and fingers as clumsy as sausages. His determination giving him a patience beyond his years. "Cut out the broken parts, spliced the wires, rewound it. Snapped it all back together. It still didn't work."

He had screamed until his throat burned. His mother and her friend had left him locked in his room. No food, no water. Nothing, they said, until he learned how to behave. The boy had had to pee in a plastic firetruck. His legs could barely support him, so sore were the backs of them.

"So I looked at it again. Very carefully." For four hours he had turned the motor over in his hands, looking for something he wouldn't recognize, didn't understand. Four hours as night fell and he heard the sounds from his mother's room, her terrible gasping. What if she died while he was locked in his room? What if no one found him? What if the one to find him was his mother's friend? What if his mother's friend did the worse thing to him? For four hours, he sat and calmly looked at the motors.

"There was a small piece of burned wire that had fallen into one of the gears on the motor. I took it out. Reconnected the wires. The motor worked." In two hours the toy was reassembled. Its plastic shell was held together by tape and elastic bands, but the three motors now worked, the same way, to give three different movements.

"I remember looking out the window later, seeing cars and trucks, thinking of the washing machine, airplanes . . . And I remember thinking that they were all different, but that somewhere underneath them all, there was always something that was the same, and *I* knew what it was." He touched Duvall's peaceful face. "I liked that feeling."

It offered protection. It offered power. It was something he could do in a locked room, listening to the sounds from his mother's room.

"How old were you?" Duvall asked, tracing the line of his shoulder.

"Ten or something," Cross said, lying.

"Pretty smart ten-year-old," she said.

But the boy had been four years old. Beaten. Hungry. Afraid for his life. Yet he had taken apart and repaired his toy. Learned several valuable lessons. Lessons that served him well when the cat had died.

"What else are you thinking?" she asked.

"Thinking of you," he said. His mother had a cat. Fat, old, and orange. Cross wasn't allowed to play with it. He was a bad boy.

"What are you thinking of me?" She put her finger on his lip. He chewed it tenderly, comically, making great gnashing sounds. She laughed. He held her hand, licked her finger. "I'm thinking: I wonder what the rest of you tastes like?"

Her eyes seemed to shudder, to scintillate. Cross couldn't get over how she could feel this way about him yet not care who he was, what he was, which one he was.

"Oh, honey," Duvall said, her voice a whisper.

"I think I have to find out," Cross said. He leaned forward over her, forcing her back, kissing her deeply. Then he pushed himself up on his hands and knees over her, moved down, tasting every part of her. She spoke to him, but her words made no sense. He moved against her, kissing and tasting. Her hands moved to his head, guiding and directing. He was confused, caught up, folds and fissures, wet and dark. The instant of transition loomed, building in the trembling of her muscles as she pushed herself against him.

He wanted a cat and his mother denied him. But one day in the field out back he had found an old tom in a dark corner where weather-rotten wooden crates had been piled against a gray wooden post. Cross had seen the cat's eyes gleam at him from the darkness of the lair, the lure of precious stones in a cavern. The boy had squatted by the entrance to the little hideaway, watching the cat watch him.

The cat was sick, no question. It panted. The inner corners of its eyes were partially covered by a white membrane. Cross came nearer to the entrance. The cat mewed softly, tried to stand but only succeeded in moving a few inches.

Cross pulled away the protective crates. The cat mewed again, tried to hiss, but the boy was able to pick it up and take it to the house and smuggle it up to his room because no one was home and he was alone.

Duvall cried out and Cross felt the world fall on him, the images lost from his eyes. He thought it might have been a cry of pain. Of the boy's pain.

"No, no," Duvall said thickly. Her hands pushed him back. "Don't stop. Not yet."

He kept the cat in his closet, surrounded him with bowls and plates of food and water. When he pushed the water dish close to the tom, a pale pink tongue would come out, stop just above the water, then the cat would sigh and lie down. But he was Cross's cat. His mother couldn't take that away from him. The tom moaned when Cross touched his swollen abdomen, the tom panted, the tom wouldn't eat or drink and his eyes eventually lost focus and were covered almost completely by the white membrane of his inner eyelid. But he was the boy's. All the boy had. All the boy could have.

The tom died as Cross petted him, twelve hours after coming home. Cross kept petting him, shaking, fighting tears, trying to understand. Struggling to understand. Everything could be understood. Everything must be understood.

His green monster watched him from a corner of the closet, painted eyes unblinking. The Great Garloo, three motors the same, three actions, different. Compare and understand. Isolate and define. Control and command.

Three days later, he found his mother's cat in the kitchen. He took it upstairs. It howled and mewed and in the end he had to tie it down in place beside his very own cat.

He was determined. He was driven. He knew what to do with his very sharp knife. He was four years old, and even though it was never intended to be opened up ever, he took his mother's cat apart.

Duvall came with explosive force against him, grinding herself into his lips, against his tongue and teeth. He gasped for breath with her, confused as to the place and time and partner.

He looked up past the angles of her hips, the smooth darkness of her stomach, the soft curves of her breasts. Her eyes were full and wide and soft. "I think my particle's been accelerated," she said dreamily and they laughed. She called him up to her.

"It's all right?" he asked, not knowing what to say, not yet understanding the mystery of her.

"It's more than all right, sweet," she said, moving her hand to him. He grew hard without thinking of it, without calculation. "Now what can I do for you?" she whispered into his ear. "What would you like me to do for you most of all?"

He couldn't speak. He didn't know. Her nails lightly raked him. He was covered in sweat, trembling, torn. "Would you like this?" she asked and he moaned his answer.

The small tiny heart in his mother's cat was still beating when he knew he had found what the difference was. In the tom's abdomen was a brilliant red sac, swollen like a water bomb the size of a baseball. In his mother's cat, in the same place, was a small pale white swelling the size of a golf ball. Cross poked at the tom's swollen red sac with his very sharp knife. A thin stream of pungent, dark yellow urine shot out from the puncture, falling back into the open body of the cat. When Cross punctured the small white sac in his mother's cat, a thin trickle of clear liquid ran out and the heart jumped crazily, then stopped.

Then his mother and her friend opened the door to his room and the friend said something slow and slurred about something smelling so bad and then his mother had screamed, had screamed, had screamed until the boy knew that her throat must feel like his, and then they had started beating him again so much and so badly that when he came back he was in a hospital and they told him he had fallen down the stairs.

He rocked his hips in time with her movements, feeling the heat of her mouth at the center of the growing vortex. The cats lay open before him. The thin stream of urine arced into the air. Mixed with the blood. He felt her finger enter him, felt his climax building. At the hospital they asked him how he fell down the stairs. He fell floating, soft and safe as the whipping belt came down, as the cane came down. Slipped on a shoe, he told them at the hospital, feeling the quake in his hips, the pressure of her mouth, the dead cats and the three motors and all the lightning, all the socks, and going away, to the moment of understanding, the moment of transition, the seat of their souls and their understandings, all the brains and the blood and the lessons and he knew, just *knew*, that the time would come when he would have to take his mother's friend apart to find out why he was so bad and he came exploding torrents of himself into some soft night with small arms that reached to him and comforted him as the four-year-old boy cried over the loss of his one pet, his one friend, the loss of everything, and his total complete ignorance to know why everything had happened to him.

"Shhh, honey," he heard Duvall whisper as he cried a lifetime's worth of tears. "Shhh, sweet child. Everything's all right. Everything will be fine, now."

But Anthony Cross continued to cry. Anthony Cross continued to sob, not for all that had happened but for all that had not. He cried that Duvall hadn't been there thirty years ago. Cried that she hadn't been there ten years ago. Cried that no one had ever been there. Cried that no matter what she said now, no matter what he hoped for now, nothing was ever again going to be all right.

The moment of the possibility had come and gone too long ago. And that moment had passed. And within himself, he was alone.

TWENTY-FOUR

Duvall awoke serenely and peacefully in the morning light, slowly taking stock of her body's gentle aches and pains. She was encompassed by the soft warmth of the comforter and the extra duvet and pillows she had brought down to the den so she and Cross could sleep together, away from the bedroom she once shared with Jesse. The time to think about what she had done would come later, but for now . . . she reached across the tumble of duvet and pillows for Cross, sighing almost in relief. She had slept so well and so soundly. Her body was wonderfully limp and relaxed, a day at the beach, of sunshine and swimming. Cross was gone.

She opened her eyes, blinking in the sunlight easing through the shutters of the den. She heard footsteps in the hallway, heavy, a man's. She decided that was what had woken her up. They were footsteps in shoes. Hard-soled shoes, not sneakers like Cross's. Hard-soled like Jesse's. All peace left her. She pulled the duvet up around her, called out, "Hello?" She wished her gun was nearby in case it wasn't whom she feared it would be.

A man in a suit walked into the den, stood in the doorway, not filling it. It was Nogura.

"Katherine?" he asked. "You okay?"

Duvall was awake instantly. She clutched the duvet to her as she sat up, glancing quickly around for any evidence of Cross still being in the house. But all she saw were her own clothes balled up at the foot of the couch.

"Yeah, sure," she said.

Nogura looked apologetic, but she saw his eyes play over the room as well, instinctively looking for an interruption of pattern and order. "I rang and I knocked. No answer. But I saw your car was in the carport, and . . ."

"What time is it?"

"Six-thirty. About."

"What are you doing in here?"

Nogura looked pained, tired, shaken. "There's been another murder. The Boy Scout."

"Let me get dressed, okay?"

Nogura turned for the kitchen. "I'll put on some coffee," he said.

Nogura was at the kitchen table with his hands folded when Duvall entered. The muscles in her legs protested each step. She hadn't had a night like that for years. Maybe ever. He just hadn't stopped. She poured coffee, but Nogura didn't want any.

"I've been up all night," he said. "I'll have to get some sleep soon."

"So where was it?" She sat down at the table. Perhaps Nogura would simply think that she fell asleep watching television, the quirk of a newly single wife without her husband. She wondered when Cross had left.

"Hollywood again. Apartment on Fountain."

Duvall nodded, feeling an odd excitement. The best odds for solving a murder were always within the first twenty-four hours. They knew whom to go after: Neale and Covington. The odds were finally on their side. But what was Nogura doing?

"Why are you looking at me that way?" she asked.

"I'm not," Nogura said, and turned his head away. "What else do you want to know?" His voice was odd, strained.

"Blond? Built? Same as before?"

He shook his head. The pattern had changed again.

"Then what was the victim?"

Nogura spoke to the floor. "Female. Slim. Five eight. Short black curly hair." He looked at her, into her. "She was black, Kate."

The sensations of the night before fled from her, leaving her with a cold stone weight in her stomach, growing. "You're describing me, Nuke."

He nodded.

Duvall placed her hands flat on the table before her. She could see that it made sense. Neale and Covington knew that Duvall was on to her. So they changed their system. They'd start killing black women who looked like Duvall. Then they'd kill Duvall, making it appear as if Duvall was one more random victim of the Boy Scout, with no connection to the murderer. But they had chosen their strategy too late. Duvall hoped.

"So," she said, sighing, "do you think I'm in any danger?"

"From the killer?"

"Killers," Duvall corrected.

"No. Not from the killers."

She didn't like that qualification. "What's going on, Nuke?"

Nogura looked at her from under a wrinkled brow. "They found evidence last night, Kate. Or this morning. An hour or two ago, anyway."

"What kind of evidence, Nuke?" Fear roiled up in her, ice cold.

"There was nothing in the apartment again. Bloody gauze pads. The tape, the ropes. Things like that, like before. Untraceable. But outside, in the alley behind the building, about a half block away . . ."

"What, Nuke?"

"They found a bag in a dumpster. It had wet bloody bandages in it. Scalpels. Rolled-up surgical gloves soaked in blood. ID tried dusting on the scene. Whoever wore them didn't sweat too much. They're going to be able to get prints off the inside of the gloves, Katherine."

"Well, that's good, isn't it?" But Nogura didn't look as if that was good. "What the hell's going on, Nuke? You're trying to say something here but it's not connecting."

"It's the bag, Kate . . . it's like an exercise gear bag. Red vinyl. Looks like leather. Yellow stripe."

Duvall's eyes widened.

"The name and address card was missing. But . . . I recognized it. From the division tennis tournament a couple of months ago."

"No," Duvall said.

"Yes," Nogura answered.

"That bag's been in my car trunk for months. I just saw it . . . oh, Jesus."

"What?" He pounced on her hesitation.

"My car wouldn't start that day I went to SHARP. Anthony had it towed to the gas station they use. It was there the night. Anyone could have taken the bag."

"Oh." He said it in such a hollow way.

"Come on, Nuke." Duvall didn't know which was greater, her fear or her sudden anger. "If I was the killer, you think I'd put evidence in a bag that could be linked to me?"

"No one leaves evidence around on purpose, Kate," he said quietly. "Unless they somehow want to be caught. To be stopped."

She stood up. "Jesus, Nuke. I'm being set up." Her eyes searched the ceiling as she remembered. "It was a pin in my carburetor. Neale could have pulled it out knowing I'd go to the nearest gas station."

"Living alone, the way you do, are you going to be able to come up with an alibi for the Riley and Frost murders?"

Duvall exploded. *"What!?* Why not ask me for my alibi for the other seventeen murders while you're at it?"

Nogura remained calm. "There's still no proof that those other murders are anything but a statistical glitch, Kate."

Duvall tried to find some hint of understanding in his eyes. "You can't honestly believe that I'm the . . . killer, can you?"

"It's not up to me," Nogura said.

"Then what is it up to?"

"The prints in the gloves." He checked his watch. "The computer will have a match within the hour."

"The prints in the gloves," Duvall repeated angrily. "The prints in the gloves." Then it hit her. "Oh, Jesus, Nuke. We all wear surgical gloves at a murder scene. They could be the ones I wore at Cassie Riley's apartment. I told you someone was stealing evidence. They could have stolen my gloves from the garbage."

Nogura nodded. "Do you have an alibi? For last night?"

Duvall closed her eyes, seeing Cross's face against her skin, electric in its contrast. "Yes," she said.

"Who?"

"A friend was—"

"*Goddammit, Katherine!*" Nogura's fist hit the table. "I'm trying to *help* you here. Seabrook thought the bag looked familiar. He should have come here himself to take you into custody. But he's trying to give you a break. He wants to find out that those *aren't* your prints in the gloves."

"You . . . aren't official?"

"Not till the computer comes up with a match," Nogura said. "Now help me here. Help yourself. Who was with you last night? Which friend?"

"Anthony Cross." She felt relief to admit it.

"Jesus Christ, he's a suspect!" Nogura moaned and put a hand to his face, covering his eyes. "Is that why you didn't go off with Jesse? One last fling?"

"No!" Duvall said, hurt by the accusation. But even as she spoke the word she knew in some way it was wrong. "I mean, no, not at first. I . . . no. I wanted to close the case. That's all. He's not a sociopath and he's not a killer, Nuke. Not after last night."

Nogura took his hand from his eyes. "Did you know Neale and Cross live together?"

"What?" The shock was so great she felt she had been hit.

"Guess not. Want to guess what Neale's motive might have been? If she is setting you up. With Covington's help. *Or* Cross's."

"How long . . . ?" She couldn't breathe.

Nogura shrugged. "Since before they came out to work at SHARP," he said. "Christ, Katherine, that was in the transcripts of Seabrook's first interview with Neale."

"I didn't . . . know . . ." She would not let herself cry in front of Nogura. Cross had seemed so open, so pure. How could he have kept that from her? Unless he was afraid to. Unless he suspected that Neale was the killer and he didn't know how to leave her. *And what am I complaining about?* Duvall thought. *Separated four months and I still don't know how to let go of my husband.* "I'm sorry, Nuke." It was all she could say.

"Yeah, I know." He waited for a few seconds, but she said nothing else. "How do you want to handle this?"

"They're going to find my fingerprints in those gloves, aren't they?"

"If whoever's behind it has someone helping them in the department, then there's a good chance they will."

"What's Seabrook going to do?"

"What can he do, Kate? He has to arrest you."

"Even with an alibi?" Cross's skin so pale, body so hard, loving so good.

"What time was he here?"

She remembered reaching into the refrigerator for a beer. She looked at the clock. "Eleven thirty-five to . . . sometime this morning." His visit was like a dream now. He was like a ghost.

Nogura shook his head. "Doesn't help, Kate. Coroner put the time of death at between eight and nine last night. Doesn't help at all." He looked at her, grim. "This is about as serious as it gets. How do you want to play it?"

"Anthony will need help," she said. That was first in her mind. "Protection. Can the task force—"

"Not possible," Nogura interrupted. "He's not connected to the case except as a suspect, and there's not enough in the files you gave me to bring him in under protective custody."

Nogura was right. But still, Cross couldn't be abandoned. Not without being given a chance to explain himself to her. "Can you give me a day?"

Nogura was silent for a long time, thinking her request through. "You won't try anything stupid? Like blowing out Neale's brains or anything?"

"No," Duvall said, though the thought had been sitting at the edge of her consciousness. "I just have to get to Anthony." *Have to ask him why he didn't tell me about himself and Neale,* she added for herself.

"What good will that do?"

"Maybe nothing," Duvall said, and offered nothing more.

"A day will be all you can have," Nogura warned. "They'll have your picture in the morning papers tomorrow. Might even make the news tonight."

"Can you slow them down?"

Nogura tapped his fingers on the table, considering. "I can tell Seabrook we talked. I can tell him you promised you'd turn yourself in tomorrow morning."

"Then you'll have to tell him everything we've been doing together," Duvall said. "There's no way you won't be involved."

"I already am involved."

Duvall smiled. "Guess you are."

"Just one thing." Nogura leaned forward. "Give me your gun so I can give it to Seabrook. It'll make him feel better. Prove you aren't dangerous or up to anything."

"He's already got my gun. And my badge. Took them both when he and Erhlenmeyer came here to suspend me."

Nogura winked at her, but it was heartless. "You're a cop. You've got a backup. Christ, maybe you've got five backups. All I need is one for Seabrook." His eyes grew cold. "Unless you *are* planning on using it?"

Duvall sighed. She wasn't and she wouldn't. "It's in the closet in the hall," she said, getting up. "Not very imaginative. Just another .38 special."

He followed her into the hallway as she pulled the revolver out from between two boxes on the shelf in the closet where she had slipped it last night. She broke the cylinder and emptied the cartridges from it. Then she handed the gun over with the handful of ammunition. "Eight years, and I've never even had to pull out my gun."

"I did once," Nogura said, slipping the revolver into one jacket pocket and the cartridges into the other. He smiled at her. "But that was in the service. Anything I can do?" Duvall shook her head. "Then I'd get out of here as soon as you can," he said. "ID was going to do the gloves ASAP."

"Thanks, Nuke."

"For sharing that with you?" he asked, trying to ease her mood.

"For . . . understanding," she said, then remembered their first conversation in that hallway. "For being nice to me."

"It'll work out," he said. He opened the door.

Duvall suddenly looked around the floor. "Did you see Briggs when you came in? The cat?" He hadn't been whining for his breakfast. An unusual occurrence.

Nogura shook his head.

"Was the door open?"

"Shut, but not locked. Why?"

Duvall swore. "He probably ran out when Anthony left." She stepped out onto the porch with Nogura and called the cat's name.

"He'll be okay," Nogura said. "There're lots of birds around."

"He's not an outdoor cat," Duvall said, part of her wondering why she could be so concerned about the stupid animal at a time like this.

"Kate," Nogura said, putting both hands on her arms. "Go inside, get ready, leave."

"Yeah," she agreed. "I have other things to worry about, don't I?"

"And so does your cat," Nogura said lightly, and he smiled.

TWENTY-FIVE

H e had returned to SHARP in the early morning, while the sky was still caught in the dark cobalt before the dawn. He walked through the dry scrub of the hills with his packages, climbed over the low wall of his private terrace, entered through the doors to his private office, avoiding everyone. He was close to his goal but there still was much work to do. The Work.

Now, an hour later, Anthony Cross sat at his desk, hands folded, knowing that in his private workshop he was only a moment away from success, but knowing that that final moment was an eternity, an infinity, a timeless fall through an event horizon where all time slowed to *tau* zero. There was still a problem.

He thought of the Greeks again. So many of their questions remained to be answered thousands of years later, a sign of the worthiness of their thought. He remembered the paradox of movement. Xeno's paradox. Before a man could take a step of a certain distance, he must first move his foot through half that distance. Yet before he could move his foot through half that distance, he must move his foot through half that new smaller distance. On and on the progression went, the distance halved and halved again, ever smaller, into infinity.

Mathematically, there was no paradox. If one quarter were added to one half. Then one eighth added, then one sixteenth, and on and on forever, each new number one half of the one preceding, then no matter how many times the operation was completed, the sum of them all would always be less than one. The single step could never be completed. But demonstrably, in the real world, the paradox didn't work. People were always taking steps of a certain distance, and that implied that it was not possible to infinitely divide a distance into smaller and smaller distances, nor space into smaller and smaller volumes. At some point, there must be a limit to how small space could become. And there was.

Max Planck had described it in his search for mathematical absolutes. He had given science h, the Planck constant, the precise measurement of the smallest amount of energy any quantum of radiation could have and exist. There was no partial amount possible. A quantum equaled h, or an integer multiple of h, or it did not exist. It was either the whole thing or nothing. One or the other. A quantum distinction. From h had come the measure of the Planck mass which gave the Planck temperature—the inconceivable temperature that the universe had been when it had existed for as long as the Planck time, 0.00000000000000000000000000000000000000000054 seconds.

Planck had defined that time mathematically, described that time, but Cross could see it, could experience it, could sense its passing in the universe around him. To other scientists, it was the Planck wall, the time beyond which their science and their physics couldn't reach, couldn't predict, couldn't understand. Beyond the Planck wall, past the Planck time, higher than the Planck temperature, the universe was too hot, too small, too dense for anyone to know. Except Anthony Cross.

He knew that there were limits where no one could see them. He had seen the fundamental units of gravity, held the smallest possible quanta of spacetime in his hands. Existence was *not* infinitely divisible. The quantum held for all things. Individual, discrete, caught in Heisenberg's uncertain wild flux from existence to nonexistence and back again, but it was there, comprehensible to anyone who would take the time to look, to see, to be inspired as Anthony Cross was inspired.

He clenched his fists at his desk, driving the nails of his hands into his palms. He was so close. He could see the gridded intersections of spacetime, of gravity, just as he had seen the gridded paint patterns on the wall of the abandoned flat in Stockholm, the student's life steaming into the frigid air. But how to attach himself to that grid? How to move along that grid, bend it and twist it as he bent and twisted his wire, as he bent and twisted the laser beam and the accelerator in Lab 2 by the simple act of observation? He saw the mystery before him. He saw Katherine Duvall's face before him. Heard the roar of the quantum, the cry of her passion. Felt spacetime flow around him, its master, felt her flow around him, her lover.

"Why?" he cried out to his empty office. Blood ran from his hands. "Why?" he cried as his toys broke and his cat died and the belt and the cane descended. "Why?" as he was abandoned. "Why?" as he slipped into the quantum. Why the folds and the fissures, the twisted wires, the copper intersections of hidden golden treasure to take him away from everything, to see things no one ever saw before, to know the one thing no one could know. The reason why for everything: the Beginning.

He saw Katherine Duvall's face, bright, and black, and intelligent. And she was a cop. A detective. By tradition, a man's job. And with that he saw the answer, knew the path to his final inspiration, just as he had dealt with the mystery of Kwong and his confusion of female and male.

Cross took a breath. He knew the rules he must follow in this world. He was . . . fine, now.

Cross reached for the phone on his desk, ignoring the sprinkling drops of blood that dripped from his palm. He punched a button, waited for only a few seconds, and then the proper part of him was there to speak the proper words in the proper way.

"Hi, Rich. Dr. Cross here. Listen, you heard about the big mess in Lab 2, didn't you?" Daystrom was muddled on the other end of the line, just waking up after another long night in his lab. "Yeah, completely unexpected," Cross answered. "Anyway, I was wondering if you could meet me there in about five minutes or so. There's some equipment I'd like you to take a look at. Get your opinion on a couple of things. That be okay?" Cross's face was wooden, unmoving, but his voice was warm and friendly. He had learned many lessons in his life. "Thanks, Rich. Knew I could count on you. See you in a bit."

He hung up. He stood up. He wiped his hands on his slacks, leaving dark bloody streaks. Then he went to his private workroom and hefted his packages, ignoring the hissing of Duvall's black-and-white cat encased in the full sphere of copper wire, though not yet completely installed within it. By stretching his hand to its limit, he was also able to carry the small black kit with the scalpels and the gloves, the gauze bandages and the tape. And the drill. He could fill the water bottle from a drinking fountain once he got there.

Cross smiled, remembering the excitement he had felt as a teacher preparing a lecture on a brand-new topic. He was certain of it. It was going to be a good lesson.

Neale stared at the figures on her computer screen in her office at SHARP. They made no sense. No matter how she changed the parameters of the equipment simulation program, no matter how she adjusted the power levels of the accelerator and the microlaser that had been destroyed in Lab 2, she couldn't coax the program to produce the same results as she and Covington, Paine, Kwong, and Weinstein had witnessed yesterday. For the equipment to have done what she saw it do— pump a laser strong enough to slice through concrete and steel, form a point source of gravity that had teetered on the brink of a singularity— was impossible.

But then there was the cat. The body of the cat, grotesquely embedded into a complex web of wiring and, as Kwong and Weinstein had discovered, intricate microcircuitry. Thin tendrils of connecting wires had been carefully inserted into the cat's brain, its heart, some organs and not others, as if Cross had had a purpose in mind.

Neale closed her eyes, leaned her head into her right hand. Her left arm was thickly bandaged over the long line of stitches closing her jagged cuts. On that hand, only two fingers and her thumb were free. Her shoulder ached from the tetanus shot. Her eyes felt heavy from the antibiotics she had been given. But she had to work. She had to understand.

Up to now, there had been nothing that Cross had come up with that she hadn't been able to grasp, to refine, to package and present to the world. He might have the insight, but she had the skill. She had made Cross possible. But the creature that he was now had wired a living cat into a mad machine. And the frightening thing was, the terrifying thing was, that somehow, within that atrocity and that madness, was a germ of an idea, a technique or a breakthrough that had apparently worked.

Neale wanted to sleep. She wanted to go back to the hospital and accept the offer of a bed. But, more than that, she wanted to *know*. She had to follow Anthony Cross as far as she could, beyond all limits. Because—the awful realization had come as she had watched Weinstein and Kwong, hands shaking, dissect Cross's circuitry from the cat's body —just as she had made Cross possible, so he had made her.

Neale understood that condition clearly. She was bound to him as surely as electrons were bound to atomic nuclei. The only question remaining was how large was the value of the quanta of energy which could displace her. If it was infinite, as she feared, then they were bound forever.

She heard someone enter her office. Covington, she thought, come to ask more questions or, perhaps, to tell her he could arrange for a never-ending supply of government-approved cats if she would care to continue Cross's work.

"What do you want, Parnel?" she asked as she opened her eyes.

It was Cross.

So many things to say to him and all she could manage was the obvious. "I asked them to call me when you came back. If you came back."

Cross shrugged, standing in the middle of the floor. His clothes were wrinkled, streaks of blood on his pants where he had wiped his hands, hair mussed and unwashed. But his smile was as pure as ever. "They don't know I'm here," he said. "I wanted to work . . . undisturbed."

Neale turned away from her workstation. "We found the cat, Anthony."

He looked down at the floor, caught in remembering. "Which one?" he asked.

Dear God, Neale thought. How many were there? "In the target chamber."

"Oh," Cross said. "Misty. As it turns out, it wasn't really necessary."

"How about the wiring, the circuitry? Was any of that necessary?" She stayed behind her desk. She wanted to go to him.

He looked sad for a moment. "Not now," he said.

"Why, Anthony?" It was quiet in the office, only the low hum of the air conditioning.

"It's almost finished."

"What is?"

"My Work."

"What work is that?" Afraid to ask, but forced to.

He smiled at her. "You know."

"I don't think I do anymore."

He nodded at her, encouraging her, chewing on his bottom lip. "I owe you a lot, Charis. You've been very helpful. With Parnel. And SHARP. And . . . everything. Because, I know, you see. I know that you've been . . . cleaning up for me. You and Parnel. I've found it very liberating, just as Parnel promised. A hundred percent of my time dedicated to my Work. No worries about mundane things like paying the rent. Or leaving behind evidence."

It was an ending. She could sense it. She feared it. She stood up, went to him, stood apart from him, alone in the center of the floor.

"I don't think we can help you any longer, Anthony."

"But you can," he said softly. He held out a hand to her. "Without you . . . I'm nothing. You know that. You've always known that." His eyes were wide, imploring. "It's always been your work, too. You've just let me be the one to go first. But I know you want to follow. I know you have to follow, don't you? You have to see what I see. I know you understand that." Their hands touched. "Tell me that you understand."

"I want to understand," she said, feeling her hand tremble in his. "I might have died in the lab when you . . . did that experiment, the singularity."

Cross sighed, studying her hand, moving his fingers over hers as if noticing their structure for the first time. "I don't think we can die. Second law, you know. Energy cannot be created or destroyed. I think we just . . . go on. We just . . . keep looking." He squeezed her hand. "We become . . . more." Long silence in the office, the hum of hidden machinery, the beating of hearts, gentle breathing. "I don't think we can die. Not alone. We talked about that in a desert once, remember?"

Neale closed her eyes again, unable to look at the sudden depths of pain in his face. She focused all she had on the grip of his hand on hers, their interaction, all the things that might have been if other things had not. "I understand," she said, a whisper, a cry.

"I need your help, Charis. One last time."

She opened her eyes. "What?"

"You know," he said, smiling, embarrassed, the small boy returned.

And poor Charis Neale, she did know.

They walked through the corridors of SHARP that early Sunday morning, hand in hand, not speaking, two lovers going off to a picnic. Neale could not say anything, Cross never offered. They came to the security doors that led to the restricted parts of the facility. Cross stood in front of the scanner and the doors opened. He pulled her through.

"Don't I have to use my card?" Neale asked. "Don't I have to have my palm scanned?"

Cross shook his head. "They're just machines now. Like the laser and the accelerator. I understand them now. I know how to observe them."

They came to the doors to Lab 2. The corridor floor was still puddled with water that had leaked out from the sprinklers. Cross pushed on the doors. The lab remained in shambles, dimly lit by emergency fixtures. He took her inside. She could still hear dripping.

"It's the scientific method," he said as he guided her through the rubble and the wreckage, making his way to the back of the lab where a dozen light bulbs in wire cages hung from the wreckage, brightly illuminating one hidden corner. "Hypothesize, test the hypothesis, refine the hypothesis, communicate the results, start again."

"An endless cycle," she said.

"No," he countered, "not endless. Chemistry is closed, isn't it? The field is understood. There are specific questions to be answered but nothing major, nothing fundamental. Chemistry is for engineers and technicians now. It's monkey work, just like quantum physics."

"Physics isn't closed," Neale said, stepping carefully over wire conduits that had peeled off from a wall, ends cut and fused by impossible laser light.

"It will be," Cross said. "We know how the three forces came out of the one force. And now I know that gravity is not a force."

"What is it then?"

Cross spoke as if in a trance as he led her deeper into the lab. "Spacetime is made of discrete granules, Charis, the smallest possible division of spacetime. They're the dark matter of the universe no one has been able to find. They respond to the curve of mass as springs in a mattress respond to a sleeper. Gravity is a shuffling of those granules. It doesn't move as a wave or a particle. It moves as electricity moves through a wire. One electron enters the wire and displaces the first it meets. That electron displaces another which displaces another until a completely different electron emerges from the wire's other end.

"That's the way the curve of spacetime is transferred from one granule to another as they move against each other. Physicists are wasting too much time looking for waves that don't exist. They should look deeper into the quantum as I have. They should bring more inspiration to their work." He smiled. "Almost there."

Cross clambered over part of a magnet housing, then turned around and helped Neale over. They were in the farthest corner of the lab, by the access doors leading to the generator room. Three piles of debris were neatly covered over with canvas tarpaulins, casting strong shadows in the light from the hanging bulbs.

"I just have one more hypothesis to test," Cross said, walking around the piles. "One more to refine. Then everything there is to know . . . will be known." He pulled the tarp off the largest pile. "Isn't that right, Rich?"

Rich Daystrom was tied to the surface of a crooked, blast-damaged desk. His legs and arms were thick with coiled rope, nylon, white and yellow, and further held in place by yards of duct tape. White cloth strips, torn from lab coats, dug into his open mouth, pulling down on the soft flesh of his cheeks, disappearing beneath the desktop, holding his head in unmoving position.

"Rich is going to be our assistant today," Cross said.

Daystrom moaned, his eyes desperately wide and wild, sweat glimmering on his uncovered head, bright, black, intelligent.

Cross reached down beside the desk and lifted up his black kit, snapped it open, pulled out a pair of surgical gloves. Neale looked down to the smaller of the two canvas-covered shapes. It had the size and shape of . . . an arm? "What's that?" she asked. *Who's that?* she wondered.

Cross smiled encouragingly. "That's for later," he said. "When the lesson's over."

A cat cried suddenly, piercing, startling. The smaller canvas-covered pile shook.

"And so is that," Cross said, snapping the tight-fitting gloves against his wrists. "Batteries, so many batteries," he said, smiling down at Daystrom's face. "I've told you about power supplies before, haven't I, Rich?"

Neale stepped forward to Cross. "Please, Anthony. You don't have to do this again."

"Scientific method," Cross said. "Replication of results. Just because it worked once is no reason to believe that it will always work." There was a scalpel in one hand, a large butcher's knife in the other.

"It's worked nineteen times before, Anthony."

"Twenty," Cross said. He smiled at Neale, brushed her face with his rubber-gloved hand. "Twenty times, now. That they know about."

He looked down at Daystrom. He held the butcher's knife in front of the man's face, drawing his attention to it. Then, beyond Daystrom's vision, Cross poked the man's forehead with the scalpel. Perfect beads of blood grew at each puncture.

"The local anesthetic has taken hold," Cross told Neale. He put the butcher's knife down. "He won't feel anything now."

Neale put her hand on Cross's, holding back the scalpel. "No, Anthony."

"Why not?" He sounded genuinely puzzled.

"You . . . don't need to."

"But I do. I have to finish my Work." He took her hand from his. "Our Work, Charis." He waved to the ruined room around them. "Look at this lab. Remember what happened. I wasn't quite in control then. I didn't quite know how to focus my observations to make what I wanted to see become real. But I've made some more adjustments to the instruments and I'm close now. We're close now. Almost finished." He looked at Daystrom. "Aren't we, Rich?"

Daystrom moaned, high and loud through his gags.

"Won't be long now," Cross said, patting the man on his shoulder. Then he turned to Neale.

"You can leave, Charis. You can abandon this, and all that has come from it. But you'll be turning your back on knowing what I know, seeing what I see, understanding all that there is to understand."

"I can't go through with it, Anthony." Neale was trapped. Her whole body felt as wrapped and as warm and as immovable as her left arm.

"You've been through it so many times before, benefited from it so many times before . . . the only difference is that now you're here with me instead of hiding out on the street where you think I can't see you, hiding so you can run in and clean up for me before I call the police and tell them what I've done. But you don't have to clean up for me this time. Don't you see? This is the last. The final. And what's important, what's so important now, is that you are here with me where you belong at last. Here beside me, sharing this with me, being inspired with me. Becoming one with me. Being *more* with me."

"No, Anthony." But her voice was uncertain.

"I don't want to be alone, Charis. Not again. Never again."

"Please, no."

Cross reached into his bag. "I know. You want to understand the way I understand. You want to look inside the quantum, understand the quantum, feel time itself in each discrete particle, slipping from one moment to another." His voice flowed like a dream, water running downhill, trapped by gravity. Cross withdrew his hand. He held another scalpel. "The moment of transition, Charis. Into the Planck time, Charis. To see all that I have seen, to be inspired as I am inspired." He held the scalpel out to her. "To know the answers. *The* answer. The way I know."

Charis Neale had reached her moment and she knew it. Each decision of her life had inevitably led to this. Each desire, each secret, each of Cross's murders that she had hidden. The transition had already occurred without her knowledge. The wall had already been passed. There was nothing more to do but continue in her path, in her orbit. Nothing more to do but to understand all that she wanted to understand in the only way that she could understand, the only way that was left open.

All or nothing.

Cross smiled.

She took the second scalpel.

"Into the quantum," Cross said, eyes full of love, all loneliness gone. He looked down at Daystrom. "Now, remember how we were talking about power supplies, Rich? And you wanted to plug the board into the computer's supply and I said, oh no, I already had batteries. Special batteries. Remember that?"

Daystrom howled beneath his gags.

Cross shrugged. "In that case, Rich, you better let me explain it to you again."

The lesson began.

TWENTY-SIX

Duvall's white car sped up the long driveway to the SHARP building. She could feel Nogura's deadline ticking away, like a clock counting down. If she didn't follow through on her promise to him, then by tomorrow morning at the latest her face would be in all the papers, on all the news shows. "Cop wanted for brutal serial slayings." It had happened before in this city. She wouldn't last a day.

The parking lot was half full, which surprised Duvall for that early on a Sunday morning. She was disappointed when she couldn't see Cross's Mercedes, though she knew it would have been too much to hope that he might be that easy to find. Duvall knew she was going to be fortunate to get out of SHARP with at least Cross's home phone number, but she had to start somewhere, anywhere, to find out why he hadn't told her about himself and Neale. What other things were there for her to learn about him?

Inside the airy, open lobby, a uniformed security guard stood up behind his counter as Duvall approached. Fortunately, he was a weekend replacement as she had counted on, and not one of the guards she had met on her first trip. Duvall wore jeans and sneakers, a light linen jacket over a matching blouse, and carried her leather satchel. She hoped she looked like anything other than a cop.

"May I help you?" the guard asked. He was young, well built, cautious but friendly; a pale blond mustache was trying to establish itself on his upper lip. He wore a SHARP ID badge that said his name was Jeff Heaslip.

Duvall went into her routine without pausing to catch her breath. "Hi there . . . Jeff. Kathy Burns to see Dr. Anthony Cross." She put her case on the counter and checked her watch. "I'm a few minutes late." She smiled and waited expectantly.

"I'm sorry, but Dr. Cross isn't in." Heaslip's friendly smile faded slightly. He could tell she expected him to say something more, but he obviously didn't know what.

"Ah, good," Duvall said with what she hoped sounded like relief. "Then he's late, too." She pulled an old notebook out of her case and slipped a pen out of the book's wire binding. "May I wait in his office?"

The guard glanced down at his work area behind the counter, perhaps looking for a note. "I don't think he's expected in today, Ms. . . . ?"

"Burns. Sure he is," Duvall said happily. "To be interviewed by me." She leaned over the counter. "Is there an appointment list back there, Jeff?"

Heaslip looked again. There was nothing. "Sorry."

Duvall frowned. "I guess things got mixed up over that explosion in the lab, huh?"

The guard was surprised. "You know about that?"

"Sure," Duvall said, trying to be chatty and open, completely nonthreatening. "Dr. Cross told me about it. I heard that Kwong and Weinstein might have been badly hurt."

"Dr. Cross told you Professor Weinstein was present?"

"Sure. Wasn't he supposed to? I mean, I'm interviewing them all. You know, Nobel Prize winners in Lotusland. Almost four years later. All that stuff. For the *Times* Sunday magazine." She leaned forward on the counter.

"Sorry," and Heaslip seemed to be telling the truth, "but no one said anything about an interview. Professor Weinstein and Dr. Kwong will be here later on, but I'm afraid we're just not expecting Dr. Cross."

"He said he'd be here by now."

"When were you talking to him?"

"Yesterday, after the explosion." Duvall snapped her fingers. "Say, Jeff, why don't I give him a call at home? Maybe Dr. Neale will know if he's on his way over." If her setup worked on the guard, then all the inside information she was dropping would make him feel that she was on the inside, that she could be trusted.

"Oh, Dr. Neale's in," Heaslip said, happy to finally be able to contribute something. He reached for his desk phone. "I can call her."

Great, Duvall thought, keeping her expression pleasant. "Sure, and if she doesn't know, I can call him at home." Duvall had no choice but to play the charade through so that, when the time came to actually make the call to Cross's home and she discovered she had "accidentally" left her address book behind, Heaslip might be willing to give her the number, no matter what the company's policy was. Then a quick phone call to PacBell's reverse directory office would give her the address to go with the number, even if it were unlisted.

Heaslip frowned. "No answer in her office." He hung up the phone and typed on a keyboard behind the counter. "I'll see where she used her pass card last."

"That's okay," Duvall said. She didn't care if Neale couldn't be located, would prefer if she wasn't. "Why don't I just—"

Heaslip swore, typed again on his security keyboard, then swore again.

"What is it?" Duvall asked.

"The security pass card system crashed." Heaslip's eyes moved anxiously over his screen. "And no alarms, no nothing."

"What's that mean?"

"It means we're wide open," Heaslip said. He reached for a walkie-talkie mounted in a recharge base. "Desk to Rover Four. Desk to Rover Four. Come in, Four."

Duvall waited by the counter while Heaslip made contact with the other guards on patrol. None of them had known about the card system not working but none sounded concerned. Duvall thought nothing of it.

After Heaslip had made sure that his coworkers weren't shot and bleeding in the hallways, he glanced up at Duvall and smiled. "Hey, Desk to all rovers. Has anyone seen Dr. Neale in the last few minutes?"

The walkie-talkie crackled as Rover Two responded. "Yeah, I saw her and Dr. Cross heading down to Lab 2 about twenty minutes ago."

Duvall and Heaslip reacted immediately, but Heaslip had the walkie-talkie.

"Are you sure it was Dr. Cross?" Heaslip asked.

"Absolutely."

Heaslip looked up to Duvall. "I guess he didn't come through—" He stared into the LAPD business card Duvall held in front of his face. She prayed he wouldn't ask to see her badge.

"I'm a police officer," she said, talking quickly, no more pretense. "Dr. Cross is in great danger. Call the number on this card. Ask to speak to Detective Adam Nogura. Tell him that I'm here and that Cross and Neale are together. That's my name on the card. Then have the rest of your guards meet me at Lab 2."

Heaslip blinked at her as if he hadn't heard a word. "I thought you were a writer or something."

"Someone's trying to *kill* Dr. Cross," Duvall said urgently. "Now call!"

Heaslip picked up his phone and began punching the number on Duvall's card.

Duvall ran through the north corridor till she came to the huge, glassed-in central lobby, filled with trees and dozens of recessed and sunken alcoves. She saw signs listing Lab 2 and followed them. There was a card and hand scan station in the middle of the corridor she had chosen, but the sliding doors were open and she walked through without challenge. The doors to Lab 2 were the second last set on her right, studded with warning signs. This time, she didn't bother to read them.

The lab was unrecognizable. Before, it had been brightly lit, the equipment clean, the metal surfaces gleaming, but now everything was twisted and burned, the floor was wet, water dripped, and the only light came from wall-mounted emergency lights, dim and orange. Duvall felt she had stepped into another realm, another time, where a war had been fought and still continued.

Then, in the farthest corner, she saw an area of brighter light, etched like the rising sun against the ragged black silhouettes of destroyed equipment. From that corner and that light she heard a sound, long, wheezing, rising and falling, a rasping scream, a desperate plea. It was a human sound, and instinctively she knew what it meant: Someone was dying.

She moved carefully through the ruins of the lab, toward the farthest corner, wishing she had kept one of her guns, wishing she was not going to see what she knew she would see as she climbed past the final charred magnet housing.

But she saw something else, insane, unexpected, burning into her eyes and her mind like the strobing flashes from a forensic photographer's camera.

She saw Neale. She saw Cross. Their hands were joined, entwined.

And reaching into the open skull of a black man tied to a damaged desk.

Thick matter and dark blood and all that had been the man welled up around the hands and fingers of Neale and Cross as they pushed in, eyes closed, forcing their way into the brain and the life of the man, blood drenched, mouth frozen open, body caught in the moment of his death.

"Yesss," Cross sighed.

Neale sighed with him.

Two lovers joined.

Duvall could only stand and watch. No words came. No scenario made sense. There was only the picture without detail.

"Did you feel it?" Cross asked. "The moment?"

Neale did not answer.

"Did you see it?" Cross asked. "The Beginning?"

Neale did not answer.

Duvall heard the slick, clicking, liquid sounds of their hands being withdrawn.

"Hello, Kate," Cross said. He hadn't opened his eyes. He hadn't seen her.

"What are you doing?" Duvall's voice was dry, gasping. Her stomach twisted. Her eyes burned.

"It's all done," Cross said. "All done." He wiped his hands on the dead man's shirt. He helped Neale wipe her hands, too. Neale's eyes were open but she did not see either.

"It was you all along," Duvall said.

Cross shook his head. "It was someone else." He lifted a crumpled tarpaulin from the floor and cleaned his hands more thoroughly.

"You lied to me," Duvall said. It was what she felt, betrayed by her heart, by what she wanted to believe, had to believe.

"It was someone else." He smiled at her. The Cross she had

known was absent. This one was a stranger. "My name is Legion, now. Don't you think that's appropriate? My eyes encompass the multitudes, the manifolds . . ." He turned to Duvall. His eyes seemed absolutely black, empty, forever deep. "All I must do is observe and collapse whichever probabilities I choose. I observe and I make real." He turned back to Neale and held the tarp to her hands, helping her clean herself as if she were the child now.

"Anthony, the police are coming," Duvall said. She knew she couldn't approach him. She couldn't do anything to stop him. She was afraid to try.

Cross looked up to the shadowed ceiling, considering her words. "Yes and no," he said. Then he took Neale's hands and led her a few feet away from the body, took her to a small familiar shape on the floor, hidden beneath another tarpaulin. "We're finished now, Charis. I just have to make the final adjustments. Now that I know how." He bent to the tarp. "Now that I've been inspired."

Duvall tensed, afraid to know what was hidden beneath the shroud.

Cross pulled away the covering.

Duvall didn't understand what she saw. It was a sculpture of some sort—a three-dimensional image of a hand and forearm, thicker than anything real and glittering with pinpoint metallic reflections from the lights.

Cross lifted the object lovingly and as it moved in his hands, Duvall could see the shape was a hollow framework, its outer boundaries crafted in geodesic twists of copper wire. She stared in wonder at the intricacies of the folded webs of metal. No pattern repeated in its mesh yet somehow an order was present, somehow a plan was maintained.

"Do you like it?" Cross asked. "Can you see it? Do you know it?" He placed the sculpted hand on Rich Daystrom's unmoving chest and the bare copper wire seemed to glow with more than the light that illuminated the corner.

Duvall saw that the sculpture was studded with black plastic shapes which looked like plugs for some type of computer connector. She felt the fear of ignorance, the fear of not knowing what was going to happen next. "Stay away from it, Anthony," she said, a plea.

Cross ignored her. Quietly, he rolled up a sleeve on his blood-spattered shirt, then reached for the construction. Neale stood silently, one limp hand still dripping with something that had once been Rich Daystrom. Cross held the wire form in his right hand. He slipped his left inside, pushing hard until the wire bit into his flesh, making his skin rise and swell to its pattern.

Duvall saw some of the purpose of it now. It was a glove, a technological version of armored gauntlets once worn by ancient warriors. "Anthony, don't," she said, but she wouldn't go near him. His expression had changed in an unreadable way, descending into depths unimaginable, or heights unattainable, as he moved the copper wire gauntlet back and forth, flexing and bending, testing its fit and the grip it had on him.

Cross lifted a circular object from the floor where it had lain beneath the canvas. It appeared to be a large, solid copper bracelet which he fastened around the upper edge of the gauntlet like a cuff below his elbow. Duvall could see colored, insulated wires dangling from the cuff, ending in more black plugs. Cross joined them to the receptacles in the gauntlet's structure. Then a small blue light glowed on the cuff and Cross's left hand seemed to shimmer, only for an instant, as if it had suddenly passed behind a wall of wavering hot air.

Cross held out his gloved hand to Duvall and made a fist. She was amazed that the wire was so supple, bending with his muscles and his skin, moving like metal flesh with a new network of nerve paths. His hand and fingers bulged with the bite of the wire, blood swollen and purple. His encased flesh seemed to glimmer in the light, as if blood were drawn forth to coat it, pressed out by the wire, the old life replaced by the new.

"This is my Work," Cross said. His right hand moved over the surface of the gauntlet and the cuff, closing final gaps in the pattern with subtle twists and reshapings. "This is my Work and it is done. At last I shall know the Beginning."

Then Cross stood still, staring at the fist before him, his task complete. Neale also remained motionless. At one point she had turned her head to look at Duvall, but her expression was without meaning and she stared at the floor. Whatever had been dripping from her hand had run out.

Duvall didn't know how long she watched Cross. She remembered the security guards only when she heard footsteps behind her, picking their way through the rubble. Heaslip was suddenly beside her, walkie-talkie in his hand, weapon holstered.

Duvall heard the shock in Heaslip's voice as he looked at the dead man. "Oh, Jesus, that's Daystrom." He held the walkie-talkie to his mouth. "Daystrom's dead. Cross is carrying some weird kind of equipment. Neale is with him. Come through the access doors from the gennie room." He looked at Duvall. "Are you all right?" Duvall didn't bother to answer. "It's okay," Heaslip said. "Your friend's here. That detective."

So soon? Duvall thought, but still couldn't speak. Cross knelt down to the ground, picked up something else from the floor. It was the size of a large book, thinner, studded with dark rectangles; it looked like the insides of a computer. He clipped the object to the side of his gauntlet, connecting it to the last of the connectors embedded in the wire.

The doors to the generator room behind him opened slowly.

"Hello, Parnel," Cross said, not looking up from the board on his forearm. "Hello, Lee. Hello, Adam. Hello, David." Cross looked up, straight at Duvall. "Hello . . . Nuke," he said.

Duvall looked over to the open doors. She saw the tall, thin man, Covington, standing with Kwong, the oriental scientist she had seen before and two other men she had not. Kwong operated a small video camera, keeping it trained on Cross. Beside Kwong was Nogura, revolver drawn. He was without backup. She did not know why.

"What has he been doing?" Covington called out. No answer. "Detective Duvall, what has Dr. Cross been doing?"

"Wiring in the timing board," Cross answered instead. "It's all in the timing, Parnel. It's all in knowing when to dip your sail into the quantum sea and when to pull it out again. That's how the universe was born." He didn't take his concentration from the board; his fingers never faltered.

At last faced with something familiar, Duvall found her voice. "Where's your backup, Nuke?"

"It's all under control," Nogura called back calmly. He holstered his weapon.

Duvall was surprised by his action. "Nuke, it was the both of them. They both killed the man on the table. I saw it."

"That's all right, Kate," Nogura said. "We'll take care of it." He called to the security guard beside Duvall. "Jeff, please bring Dr. Neale over to us."

And it was then Duvall knew who had stolen the evidence, who had hidden the details, who had protected the murderer's secret. Nogura worked for *them*. The realization made her feel hollow, empty, used.

Heaslip hung the walkie-talkie on his belt. Duvall saw the flicker of fear in his eyes.

"It will be all right, Jeff," Nogura encouraged him. "Just do it."

The guard advanced.

"No. Don't do it," Cross said. He raised his voice. "Charis doesn't want to leave yet, Parnel. She's been so helpful to us all that it's only fair that she share in this final moment. Don't you agree?"

"It's not a final moment, Anthony." Covington stepped a few feet farther into the lab. "There's still a lot of work for you to do. A lot you must explain to us."

Cross laughed. He turned to face Covington. Heaslip began to move toward Neale behind the madman's back.

"Do you see what I'm wearing, Parnel?"

"Very impressive," Covington said. Heaslip was halfway to Neale. "What is it?"

"What isn't it?" Cross asked in return. "It generates a quantum field, Parnel, if you understand that."

"I don't, Anthony."

Heaslip moved closer.

"Would you like a demonstration?"

"Yes, I would. Very much."

"Of course you would. You always like what I do, don't you? Always wanting to get your piece of me, aren't you? Well, watch this, Parnel!" Cross wheeled like smoke in the wind and his hands closed on Heaslip as if the guard's exact position had always been known to him. Heaslip struggled. Duvall could see him attempting to use Cross's hold as leverage, but Cross was like a cast-iron statue bolted to the floor. The guard couldn't budge him.

Cross spun the man to hold him from behind, his right arm locked against Heaslip's throat, squeezing until Heaslip's hands fell uselessly to his sides in defeat. Cross's left hand, in its gauntlet, was poised at the side of Heaslip's head. "I have Rich to thank for the timing board. I have Rich to thank for the final inspiration to know how to use it correctly. Watch this, Parnel. See how fine the resolution of spacetime is. See how easy it is to align a quantum field to the pattern, then slip between the lattice of existence."

For an instant, Duvall thought that the gauntlet had suddenly fallen from Cross's hand. The gleam of the metal had disappeared. But as his hand moved in toward Heaslip's head, she saw the gauntlet was only lost in a shadow from the light spilling from the doors to the generator room. Yet the gauntlet looked oddly darker than the shadow, as if it had no depth and was only a black cutout.

Cross placed his hand on the guard's temple. There was more than fear in the young man's glazed eyes but his crushed throat could make no sound. Duvall was astounded that no one moved to help.

"No!" she shouted. "Don't do it! Don't let him—"

Cross's hand pushed against the guard's head and the guard howled. His body twitched and arched as if lightning coursed through him. There was a sound of sizzling heat, a high-pitched whine and buzz, the sputter of interference. And Duvall stared in horror as Cross's hand disappeared *inside* the guard's head. She looked in panic at Nogura and the others by the door, but the way Cross was angled they couldn't see what she saw.

"Yesss," Cross sighed. He withdrew his hand. He let go of the guard.

The body collapsed limply to the floor, half its head raw red and blistered.

"Did you feel it, Parnel? The moment?"

"No, Anthony," Covington answered.

"Did you see it, Parnel? The Beginning?"

"No, Anthony, but I want to. I know you can show it to me. I know you can show the world."

Cross lowered his hand, still black and indistinct, the copper gone. "I know that I can, too, Parnel. The question to be answered now is: Do I want to?" He walked over to a smaller shape beneath another tarpaulin.

"Of course you do, Anthony," Covington said. "You must. What else do you work for?"

Cross knelt by the smaller shape. He paused. "What I have always worked for: to know the Beginning." His voice sounded tired and sad.

"And now, I suspect I will." He pulled off the tarp. Duvall heard a cat hiss. It was Briggs.

"God, no," Duvall said and ran unthinking to her cat. The animal was enclosed in a spherical cage of copper wire, as intricately woven as the gauntlet Cross wore. "What are you doing with him?"

Cross held up his black hand. Even at only three feet away, Duvall could still not see detail or form in it, only an outline, a two-dimensional shadow cast against the air.

"There are so many things still to understand, Kate," Cross said. "Physics is closed now. The fundamental questions solved. But there are still little things, still tiny questions."

"Leave the animal alone, Anthony."

"I need batteries," Cross said. "Talk to Rich. He knows all about power supplies. Now."

Cross's gauntlet touched the cat's cage and blackness swept across it like a wave. Its shape and form were gone. Only a circular hole remained, black and flat.

Duvall shot her hand out to the altered cage. Her hand passed into shadow, swept through empty air back into the light.

"Where did he go? What did you do?"

"Nothing," Cross said. He hefted the black shape as if he held an invisible cage. Duvall heard her cat screech, heard the sound instantly muffled. Cross dropped the sphere to the floor. The black was gone from it. And so was Briggs.

"Ahhh," Cross sighed. "It's all in the way you look at it."

Duvall swung at Cross, not thinking, not caring. He caught her fist in his black hand. She heard the sizzle of meat on a skillet, felt numbing cold in her hand and screamed.

Cross released her. Her knuckles were burned, the surface skin raw and bleeding with the imprint of his fingers.

"There are still some details to be worked out," Cross said.

"We can help you work them out," Covington offered. "Whatever you need, whatever it takes."

Cross shook his head. "I already have it all, Parnel. Can't you see that?"

Cross's bare hand moved to his gauntlet again, touching and prodding the timing board. "I have it all," he repeated, then turned to Duvall. His eyes fixed on her intently, sadly, passionately. His black hand reached out to her face, gently, caressing her with the chill of empty space. This time, there was no sound. No pain.

"I have it all," Cross said again, "except you."

"We'll let you keep her." Covington walked slowly through the rubble toward Cross. "Whatever you want, Anthony. Whoever you want. We'll get it for you."

Cross withdrew his hand. "Tell him, Kate. Tell him it doesn't work like that. Tell him what you told me."

"What, Anthony?"

There were tears in his eyes but Duvall didn't know why. Then Cross spun and ran.

"Stop him!" Covington yelled.

Duvall backed out of the way as Nogura sped forward, followed by Kwong, who ran with his videocam still held before him. Cross had run behind the shell of the ruined accelerator target chamber. Great blue sparks suddenly crackled into the air from behind it.

"Careful!" Covington warned as Nogura eased around the corner of the chamber. "He's got his hand wired up like a cattle prod or something. Don't let him touch you."

"It's *not* like a cattle prod," Duvall said to Covington as he came up beside her. "He put his hand right *into* that guard's head. He pushed it right through his goddamned head like it . . . it just wasn't there."

"Really?" Duvall was stunned by the excitement she heard in Covington's voice.

Nogura cried out. Three gunshots exploded. Duvall heard a low electrical crackle and saw a flurry of sparks erupt from another spot in the lab.

"He's heading for the main doors!" Nogura shouted. "Block him! Block him!"

Covington and the other men ran back for the lab's entrance. Duvall stayed by Neale but the physicist still gave no indication that she was aware of what went on around her. She only rocked slowly from foot to foot, staring at the floor.

Duvall heard Covington cry out excitedly. "There he is!" She looked back at what she could see of the main entrance. Cross stood backlit against the partially opened doors to the corridor, watching the others converge on him.

"Please, Anthony," Covington said. "We don't want to hurt you."

"No," Cross agreed. "You don't want to do that at all." And then he crouched down and slapped his gauntlet against a twisted sheet of steel which had once been part of the accelerator's wall. Duvall saw the sparks fly from the glove, heard a dull rushing crackle, and then saw a line of sparks flicker along the steel plate toward Covington and the others like a long circuit shorting out.

The electrical arcs jumped from metal debris to steel plates and dangling wires, closing in, moving faster. "Get back," Nogura cried. "Away from the metal—"

There was a flash like lightning. A rumble like thunder. Duvall heard a man scream and when her vision cleared, all she could see was one lab door slowly swinging back and forth.

Nogura was in the corridor beyond, gun in hand, frantically looking back and forth. "No good!" he shouted back inside. "He's gone."

"But how?" Covington snapped. "Where could he go so quickly?"

"That's easy," Neale said softly behind Duvall.

Duvall turned to the scientist. "Do you know?"

Neale nodded her head, shared her secret. "To the Beginning."

TWENTY-SEVEN

T hey wouldn't tell her why they called their group Cathedral Three and, in the end, Duvall didn't care. In fact, she found she didn't care about anything, except one thing. She had been betrayed by her department, allowed herself to be used and betrayed by a madman, and had cut herself off from Jesse, the one center of normalcy her life had held. Yet what she cared about now, what she cried over, was the last plaintive wail of her cat as it was consumed by the blackness of Anthony Cross.

Because the cat was the one element that could not know what was happening. The cat had been innocent and Duvall had failed to protect it, failed to change things, failed to make a difference. To make a difference was the reason she had chosen her career and she had not lived up to her choice. Instead she was the prisoner of people just as crazed and as mad as the maniac they tracked. She was a prisoner of Cathedral Three and she didn't even know what it was.

"We have to get him back," Covington said. "At any cost."

They sat around a long walnut table in a conference room at SHARP. *Like a board meeting in hell,* Duvall thought. She was held by Nogura's handcuffs, her hands looped through the arm of her blue-padded executive chair. Near one end of the table, isolated from the others, Neale sat, still stunned. Her hands were folded in front of her, nails dark with dried blood, her skin stained with it. Closer to Duvall, Kwong rocked constantly in his chair, the video camera on the table in front of him. The old man with the yarmulke, Weinstein she had heard him called, was pale and shaken. But Covington and the vaguely familiar white-haired man, David Paine, were electrified, like dogs sniffing at the spoor of a wounded animal, closing for the kill.

And sitting quietly across from Duvall, face composed, sure and certain of his role, was the man who had said he wanted to be her partner, the man who had tried a dozen times to steer her away from this case, the man who had lived a lie and now, perhaps, would be responsible for her death.

"What did he tell you about that thing he was wearing on his hand, Detective?" Covington glared impatiently at Duvall. She could tell he would feel better if he could hit her.

"He didn't tell me anything about it," Duvall said wearily. "I saw it for the first time in the lab just before you came in."

"He must have talked about his work with you." Nogura leaned forward, trying to be helpful.

"Catch fire, Nuke. And this time I really mean it."

"You don't understand your situation, Kate," Nogura explained. "By now, ID has confirmed that your fingerprints are in the surgical gloves. The gloves are covered in the blood of Cross's last victim—the victim he murdered an hour before he came to visit you. As soon as you're not useful to Cathedral, Kate, I can bring you in with a bullet hole in your head. And I'll be a hero because of it."

"Why, Nuke? How did you get involved with this shit? What—"

Covington interrupted. "Time is short, Detective. It's your place to answer our questions."

Paine spoke next. His voice was deep and controlled. "Detective Duvall, as your colleague has pointed out, if you have nothing to contribute to our endeavors here, then you are quite expendable. On the other side, however, is the certainty that *if* you are cooperative, *if* you can help us, then you will be rewarded."

Duvall shook her head. "Give me a break."

"Why be that way, Kate?" Nogura asked. "They've been good to me."

"Nuke, you've let a murderer walk around free. You've let him commit additional murders. You've destroyed evidence. You've set me up with false evidence. How can I ignore that? How good can they be?"

Paine stopped Nogura from replying. "Detective . . ." He smiled, correcting himself. "Kate, a hypothetical question for a moment: If you, in the course of your duties as a police officer, were being shot at by someone who wished to kill you, would you be justified in firing back, perhaps even killing your attacker?"

"This is different," Duvall said. Why were they wasting so much time on her?

"I think not," Paine said. "I think your department specifically allows you to return deadly force with deadly force. I think also that if you were in a situation in which deadly force was threatened against another person, an innocent civilian, a child perhaps, then once again your department allows the use of deadly force to prevent the death of innocent people. My point is that, in order to meet certain goals, some authorities have conceded that certain deaths are permissible."

The guy is slimy enough to be a defense lawyer, Duvall thought. "Are you telling me that Cross was only killing bad guys?"

"No," Paine said. "But what I am saying is that certain authorities have conceded that, in order to achieve the goals made possible by Anthony Cross's work, some deaths, even of innocents, are . . . acceptable."

His words sent a chill through Duvall. "Certain authorities?"

"The highest authorities," Paine said.

"You bastards," Neale muttered. "You *are* the government, aren't you?"

Paine ignored her. "In any war, Kate, a certain level of civilian casualties is deemed acceptable."

"Have I missed something here? When was war declared? Who are we fighting? The United Soviet Republic of Office Receptionists and Hookers?"

"We must be prepared," Covington said.

"Oh, of course, forgive me. The Boy Scout killer. He was doing it to keep us prepared."

Nogura stood up. "Kate, last chance. Are you going to help us?"

"Nuke, last chance. Are you going to help me bag these assholes?"

Nogura glanced at Paine. The white-haired man nodded once.

"Sorry, Katherine," Nogura said as he unlocked her handcuffs. "We would have made a great team."

He led her from the meeting.

Thirty minutes later, the metal door to the equipment storage room opened and Nogura brought Charis Neale in to join Duvall. Without saying a word, he handcuffed the physicist to a thick yellow pipe running up the unfinished cinderblock wall. Duvall was handcuffed to three smaller black pipes running along the opposite wall. If they both stretched out, they might have been able to touch their feet together. Nogura left. The women sat on the concrete floor, hands caught up around the pipes that restrained them.

There were a thousand things Duvall felt like saying, but she forced herself to concentrate on the immediate situation. "Why are you in here?" she asked.

Neale's eyes were shadowed, her hands still stained. "They're government," she said bitterly. "I kept asking Parnel, he kept saying no. You know what their name means? What Cathedral means?"

Duvall shook her head.

"Nothing," Neale said. "Absolutely nothing. Don't you get it?"

"No." Duvall wondered if the other woman was still aware of her circumstances. She seemed to be talking to someone else in the room, her eyes staring at an empty corner.

"It's just random. A random code from Pentagon computers. A black project designation. Advanced weapons research. That's what it's been all along. From the beginning."

That the government was interested in what she had witnessed was not a revelation to Duvall. "You saw what that glove thing could do. Why are you so surprised that the military would be interested?"

Neale's shoulders sagged. Her arms slumped, held up by the handcuffs. "We were supposed to be theorists. Basic research. Science pure and unsullied."

"You have blood on your hands, Dr. Neale."

"Don't you think I know that? Don't you think I know about Anthony? I've always known about Anthony."

"How long?" Duvall asked. She kept her fingers locked together, supporting her arms with her own strength.

"Since Harvard," Neale said. "Nine years, ten years. I'm not sure anymore."

"And you always helped him?"

She nodded her head. "I followed him one night. Saw him go into this student's apartment. Saw him come out. I was angry. I was jealous. I went in to confront her. I saw . . . what he had done. At first, I didn't believe it had been him. I took care of the evidence, though, just in case he had seen what had happened, left his fingerprints or something behind, and run out. But later . . . the others . . . I just just kept taking care of . . . everything after that."

"Then what?"

"Parnel Covington. SHARP. They wanted Anthony to bring prestige to Shannon Industries. Cathedral was supposed to be an industry-wide consortium, low key and secret to avoid the antitrust laws." She laughed. "And I believed it." The laughing stopped. "But then, I had to, didn't I? I couldn't keep him safe on my own anymore."

Duvall could see the scenario unfolding. "So you told them what Anthony was doing."

Tears suddenly burst from Neale's eyes. Her sobs were cold and lonely in the bare room. "They already knew. They already knew." She turned to look at Duvall for the first time. "And it was *acceptable* to them. They said they could even do a better job than I had been doing. They had friends, they said. Certain authorities. Certain rights conceded. They had military personnel transferred into the police force. Contingency planning, they called it." She took a deep breath, closed her eyes, leaned her head back. "You would have done it, too, Detective. You would have done it, too."

"No," Duvall said. She knew she wouldn't. She hoped she wouldn't. Then she realized that in her own way, by not questioning Cross, she already had.

Neale smiled. "I said that to myself at the time. When I found out about the first time. But I did it one more time. And one more time after that. It became very easy after a while. Especially when I saw what it did for him—freed him, opened up his mind. Each murder, Detective, *each* one was followed by an incredible advancement in his work. And then he started his affair with Cassie, trying to remake her into me. So he could 'understand' me. Be inspired by me. And I still kept helping him." She looked at Duvall again. "I used to think that there was something wrong with me, because I would help Anthony like that. But then I realized that no, there was nothing the matter with me. What I did was nothing that anyone else wouldn't do, under the right circumstances, given the right motivation. You're a police officer. You know people, why they do things. And you know I'm right. We all have it in us, don't we? We just need a reason, that's all."

"Some people have different reasons. Better reasons."

Neale laughed. "You spent the night with Anthony, Detective. You listened to him. You fucked him. You probably even heard him cry. Helped comfort him. What better reason than that?"

Duvall said nothing.

"He's a genius. In physics, and in manipulating people. I think we're all as predictable as billiard balls to him. But he's probably the greatest mind we've ever known, so isn't that worth the greatest sacrifice?"

"He's insane."

"He created artificial gravity. He built a quantum field generator."

"He's killed more than twenty people."

"Acceptable losses, our government says." Neale closed her eyes again. "You know there were American prisoners of war in Hiroshima when the A-bomb was dropped there? You know they're going to kill us, don't you?"

Duvall hadn't wanted to think that they would make up their minds so quickly. "I thought they wanted information."

"They're fairly certain they can figure out the glove—if it can do what you say you saw it do. They have some of what it did on Lee's videotape, sparking mostly, and the sketches of the timing circuit board Rich put together.

"You know, they won't even have to put bullets in our heads. They can just make us disappear. Probably drop us into a black hole. A fucking literal black hole. They'll be able to build one now, a gravity well. Just like the one Anthony made in the accelerator."

Duvall flexed her hands. They felt cold. She leaned back against the wall, trying to think of some way out. "Anthony said he was the only one who understood gravity."

"He said he was the only one who could understand a lot of things."

Duvall closed her eyes, remembering the look and the feel of him.

The words he had spoken. "But gravity was different. He said it wasn't like the other three things."

"What three things?"

"The forces? Yeah, the three forces. Everyone thought that gravity was going to be another force but he said it wasn't. He had 'seen' it."

"That's odd," Neale said. "That doesn't sound like Anthony at all. Did he say what he thought gravity was?"

Duvall shrugged. "It was space, it was time." She shook her head, stretched her arms. "The other three moved inside it, or something. Something to do with the earliest moment of the universe. Planck time? Dark matter? I guess I wasn't paying attention." *I wonder why?* she thought.

"Is that how he said the glove worked?"

"He didn't tell me about the glove. He . . ." Duvall turned to Neale. There was far too much awareness in the physicist's eyes. "But I already said that the first time you assholes questioned me, didn't I?"

Neale watched Duvall for a few seconds, then said, "She was telling the truth. He didn't tell her anything."

The door to the equipment room opened again. Nogura and Covington stood outside. Duvall could see a suction microphone stuck to the door. The wire from it ran into a small tape recorder Covington held.

Nogura unlocked Neale's handcuffs. "We had to be sure," he said to Duvall. "We had to know what he told you."

"Is what you're doing worth it, Neale?" Duvall asked suddenly. "Is your reason good enough?"

Neale stopped in the doorway. "I love him, Detective. What other reason can there be to make all this . . . worthwhile?"

As the door swung shut and she heard the click of the lock, Duvall could not think of an immediate answer. But she knew that if she were ever to be able to believe that she was different from Neale, there had to be another reason.

There had to be.

TWENTY-EIGHT

He *was* Legion. His probability wave spread throughout the universe. He was everything and everywhere, stretching backward to the ultimate moment beyond the Planck time when all things were one, when all matter and energy were connected in one point at one time. And he felt that connection hold as the universe expanded through its billions of years. That primordial instant of unity was why the Einstein-Podolsky-Rosen electrons were correlated. It was why life had arisen to contemplate itself. It was why protons were eternal and gravitons nonexistent.

It was why Anthony Cross existed.

The universe was all the same, all one particle, all one time. The barriers humans saw were illusions. But Cross saw beyond them. He knew he was not human any longer. As he had always known he would become, he was *more*.

Cross was in Lab 2 and no longer wished to be there with Neale and Duvall and the others. And since all places were the same place it was the most trivial of problems to know how to be someplace else. And he was. The pool car he had taken from the SHARP lot, the second car he had stolen from Smokey's garage, and all the other cars he had taken to disguise his journey were just an illusion. He knew that the secret to true movement lay in realms other than the physical world and in time he would solve the tiny problem that would allow him to abandon illusion altogether.

But for now, after the sunset of the third day since his Work was completed, Cross was by the house, *the* house where he had first thought and where all his different aspects had first become aware. Now the house was boarded and shuttered, silent in the night. Condemned by the small town for the atrocities that had been committed there, forgotten over the years, now just a relic. But since all times were the same time, it was the most trivial of problems to know how to be somewhen else. And he was.

He saw the house re-form itself before him. The curls of paint flattened against the wood. The weeds receded, replaced with grass. The porch straightened, the glass returned to the windows. People were alive again within it. Anthony Cross moved forward, a shadow slipping through the air, to look past a window, to collapse a wave by the act of observation.

The boy was five years old. His mother's friend lay on the living room carpet. His mother's friend had been easy to fool, an innocent magic trick with a rope gone wrong, and the rope would not come off the man's hands. The boy was just a child. Why would the friend suspect?

Then the rope went around the man's feet, in socks now, his shoes on the mat in the hallway by the door where he usually left them. The boy had read a Boy Scout book about knots. The ones he had tied tightened with each of the man's struggles. Within seconds the man was on the floor, bellowing with rage. But the boy's mother was not at home. And even the boy was not there. Young Anthony had gone away again and someone else had taken over. The someone else who always came when the boy was being beaten. The someone else who protected the boy, suffered for the boy, plotted revenge for the boy. The someone else who shared nothing of the boy's except an insatiable curiosity. It was the someone else who wanted to know *how things worked.*

The older Anthony Cross, bound by his memories as surely as the planets were bound by the sun, watched like a shadow in the window as the boy inside the house left the man on the floor, went to his room, and returned with his baseball bat.

The young Anthony had not been strong at age five. It had taken eighteen blows until the man no longer tried to crawl away. Five more blows until he no longer tried to scream for help.

Then the boy went to the kitchen and got the knives and the drawer of household tools, and the spool of copper wire, and he sat down on the carpet in the silent house, and calmly and methodically, and with a great deal of skill (he had read a book about anatomy), took the man apart to find out why he was bad.

It had been so easy, Anthony Cross remembered as he watched the flesh of the man part again. Easier than toys, easier than the cats a year before. The heat and the wet and the thickness had felt so good as he had reached inside the man's body. And the act had made so much sense. To understand, to truly understand, young Anthony realized, it was necessary to peer beyond the barriers, to get inside, to find out firsthand how things worked.

A few hours later, the boy had had the first of the revelations to be brought on by his explorations, by his Work. A few hours later, after his mother had come home, after she had screamed and shrieked and at last fallen silent on the long gleaming curve of the carving knife, after the boy had dragged her to the carpet and taken her apart, too, he realized, looking from one open shell to another, from his mother to her friend, that they were both the same, they were all the same. They were empty shells with only one purpose: to help him understand.

A shadow flickered at the window but the boy didn't see it as he dug in and reached in and felt the hot meat slip through his fingers. The older Anthony Cross, bound by his memories and his genius to all time, could only be an observer. The images he saw were created solely within his mind.

The passage of this past time increased. Cross saw the others come to the house. He saw the police take the boy away. He saw the therapists and the case workers and all who tried to help. Fortunately, though, young Anthony had read books about these things and parts of him knew what to say, knew how to act, and in time the grown-ups had pronounced him cured and safe and had sealed his records so no one would ever know, not even reporters from *Time*, and had given him a new name and a new family: a man and a woman pleased to have such a smart young boy come to stay with them.

The smart young boy was happy to be in a house where he wasn't beaten. He was entranced by the endless supply of books his foster parents provided. Young Anthony had changed. He was not as he had been before. He had learned to be careful. He had learned how not to be caught.

When he entered the university, a prodigy at the age of eleven, the boy was supported by his foster parents no longer, only by a trust fund. None of the other empty shells who inhabited his world ever suspected how that man and woman could die so tragically, so easily, so unexpectedly. Never suspected that his foster parents' deaths in a car without brakes had been anything other than an accident. Because by the age of eleven, Anthony Cross, and all the other disparate aspects of him, had even learned how to cry when it was necessary. How to laugh, how to smile, how to hug, even how to look like a child in need of help and understanding. But inside the boy, unknown, unfelt, there was nothing except his brilliance and his hunger to know how things worked, how everything worked. In that there was power and solace. In that there was lonely control.

And now, dissolved in the quantum that underlay all things, Cross did know.

The dream images of his memory vanished and he was by the old house, boarded and shuttered. He sat on the warped porch. He rested his elbows on his knees, his head on his hands. He had done what he had set out to do and now he had come home.

To his beginning.

But there was no one there for him.

He no longer felt the bite of the wires of his gauntlet as they moved like second skin across his hand and arm. He was too caught up in trying to decide on another question, another goal.

What was there for him now? He knew how everything worked. He knew how everything had begun. Physics was closed. All science was closed. Did that mean his life was closed with them? Was there nothing more?

And then it came to him. There *was* another question to be explored. It was true that he knew how everything had begun—but what was still a mystery was how everything would end.

"Of course," he said into the silence of the night. He stood up on the porch of his house, where his journey had begun. As easily as that, he had a new goal now, a new quest, new meaning.

There was something more for him to become.

But first, he knew, he would need some help. First he knew, he would need to be *inspired*. And he knew just where to go for that.

This house had been only one of his many beginning points. There had been others. He would go to them. And then, he knew, he would be able to leave the cars and all the other illusions behind. Because soon there would be only one reality for the entire world.

His.

TWENTY-NINE

When Nogura brought her a cot, some blankets, and a tray of plastic-wrapped sandwiches from a vending machine, Duvall decided that Cathedral was not going to put her into a black hole right away. And since she knew they had no compunctions about killing, and that by connecting her to the Boy Scout murders they had arranged for her death not to be questioned, Duvall further concluded that Cathedral believed she still had something to offer them, though she didn't know what. At the very least, their decision gave her the time she needed to plan her escape.

On Wednesday night, the fourth day of her captivity, Nogura and Paine opened the door to the equipment room where Duvall was still held. By the rules they had established for her, Duvall sat on the cot against the far wall, twelve feet away from the door. The chain that Nogura had cuffed to her hand at one end and to the pipes at the other dragged noisily on the floor, but it gave her some freedom of movement and the chance to use the portable toilet they had provided. Duvall felt as if she were in a dungeon.

"We have a few more questions for you," Nogura said. He carried a rolled-up sheet of paper in his hand. Both he and Paine remained just inside the open door, beyond the reach of her chain.

"Why should I answer anything?" Duvall didn't want to risk giving up whatever information she had that made her valuable.

"To do what's right," Nogura said. "To bring Cross to justice."

"*Now* you want to bring him to justice? I thought you gave up on being one of the good guys, Nuke. I thought selling out was more your style, now."

"Cross has done what he set out to do," Paine said. "There's no need for him to continue to be free. To continue searching for . . . inspiration."

"Is that what you call it?" Duvall pulled her knees up to her chest, dragging the chain against the floor, getting them used to seeing it move, hearing it slide. If they did come closer and she managed to get the chain around someone's neck, preferably Nogura's, then the links would act as ratchets. As long as she kept the pressure on, the chain could only get tighter.

"Inspiration is what Anthony calls it." Paine might have been describing the operation of a car engine. "He believes he gains insight into the universe whenever he feels the life pass from someone."

"I'll remember to try that the next time I need some inspiration for redecorating my house."

"The fact remains," Paine continued, and there was anger growing in his voice, "that each of Anthony's major breakthroughs, in theory and in application, has been preceded by such an act."

"His murders, you mean."

Nogura broke in before Duvall and Paine began yelling at each other. "Kate, you've worked Homicide longer than I have. I want to ask you some questions about Cross. As a murderer. A pattern killer. How he kills."

"Gee, Nuke, I thought you knew. He puts his fucking hand through people's heads like he was a ghost or something. What's more straightforward than that?"

"He's not a ghost," Nogura said calmly. "He is able to tunnel his hand into his victims' bodies."

"Tunnel, Nuke? What's that mean, like a mole?"

"Like an electron in an Esaki diode," Paine said. "It makes a quantum jump from one position to another without traversing any of the space in between. We believe Anthony's glove is wired to somehow create a field which enables him to make his hand behave as such a particle, under his conscious control."

"You didn't believe me the first time I told you what I saw him do with the glove. How do you know he didn't just wire up some sort of super heating coil and *burn* his way into the guard?" Duvall shook her head. She didn't see what they were getting at. And then, "Hold on, did you say 'his victim*s*?'"

Nogura unrolled the paper he had in his hand. There were several sheets. Duvall recognized them as police faxes: case inquiries.

"How many, Nuke?"

"Three or four that we know of. He's stealing cars. Or was. But we've managed to gather enough preliminary autopsy results to know that the people he stole the cars from didn't just die from a heating coil. The disruption of flesh and bone extends several inches into the skull and brain. It's like nothing we've ever seen before. And it's getting hard to keep it quiet."

"What's he stealing the cars for? Is he headed someplace?"

"We suspect it has something to do with finding . . . the Beginning," Paine said.

Duvall studied the white-haired man, wondering how much she should share, how much she should hold back. But Cross was still killing people. She had her duty. "He did talk to me about that being what he wanted to find out. The Beginning of everything."

"We think perhaps he's after a different type of beginning now. His own."

"I don't get it."

Nogura shuffled through the faxes. "The last stolen car reported was found near a house in Larkin's Mill, Pennsylvania. The house had been abandoned years ago. Last night, it was torched."

"I've read about Larkin's Mill in *People*, Nuke. People say a lot of strange stuff happens there."

"The house used to belong to Cross's mother. It was where he lived as a child. It was where he murdered his mother and her boyfriend."

Duvall whistled. "How old was he?"

"Not important," Paine said before Nogura could reply. "Young enough that his files were sealed. The thing is, we believe he went back to that house as part of his . . . quest I suppose you'd call it, to understand *his* beginning."

"Yeah, so? He did and you didn't get him and now what?"

Nogura and Paine looked at each other for a moment. Nogura answered. "There's a chance we might know where he's going next. And . . ."

Duvall at least knew the detective well enough to know what he was going to say next. "And you want me to help you. I don't fucking believe it."

"You have to, Kate," Nogura said.

"You're going to kill me, Nuke. I don't have to do anything."

Paine cleared his throat. "I am in the position to grant you full immunity," he announced.

"From *what*, for God's sake? I haven't done anything."

"All you have to do," Paine continued, "is swear an oath under the Official Secrets Act that you will not divulge any information you have about Cathedral and . . . you will be free to go."

"Everything will be cleared up at the department, too," Nogura added.

"And," Paine continued, "a cash settlement of one—"

"What the hell is wrong with you guys?" Duvall shouted. "You don't control the whole goddamned world, you know."

"No, we don't," Paine agreed. "But, unfortunately, if Anthony Cross continues on in this manner, we believe that there is a chance that *he* could."

"Help us, Kate," Nogura said. "We've started on a plan, but we need to know what you know about people like Cross."

Duvall slammed her feet and her chain back down to the floor. "Nuke, you're full of shit. You don't need me. You could get fifty behavioral experts from the FBI or some psych hospital to tell you all you want to know about psychopathic killers."

"We could," Nogura said calmly. "But they don't know Anthony . . . the way you do."

"What drives him, Kate?" Paine asked.

"You assholes made him what he is today. You tell me."

Paine took her question seriously. "Well, he's a scientist. They all live for the day that they discover something unknown to everyone else. And he's brilliant beyond labels, so he chose for himself the ultimate discovery—the marriage of relativity and quantum physics, the unified field theory, the creation of the universe."

"To find out things no one has ever known before," Duvall quoted softly.

"Is that something he told you?" Paine asked.

Duvall nodded.

"Anything else?"

"Look, there is no one accepted theory to explain why serial killers do the things they do," she said at last, realizing that perhaps she did have something to offer. "If Anthony has said that he somehow finds inspiration in the process of murder, then that could be reason enough. For some reason, he's come to associate death—the specific way he causes death at least—with a particular way of thinking that is rewarding to him."

"All his thinking was dedicated to one goal," Paine said. "And he apparently has achieved that goal. So why is he continuing?"

"That's obvious," Duvall said. "He's got a new goal."

Paine threw up his hands. "If he's solved the fundamental mystery of all creation, Kate, what's left?"

"Everything's left. I mean, every psychopath has a purpose, some path he follows, some mystical achievement to be won despite what the rest of the world thinks. Only in Anthony's case, it's not so mystical, is it?"

"But why won't he stop?" There was no anger left in Paine, just fatigue.

"What you have to remember," Duvall said, "is that no matter how brilliant his accomplishments, Anthony is insane. He might have all sorts of complicated reasons for doing whatever it is he's done in the past and whatever it is he's still doing, but we can't expect that those reasons would ever make sense to us. He's playing by his own rules now. He's in his own world."

"Can you make a guess, Kate?" Paine asked. "Anything at all that might help us understand what he's up to."

"Why is that important?"

"I told you. We have to catch him," Nogura said.

Duvall laughed. "You don't want to catch Cross. He's filled his purpose for you. All you want is his glove, the quantum whatzits generator."

"Who would you rather had that device, Kate?" Paine asked. "A team of specialist military researchers responsible to Congress, or a murderous psychopath?"

"There's a difference?"

"If I were you, Detective," Paine said, "I'd certainly hope so."

"So we're all agreed?" Covington asked. Neale watched him look around the conference table, checking with each member of Cathedral present. She could tell Covington was enjoying this; he had played at being an ordinary businessman too long. He needed action, no matter what the price.

"If any of it comes into the open, SHARP's cover will be completely exposed," David Paine said, staring contemplatively at his hands on the dark wood of the table. "There will be hearings into funding, responsibility, that sort of annoyance."

Covington nodded. "I think that will be seen as an acceptable trade-off, David. It's also quite likely that all that information will be declared Most Secret."

"If the ambush works," Kwong said.

"If it doesn't work," Covington replied, "then SHARP will not be compromised. Of course, without Anthony we'd have to shut down anyway."

"And what about us?" Weinstein asked. Neale could see that his color had come back to normal after a few days' rest and a visit from a doctor, but the old man was still shaken by what he had witnessed in the ruins of Lab 2, beginning with the cat and ending with the demonstration of Cross's device. "What about our professional reputations? We brought Cross into this, after all. And by now, he knows it, too."

"If it doesn't work, Adam," Covington said, "I expect both you and Lee will be employed by an appropriate defense contractor to lead the effort to re-create Cross's work."

"And you should have a much easier time than Cross had," Paine added, "because we have the timing circuit diagrams and the wiring design on the videotape. Plus, you know it can be done. That's half the battle right there."

Kwong chewed on a thumbnail. "Listen, are you honestly convinced that's where he's headed?" Kwong obviously wasn't.

"He's trying to track down his own beginning, Lee," Covington said. "He's been to where his life as a child and as . . . a killer began. I think we can be hopeful that sometime in the next few days he'll arrive at where he first became a scientist. Of course, we're happy to hear any other ideas about stopping him."

"What other ideas?" Kwong grumbled. "If that *is* a quantum field generator, then nothing will stop him."

"That's what worries me," Nogura said, finally having something within his range of expertise on which to comment. "Assuming that he does show up and he's still wearing the glove, it's not as if we can slap cuffs on him or anything."

Covington stood up at the head of the table. Neale could see the enjoyment in his eyes, the hunger she knew so well. "I wouldn't worry about stopping Anthony, Detective," Covington said. "In my father's house are many mansions." He smiled, enjoying his vision of what was to come. "And as should be obvious from our name, more than one Cathedral."

THIRTY

Anthony Cross remembered Harvard at dawn. The low angle of brilliant sun sending long shadows across dew-sparkling grass. The full trees overhead, leaves motionless in the still morning air. The smell of green, the quiet, the empty buildings poised on the brink of day. He remembered the Charles River, silver with morning light, the dark angles of the Boston skyline, dark towers studded with scintillating pinpoints of light, silhouetted against the brightening sky.

Anthony Cross remembered Harvard at dawn and he was there, his passage through the physical world an illusion. All that mattered was that he was at the starting point of his education, in a narrow corridor on the top floor of the Jefferson Physical Laboratory.

He breathed the musty smell of hundred-year-old wood paneling, the scent of coffee too long on a hot plate. He heard the tired laughter of graduate students who had worked through the night. He remembered that this was where his own student office had been when he had worked with his data from the abandoned A-bomb test sites. He had returned to where what he now thought of as the first phase of his search had begun. Perhaps, he hoped, it was where the next phase would end.

He listened in the stillness of the morning and could hear voices from an open door down the corridor. He moved to that door and those voices, seeking inspiration.

There were four students clustered at a computer workstation in the cramped office, three men, one woman. The computer screen showed a starfield against which two fleets of spaceships moved. The students laughed again as one of the spaceships blew up.

Cross twisted the cuff on his gauntlet and a single blue light glowed on it. He rested his left hand against the doorframe. The surface of that hand and forearm, bound in copper, had been resculpted with the whorls and patterns of the wire's pressure, and the flesh was dark and swollen.

"Who knows about de Sitter space?" he asked.

The four students jumped and spun around on their cheap office chairs. He saw their eyes go wide.

"Who knows about de Sitter space?" Cross repeated.

"What's wrong with your arm?" one of the students asked.

"In this time you have wasted for me," Cross said angrily, "the universe has expanded by another four million miles. We must hurry! Do you understand?" he asked.

The woman turned to the man at her side and smiled. "I bet this is Kingsburgh's idea for getting us ready for our orals," she said. "She's wacky enough to make a getup like that." She stood up. "Okay, I'll go for it."

"I don't know, Beth," the man beside her said. "He looks pretty *wired* to me."

All the students laughed. But Cross could see something else in the woman's eyes, something other than humor. He hoped it might be that meaningful contact so important when seeking to inspire true understanding.

"Do you understand de Sitter space?" Cross asked the woman.

"Willem de Sitter," the woman said, smiling tentatively. "Dutch physicist. Defined de Sitter space in 1917. He and Einstein redefined it in 1932."

"Good," Cross said. "Continue."

"He, uh, introduced a cosmological constant to describe the universe's uniform infinite expansion. Einstein later called the inclusion of a cosmological constant in his work the biggest mistake of his career. The postulates of de Sitter space are that the universe is isotropic and homogenous, that the universe does not change over time, that . . . *did* Professor Kingsburgh send you up here?'' The woman stepped back hesitantly.

Some past part of Cross came up with the lines that were needed, the inspiration the woman might require in this place and this time. ''Do you want to earn your doctorate, young lady, or would you rather be sent down with a master's?''

The woman blinked, glanced at her companions, then turned back to Cross. ''Uh, okay, so today there is not enough observational data to confirm whether or not our universe exists as de Sitter space though most workers accept that the residual radiation of the big bang . . .'' The woman's smile was gone. Cross could feel blood dripping from his arm, released by the movements of his hand stretching the tightly drawn wire.

''You're hurt, man,'' one of the students said weakly.

Cross took a step forward. ''What are the options?'' he asked the woman.

''Uh, if there is enough mass in the universe, then the universe is closed. That is, sometime in the future, the force of gravity will be enough to reverse the outward expansion of the big bang and eventually pull all the universe's mass back together into a big crunch.''

''And what if there is not enough mass?'' Cross asked. ''What happens then?'' That was the next phase.

One of the men stood up beside the nervous woman. ''Hey, bud, you're dripping blood all over the place. Maybe you should back off a little and head to the infirmary. This isn't funny anymore.''

''It was never supposed to be,'' Cross said. He looked at the woman again. ''Tell me about the open universe. Tell me all that you understand.''

''Uh, if there's not enough mass, then the expansion of the big bang continues indefinitely. The stars use up all the available fuel in the universe until fusion reactions are no longer possible and they all die. Eventually, all energy is evenly distributed throughout the universe in total entropy. And nothing more happens, ever.''

''And is there no way out?''

"Black holes?" the student suggested nervously. "If any form with enough mass, then any one of them might trigger the creation of another universe . . . uh, somewhere else in superspace."

"Another universe," Cross said. "Yesss." His hand flickered randomly with the blackness of chance.

"Holy shit," a student whispered. "Look at his hand."

The woman continued. "Uh, but each universe would be closed off like a singularity, unable to ever contact—"

"Enough mass, yesss." Cross moved closer again. "Singularity."

"But that's only if . . . only if . . ." The woman faltered.

The man stepped forward again. "That's enough. I'm calling security, bud."

He brought his hand up to push on Cross's shoulder but Cross brought his left hand up to block the blow. The gauntlet flickered with uncertainty, its possibilities expanded. The man's open hand fell into it as if he had met empty space. The man gasped, withdrew his hand. His face was white.

The woman gaped at what she saw. The two other men stood up, confused.

"I'm not here to hurt you," Cross said. "I only want to see that she understands."

He reached out his hand, flickering it to solid, impenetrable black. He brushed the probabilities of his fingers against the woman's forehead. He pushed deeper.

"I only want to see into the quantum," he explained. Deeper, through the atoms of her skull. "Beyond the event horizon." Through the atoms of the nerve-webbed membranes, the folds and fissures of all that she was. "Into the singularity."

He made a fist in her head and collapsed the probability waves that made his hand be there, fully formed inside her.

A moment passed.

From life to lifelessness in that one instant.

She didn't scream. She only slumped as the sound of sizzling flesh, the sound of solid interference hummed through the room. The lattice of his existence impinging on her own.

"Yesss," Cross sighed. He had felt it. "Yesss." The moment of her transition. He returned his hand to an indeterminate state and she slid from the lost solidity of his fist, crumpled to the floor, her head a bloodied pulp of disruption.

The man beside the woman's body roared in anger, not knowing what he had seen. He drew back his arm and swung at Cross. Cross flickered his chest, bare of wire. The fist swung through emptiness.

The students stared at the body on the floor.

"What happened?"

"What is it?"

"Just fucking get him!"

The three men jumped at Cross, so quickly that they caught him unprepared. He felt their hands and arms wrap around him, squeezing, forcing him to the wall. Their voices joined together in frantic cries for help.

Then at each point of contact, Cross flickered. But only once.

Their hands and arms passed through him, into him, and then were caught, intermixed, interference. Their voices were shrieks of agony as they writhed around him, fixed solidly within him.

Cross expanded his wave again and released them. They fell to the floor, hands and arms bloody stumps of twisted bones and ruined flesh. Cross leaned over one student, grasped the student's hair to pull his head up, looked in his eyes.

"Do you understand?" Cross asked. The blood from his wire-wrapped hand dripped on the student's face.

The student blubbered. Cross reached into the man's skull, made a fist, collapsed it.

"Do you understand, *now?*" Cross asked as the student passed through his transition.

Cross expanded the wave of his hand and the student fell back to the floor, scalp frozen in the bloody ripples of quantum disruption. Within a minute, Cross had seen to it that the other two students understood as well.

Behind him then, coming down the corridor, he could hear the sound of running feet and anxious voices, responding to the students' calls for help and their cries of ultimate understanding.

Cross stood up and faced the open doorway, expanded the wave of his hand and felt the blackness of its field rush over his body, encasing his entire being in infinite possibilities.

"Yesss," he said.

And when the rescuers came speeding through the doorway, rushing into the office, they ran right *into* him.

Dr. Anthony Cross was back on campus, and everyone had a lot to learn.

THIRTY-ONE

After the preciseness and the newness and the freshness of SHARP, the scarred wooden desks, jammed bookshelves, and decade-old computer terminals of Harvard made Charis Neale feel as if she had traveled to a primitive land in which she did not belong. She wondered if she would ever feel she belonged anywhere again.

"Has it changed all that much?" Covington asked as he watched her stare out the window at the dawn over the commons.

"I don't know," Neale answered. She had spent eight years at Harvard, earned her two doctorates here, but her old office seemed as alien to her as did her purpose for returning to it. "Is Adam going to be all right?"

Covington frowned as he folded himself to fit in a small metal stacking chair across from the desk that once was Neale's. Weinstein hadn't wanted to come with them. He had been dragged on board the Shannon jet in Los Angeles, crying that he didn't want to be bait for the trap. "We gave him a few hours to recuperate at the hotel. He and Kwong should be arriving in a few minutes."

"Adam's an old man," Neale said, as if she might care.

"He's just feeling guilty, that's all. Adam and Lee both think that everything that's happened is their fault because they're the ones who set up Anthony back when Shannon was trading research grants for . . . inside information. They're afraid of what Anthony's reaction is going to be when—well, when he finds us here and learns that his work is about to be usurped by them. If he doesn't cooperate."

Neale stepped away from the window. There was nothing to see other than a few early morning joggers. The watchers surrounding them were unseen, invisibly protecting the perimeter of the Jefferson Physical Lab building. *"Will* you use them as bait?" she asked.

Covington held up a finger and listened intently as he pressed a hand to his ear. A thin white wire ran from it to the collar of his open blue windbreaker. "Sorry," he said after a few moments. "Just a routine check. Nothing yet. What did you say?"

"Adam thinks that he and Lee are bait for the trap."

"Whatever it takes, Charis. We all knew that going in. And if not Lee and Adam, then . . . whatever else it takes."

Neale sat down in the chair behind the desk and folded her hands on it. In her day, this row of offices had been part of the Physics Department. Now it belonged to History and she didn't recognize any of the books on the shelves. Paine had made arrangements for the faculty to work elsewhere for the duration of the operation. He was a versatile man. He seemed to be able to arrange anything.

"Whatever it takes. Even if it's Duvall? Or me?"

"It won't come to that. If we're lucky." Covington leaned forward in his chair and placed his hands on the desk near Neale's. "Why do you seem so nervous, Charis? Cross is a psychopath and that's what makes the trap foolproof. He can't escape his compulsion to return to his beginnings, so eventually he *has* to come here. Every stop he's made across the country confirms that this is where he's headed. And when he does arrive, tonight, tomorrow, whenever, he'll be . . . neutralized and we'll have the field generator and the beginnings of quantum technology. It's everything we always wanted."

"I only wanted . . . Anthony." Neale moved her hands away from his and slipped them inside the pockets of her own blue windbreaker. Covington had said the jackets would make it easier to identify the Cathedral team in the event of confusion, and Nogura had said the jackets would be better for hiding the body armor they had to wear. In case the operation did manage to escalate to the second stage.

Covington spoke softly, trying to be gentle. "What you wanted was knowledge."

"That came with Anthony."

"You wanted power."

"*You* wanted that, Parnel. That's all you ever wanted. You told me Cathedral was part of Shannon Industries' long-term R&D commitments. An industrial consortium. Ha." She looked across at him, her employer for almost four years, her confessor for the same length of time, the man who shared all the secrets she could not share with Cross, the man who had shared none of his secrets with her. "Has there ever been anything you told me that was the truth?"

"Four years is a long time," Covington said. "I imagine that once or twice, I did. And I'm sure you remember the times."

"Sometimes I wonder whether you brought me on for Anthony or for yourself. Maybe you thought he'd get tired of me and you could take his leavings. All you'd have to do is show some pity for the girl scientist who thought she could think like the big boys before they took her off to the freak show for abnormal IQs." All her bitterness flooded from her, as if she knew she might be running out of time to let it out.

"Don't pretend you don't want to be part of this, Charis. And don't pretend you've never thought about me and what it might be like if Anthony was out of the equation. You don't have to keep cooperating with me. Just like you didn't have to try and get that information from Duvall."

"I wanted other information from her."

"And you still don't have to go through with what we're doing here."

"What choice have you left me?"

"All the choice in the world."

She shook her head. "Anthony had that once. I don't. Never had."

Covington stretched one long arm across the desk to grab her hand from her pocket. "If this works and we get that glove, then you could gain the same choice that Anthony had. And that *is* what you've always wanted. I don't care what you say. More than being Anthony's lover, more than even being a woman, you're a scientist. You want that knowledge more than anything. Ultimate knowledge, Charis. Ultimate power. And I can give you that. Think of it. The power of the quantum field. The power to do whatever you want, whatever you choose."

"Whatever I choose?" She put her free hand over his and leaned forward, staring into his eyes, capturing his hand beneath her breasts.

Covington's eyes burned. "Absolute power is absolute freedom. It can be yours." He slowly moved his hand beneath hers, pressing into her.

She rubbed against him. "If that happens, Parnel . . ."

"Yes?" He began to move his other hand toward her.

"If I were you, I'd start to run." She raked her fingers across the back of his hand and felt skin peel off beneath her nails. "And I wouldn't stop."

Covington wrenched his hand back and held the wounds to his mouth. But he smiled at her, even as the blood flowed past his lips. "You see, you fucking little bitch? You know what power feels like. And that means that no matter what you say, we've been on the same side all along. The same fucking side."

He left her then and she waited in the office, full of fear for what might happen when Cross came, and full of fear for what might happen, what she might choose, if what Covington had said was true.

Nogura and Duvall had an understanding. If she wouldn't scream for help, he wouldn't gag her; and if she wouldn't try to get away, he wouldn't shoot her. They were both professionals. But he did cuff her hands behind her back, just to make things a bit more difficult in case she had a lapse of judgment.

They sat in a small office with bookcases which reached shakily from the floor to ceiling. Duvall was certain that two on the opposite wall were on the brink of tipping over onto her. Near the back of the room, two desks were jammed together, front to front. One was buried beneath stacks of paper all tumbled against each other, the other was covered by Nogura's surveillance equipment.

The camera pickups were outside, covering the walks and doors that led to the building. Duvall hadn't seen any of the personnel involved in the operation. She only knew they were present because of Nogura's intermittent exchanges with them over his walkie-talkie. Other than a few morons who thought jogging in the early morning was somehow good for a person, the images on the three black-and-white television monitors on the desk showed no one outside within range.

Duvall leaned her rickety wooden chair back against one of the bookcases, to help hold the bookcase up as much as make the chair more comfortable. "So how long do we stay here, Nuke?" she asked. "I mean, are we here for keeps? Do you chain me up in the hotel basement every night? Start teaching classes here, maybe?"

"This was an important place for Cross," Nogura said, adjusting the images on the monitors. "He'll come here. And he'll come here soon so we can do our job and leave."

" 'Do our job'? Christ, how can you say that? It's Covington's fucking job. You're a cop. You used to be, anyhow."

Nogura looked sad. He acted as if he no longer had to keep his feelings hidden; the time for secrets past. "I'm a soldier, Katherine. Always have been. The LAPD was just another posting."

"A posting? So you could hang around and wait to cover up Cross's murders?"

Nogura nodded.

"How many?"

"On my own, just three."

"There were others in the department? Like you?"

"A couple," Nogura admitted. "In other divisions, other states. We tried to keep up with Cross's movements. Did a pretty good job, too."

Duvall felt sick. She had let Cross touch her. Let him inside her. "How many murders, Nuke? How many were covered up so he could build that fucking wire thing?"

"I don't know. I'm just a soldier." He made it sound like an apology. "But I do know that you were the first cop to get so far, connecting the murders in the national databank. That was good work, Katherine. I really mean it."

"I know you do, Nuke," Duvall said sadly, feeling a wave of realization wash over her. "And you know how? Because you called me Katherine. Jesus. You've been doing it all along, haven't you?"

Nogura's face returned to stone. "Doing what?"

"Your tell, Nuke. When you lie to me, you always call me Kate. Guess you're trying to put on a show, act like one of the boys. But when you tell the truth, it's Katherine. Nice and polite. Sure wish I had figured that out a couple of weeks ago."

Nogura looked embarrassed. He hadn't realized what he had been doing. "I'm glad you didn't. I could have been fired."

"You should have been fired for the way you were helping me dig up information on Cross's activities." She felt a wave of new knowledge strike again. "But I was doing your work for you, wasn't I? You were using me to dig up all the loose ends that might have been lying around, sending me off in all sorts of directions, laying it out in front of me, telling me to watch out for Cross and then, like I just fell off the biggest goddamned turnip truck in the world, I handed all my files over to you. Jesus, that was smooth. Gutsy, too."

"Personally," Nogura said quietly, "I'm sorry it had to go down like that."

Duvall dropped her voice, too. "There's still time to change the way things are, Nuke."

"You're not being realistic . . . Katherine."

"I'm not a soldier, Nuke. I'm a cop. We're not supposed to be realistic. We're supposed to believe that the good guys always win, that the bad guys always get what's coming to them, and that the innocent are always protected."

"That's not the way the world works. You know that." Nogura adjusted the image on center monitor, making it sharper as he kept making frequent glances in Duvall's direction.

Duvall leaned her head back into the books and sighed. She wasn't getting through to him but she'd be damned if she was going to give up. "Yeah, Nuke, I know that. I've worked for Erhlenmeyer for three years, remember? I grew up in the projects knowing the way the world works every fucking day of my life. But it doesn't mean I have to give up trying."

"Trying to do what?"

"To make a difference."

On the monitor, Duvall saw two students with book bags walking up the path to a main door. They stopped at the steps and kissed. The girl squeezed the guy's backside. Duvall wondered how the couple would feel if they knew every move was being watched by what she guessed was a fully equipped SWAT team.

"Well, Katherine," Nogura said, sitting back in his chair. "In a little while, you might just get your chance to make a difference."

Duvall didn't like the way he had said that. "I'm not just here for the ride, am I. What've you got planned for me, Nuke?"

"It's not up to me," Nogura said. "It never has been."

"Then who is it up to?" But as soon as Duvall asked that question, she saw the desolate look in Nogura's eyes and knew what and who his answer would be.

Her life was in the hands of Anthony Cross.

Neale couldn't stand the waiting. She left her office, heard voices in the corridor, and found the small cubicle where Nogura sat hunched over surveillance monitors and Duvall appeared to be trying to go to sleep in her chair.

"Anything?" Neale asked, standing in the doorway.

Nogura wheeled in his chair, making it squeak against the cheap tiled floor, one hand heading for the inside of his windbreaker. Duvall only opened her eyes.

"We're not expecting him in the daytime," Nogura said, adjusting himself in his chair. "Too many people around. We think he'll want to stay hidden. At least that's the way he's been operating so far."

"Then again, he might have already been here," Duvall suggested. "So maybe we should call it off."

Nogura frowned at Duvall. "Harvard isn't exactly a deserted house on the edge of a small town. If he already had been here, there would have been reports. We'd know it." He looked up at Neale. "How are you doing, Dr. Neale? Can I get you anything?"

Neale shook her head.

Duvall rocked forward in her chair to bring all four of its legs to the floor with a thud. "So, you went to school here?"

Neale nodded, hands in her pockets. "For a long time."

"Why?"

"I beg your pardon?"

Duvall shrugged, still asking questions like a cop. It was a hard habit to break, never knowing when a small piece of information might be useful. "Well, Anthony wanted to find out about the Beginning of everything. What did *you* want to do? What made you be a scientist?"

Neale was confused by the question. It had been such a long time since she had thought about it. "I, uh, liked science. I was good at it."

"So you could feed the starving millions and solve all the world's problems, right?"

"No. It's not like that." Neale walked into the room and stood across from Duvall and didn't know what to say. The detective was a layperson, a foreigner who didn't speak the language, didn't know the customs. She was one of those who believed that science was a religion, the pure unassailable word of God, and that scientists were its priests unspoiled by human flaws. But that belief was wrong. Despite its superficial logic and the elegance of its theorems and equations, science was the most human of endeavors, an interpretation of reality to be shared like ghost stories told around a fire, punctuated by frequent nervous glances over the shoulder, to try and see what really waited out there in the darkness, beyond the feeble light.

Neale stared into Duvall's questioning eyes and had no doubt that soon the detective would know how human a process science really was. Einstein had shown the world a gentle science, Curie a courageous science, Oppenheimer a moral science, with each version a personal and unique combination of the scientist's own genius tempered with the influences of his or her society and upbringing. And soon Anthony Cross would show the world *his* version of science, his own genius combined with the unique violence of his shared society and the unknown personal rage and madness in which he had been forged.

"It's not like what you think at all," Neale said. *Though whatever you think science is,* she thought, *once Anthony arrives, it's never going to be the same for you again.*

"I guess it doesn't matter what I—" Duvall stopped talking as the sound of running feet came from the corridor.

Neale turned to see two students tear by. She heard sneakers skid on tiles. One of the students reappeared in the doorway. Breathless and frightened. "Get outa here!" he screamed at them.

Nogura was on his feet. "What is it?"

"There's some freak upstairs . . . some . . . oh, fuck, just run. There are dead people up there, man. Fucking dead people!" The student shook his head as if to clear his vision, peered over his shoulder, then took off again.

Neale felt a long stream of ice cold fear pour through her. She put a hand to a bookcase to steady herself. A dark shape appeared in the doorway and she gasped.

It was Covington. He carried a dull black handgun. "He's here."

Nogura waved at the monitors. "But how? The whole building's covered."

Someone screamed from far away in the building. It lasted a long time.

"I don't know," Covington said. His eyes were wild. "It doesn't matter. Have Lee and Adam arrived yet?"

Nogura nodded. "They're on the paths."

Covington grabbed Neale's arm. "Good, keep them here until you get my signal," he told Nogura. "Then send them up."

"Where?"

Another scream, bloodcurdling, pleading. Abruptly cut off.

"You'll know," Covington said.

As Covington dragged Neale from the room, Nogura turned back to the monitors to see armed men running up to each of the building's entrances. They wore windbreakers, baseball caps, and carried automatic assault rifles. Duvall couldn't recognize which model of rifle on the small screens. They looked customized, heavier than she might expect. Kwong and Weinstein were being half dragged along a bricked pathway by two other men without apparent weapons.

"Gee, Nuke, looks like Cross waltzed right by Paine's SWAT guys," Duvall said. She paused as she heard a short staccato of gunfire bursts, followed by two more screams. "Offhand, I'd say you guys were fucked."

Nogura reached into a pocket and brought out the flat silver key for Duvall's handcuffs. "Out of the chair," he said.

Duvall stood and faced the bookshelves. She heard another distant scream followed by the sounds of more running feet. When she turned around again, her hands were free but Nogura stood out of reach, a gun like Covington's in his hand, not his Beretta. Then the overhead lights flickered and the images on the monitors dissolved into static.

"Why's Covington want Neale up there with him?"

Nogura held his hand to his earphone. Duvall could see he wasn't hearing anything intelligible.

"Come on! What's the plan, Nuke?"

"She's to distract him," Nogura said. "To give him something to focus on."

"Don't you think it might be safer if you focused him on something else? Like a deserted island in the Pacific?"

Nogura pointed to the chair. "Just sit, will you? It's going to be okay. We're going to get him."

Duvall flopped back onto the chair. "Is that right? You and what army?"

"Cathedral Two," he said grimly. "Cross doesn't have a chance."

THIRTY-TWO

Covington dragged Neale through the corridors and up the stairwells as if she were a gun or a radio or any other piece of equipment he owned. She couldn't blame him. Equipment was exactly what she was to him. That was all she ever had been. Just another something else to be used by people she'd never met, in ways she couldn't imagine, to win a war she had never even known was being fought. A war for Anthony Cross. A war she had thought she had won years ago because no one had ever told her what the rules really were.

A blue-jacketed man with a rifle and a baseball cap met them on the fifth-floor landing. He was one of Paine's soldiers, drenched in sweat. Neale had never seen a rifle similar to the blocky, black metal one he carried. The sight on it was huge.

Both men watched the closed door leading to the fifth floor. Covington spoke in an urgent whisper. "Have you figured out how he got past us?"

"He must have come down from the roof," the soldier answered, also whispering.

"But how could he get on the *roof* without us seeing him?"

"Maybe he was hiding here from yesterday. Maybe he had a helicopter." The soldier adjusted something on his rifle and it made a dull metallic clank.

"Maybe he flew," Neale said.

"Yeah, right," the soldier answered, as if she had made a joke.

Covington squeezed Neale's arm. "Is that possible?"

"Why don't you ask Anthony?"

Covington pulled her toward the landing door. "Oh no, that's your job."

Two more soldiers crouched in the fifth-floor corridor outside the door to the landing. Both had duplicates of the first rifle Neale had seen, and one had taken apart the sight and was adjusting something in it with a small tool. The sight appeared to have circuitry in it. She didn't think rifles needed that. She wondered what weaponry Cathedral Two had been assigned to develop.

"Is he still on this floor?" Covington asked the soldier whose rifle was intact.

"Yes, sir. There's a big lounge or something down this corridor and off to the right. He knows we're here but he's not moving. Like he's waiting for something."

Covington looked at Neale. "Or someone." He glanced at the disassembled rifle the other soldier worked on. "Has anyone tried to shoot him yet?"

"The first team did. At least we heard gunfire. But . . . the first team's dead, sir. Their bodies are in the lounge."

"How?"

"Don't know. No one saw it happen."

"Then how do you know their bodies are there?"

"The lounge has a wall of windows, sir. Mr. Paine and the second-stage team are on the roof of the building next door. They can see the bodies and Cross."

"Do they have a clear shot?" Covington asked.

"Yes, sir. As long as he doesn't have hostages. There're already a lot of dead students on the upper floors."

"I'll worry about hostages." He turned to the other soldier. "Tell everyone to stand down and wait for my signal for the second stage. We're going to go try to talk to him. And tell Paine. He might want to get in on it."

The soldier looked skeptical but he pulled a walkie-talkie from inside his jacket. "Very good, sir."

Then Covington checked a small switch on the side of his gun, pulled on Neale's arm again, and took both his weapons into battle.

Neale recognized the large, wood-paneled student union lounge from her earlier days, with its pub band posters, the Earth Day photos, the overcrowded bulletin boards, and long computer-printed banners. And she recognized Cross when she saw him waiting for them. She had been worried that she wouldn't. That he might have changed too much.

"Helloooo, Parnelll!" Cross called out from the other end of the lounge, thirty feet away. He was sitting in a beat-up armchair by a small table with a coffeemaker on it. The coffeemaker was bubbling. Other mismatched chairs, sofas, and tables were scattered around the room. So were the bodies of five soldiers, their heads and faces disfigured as if they had been savagely beaten. There were strings of large bullet holes in the far wall, several close to where Cross was sitting. But Cross was unhurt. At least, the parts of him Neale could see looked uninjured. His left arm, though, was wrapped in a blue windbreaker taken from one of the dead soldiers.

"Hello, Anthony," Covington answered. He walked casually to a section of the lounge where the expanse of windows was interrupted by a five-foot stretch of exposed brick wall, bringing Neale with him.

"And helloooo, Charis. Were you the one who figured out that I'd come here?"

"We all did, Anthony." The Cross she knew best was present. Whatever had happened here earlier had been done by another part of his personality. She knew even she wouldn't be safe if that part returned.

But Cross seemed disappointed by her gentle reply. He shifted the windbreaker around his arm. "Am I that predictable?"

"It was just a lucky guess," Neale said. She tried to push Covington's hand from her arm. "I'm here, aren't I?" she whispered angrily at him. Covington let go and Neale stepped away from him.

"How's the arm, Anthony?" Covington asked.

"You mean, how's the quantum field generator, don't you?"

Covington put his hands in his pockets and walked to the wall opposite the windows, as if he were just pacing. "Do you still have it?"

"I have it."

"Does it still work?"

Cross stood up, cradling his blue-wrapped arm. Neale could see blood on his shirt but couldn't tell whose it was. "Of course it does." He went to the table with the coffeemaker and with his right hand poured coffee into a yellow ceramic mug, then sprinkled it with something from a jar. Neale could smell cinnamon with the coffee. She remembered having smelled that combination before, a long time ago, in an abandoned apartment in Stockholm. Cross kept his back turned to Covington. Neale saw it for the dare it was.

Covington looked out through the multipaned windows that ran along one wall of the lounge. They were small panes of old glass and the view was distorted through them. Neale followed his line of sight. She saw no one on the roof of the nearby building. But she knew they were there. The second stage. She wondered how far Cathedral was prepared to go.

Cross turned around and sipped his coffee. He pressed his left arm against his chest to hold the jacket in place. "You didn't try to shoot me, Parnel. I'm surprised."

"Why would I want to do that?"

"They did." Cross glanced down at the bodies of the soldiers.

"A mistake," Covington said.

Cross held his cup in a salute. "I'll say."

Covington paced again, slowly moving closer to the wall between the windows. Getting in position to give his signal, Neale presumed. Covington coughed to clear his throat. "Anthony, we would like you to come back to SHARP with us."

Cross took a step away from the windows, as if a chess game were in progress and it was his turn to counter Covington's attack. He winked at Neale. "And why's that, Parnel?"

"To work on your generator. Perfect it. We've been studying the tapes we made of it in Lab 2. It's really quite magnificent, you know."

"Ah, but it's primitive now, Parnel. Obsolete. Last year's model. How are you, Charis?"

"Paine and his men are on the rooftop next door, Anthony. Parnel has a gun."

Covington moved toward her. "You *bitch!*"

"YOU DON'T WANT TO DO THAT, PARNEL." The windows

vibrated from the deafening volume of the words. It had been Cross's voice but it was as if he had bellowed through a monstrous PA system.

Covington stopped dead.

"Thank you, Charis," Cross said, his voice normal again. He carried no microphone or other equipment that Neale could see which would account for the loudness of his warning to Parnel. She was afraid to guess how he had managed it. "But I already knew that Paine and his people were there. I already know so many things." He stared at Covington. "Would you like the generator, Parnel? To have for your very own?"

Covington glanced at Neale and she could see the confusion in his eyes. It might be a trick, but Cross *was* insane. Perhaps he *would* give up his secrets this easily. Neale offered Covington no help. It had to be his decision. He licked his lips and turned back to Cross. "Yes, I would, Anthony. Very much."

"Then get my erstwhile partners up here."

"Lee and Adam?" Covington asked innocently.

Cross's right hand splintered the mug he held, spraying coffee into the air. "They're downstairs with Kate and her detective friend. There are five men on the opposite roof. Three men in the hall. One man covering each of five ground entrances into this building. Want to know anything else that I know? Want me to *show* you some of the things that I know? Like I showed *them?*" He threw the coffee mug shards at the bodies of the soldiers. Neale didn't see any blood on his hand, but she could feel the rage building in him. She knew Covington could feel it, too. Whatever Paine and Covington had planned had better happen quickly.

Covington snapped the walkie-talkie from his jacket. "This is Blue Leader. I want Lee and Adam to come up to the fifth-floor student lounge."

"That's right," Cross said. "We're going to have a trade. You know, Parnel, the sort of thing you're so good at—a *business* transaction."

"So that I get the field generator . . . ?" Covington asked.

"That's right," Cross agreed. "And I get . . . everything else."

THIRTY-THREE

When they were out of sight of the soldiers in the corridor but still not near the lounge, Nogura put his hand on Duvall's shoulder and made her stop. When she turned to him, he held out a pistol. Grip first.

"What are you doing?" Kwong asked, voice trembling. Both he and Weinstein were pale and panting after their run up the stairs. "You're not supposed to give it to her yet."

Nogura glared at him. "It's insurance, asshole."

Duvall stared at the gun, without reaching for it. "He's right, Nuke, how do you know I won't blow your head off with it?"

"Because I'm the closest thing you've got to a good guy around here. And no cop likes to work without a partner."

Duvall took the gun. It was Nogura's Beretta. She slipped it into the waistband of her jeans at the small of her back where her linen jacket would hide it. "What are you going to use?"

"This." He held out a second handgun. Blocky and black like Covington's. "Whatever happens, don't take this one. Or any others like it. Stick with the Beretta."

"You are making a big mistake, Detective," Weinstein wheezed. The old man's stringy gray hair was plastered to the sides of his head with sweat. The blue jacket he wore was too small and the outline of his body armor could be clearly seen through the stretched fabric of his white shirt. "It could ruin everything."

"I think you two have already cornered the market in big mistakes," Nogura said.

Duvall ignored the scientist. "Why stay away from that kind of gun, Nuke?"

Nogura motioned them forward. "Just do it." Duvall hoped there would be time for questions later.

The first thing Duvall noticed when she entered the lounge was the smell of coffee mixed with cinnamon. And Cross, Neale, and Covington looked so calm and ordinary that for a moment she wouldn't have been surprised if she found out they had all been sitting around having a coffee break together. Then Covington drew his gun and aimed it at Duvall and she knew that nothing had changed.

"What's *she* doing here?" Covington demanded.

"Would you rather have her downstairs all by herself?"

"Then she's your responsibility, Detective."

"I know," Nogura said.

Covington lowered his gun but did not put it away. Nogura pulled Duvall off to the side and Duvall didn't fight him.

Cross nodded at Duvall. "Don't worry about Parnel, Kate. He's just being dramatic. I don't think he trusts me, either. Put the gun down, Parnel. You've brought me what I want, hasn't he, Lee? Hasn't he, Adam?"

Weinstein looked as if he would not be capable of speech even if Covington held a gun to his head. But Kwong was seething with anger. "Why do you want us here? What are you going to do?"

Cross seemed to capture that rage, absorb it, and magnify it. "Whatever I want to do, Lee. Don't you know enough about the quantum to figure that out? When the scale is right . . . when the observation is right . . . then the possibilities are infinite."

"You—you are *insane!*"

Cross's eyes became dark and dull as something changed within him. "That's not the issue here, Lee. The issue is who created the corollary? Who applied it? Who understands the most, first? And who are the two miserable, ignorant, brainless shiteating fuckers who made all this go wrong and turned me in and—"

Duvall was amazed by the sudden fury she saw appear in Cross. Had it been there all along? She was relieved when Covington shouted to break Cross's tirade. *"Stop it, Anthony! You got what you wanted!"*

Cross blinked, as if remembering where he was and what he had set out to do. "That's right, Parnel. That's right. And now it's time for you to get what you want. The generator."

"You'll take it off now?"

"I've already taken it off." Cross walked over to an easy chair with worn upholstery, reached behind it, and brought out the gauntlet with its timing circuit board and cuff still attached. "It was giving my hand some trouble."

Duvall stared at the rolled-up jacket Cross had around his left arm. From its bulk, she had assumed he wore the gauntlet beneath it. And from the expressions on the other's faces, they had, too.

Cross walked over to a large sofa with tattered cushions and dropped the gauntlet on it, then went back to the far wall by the coffeemaker.

"What sort of trouble, Anthony?"

"Kind of you to ask, Parnel. Stiff, sort of. The wire can be . . . constricting."

"I want to see your hand."

Cross returned Covington's stare. "Are you afraid, Parnel?"

"Take the jacket off your hand."

"This wasn't part of our deal."

Duvall was surprised at how collected Cross appeared to be once more. He didn't seem to be angered by Covington's unexpected demand. Unless he had wanted Covington to act that way. Unless he was manipulating the man.

"It's part of the deal now." Duvall wondered what Covington could possibly do to carry out the threat implicit in his words. There were five dead soldiers on the floor.

"Okay," Cross said simply. "Here you go." He held out his left arm, waved it around, and pulled the blue jacket from it with a flourish.

Duvall cringed at what was to be revealed.

But his hand was fine. Not a mark on it. All fingers in place and working normally.

Cross laughed at Covington. "The way I see it, Parnel, I got better. Now go ahead. Try it yourself."

Covington went over to the couch and picked up the gauntlet.

"It's all hooked up, ready to go," Cross said.

"Where are its controls?"

"Pressure studs lining the inside of the fingers. See them in there? Hold it up to the light from the windows. That's it. Just like a Nintendo Glove, isn't it?" He snickered. "Think what the Japanese could do with it. Probably end up selling them for nineteen ninety-five on the Shopping Channel."

Cross's rage had slipped beneath the surface as quickly as it had appeared and the way he joked with Covington reminded Duvall of the Cross who had come to her house; the lover who had captured her heart and soothed her body. Yet she knew he was a monster and a killer and she loathed him for what he was even as she ached for what he once had been to her, what he might have been if only some things had been different. If other choices had been made.

"Go on, Parnel, put it on."

"I'll take it back to SHARP for that." Covington held the gauntlet in his free hand and began to move back toward Neale. Kwong and Weinstein waited nervously, not sure what was expected of them but obviously not wanting to be left to Cross. Duvall and Nogura were unnoticed in their corner.

"But how do you know it's the same one?" Neale asked as Covington approached. "And if it is, how do you know it still works?"

Cross thrust out his bottom lip. "Charis, don't spoil it for me. I was just about to out-business the businessman."

Covington was silent, staring at the gauntlet, looking back at Cross, weighing the odds, considering all the possibilities.

"That's all right, Parnel. I'll take it from here." David Paine was in the doorway to the lounge. He put a black, blocky handgun into a shoulder holster beneath his jacket and held out his hand to Covington.

"Ah, Mr. Ambassador," Cross said. "What a surprise." But from the way he said it, Duvall suspected that Cross had known Paine would arrive exactly when he had.

Paine went to Covington and took the gauntlet from him. "This is what it's all been about, isn't it, Parnel?"

"Is this wise, sir?" Covington asked.

"*His* hand is fine. I'll be fine, too." Paine rolled up his sleeve, and pushed his left hand into the gauntlet. His hand was larger than Cross's but the complex wire mesh seemed to stretch around him, conforming to his larger dimensions.

"Feels nice, doesn't it?" Cross leaned against the wall, hands in his pockets, one knee bent to rest his foot against the wall as well.

Paine studied the gauntlet on his arm, checking the fit, touching the black plugs to ensure they were connected. To Duvall, it looked as if the man caressed himself and not the device. "What's the control sequence to turn it on?" he asked.

Cross waited until Paine looked away from the gauntlet and toward him. "Just make a fist, Mr. Ambassador. Squeeze real hard. It'll feel hot for a few seconds as the wire warms up. But then . . . everything will be fine. Of course, I'm sure Lee and Adam could explain it much better than that, considering they know so much about my work. Isn't that right, gentlemen?"

Weinstein looked unsteady and made his way to a couch against the short solid wall between the two sets of windows. Kwong followed him.

Paine checked the room. He looked at the gauntlet. Duvall could see he was trembling with anticipation. Then he made a fist and Duvall saw the gauntlet shimmer as it had in the lab, caught for an instant behind a wall of heated air.

"You've got a blue light glowing on the cuff," Covington reported.

Paine twisted his arm around so he could see the light for himself. "All right, what do I do now?"

Cross scratched at his ear. "What you've always wanted to do. Anything you want."

Paine held his copper-wrapped fist before him. The gauntlet flickered with blackness.

"That's right," Cross encouraged. "Once more."

The gauntlet flickered again, stayed black longer.

"Very *good*, Mr. Ambassador. You can do it."

The gauntlet turned black and stayed that way. Flat, featureless, as if a two-dimensional hole had been left where Paine's forearm and hand had once been.

Tentatively, Paine used his right hand to touch the surface of the glove, but didn't appear to make contact. Then he waved his right hand completely through the shadow. There was no resistance. Paine looked excitedly at Covington. "Dear God, it works," he whispered. He held his fist up and Duvall saw the shadow take the outline of an open hand. For an instant, a brief tracery of blue light burst from it.

"Well done," Cross said. "You're getting the hang of it." He began to applaud slowly. "And now, I'd like to have my little chat with Lee and Adam. A deal's a deal, after all." He held out his hand to Kwong and Weinstein, motioning to them to get up from their sofa.

Covington glanced at Paine. Paine nodded. Covington took the walkie-talkie from his jacket. "This is Blue Leader. We can proceed to the second stage now."

A flurry of red dots suddenly appeared on the wall around Cross, then instantly swept in to converge on his chest. Cross looked down at them, intercepted some of them with his open hand. Stared at them with puzzlement.

Laser targeting, Duvall thought suddenly. She felt Nogura's hands dig into her shoulders, felt him spin her around, throwing her to the ground. But he was too late.

The far end of the wall of windows erupted like a tidal wave of shattered crystal. Duvall saw Cross disappear within a multitude of brilliant explosions. She felt the concussions hit her. Saw the explosions streak across the wall opposite the windows. And then she was flat on the floor, hands over her head, Nogura on top of her, pressing her down. The building trembled and bucked beneath her as if it was about to be swallowed by the earth.

The attack could have lasted only seconds, but to Duvall it felt like hours. When she finally realized that the sound she still heard was the ringing in her ears, she raised her head. The lounge had been transformed.

Most of the wall Cross had leaned against was gone. Small flames danced on the edges of the hole that had been blasted through it and part of the ceiling had caved in above, no longer supported. Billows of plaster dust and fire smoke blew in the breezes that entered through the empty window frames. Covington and Paine—black fist raised—still stood in the protected section of the room, safe behind the small patch of solid wall. Obviously, they had chosen their position with care. Weinstein and Kwong cowered on the sofa against the wall, similarly protected. In a more exposed area, Neale slowly got back to her feet, glass fragments clinking from her back. Just as obviously, she had not been told what was to happen. Cathedral had found her expendable.

Duvall felt Nogura roll off her. "What the hell was that?" she asked, and her voice sounded small and tinny after the roar of the explosions. She had to cough to clear the dust from her throat.

"Cathedral Two," Neale said dully. She stared at where the wall used to be. Where Cross used to be. "Antitank weapons. Liquid-core projectiles. Magnetic propulsion. Who knows what else?"

Duvall got to her knees and looked out at the roof of the next-door building. She saw five men standing there holding long rifles with thick barrels. "Good shooting," Covington said into his walkie-talkie. One of the men on the rooftop waved.

Duvall turned to Nogura. He had probably saved her life. "Thanks, Nuke, I—" He lay centered in a pool of spreading blood.

Duvall ignored everything else. Nogura coughed blood, his eyes vacant. She checked the ragged shrapnel wound along his neck and head with icy deliberation, knowing there was nothing she could do.

"It's going to be okay . . . partner," she said. The blood flowed from a dozen wounds, life running out like sand in an hourglass.

Nogura gripped her hand but his eyes stared far over her shoulder, seeing nothing he could describe. "Aren't you . . . going to . . . tell me to catch fire?" He smiled and blood curled down from the corner of his mouth.

"No," she said, heart cold, not knowing how or where to release her anger.

Nogura's hand squeezed hard. "Katherine!" His eyes cleared. "Don't take the guns! The NavStar system. They . . . want you to go." He made it sound as if it was the most important thing he could say.

"Go where, Nuke?"

His eyes fluttered, seeing other things again. "With him . . . with Cross. Wherever."

"Why would I?" Cross was dead. Too bad his keepers weren't taken out with him.

"Good," Nogura coughed. "Good. I was worried . . . you were going to try . . . to make a difference . . ." He attempted another smile. Tried to show her something of what he felt. "See," he rasped. "I told you you were going to wish you'd gone to Hawaii." He didn't cough again.

Duvall put his hand down gently. She was aware of someone standing behind her. She felt a gun barrel press into her back.

"Tough break," Covington said. "But, on the bright side, he's one loose end fewer to deal with. Maybe you and I can talk about you taking over for him."

Duvall got to her feet, putting her hands on her head as Covington directed her with the gun. "Maybe you and I can talk about you crawling up your own asshole where you belong."

Covington cocked his gun. *Please let him forget I'm wearing armor,* Duvall thought as she tensed for the impact of the bullet. *Go for the stomach, you bastard.*

But Neale stepped forward and put her hand on Covington's arm. "Don't you think he should turn it off?"

Covington looked over at Paine. Duvall exhaled quietly and dropped her hands lower behind her head to her neck. It would take her a second to pull out the gun Nogura had given her. It would take Covington a half second to shoot once he saw her move. She watched for what Paine might do next, choosing her time.

Paine stood alone, enraptured by the device he wore. He opened his fist. The gauntlet remained a black outline. He tried the move a few more times. Nothing changed. He looked over at Neale and Covington. "I can't make it . . . do what it was doing before."

"Can you disconnect any of the wires?" Covington asked.

Paine's right hand passed through the gauntlet's shadow. "Can't get hold of any of them."

The white-haired man shook his left hand in frustration. Blue sparks crackled off from the blackness of it. He made a sound of pain.

Covington pulled out his radio. "This is Blue Leader. We've got a problem with the glove."

The three soldiers Duvall had seen in the stairwell and the corridor ran into the room, stopping to stare helplessly at Paine.

"Forget it," Paine told them. He waved over to the ruins of the wall. "Go find whatever's left of Cross's body. See if he had another part for this thing." He started to move his right hand along his left arm, feeling carefully for the first sign of the black field.

"Can we go now?" Kwong asked. His voice was broken by silent sobs. He was on his feet, but beside him, Weinstein was slumped against the sofa's arm, eyes closed, lips moving in silent prayer.

"Not yet," Covington snapped. "We're all going together." He approached Paine, turning so he could keep one eye on Duvall. "No 'off' switch?" he asked.

Paine's mouth twitched into a brief smile. "Should have remembered to ask. And it's heating up. Or getting tighter. It's doing something." He tried to shake the gauntlet off again, but all he accomplished was to shed blue sparks like drops of water.

Paine called Neale over. "Where's its power coming from? Will it run out?"

I know where the fucking power is coming from, Duvall thought bitterly, remembering Cross's "battery." But she remained silent. Covington was becoming too interested in the gauntlet. With the soldiers at the other end of the lounge, she wasn't going to risk going for her gun. What she needed now was an opportunity to make it out of the room without anyone noticing. If the smoke from the spreading fires caused by the explosions continued to increase, then she'd have a good chance. She wondered if Cathedral had any operatives in the Boston police force. She didn't care. She was going to the papers first, just to make sure her story was on record before she disappeared into any black holes, bureaucratic, conspiratorial, or literal.

Duvall remained motionless and watched Neale wipe at the streaks of white dust on her face. Her eyes were red and watering badly. "If the field generator *is* powered by vacuum fluctuations, then it's got a potentially infinite supply. Power created from literally nothing. However, we might be able to disconnect it from its . . . control source."

"Disconnect?" Paine asked. "How?"

"Amputation."

Paine stared at Neale in shock. "I am not a 'control source.'"

Duvall could see that Neale enjoyed Covington's reaction. "Then again, if the glove responds to gravity, then in its insubstantial form it could fall through the earth if it's no longer anchored to his body."

Paine shook his head wildly. "I *can* shut it off, Charis. All I have to do is . . ." His right hand reached for the gauntlet one more time. The glove flickered, sparkled with blue. Duvall heard the same sizzling noise she had heard when Cross had grabbed her hand in the lab and burned her. "A tiny detail," Cross had told her, "that still needed to be worked out."

Paine screamed. His right hand was fused to the gauntlet's black surface and he couldn't pull free. Duvall could smell the stench of burning flesh even where she stood.

"Jesus," Paine moaned. "It's . . . it's . . ." He pulled both hands against his stomach to cradle them. But the sizzling sound intensified as the gauntlet made contact with the rest of his body. This time he shrieked, unable to pull it away again.

Paine fell to his knees, doubled over, twitching, writhing. "Anthony!" he screamed. *"Anthonyyy!"* He rolled onto his side, legs drawn up, shuddering terribly. His face was pale.

Neale watched impassively. "Don't worry, David. After it's over, why, Parnel and I will clean everything up and no one will ever know what happened. Just the way you like it."

"Listen, shouldn't we do something?" Kwong asked from the sofa.

But Covington shook his head. "Do *you* want to touch that thing?"

The gauntlet flickered to blue, then black. The sizzling noise became a roar. Paine screeched. And then the trembling left him along with the blackness.

His left hand was embedded in his stomach like a candle melted on a griddle. What could be seen of his forearm was encased in intricate whorls of woven copper. The blue light on the cuff winked out. He was dead.

"Fuck you, Mr. Ambassador." Neale kicked his body, then turned away.

"Well, at least it's off," Covington said to no one in particular. He called to the soldiers at the far end of the lounge. "Hey, any sign of the body?"

There was no answer from the smoke.

Covington called out again. "I said, is there any sign of . . ."

The smoke shifted and, sudden and whole as if he had formed from the swirling billows themselves, Anthony Cross came forward. His feet and legs had not appeared to move. He was unmarked, uninjured, completely untouched by the explosions that had disintegrated the wall he had stood by.

He is dead, Duvall thought. *I saw him obliterated. I saw him disintegrate with the wall behind him. Dead. Dead.* She was numbed by what she saw, left with an inexplicable clarity of thought, devoid of fear or panic. The emotional safeguards that let her function in a job where children were slaughtered by their parents, where gun-blasted brain tissue adhered to walls, where her sneakers left tracks in human blood, protected her. Later there would be time to understand what she witnessed, but for now, it was enough just to function, and to stay alive.

Cross bared his teeth at Covington, and it was like no smile Duvall had ever seen before. But when he spoke, it was with a voice of calm and reason and control.

"Now do you understand?" Cross asked those assembled before him.

To Duvall, he sounded just like a teacher.

THIRTY-FOUR

Charis Neale was not surprised that Cross lived. She knew the two of them were linked. He could no more die without her than an electron could spring into life without its antiparticle or be transformed into energy on its own. Their fates were as inextricably linked as all the laws of physics.

But Cross ignored Neale where she stood by Covington. Instead, he went to Weinstein and Kwong.

"Stand up! Stand up, you fatjewcocksuckingchinkshit," Cross bellowed in a voice of thunder, on and on until Neale's ears rang and there was no sense left to his words. She felt the explosion building in him. Felt the fury and the wrath erupting. Knew the killing rage that would follow. Cried because she knew she could control it in him. In the way she always had.

Kwong rose unsteadily to his feet. He held out his hands to help Weinstein stand beside him. Both men stared past Cross, pleading with their eyes for Covington to help them. But Neale knew he wouldn't. He was running an experiment: how much further could Cross go?

"Everything you are is because you have stolen from me!" Cross shrieked at the cowering physicists. "You are useless! You are thieves!

Time wasters! Frauds!" He stepped closer to them, raised his arms. He wore no gauntlets of copper, but both hands flickered with the blackness of the quantum just the same. He had gone that far. No wonder the explosive shells hadn't touched him.

"I'm sorry!" Weinstein called out. "Lee made me report you! Lee made me set you up with Parnel!"

"No! No! No!" Kwong shouted. "Listen to me, Anthony! It was Adam! It was all his idea to set you up! I tried to stop him!"

But Cross ignored their shrieks. Neale watched his hands flicker faster, losing their detail, going to solid and impenetrable black. One hand grabbed each man at his shoulder, sank into the shoulder, solidified in each shoulder with a hideous sputter of heated flesh as Kwong and Weinstein screamed their pain.

Cross pulled them closer to him as if they weighed nothing. He stared into their contorted faces.

"Like I always said," he thundered at them, "you'd be lucky to have one brain between you."

Neale saw black disks form on each man's shoulder, emanating from the point where Cross's hands were inserted. The black grew over the men, encasing their necks and their heads. Their screams became indistinct, muffled, beating with a strange harmonic.

Cross pushed them closer together, moving the blackened silhouettes of their heads against each other, into each other.

And left them there.

He withdrew his hands. The two bodies fell back to the sofa. The black flickered like the surface of dark water, then left as the men solidified again.

Joined.

Fused.

A single swollen face with four eyes, four nostrils, two shrieking, gaping, blubbering mouths screaming for release from a single skull.

There was a drawn-out sound of sizzling, the interference of matter overlaid on matter. The voices faded. Two bodies on the sofa. Now one body. One brain.

Cross laughed, the thunder of lightning. He turned to Covington. "And now, Parnel, I think we have some business of our own to discuss."

Covington aimed his gun at Cross. Neale laughed.

But someone else spoke. "Stop it, Anthony." It was Duvall, standing beside a knocked-over chair.

"Ahhh," Cross said, and with that sound, his voice modulated down, close to normal. "Hello, Kate."

Duvall walked slowly to Cross, ignoring the grotesque fusion of Kwong and Weinstein. She made a show of tossing away her gun. As if it could possibly be any sort of threat. Or protection. "Why are you doing this, Anthony?"

"Because he *is* insane!" Neale said. She coughed again from the smoke and the dust.

"Charis?" Cross said, and he sounded hurt.

Duvall stopped within arm's reach of Cross. "Anthony, answer me. *Why* are you doing this?"

Cross turned from one woman to the other.

"Why, Anthony?" Duvall asked. Neale was astounded that she could see no fear on the detective's face. Didn't she know she wasn't talking with Anthony Cross? She was talking with a fundamental force of nature.

Cross held a flickering black finger to his temple. "It is what I see," he said. "Beautiful. So beautiful."

Duvall pointed to the fused bodies. "Is that what you see? Is that beautiful? What happened to your dreams, Anthony? All those things you told me about? The forces and the universe and . . . and the Beginning of everything. Your dreams were of birth, Anthony. This is death."

Cross watched her but said nothing. Neale could hear him breathe in great, deep gasps.

"He *is* death, now," Neale said. Why couldn't Duvall understand that?

"No," Cross said. He sounded confused.

Duvall stepped closer. "You said you could make me see what you saw, Anthony. You said you could help me see into the quantum with you. Remember?"

"You don't know what you're saying!" Neale shouted. Those were the words Cross used to seek for inspiration.

"Yes, I do," Duvall said. She reached out her hand to Cross.

"Don't touch him!" Neale said. "You don't know him!"

"Yes, I do," Duvall said. "Isn't that right, Anthony? Cops and scientists?"

"Seekers of truth," Cross said. He sounded tired.

Duvall's hand touched Cross's shoulder. His flesh didn't flicker, her hand did not disappear.

"I know a different part of you, Anthony. Bring that part back. Please."

"Yes," he said. "I could do that."

"You can do anything, Anthony. But of all the things that you can do, that is the one thing that you must do now."

And then Neale saw what Duvall had planned and was stunned by the logic of it. Cross had conquered the quantum—the underlying basis of all reality. He could alter the nature of all matter and energy. Why not turn that power upon himself? Why not use his power to change himself? To remove the power? To return himself to what he used to be? It was possible. Cross could do it. He could be saved.

"Yes," Cross said slowly, nodding his head. "I understand." He closed his eyes. His hands and arms flickered and the black fell from them. He sighed. He opened his eyes. And Neale recognized the expression in them. It was the Cross she knew best. The dreamer, the seeker, her lover. He smiled at Duvall, embarrassed, the boy returned.

"There," he said, such relief in his voice. "Kate, you were right. You were—"

His chest erupted in a spray of blood. Neale felt the heat of it splatter across her face.

Cross's eyes bulged in pain and shock. A soft gasp came from his open mouth.

Covington stepped forward, his black, smoking gun in his hand. "The last of the loose ends," he said, and pulled the trigger again.

Neale saw the blood burst away from Cross's back as he screamed. She saw each drop of blood in perfect detail, rich and glossy, arcing into the smoke behind him. She felt she sensed the world with the heightened awareness of madness. She watched the spray of blood move slower and slower.

She saw the blood stop in the air.

Neale heard Duvall swear. It was not heightened awareness.

The blood arced back. It was not madness.

It was Cross.

Cross stood up straight, reassembling. Rivulets of blood ran back across his ruined shirt. Beneath the fabric tatters, the flesh deformed by heat and impact drew together. Even time bent to his command.

Covington fired again. Again and again. And with each new shot a small circle of black appeared on Cross's body, and nothing more. The gun clicked empty. Cross held out his fist. It was black. He opened it. A rain of spent bullets fell to clatter to the floor.

"I don't think you'll ever understand, Parnel. Till your dying day, you won't understand anything."

Covington made a senseless sound, a whimper. He stumbled backward. Tripped over debris. Scrambled back to his feet and ran from the smoke-filled lounge. Neale could hear his footsteps echoing away. She heard nothing else. No alarms. No soldiers. Things had progressed too far for anything ordinary to be useful. That meant the planners of Cathedral had only one more option. Inevitable. Predictable. Chaotic.

"Time to go," Cross said softly.

Neale and Duvall both looked at him, slowly realizing that this nightmare still could end. But then Cross reached out and grabbed both by their arms.

"All of us," he said. "I still have some work to do before we can *all* understand."

Neale sobbed as she saw the black field take form over Cross's entire body, without the need for the gauntlet, without the need for anything except what lay within his own mind. She tried to pull away from him as the blackness flowed down his arm, through his hand, and across to hers. She looked past him and saw Duvall's arm already disappearing within the field as the black flowed up around her.

"No!" Neale pleaded but the field grew, each part of her it touched numbed instantly as if her nerves no longer connected within her. "No," she whispered as the field crawled up her neck, through her mouth, drowning her in lost sensation, filling her eyes with nothingness, reaching up and engulfing her completely as she fell through the lattice of spacetime, into the realm between each possibility, down to the gaps between moments, and into the quantum sea.

Three

ATOMIC CITY

ONE

Katherine Duvall awoke in the Atomic City, breathing the dust of Armageddon, hearing the wind sigh from the desert and whistle through ruins scorched by radiation the equal of any sun.

She pushed against the crumbled concrete that she lay on, feeling each limb in turn, stretching her fingers, moving her toes. She made a sound, rough and strangled in her parched throat. She rolled over, sat up, and remembered the blackness that had swallowed her, and nothing else.

The room was a bare concrete cube, one empty window open to the outside, one door open to the darkness of the inside. Through the corroded metal frame of the window, Duvall saw skeletal outlines of blast-damaged buildings, oddly familiar hulks of sand-scoured cars. The sky behind them was faded blue and cloudless without moisture. She heard only the wind and remembered her words to Cross. "You can do *anything.*"

Duvall went to the window. A wide street of cracked asphalt and crumbling sidewalks, half-buried by drifting sand, led through a handful of structures and within two hundred feet faded at the edge of an endless flat tan desert. She feared for what Cross might have done.

She heard something moving behind her, soft crunchings on the hard floor. She turned to see a shape appear in the skewed opening of the twisted doorway. A human shape. It was Neale.

"Are you all right?" Neale asked, stepping forward from the shadow of the doorway, into the light from the window. She still wore her blue jacket, now filthy with smoke and blood and the dirt of that place. Her face was streaked with the same markings. Some of her blond hair was tied back, most floated erratically around her head. Her face was grim.

"Do you know what happened?" Duvall asked, afraid to learn the answer. "Do you know where we are? What he's done?"

Neale looked out the window at the modern ruins. "It's not what you think," she said. "We're in New Mexico. Atomic City." Her voice was harsh against the hard walls of the room. "Built for the bomb tests in the forties and fifties." She walked over to the window to peer up at the sky, watching for something. "Anthony and I did some research here, years ago. We were both students. It's where we met. It's where his theories began."

"He brought us here?" Duvall went to the window to stand beside Neale.

"Yes." Neale sat on the ledge, exhausted.

"By . . . tunneling?" Duvall asked.

"I assume so," Neale answered. "I don't remember what happened after the field spread from him onto me, except for waking up here."

"He's not around?"

Neale leaned her head against the wall. "Who knows? We might have been here for a day or two. He could be . . . anywhere." She straightened up suddenly. "Let's go outside."

"Why?" Duvall asked.

Neale pursed her lips, thinking of something else. "To see the sun," she said, then left the room.

For a moment, Duvall hesitated, thinking that she felt safer inside. But then she remembered what Cross was capable of and decided it didn't matter where she was. She followed Neale.

The Atomic City spanned only two blocks on each side. Neale told Duvall it was one of five sites where buildings of various materials and designs had been constructed to measure their response to test explosions of fission and fusion bombs. Duvall found it unnerving to see structures so modern in shape look so old and weathered. "It makes me feel like our world's already a thousand years in the past," she said, sitting a few feet from Neale on an angled slab of concrete, once part of a wall.

"Someday it will be," Neale said. "If it lasts that long." She watched the sky. Duvall listened to the wind.

"We should be doing something," Duvall said. "Build a fire for a signal. Walk out to a road."

"Anthony brought us here for a reason," Neale told her. "If we go anywhere, he'll just bring us back. So there's no place we can go."

"You just want to wait?"

Neale sat forward and reached in behind her jacket. She pulled out a black pistol like the ones Paine and Covington had used, the ones Nogura had warned her not to take if she went with Cross.

"May I?" Duvall asked, holding out her hand, prepared to take the gun from Neale if the physicist hesitated. But Neale shrugged and passed it over unconcerned.

Duvall studied the gun, much lighter than she had expected it to be. She read the manufacturer's name. "A Glock," she said, hefting it in her hand, finding the safety. "Mostly plastic."

Neale paid no attention.

"Covington didn't have much luck with this," Duvall said, finding the magazine release and thumbing it. "I don't think it would be a good idea to—"

The magazine dropped out of the gun's handle. It was filled with cartridges but in the space where the last four should have been, Duvall saw a small, flat, metal box with rounded edges. She pried back the follower and slipped the box out. It had no markings, but a small green LED glowed in one corner.

"Do you know what this is?" Duvall asked, holding the box out to Neale.

Neale didn't look at it. "A NavStar locater beacon."

"NavStar?" Nogura had said something about that. Another warning it had sounded like.

Neale pointed up. "Satellite navigation system. That beacon is transmitting our location, accurate to within ten feet. The signal passes

right through the gun's plastic handle. Would've worked anywhere in
the world Cross might have taken us."

"So they know where we are," Duvall said. No wonder Neale
didn't want to leave the area.

"That's right," Neale said. "They know where we are."

Duvall looked at the locater and the gun in her hand, remembering
something. "Was there one of these locaters in each of the guns you
people carried?"

"That's right," Neale said.

"So they could track down whoever Anthony took along with him,
just in case he got away?"

"That's right."

"Then why didn't Nogura want me to take one?" Duvall was suddenly concerned. Nogura's request had been more urgent than his dying.

"He was your friend. He was trying to save you."

"From what?" Duvall asked.

Neale just looked at her. A question which needed no answer.

"You don't seem to care about any of this," Duvall finally said,
slipping the locater into her pocket and reloading the Glock.

"I don't."

"You used to care about Anthony, didn't you?"

Neale said nothing.

"I didn't know about you two when . . . I'm sorry," Duvall said.
All at once, all the anguish, all the horror she had undergone welled up
in her, broke through her professional detachment. She had no more
words, no more plans, only what she *felt* was real.

"How can you think that matters now?" Neale said. She turned
away from Duvall.

"Something's got to matter, doesn't it?"

Neale's body rocked gently in silent crying.

"Doesn't it?" But Duvall's voice was lost in the wind that the dead
city breathed, and there was no answer.

The sky was red with sunset and the temperature was dropping. *Blood
and cold*, Duvall thought, *the death of the day.*

Neale had said nothing more to her during the wait on the slab of
concrete. Twice Duvall had seen a high-flying jet pass over; she thought

it was their rescuers, but nothing more had happened. She still couldn't understand why Nogura had not wanted her to take Paine's gun with its hidden locater if it meant rescuers could find her.

About an hour before sunset, Duvall had told Neale she was going to try making a fire. There were wood supports in several of the smaller buildings, the wood exquisitely dry, some timbers already splintered to provide good kindling. Duvall figured she could break open one of the cartridges from the Glock, sprinkle out the black powder, and get a good start going on a fire with just one or two sparks. She didn't think that it could take much longer for the locater to work. She doubted they would spend the night there.

Duvall piled the wood in the sheltered overhang on the other side of the concrete slab Neale sat on. The scientist hadn't moved for hours.

"I don't suppose you have any matches, a lighter, anything like that?" Duvall asked.

Neale shook her head.

"Kleenex? Paper? Thousand-dollar bills?"

Neale had nothing. Duvall sat down beside her. "Well, you let me know when you start to get cold and I'll see about getting the fire going. Any idea how long the satellite stuff takes to find us?"

"Oh, they've found us by now," Neale said. "There's one overhead every half hour or so."

"Then what are they waiting for?"

A small dust devil sprang up a few feet from the slab, spinning in a whirl of dirt and sand. Duvall was distracted by it. She watched it grow, slowly realizing that it was becoming larger than any dust devil should be in the gentle wind that was blowing, slowly recognizing the deep black shadows that writhed inside, sucking in all light.

"There," Neale said quietly. "That's what they're waiting for."

Neale was not frightened by Cross's arrival. How he appeared now was how she had first seen him: stepping from the chaos of a swirling wall of sand. She had accepted the inevitable, and with his return, the inevitable was only a handful of minutes away. There was nothing that could frighten her now.

The dust that formed the miniature cyclone was sucked inside the solid blackness coalescing at its center, each grain of sand becoming a flaring spark as it was consumed, and Neale could see that he had

changed again. This time, as Cross's outline formed, his blackness was
no longer devoid of detail. The sparks seemed to fly within it, giving the
impression that his shape was coated with an inky slickness in which
stars were born, lived, and exploded in death. Night flowed within his
glistening shape, and the setting sun streaked red highlights along his
contours.

Cross's features came out of the blackness, oil-coated and glossy.
"Hello, Charis. Hello, Kate," he said. Sweetly, almost.

Then he pulled something long like a thin metal rod from . . .
somewhere else beside him that Neale couldn't quite see. He held it out
to the women, like an offering. The slick blackness slipped from it and
a large rectangular shape grew from one end, as if it were being un-
folded from an impossibly narrow case.

Cross stuck one end of the rod into the sand before them. It was a
flagpole, Neale realized, but the flag, supported by a second metal rod
extended at right angles from the top of the first, was ivory white,
without apparent detail. Then she saw the flag flutter stiffly in the light
breeze and the shadows from the sun near the horizon finally revealed
that there was a pattern on the flag, stitched out of pieces of cloth in all
the same bleached color. She saw stripes on the flag, stars in a box in
the corner. Neale didn't understand what a white American flag meant.

"Tranquility Base," Cross said, almost sadly. "The Eagle has
landed." He smiled at them, his face losing the shiny blackness of
whatever surrounded him. "I observed it on television, once. So I can
observe it again." He extended his other hand held in a fist. It solidified
to flesh. He opened it. Red sand poured out, swirling in the wind,
mixing with the desert. "Mars," he said. "I saw that once, too."

"You went to those places?" Duvall asked, the first words she had
spoken.

"I think," Cross said thoughtfully, "it's more like they come to
me." He turned to Neale. "I know so much more now, Charis. Oh, the
things I understand. The places I can go." He shook his head. "The
beauty and the farness of it. The power that is within each of us."

"Do you have the answers you wanted?" Duvall asked.

Neale didn't want to hear any more. "How can you speak to him
that way?"

"What way?"

"As if he's human."

Cross frowned. The field dropped from him completely and he was solid and normal again, an ordinary man in light slacks and a white shirt. The only thing dark about him was the long shadow he cast in the sunset, stretching far across the sand, into the dead city. "Don't you think I'm human, Charis?" He sounded hurt.

"I don't know what you are."

Cross gestured with empty, human hands. "I'm your lover."

Neale shook her head. "You're a killer."

"I'm a scientist."

"You're a madman."

Cross hung his head. He turned to Duvall. "What do you think I am?" he asked.

"All those things, Anthony," she said.

He sighed. "I have done bad things, haven't I?" He spoke with the voice of a child.

"Yes, you have," Duvall said.

"Stop it," Neale snapped. "It doesn't matter anymore."

"Bad things were done to me," Cross said.

"That's no excuse." Duvall was calm and cool, a cop on the job, Neale thought. She wondered how the detective would behave if she knew that in moments they all would be dead. There was still one more Cathedral to hear from.

"Sometimes I think there's more than one of me," Cross said.

"I know there is, child." Duvall spoke like a soothing mother.

"All sorts of possibilities, aren't there?" Cross smiled at the thought. Neale wanted to scream.

"Infinite," Duvall said. "Just like all those things you told me about, all those things you saw. All those things you wanted to know."

Cross sank to his knees. Tears came to his eyes. He looked to Duvall seeking salvation. But Neale knew it would come from somewhere else. She strained to hear it approaching.

"You understand me, don't you, Kate?" Cross's fingers trailed in the sand, the soils of earth and Mars mixed together against all odds. All possibilities.

"I won't lie to you, child. I don't understand all of you, each of you." Duvall knelt down in the sand beside him. "But I understand some of you. I want to understand the others."

"Even the bad ones?"

"Yes, child."

"Why?"

"I want to help," Duvall said.

"Why?" A child's litany.

But Duvall knew how to break it. "Why do you want to know things?"

Cross bit his lip. Neale could hear an engine, soft and distant, coming from the dusk.

"I know how it started," Cross said. "I've seen beyond the Planck wall. Everything I thought before, all my theories . . ."

"Were insane," Neale said.

Cross smiled. "And so, it turns out, were the theories of everyone else." He brushed his fingers against his legs. "Waves and particles. Four fundamental forces. Entropy. All wrong. How could we stay so blind for so long? How could understand so little?" He held a finger to his temple. "It wasn't the generator that let me do those things, you know. Never the wire or the circuits or anything else. The power was always in me alone. It came from . . . what I thought. What I observed. What I made real."

His eyes stared up into space where the first stars of evening glimmered through the gathering twilight. "We evolved in a world of cause and effect. A world of Newtonian mechanics. The reality we perceive is hard-wired into our brain pathways, burned into our DNA because those were the conditions that existed in the world as life arose, and awareness of them, anticipation of them, was necessary for our survival. But for the quantum . . . for the quantum . . . we need new senses there. New pathways, new perceptions. To truly comprehend it, we must become changed. We must become . . . more."

"As you have become?" Neale asked. Her voice cracked. She was surprised by the passion that came over her. Far too late, she realized it wasn't hate that she felt for Cross. It was jealousy. He had gone by himself to where they were meant to go together.

He had left her alone.

The engine was louder. Something was coming. She buried her face in her hands and sobbed. It was all too late.

Cross wrinkled his brow, not understanding her tears.

"So many mysteries remain," he said in a voice of wonder. "You know that, Kate? I saw how the universe began. I know the fires that fueled creation. But even with that ultimate answer, I have found more questions. It's so . . . wonderful." He glanced up at the sky again. The soft rush of the approaching motor grew louder.

"What other questions can there be?" Duvall asked, looking up into the dark eastern sky.

"I don't know how it will end," Cross said.

Neale cried. Her face was wet with tears. "I do."

Duvall pulled out the locater. The green LED blinked on and off. "They're coming?" she asked. "But not to rescue us?"

Neale nodded her head, so hard to speak. She slipped down to join the others, kneeling before the onrushing night, the onrushing vehicle. A truck of some sort she could tell now, almost here. "Oh, Anthony," she cried. "SHARP, and you—we were all a project to develop new technologies. New weapons."

"I know that," Cross said, eyes fixed on the heavens.

"We were . . . we were Cathedral Three. The weapons they used on you at Harvard . . . they were from Cathedral Two."

Duvall dropped the locater into the sand, crushing it with her heel. "What's coming in that truck?" she demanded. She pointed to it, a looming shape only a few hundred yards distant.

Neale turned away. It was all too late. "Cathedral One," she said.

TWO

The sun was on the horizon, red, swollen, a minute from extinction. Duvall looked away from it, into the night. The truck was a pickup, beige, without markings.

"Do you know what it will be?" Cross asked. Duvall watched him stand up, his face set, eyes dark.

"No," Neale said. "Parnel didn't tell us. It was the last contingency, he said. Planned from the beginning."

Cross's eyes scanned the sky like tracking radar, looking for anything else that might approach. "They couldn't be sure I'd come here," he said. "So it has to be something they could use in a city. It can't be that big. It's only a pickup."

"They wouldn't care," Neale told him. "Parnel only wanted to stop you."

The truck stopped ten feet away. The driver's door opened toward them.

"Hello, Parnel," Cross said flatly.

It was Covington.

He looked years older, haggard, unsmiling. He held up his hand.

His thumb was pressed against the side of a small black box. It had a short antenna. A red light glowed on it. "No closer, Anthony. Please."

"Why you?" Cross asked.

Covington closed the door behind him without looking away from Cross. "You're my responsibility, Anthony. I created you and—"

"No. I created myself. I am the choices I made. You still don't understand," Cross muttered. "You still don't." Duvall looked at Neale, could see the same reaction in her eyes. Cross's voice had changed again. The anger had returned. A new Cross was rising to the surface. "You're just trying to hurt me again. You're always just trying to hurt me."

Duvall wanted to say "no" to him, but she knew he had gone past the point of listening. Whichever one of Cross's disparate personalities they had just peacefully encountered, his moment had passed with Covington's arrival.

"No matter what you have in there, Parnel, it can't work. It won't be enough." Cross's hands made fists at his side. They flickered with blackness.

"It's enough," Covington said. "Enough energy release to distort the fabric of spacetime over a small area. There will be no lattice to slip through this time."

"You'll die, Parnel."

"That's the problem with the world today, Anthony. Not enough people willing to take responsibility for their own mistakes. I am willing. I shall make things right again." He held the black box over his head. Behind him, the sun had set.

Cross slipped into the cloak of his new understanding. The blackness welled forth from him, coating him in obsidian reflections. Completely and abruptly, he vanished. A small puff of sand swirled up into the vacuum he left behind.

"Don't, Parnel!" Neale shouted. "You're too late."

Covington backed up against the truck, looking all around. "Oh, no, I'm not. I know him better than you think, Charis. I've studied him longer. He'll come back. And that's when it has to be detonated. When he's in the field, still forming, that's when he's vuln—"

Covington's hand was engulfed by darkness, the red light smothered. He groaned and tried to pull his hand from the air, but it was stuck, held in place by an invisible force.

A shadow appeared five feet away, flickered once, and became whole, became Cross. He held the box, holding his own thumb to it. "Is this how it works?" he asked. "I just take my thumb from it . . . like this!" He released the switch.

Covington gasped. But the Atomic City still existed.

"Think of this as your lesson, Parnel. Think of this as your final lesson in quantum physics. If I do not chose to observe the electrons which could trigger this detonator for the bomb in your truck, then those electrons do not exist. Do you understand?"

Covington wasn't listening. He was staring at his arm, locked in position, as black dripped down it. Where his hand had been was only empty air. And the blackness was spreading up his legs from his feet.

"And if I chose not to observe the particles of which you're composed, then you don't exist either, Parnel." Cross stepped closer. Covington rocked back and forth but no part of him made contact with the ground. His feet were gone, his legs disappearing, dissolving into nothingness. *Do you understand, Parnel? Do you?"*

Covington shimmered with the darkness of the field, with the madness of Cross. "I'll see you in hell!"

Cross held his hands to the sides of his face. "Parnel, you won't even exist *there! Do you understand?"* He folded his hands across his eyes. *"I don't* see *you!"*

Covington was gone. Only his dying scream remained.

Cross walked to the back of the pickup truck.

Neale looked at Duvall as Covington's echoes rolled through the ruins of the city. "Are you afraid to die?"

Duvall was surprised to realize that she wasn't. She listened as the last cry of a life faded, swallowed by the night. "I'm not afraid of my life ending. I'm just mad that everything else will go on without me." She looked down at the ground. "And I miss my cat. What a stupid way to—"

Cross pulled a tarpaulin from the back of the truck. Duvall heard him laugh, cold and heartless, a different person once again.

"Are *you* afraid to die?" Duvall asked Neale.

"Not anymore."

"Look what they made for me," Cross announced. Duvall jumped back, startled by the thunderous boom of his altered voice. This was the

Cross who had appeared in the lounge, the Cross who had killed Kwong and Weinstein.

Duvall and Neale had no choice but to go to him, to see what he had uncovered in Covington's truck.

It was so innocuous, like half of an amateur welder's set: a green metal cylinder, two feet by less than one foot, held in place on the truck bed by metal brackets bolted to the floor. It looked like such a rushed and haphazard job. Unprofessional.

"A fusion bomb," Neale said. "Tactical. Half-kiloton, maybe."

"Twenty kilotons," Cross corrected her. "Hiroshima to go. A Cathedral breakthrough." He held his hands to his face again. "Why do they always want to hurt me?"

Neale pointed to a small metal box on the side of the cylinder. Red numbers flashed in it. Counting down. "Is it disarmed?" she asked.

Cross shook his head.

The readout showed 90. Then 89. *Just over a minute,* Duvall thought. She couldn't even make it to the other side of the buildings.

"How do you know its yield? Can you sense its components?" Neale asked, and Duvall was astounded that a minute from destruction Neale could still think of questions she wanted answered, still want to know something new. Somewhere inside the woman, Duvall at last saw, was something that did care.

"I can see the way its mass stretches the lattice of existence," Cross answered. "Oh, Charis, the things I know. The things I've seen."

The numbers kept counting. *Like my bedside clock,* Duvall thought, *counting the long hours till the end of night and the release of day.* What a dawn it would be. She wondered why she did not feel more frightened.

The floor of the truck bed suddenly creaked and Duvall saw the cylinder sink into the metal, deforming it, as if it was suddenly too heavy for the truck to support. Two of the metal brackets cracked.

Neale looked concerned. "What's happening, Anthony?"

The truck bed shifted again. Duvall could hear the suspension creaking as the truck settled closer to the ground. Less than forty seconds.

"I'm changing the mass," Cross said in the calm voice of a teacher. "So simple to add mass. The quantum sail can also be a scoop, Charis. Mass is everywhere." He swept his hand across the surface of the cylinder and both rear tires on the truck blew out. "Yesss," he sighed.

"How much mass, Anthony?" The wonder had gone from Neale's voice. There was a new serious tone to it.

Thirty seconds, Duvall estimated, and Neale still had questions. But so did Duvall. She wondered if souls could survive a nuclear bomb. She wondered if she would see her gram in that last split second. It wasn't just cops and scientists, she realized. It was everybody. *We all want to know the truth. We all want answers.*

"How much mass, Anthony!" Neale's voice was a shout. Duvall didn't know why.

"How much will it need?" Cross shouted back, and it seemed that his voice came from the air all around. "Megatons? Gigatons? As much as it takes."

"No!" Neale screamed. "You can't!"

"What's he doing?" Duvall stepped back from the truck. It was still shifting, the back of it still being forced down on an angle as if a thousand cylinders had been stacked in it.

"There's no size limit to a fusion reaction," Neale said dully. "He could turn the whole planet into another sun."

"That would make them all understand!" Cross shouted, the voice of a new god, the voice of hell. "All of them, forever!"

"Stop it!" Duvall pleaded. "You have to stop it, Anthony!"

"Too late," he sighed, deafeningly loud. "It's all in there now. A chain reaction. It's all bubbling out of the foam and the sea. An infinite supply of matter and energy."

Neale was frantic. Duvall had seen the same look in Cross as he had worked in his lab. Total concentration. Total involvement. Hard at work. Twenty seconds.

"Yes, Anthony!" Neale suddenly said. She ran to him. "More mass! Bring it all out! Now!"

Cross smiled, cruel and twisted. "Yesss," he said. "You understand, too. Destroy everything! Destroy it all to teach them all."

"No!" Neale said, and she put her hands on him. "Even *more* mass, Anthony! Even more than it would take to destroy everything!"

Cross looked down at her accusingly. "You want the fireball to collapse. You want it to swallow itself, disappear without destroying anything, without teaching a lesson."

"Even more mass than that, Anthony. Even more!" Her voice was desperate. With a shriek of tearing metal, the cylinder punched through the floor of the truck bed at last, smashing to the ground. Sparks ignited gasoline from the ruptured fuel tank and Duvall stumbled back from the instant fire, falling against the sand. But what did it matter? Ten seconds, she guessed.

"How much mass?" Cross asked Neale. "How much more?"

"Ten to the ninety-third grams per cubic centimeter," she shouted.

"It will fall!" Cross thundered. "Beyond singularity. Into super-space."

"Yes, Anthony! Please, yes! Not death, life! Not destruction—"

"Creation." The word echoed through the buildings of the dead city, buildings glowing in the light from the fire that burned round the seed of ultimate possibility.

Cross looked over Neale's head. Duvall looked into his eyes. They flickered once and for a moment, a single moment, the blackness fell from them. She saw the eyes of the man who had smiled with kindness, the eyes of the man who had sought to understand, the eyes of the man who had been her lover.

"You can do *anything,"* Duvall whispered to him, not knowing if her words could be heard, but knowing that her thoughts would be understood. *"Anything."*

The moment of clarity passed. He looked down to Neale.

"Not alone," he said, the voice of the boy.

"No," Neale promised. "Not alone, ever."

"Promise?" he asked, the echo of an ancient question.

"Oh, yesss," Neale whispered. "Promise."

Cross spread his arms as the fire in the truck grew. He shimmered at the edge of it. Duvall saw his mouth open. Felt his cry of fear and pain and exaltation rock the air and the earth and the bones within her. She saw Neale wrap her arms around him, falling into him, consumed by him, consumed by the light, her cry joining his, becoming one, becoming—

Zero seconds.

Detonation.

Silence.

Cross and Neale were gone. Not even the echo of their final sounds remained. The flowing, twisted patterns of the fire were frozen in place.

The stars ceased to twinkle in the planet's thick air. Everything waited. Just for a moment.

The fire shrank back to its source. The cylinder folded in on itself like a tin can being crushed. It drew the truck after it, collapsing all around it. Duvall felt the air rush out of her at the suddenness of the collapse. She felt the earth shift beneath her as it angled upright, as all the buildings and the desert and the sky and stars above curved into impossible shapes as the path of light was bent by an awesome gravitational force, following the cylinder's retreat down some dark hole, faster and faster, receding in all directions at once, all space and time and dimensions unknown collapsing around it, dragged down into it.

But the cylinder fell so fast that nothing in existence could keep up with it. It fell so fast that existence wasn't changed.

It fell so fast, become so hot and so dense that it became its own existence.

And Duvall fell behind it, watching it escape from her, feeling the last threads of connection and causality stretch away into infinity. She felt the echoes of Cross and Neale. Saw equations as they had existed in their minds. Read them, shared them, knew what they meant.

Singularity.

And beyond.

THREE

T here was nothing, not even a void in which nothing could exist.

It was an absence beyond anything Duvall could conceive. An absolute lacking surpassing even the unknowing of death.

But there were possibilities, always possibilities in the quantum sea.

Duvall followed after them, through the superspace that was beyond human comprehension, between the event horizons that limited one universe from the next, all universes from each other, through the foam of the quantum sea, alive and bursting with universe after universe, on and on, infinity after infinity, forever and ever through all there was, all there ever would be.

Now, Cross said, and what he had created, what he had shaped and fashioned and made so impossible that it fell from the universe, in directions that did not exist in the universe, emerged into that nothingness where only chance could exist.

It took 0.000000000000000000000000000000000000000000000000054 seconds for him to construct that Planck boundary, and then all time began. As it had always begun. Again.

Do you see? Cross asked.

Neale did and she said *Now,* and from the two of them joined together gravity took its form as they grew spacetime all around them, containing all the new universe in a volume less than an atom's.

The clock ticked.

Now, Cross said at 0.0000000000000000000000000000000001 seconds. The strong force took shape in a flurry of quarks and leptons, existing among other forces undreamed of, torn by inflation and foldings unknown to all who were not a witness.

Now, Neale said at 0.0000000000001 seconds. The weak force dropped from the electromagnetic. All the new universe in a chaotic sphere the size of earth's solar system with the pattern laid for the explosion to continue for billions of years. For galaxies to form, for stars to erupt, for planets to orbit, for life to arise and see it all and want to know and understand and do it all again in its own way.

But even as the expansion raced, as particles separated from particles, as the density dropped and space itself was created, Anthony Cross and Charis Neale remained entwined.

Their thoughts faded against the majesty of their creation.

Not alone, Cross said, seeing his final answer loom. *Not alone,* Neale said, facing that answer with him.

Together, they said. *Promise,* they said. *Love,* they felt.

Duvall felt them slipping away as the event horizon formed between her universe and the new one that had sprung from it. She shared their thoughts and their minds and their dreams, seeing all that they had seen, knowing all that they had known.

I understand, she said to her teacher, and then Anthony Cross made one parting gesture, one gift of thanks to show how much they were alike. *For Schrödinger,* Cross said. *For all the possibilities that are left to you. For all the possibilities that you choose to see.*

And then the space of Duvall's universe healed.

Separate now, the new universe that Cross and Neale had created continued to grow.

It would take another hundred thousand years, another 3.15 times

ten to the thirteenth seconds, to cool enough that photons could separate from matter. But that moment would come. The process had begun
again as it had an infinite number of times before and as it would an
infinite number of times to come. And when that moment came, at that
one time that was *always*, in that one place that was *everyplace*, once
again . . .

 . . . there would be light.

FOUR

Duvall felt cool sand beneath her fingers. She saw the stars shining in the glowing arc of the Milky Way above her. The dark hulks of the dead city were silent and undisturbed. Anthony Cross and Charis Neale were gone, absolutely, fallen from this universe to the new one they had created. The desert was all surrounding. Duvall breathed the air and she understood everything except what Cross had said about a gift, given because they were so much alike.

Then she heard a sound. Soft and familiar, a gentle interrogation. She reached out, the night not dark at all beneath the multitude of stars, and touched the warmth and the softness of Cross's gift.

Duvall's cat purred. Briggs had been returned, whole and sudden, brought back from the instant of chaos, returned from Cross's madness. A possibility made real. A gift, he had said. A message, Duvall now knew.

Beneath the stars, in the center of the desert, she held the cat in her arms and, as Cross had wanted her to, she knew that she was not alone.

And that all things were possible.

She sat in the desert long that night, sorting the new thoughts and memories she had shared with Cross and Neale. She saw with their eyes, deep into the quantum. She thought with their thoughts, and understood their methods for delving deeply within it.

She saw how to control it all with the power that was within herself.

Duvall held out her hand to the stars. She knew what to do. The power that Cross had had now flowed within her, as she knew it could flow though anyone who chose to see it. Her fingers blurred before her eyes, they glowed with the soft focus of an energy so basic it had not yet been named.

She held that power in her hand. A new god. *All things are possible.* She saw within herself the same disparate parts that had ruled Cross. She heard again each hateful word that had been said to her in her life. She felt again the cruelty and the hatred and the ignorance that had plagued her life.

Her hand glowed blue against the stars. Briggs looked at it in wonder, transfixed. Duvall looked at it and trembled on the brink, knowing of the madness within the soul of humanity, but also knowing of the love, and believing with all her heart that one person can make a difference. Must make a difference. Or else, what was the point?

You can do anything.

A moment passed.

"No," she said. Her voice was small against the night, but it was loud enough.

The glow faded. Her hand flickered, becoming flesh again, and her universe had changed in such a way that the glow and the black and the power would not return again in anyone.

With both hands she held her cat, wrapping him warmly within her jacket, feeling his simple purr of unconditional contentment against her. It was enough.

A moment had passed and it was time for another to begin.

"Time to get started, Briggsy," Duvall said.

Then she set off across the endless desert, beneath the endless stars, on her way home, at last.